# Stigma: Wicked Rebirth

by Thomas Goyette
Copyright © Thomas Goyette

Join my e-mail list: StigmaSeries@gmail.com
Follow me on Twitter: @Stigmaseries

Thank you for all of your support.

*may you always strive for a great adventure :) happy reading.*

# Prologue:

Silver mist plumed as my feet crashed through, pounding the damp ground with every desperate step as I dodged the scarcely scattered trees of a forgotten forest. Though the moon hung high, veiled by a fractured mask of smoke and clouds, the flashes of guns and raining fire lit my world like day, consequence of a world at war with itself. My panting echoed through the skeletal remains of this once proud forest, as did their voices behind me.

"Stop! By the name of Commander Zanin," they'd shout, as if it was all they knew how to say. The Agents had been trained for this, genetically engineered and hell bent on cleansing the world of all those who shared the Gift. They were elite soldiers loyal to the dictatorship, Agents of Death.

Zanin had rallied his people, the Pure, who didn't share our Gift, instilling a fear that has fueled a genocide against all of those who held this power, for fear of our talents shortly after the Pulse that had first granted it. What was supposed to be a blessing from our mother Sera had quickly become a stigma that plagued our lives. With them under him Zanin assumed near complete control of the world, or what was left of it.

I held that mark, so, I could do nothing else but run until my body heaved with each step.

The soft patter of paws falling on the damp ground only pushed me forward in a desperate attempt to escape my impending doom as a pack of dogs circled around from every side. Their shadows loomed maliciously in the brush ahead of me, and behind me I could hear the steady advance of the Agents and the thunderous crash of trees falling as if they were being ripped out of the ground and thrown aside as easily as a child may pluck a blade of grass from loose soil.

My heart rate spiked as I realized my escape path was dwindling, but didn't dare to look back as I pushed forward.

As the dogs closed in my hopes of escape grew dim.

Dimmer.

Gone, until I felt it escape me completely.

Suddenly, I felt a tug, and all of my momentum stopped in a moment of sheer terror. My feet left me and I crashed helplessly to the ground before being pulled by my hair towards the Agents behind me. I grasped blindly at the heavily armored hand that had taken hold and stole a look at the man who towered over me. His thick metal armor was battered and scarred from years of war, his face hidden behind a standard issue helmet that I damned for concealing the identity of my murderer.

I drove my hand into my coat pocket, searching for my knife in a fit of panic all while trying to ignore the grim impossibility of my survival. My eyes began to swell with tears as the thought of my life ending came to the forefront of my mind.

*No*, I thought, *not today, not like this.*

I blindly found my knife and flipped it open in my pocket, unsure of what I could even do with a blade so small against an armor designed to protect against the supernatural.

The Agent pulled harder on my hair, as if sensing that I was planning to fight back.

I knew I needed to do something, and soon—desperation had kicked in.

I clutched the knife and used my free hand to grab hold of the Agent's, holding it in place. He stopped dragging me the moment I took hold, but only to bring his eyes on me as if questioning my intent. By then it was too late for him to do much to stop my escape. In one motion I brought the knife up to where the Agent had taken hold, and with a quick slice left several inches of my hair dangling in his grasp.

My body melted with a wave of short lived relief and a much needed boost of adrenaline as I hit the damp ground. Immediately, I scrambled to my feet and let out into a mad dash before he had the chance to react.

My burst of joy soon faded, as I realized once more that the towering mountain face before me would soon steal my last hope for escape. My eyes darted from side to side as I closed in, searching, hoping, for some crevice or cave that I could back myself into. I found nothing but a small, shallow indent in the rock wall that was hardly my size. I knew it wasn't enough protection, but I hoped they might overlook me in the slight veil of darkness it offered. It was that, or risk running through the gauntlet of Agents behind me.

The seconds before they found me passed like a small eternity as I sat, back pressed against the damp stone, out of breath and quivering from the cold, yet hot with the fear and anger, adrenaline coursing through my veins as I waited for near certain death.

I could fight, I knew that, anyone else with the Gift would have at least put up a decent struggle but I knew my efforts would be for nothing. Though I held the Stigma's mark, I had never shown any talent, any promise — only enough common sense to survive on my own. I'd always been a late bloomer and now, I knew, I'd never have my chance.

The Agency doesn't think very fondly of runners, preferring us to simply accept our fate quietly, never realizing people are all still animals at the core, and no animal is meant to be caged. I'd heard that those who surrender are taken back into the dome cities where the Pure live with the promise of a cure for what we are. What happens then is only known through rumor, but one thing is sure— they are never seen again. As the men approached my eyes opened, scared of what was to come yet curious of what was before me. If I was going to die here, I would die with my eyes wide open.

Four men broke the tree-line clad in thick metal plates across their chest, legs, and arms and formed a loose wall around the opening of my shallow grave, the dogs that hunted me standing by each Agent's side. Each man was nearly double my size, holding a rifle I couldn't imagine being able to carry, never mind fight with. Their helmets told silent stories through canyons scared in the thick metal, and had visors that shone bright with the glare from thin ribbons of moonlight that pierced the thin canopy of the surrounding trees. There were foggy blue displays on their visors that must have been seen clearly from the inside. Some were flashing with bright colors and shapes, while others looked like blocks of scrolling text. I had no idea what any of it could mean.

I saw my reflection in the their mask, pathetic and quivering, pushing myself back against the wall, terrified of what was to come. I could feel the warm touch of a tear rolling down my face, realizing there was no escape for this fate as an Agent towards the back sent out his order, "Kill her."

"Roger that," said one of the Agents, who stepped forward in front of my entrance, looked down at me for a moment, then raised his rifle.

I felt as if a warm blanket had been draped over me, consuming me, and I found myself okay with death. It was something oddly welcoming, familiar, as if death had been a close friend. My eyes grew heavy and my vision a blur as I came to peace with this end. I could hear only the dog's whimper, my scream, then nothing, as everything faded to darkness.

# Chapter 1:

"Hello? You've been out for some time now. Hello?" it was a voice I've heard for days now, a girl's voice, gentle, kind, and soothing in my new found world of confusion. It would radiate through the walls of the thin corridors in which I've wandered in silence, acting as my lone, though disembodied, companion.

The darkness ahead of me would twist and churn, taking abstract shapes in the distance only to flutter in and out of existence as I drew near before disappearing completely. I either welcomed, or was haunted by the sounds of past memories that called from every passing room, some warm with sentiment and heart, others, hot with pain and passion that still burns deep within my soul.

I wondered, was this death? Would I be forced to walk an eternity as a silent specter amongst the grim cinema of my life?

"How's she doing?" another voice asked, a man's voice.

"Can't say, I've done all I could. She's stopped coughing up blood so I guess that's a good sign, but her body is still under a lot of stress," the girl returned.

I rounded another corner and found myself in yet another identical hall. My hand ran along the grooved walls, feeling the protruding shapes and characters of an abstract language long since forgotten. The walls were damp, as was the ground, from thin ribbons of water that trickled down from the ceiling.

The only light here seemed to radiate from nothing, having no source, but existing nonetheless, and was only bright enough to reflect softly off the small pools that lined the walls down the entire length of the hallway. As the darkness ahead came to shape, the shadows formed into a grand double door with gyrating lines and symbols that danced amongst themselves, but fell still as I drew near. A thin white light escaped from under the doors, and I pondered the possibility of that single strand being what had lit my way through this labyrinth. I ran my hand down the rusty decay of its ice cold metal design.

"I think she's coming to, she's moving," the girl's voice crept softly through the walls.

I pressed my ear to the door to listen, but heard only the roaring crash of water pounding the earth and the faint drip of droplets as they bombed the ground from the ceiling above. Then, over it all, I could hear the deep, heavy breathing of something inside. My heart began to pound in my chest, and I covered my mouth to hold in my scream as I took a step back. I couldn't begin to imagine what could live in this drab and desolate place, but the thought of something worse than death crept into my mind, forcing me to shut my eyes in what was both fear and a desperate hope to escape it.

"Hey! Finally done with your nap?" My eyes slowly came to focus to see the young girl whose voice I was already familiar with. "I'm Ava! I've been taking care of you while you've been umm…out. You've been asleep for days you know, I was afraid you'd never wake up!" she continued with just a little too much enthusiasm.

Her eyes were a beautiful light green and her hair fell lightly over her shoulders in shining, blonde swirls, though most of it was covered by a grey hat made from a soft fur with an even softer looking white fur tracing the hat's edges. Two perky white ears that reminded me of a cat's were perched on top. The hat came down to her forehead in front and to round off flaps along the sides that covered her ears, and, dangling from each of those flaps was a single white pom-pom. Her sun-kissed olive skin brought out the color of her hair and eyes, making her look almost angelic. She had an amazing energy about her, and a tangible vibe that radiated through the entire room.

Had the Agents not killed me? The possibilities of what could have happened that night rushed through my mind. A shot of fear ran through me, dreading the possibility of my capture.

My eyes darted around the room, which wasn't a room at all but a large tent. There were other beds here, lining the walls, though all others were empty but one, where a man with a bandaged up arm silently struggled to eat from a bowl on his lap. There were wooden boxes by the foot of each bed, with a painted red cross on each. The floors were nothing more than compacted dirt. I could see no windows, and only one closed over rawhide flap of a door. This didn't seem like anywhere the Pure may have taken me, and the design seemed familiar, only expanded.

My eyes fell on Ava once more. She didn't look like anyone I'd imagine working for Zanin, unless child labor was suddenly an acceptable for the Pure. She didn't wear a uniform either, rather, a tan sleeveless top tucked inside an orange sash wrapped around her waist and I took a moment to study the swirling mint green designs in its fabric. Her harem pants were the same mint green that accented her sash and were baggy, leaving a lot of extra fabric hanging between her legs but hugging tight to her ankles. She didn't look at all threatening, and was far too young to be trusted alone with a prisoner, if I was one.

I smiled, deciding to trust her for the time being and tried to prop myself up on one arm. I was immediately brought back down as the pain shot through and grasped my arm, forcing my words through my teeth, "It—it's so cold!"

She stood up from her chair and came closer to where I lay, placing one hand on my arm and the other on my back, helping me to sit. The pain instantly began to dissolve up my veins until it disintegrated with tiny pricks in my shoulder as a green aura surrounding her hands began to wash over me.

I looked at that aura for a moment, then back to her more intently. The crescent shaped mark in the iris of her eye gave me the answer I was looking for and I damned myself for overlooking that detail to begin with. The natural color of her eyes worked so well to hide that mark.

"So you have it too?" I asked.

Ava smiled, "We all do silly! You're in a camp run by the Council. Well, we're under their protection I mean. It's the safest and best in the world, or what's left of it I hear."

*The Council?* I thought.

I took a moment to think back to the past camps I'd taken shelter in, but none were under the protection of the Council. In fact, I'd only heard stories of them, which were spoken of in the same light as the Pulse that had originally granted us our power. The stories told of armies that would fight the Zanin and those who followed him for power and land in the early days of the war. The Council had built cities all over the world much like Zanin's domed cities and fought to save us from his oppression. From what I knew, the efforts of the Council brought the closest thing to civilized life a Stigma holder had ever been given since the Pulse, with a government and culture all its own before disappearing entirely, leaving behind mere glimpses of what we could have become.

Outside the war still raged on, and those left to survive in the forgotten cities, plains, or tucked away in the swiftly growing forest were cared for mainly by members of a group called Cekrit, the organization largely responsible for the resistance today-though, other clans did exist with motives all their own. What started as a rough group of misfits swiftly multiplied, taking on anyone who was willing to fight in the name of freedom into their ranks. I've even seen exiled Pure fighting proudly beside those with the Gift. Safe camps were set up all over the world as well, and for each one that was found, and destroyed, another would rise in its place with the hope that one day they would be left in peace.

The oldest of us would stay and fight, their powers having developed the furthest, while the youngest would run for safety. That code meant that the clan's population was very young, as the oldest would often be killed while protecting the others, and even if they weren't, there are only so many battles one person can survive unharmed. Those who survived the slaughter would gather again and start over, constantly struggling to survive. It was a vicious, and seemingly endless cycle of death and despair.

The two groups had worked together once, Cekrit and the Council, in the beginning of the war. Though they shared the same mark and a common enemy in Zanin, their goals were different and efforts to work together had stopped completely. Cekrit pulled back, focusing on rebuilding order among the hordes of displaced people while the Council continued their relentless assaults. I'd always assumed the Council was killed off, victims of their own zeal, we all did.

My memories were short lived, as Ava seemed to get bubblier, doing a sort of overacted bunny hop as she clapped her hands, "Well, let's get out of this stuffy tent. I'll show you around."

As she turned to walk away, the question escaped my lips before I had enough time to even ask myself, "Wait, tell me what happened first, how did I end up here? What happened to the Agents?"

"How should I know? Demi found you just outside and carried you in. I'm glad he did too, we're going to be really good friends, I just know it! Now," Ava said as she backed out of the tent, her tone suddenly changing from overly cheery to motherly stern, "let's go."

I followed, reluctantly, to catch my first glimpse of what I would now call home, at least for the time being. Stepping out of the rawhide flap of the medical tent's door I saw no sky, felt no bitter kiss of winter breeze, nor was there any hint of the forest in which they found me.

Rather, we stood on the ground level, amongst a valley of lush green gardens peppered with smaller tents much the same as the one we had just left. A half dozen giant spires seemed to have grown from the ground, connected by an entire system of stone bridges and walkways in the space between, spiraling staircases carved into the body of each.

The protruding shapes of red stained adobe homes that lined every inch of the rock walls beyond drew my attention, offering my first solid hint that we weren't inside some simple camp that was hoping not to be found, no, this was a thriving city that rivaled the Pure's domes.

I felt short of breath, realizing that the Council truly hadn't been killed off, but had thrived in hiding all of these years, and suddenly, I felt an odd mixture of wonder and betrayal as I studied the city around me, mesmerized by its immense beauty.

"How?" I asked curiously, mostly to myself.

"That mountain, we are inside of it, it keeps us safe," Ava explained as she took my hand and began to drag me along, "Now, let's go lazy, you've done enough sleeping! We've got to get you situated."

As she dragged me along the smooth mountain floor my eyes sprang from one thing to another. On the far side of camp there was a thin ribbon of water cascading down from a cut out hole near the ceiling, probably driven by the constantly melting snow on the mountain's peak. At the base, there was a large pool of water that looked shallow around the edges, but deep where the water crashed down. The waterfall fed a running stream that meandered through the center of the city, a ready and endless supply for the farmers that would fetch their water from it.

"Where are you bringing me in such a hurry punk?" I half spoke, half laughed as Ava tugged me along.

She gave no answer, only pulled harder, which still wasn't very hard given her size.

We climbed one set of stairs running alongside the rock face, turned, and started down one of the bridges I'd seen before. Looking over the edge, I was amazed by the abundance of vibrant greens and radiant colors overflowing the mountain floor, painting a perfect picture of spring. Even the stream that cut through was sparkling like few I'd ever seen.

I was simply beside myself, with so many questions I needed answered, but too much in awe to ask.

Before that moment, I hadn't even bothered to ask myself how it was even possible that we could see inside the mountain, until it literally hit me in the face, causing me to stop short.

About a foot from me, a small orb about the size of my fist floated in place, glowing a soft orange. Above, hundreds, perhaps thousands more in green, blue, red, and yellow all drifted around us. Most lingered high up towards the ceiling, illuminating the ground below, but some dared to drift lower. Alone, they gave off a soft, faint glow, but together they lit the city like day.

I cupped my hands under the floating orb before me, hoping I would sink down and rest in them, and it did. I could feel its warmth as it touched down gently, the silky hairs that covered it tickling my hands. I tried to find its face, but found nothing, and began to wonder if it even had one. There was a soft pulse of a heartbeat that startled me at first, causing my hands to twitch ever so slightly. The orb made a soft noise and drifted out of my hands as if I'd scared it away.

I looked to Ava, who was already waiting with an answer, "they're the only things Demi has ever made that I actually enjoy. They keep us warm, help with light, and keep everything here alive and healthy. Easy to care for too, they live off of the air we breathe out, giving us new, and clean air in return," Ava said, looking over the edge of the bridge, "they're all very shy really, but I love them."

"So they're like the trees then?" I asked, impressed. It was really a stroke of genius, they kept the air clean and the only care for them was already provided just by our own natural breathing. The entire place was self-sustaining in that sense, and judging by the abundant gardens below it didn't seem like food was an issue either.

"Like what?" Ava asked, cocking her head to the side in confusion.

I shot her a curious look in return before sweeping over the city once more. I was stunned, really, to see that there wasn't a single tree, only gardens. I wondered then, if she had ever left the city.

"Oh, nothing, never mind," I returned, looking over the edge with her. Suddenly, the run down camps, abandoned buildings, and caves I'd found shelter in seemed worlds away.

I sighed, taking another moment to fully absorb the beauty all around me. For the first time in my life I felt as though a weight had been lifted off my shoulders, I could finally relax. The lush gardens below were lit softly by floating sprites that illuminated the air like an army of Chinese lanterns being pushed along in an unseen current.

Rather than the typical makeshift gathering of tents with scattered campfires I'd grown up living in, this was so much more. The adobe homes, spires, and beautiful gardens proved the security and lasting life of this city. This wasn't some place to stay in the back woods of nowhere, this was home for an entire population of people looking for a place to be normal again, a place to truly call home.

The falls were crashing down just feet from us now, and as I looked down I could see someone below in it's spring. The man had a certain stance about him, arms moving in slow, fluid motions as if he were a part of the water itself. There was movement in the water around him, a set of deep shadows that twisted and danced around and between his legs below the surface.

"There's something else down there," I said, nodding my head in his direction.

"Hmm?" Ava buzzed, "Oh, down there?" she continued, pointing down into the spring. "That's just Demi, he's always down there, he says he's training but I really just think it's an excuse to slack off."

"I should probably thank him for saving me," I said, still watching him below.

His black hair was straight, but roughly worn, hanging down mid-forehead and all together disheveled in a way that made it look like he'd just gotten out of bed. At first, I thought it may have been the light reflecting off the pool playing tricks on my eyes, but looking closer, his hair was speckled with just a few strands of snow white hair.

He wore something similar to Ava and though still baggy, his pants had far less loose fabric than hers, coming to a narrow stop just below his calf where he had tied them off. Despite that, water still seeped up his legs from the spring, darkening the light green fabric. On either leg, he had added two cargo pockets with a button flap, fastened closed. He wore a short sleeved sweatshirt, half undone, exposing a statue of the male form.

"Don't get too excited," Ava said with a slight smirk as she took my hand once more and started toward another set of stairs leading down to the spring. She seemed eager, as always, and dragged me along at a pace just a little swifter than a walk. As we stepped down, Demi eyed us for a short moment, or, rather, eyed me, before putting his attention back to the shadows, sending them away. His eyes, now a dark blue, began to lighten as they fell on me once more in a way that could only be described as silent disgust.

"Hey, look who decided to wake up," Ava said, looking at him for a moment, then back to me and I realized I'd never told anyone my name.

As I stepped past Ava, Demi's stance staggered slightly, as if he was repulsed by my presence, "My name's Sage, I wanted to thank you for saving me."

He studied me in several moments of painful silence, eyes narrow as if trying to see right through me but failing before lightening up, "You're up, great! Now you can leave," he said, turning into the falls behind him.

"Hey!" I yelled after him and started in his direction, but stopped short realizing there was nothing but a rock wall behind the falls. He was gone.

"Don't worry about him, he gets like this sometimes. He'll warm up to you," Ava said, taking my hand again, "Let's go, we need to get you out of these," she paused to look me up and down, "whatever you're wearing."

I looked down at myself, and was more than slightly embarrassed. A pair of ripped jeans with countless stains, an overly baggy shirt, and a coat that I knew wasn't mine couldn't have exactly been very flattering. The coat was slightly too big on me, but warm, and well made. I'd ditched mine in the chase so that it hadn't slowed me down, and I realized that Demi must have given me his once he found me. I smiled, despite his attitude it seemed as though he wasn't as much of a jerk as he put himself off to be.

With that we headed back up the stairs. As we scurried through the narrow roads and cut sharp turns people passed by, all staring as if they'd never seen another Stigma holder before. Dozens of open archways, which appeared to be the entrances to homes and shops, begged to be explored as we passed. I was amazed by it all, never having seen anything like it. Each shop had its own specialty, it's doors left open and welcoming. There were signs scattered about, hanging lazily above each vacant entrance with only the occasional bystander leaning against its frame.

In the Cekrit camps, everyone simply pitched in for the good of the community, using whatever skills they had to provide and never once asking for anything in return. Money meant little out there, mostly because many of us wouldn't be alive long enough to spend it. It was someone's skills that made them valuable. Here, people had settled into this life enough for shops to be open and running. It was an interesting shift to see.

There are abandoned cities from the time before the war that are set up much the same. Nearly thirty years have passed since then and nature had already begun to reclaim the land. Some trees have grown as tall as the buildings, and the streets have become little more than deep rivers of green. I remember looking into shop windows, glass broken and on the floor. Some had hard, life sized people dressed up in them, but the clothes inside had been long since stolen. I'm sure there was a name for those people back then, but the words were lost in the times. They had always seemed to follow me ominously with their eyes and often wondered if they had a soul, and if they did, what they might have thought about the world having watched for years behind those empty eyes.

I think that they would tell us stories of what was important, of how before the war they would watch as countless people entered their store, only to leave with an armful of bags and a misplaced smile. Perhaps they watched a child throw a tantrum, or a mother try to win her daughter's love with the perfect dress, or they watched someone spend their last dollar on something that they couldn't afford.

Now, the material has become immaterial, and what was once thought to be a necessity is now a burden. The stores, though raided and pillaged, are more stocked now than ever with the things that we never needed. I think that they would tell us all we ever wanted was to be loved, to find our humanity, only, we looked for those things in the wrong places and it's only now that we realize what's truly important in our lives.

How I wish they could have just told us.

Ava slowed as we rounded another turn and came upon a narrow path, a dead end before us. There was another staircase that hugged the wall to our right, and then sharply turned to run along the approaching wall above a wooden door.

"Is this your place?" I asked.

Ava only offered a disapproving nod and another smile as I drudged up the stairs behind her. When we reached the top she swung open the door that the second staircase had led to. As I followed, the door had swung back and I caught it with an open palm. The wood grain was smooth to the touch, with golden brackets holding the door to its hinges. My hand traced the deep set lines and knots in a design that looked like wood, yet felt like stone.

I stepped into the dimly lit room after Ava, who turned to face me, "This isn't mine, it's yours. Everyone in Terra Sera has a home. We built it while you were recovering."

Stumbling over my words, I tried to express my gratitude, "I— I don't know what to say. This is amazing, thank you!"

She offered only a smile and a nod to the bed, where a fresh change of clothes sat neatly folded on top. The bed was elegant and flawlessly crafted, tucked away in a darkened corner of the room. Four rounded pillars stood proudly on its corners, a lace canopy draped softly over them, creating an airy screen around the bed.

The sheets were a metallic grey silk with deep black designs rippling like an ocean wave through the folds and dips in its fabric.

Just under the overly plush pillows the sheets were folded over towards the bottom by just a few inches revealing a white underside with the same rippling black pattern. The bed begged to be laid on, and I would have, if there wasn't so much more that caught my attention.

Two dressers stood by either side, both sharing the same design and texture as the bed which sat between them. On one burned a line of candles that helped little to brighten the room. On the other, books were neatly stacked before the large mirror that took up the length of the entire piece. I could see a burst of light rays sneaking in through an open archway leading out to a balcony in the mirror's reflection.

I turned and made my way towards the balcony and the promise of a new perspective. From here, all of Terra Sera was before me; vibrant, moving, and free. I ran my hands along the smooth stone of the balconies rail as I gazed upon the city before me, taking it all in. For the first time in my life I felt something different, a sense of safety, a sense of security, a sense that I may have finally stumbled upon a place I could call home. No more running, no more fear, no more death and despair, no more war— just peace.

There was a waterfall to my right, crashing down into the small pool Demi had been in earlier, feeding a meandering stream that cut through the mountain valley, giving it life. On either side, lush gardens and fields sparkled like powdered silver with the ever present dew of the cascading falls spray. There were small foot paths dividing the abundance of green, leading to a handful of scattered buildings on the mountain floor.

There was a series of rising spires growing progressively larger as they circled the center of the city, the largest standing proudly surrounded by them. All had one main building perched on its plateau with a staircase carved into its side and each was connected to the next in line by a series of stone bridges.

Behind me, Ava was sitting on the bed swinging her legs and humming a tune unknown to me, sounding almost like a children's melody, uplifting and pure, I couldn't help but smile. When she saw I was looking she grabbed the clothes beside her and tilted her head slightly with a smile, holding her selections out toward me, "Time for *you* to get changed. These will help you blend in a bit more."

I took the bundle of clothes from her and followed her motion to the opposite corner of the room, where the bathroom was tucked away behind another door.

There was a stone sink in front of the door, making the sort of shape a mushroom cloud would when it plumes, though the top of that cloud was indented to form the bowl. Above that, protruding from the wall was a series of diagonal slabs all tilted downward toward the center. I saw no lever, no knob, to turn it on, rather, above those slabs was a soft blue circular light that seemed to shine through the wall. I reached out to touch it curiously, only to find that the circle would instantly begin to lose its form, dancing within itself before liquefying into a thin stream of water that continuously flowed down each of the stone slabs, being passed from one to the other before falling into the sink which, once filled, began to form a whirlpool before me.

As I washed the months of dirt and blood off my hands I gazed blankly into my hazy reflection in the stone, being reminded then just how worn this world had made me. My pale complexion stared back at me, and even in the orange tinted light I could tell I was still lighter than anyone I'd seen since waking up here. My clothes were badly torn, my skin covered in muddy brown smears, and my hair a disheveled mess — now more so than ever.

I'd almost forgotten I'd sliced most of my hair off to escape. Now, it was short, too short for my taste but I knew I should have kept it like this all along. I felt foolish for letting my own vanity almost kill me. I let out a nervous sigh, trying to find humor in the fact that I now looked like a pixie. I knew that it was a small price to pay for my life.

As I ran my hands through my hair I realized that I was shorter in the back than I'd thought, only coming down just past the nape of my neck to a point between my shoulder blades. Along the sides of my face my hair gradually grew longer, brushing my cheekbones, with the only length I'd actually managed to save coming down to a point just under my chin on either side. Aside from those points, the rest of my hair flared out like a wave the moment before it breaks. Even in this distorted reflection I could tell that it all needed to be cleaned up so I found a pair of scissors and went to work in an attempt to at least look somewhat presentable, cutting it so that the digression in length from front to back was smoother and less choppy. Sadly, there wasn't much else I could do about the length in the back, but I knew I would have to get over that.

"Well," I said to myself as I looked over to the clothes beside me, "in with the new I guess."

I slipped off my shirt, which had been loosely hanging across my chest from a torn shoulder, and a patchwork pair of pants kept together with whatever bit of fabric I could find to close up a new tare.

The first thing I picked up was a dark brown sleeveless shirt that hugged my body tightly, but wasn't constricting. Next, was a pair of burnt orange pants nearly identical to the ones Ava had worn. The fabric was light, and breezy, with strings to tighten around my ankles and waist. I'd never worn anything like it, but the comfort and refreshing coolness, even in the warmth of the city, made the awkwardness I felt almost worth it.

There was a mint green sash left waiting to be picked up, made with accents of the same burnt orange as my pants, and it was then that I realized my clothes matched Ava's exactly, though she wore the opposite colors. There was a dark brown sleeveless jacket as well, much like what Demi had been wearing earlier, with a hood just large enough to hang just above my eyes, clouding my face in the shadows. The sides of the jacket swooped down just above my knees to sharp points and shot back with an upward arch to rest at the small of my back.

I looked at myself in the walls reflection once more, content with the transformation. I'll admit change was refreshing.

From where I was I could see into the bedroom behind me. Ava's arms were stretched out wide as she danced around the room in circles, humming that same tune as earlier before throwing herself onto the bed.

"Sage?" she asked.

"Yes?" I answered as I turned to walk back into the bedroom.

Ava jumped off the bed to face me, "What were you doing out there all alone anyway?"

I closed my eyes and images of that night surged through my mind, even the memories I didn't want to relive. In those moments I felt so much fear, so much pain, and even joy. It was an odd mixture of emotion, and through that the only answer I could offer was a very unsure, "I don't know."

Ava seemed content enough with my response, letting the question go completely as she back up into the room to dance as she had been earlier.

"You know, for a girl your age you can be very playful," I said, watching her.

"Playful, or immature? I've heard both," she said, not bothering to stop her dance, "I'm just like every other eleven year old, I just know how to have more fun. How old are you anyway, eighty?" she shot back with a grin.

"Nineteen, thank you very much!"

"Never would have guessed," she said, laughing at her own joke. She stopped twirling to face me, "So you have to gift too, huh? What can you do?"

"Nothing," I said, my smile leaving me as I looked away, almost embarrassed to admit it, "it looks like Mother Sera forgot about this one," I continued, pointing to myself with both thumbs.

"What about you?" I returned.

"Sage, why are you alive right now? I heal people," she said, her hands starting to emit a dim green glow before fading back to normal.

Ava sighed, and sat back down on the bed, "I hear so much about Mother Sera, but I really don't know much about her really. Demi says I'm still too young to understand, but I think I do. She talks to me sometimes, I know it. Is that crazy?"

"Of course not," I said with a smile, "I hear her too, we all do."

"How?" Ava asked. "No one has ever really told me much about Mother, only that she is the reason we were granted our gift."

I nodded, "She is the reason yes, and it was because Mother loves us all. She was found many years ago and spread her power, even before I was born, when the world was at peace. This whole time she's guided us, and protects us, that is why we can hear her song."

"Why doesn't she come see us, you know, really come to talk to us?"

I came to sit by Ava's side on the bed, "No one has ever told you?"

"Told me what? Is she okay?" Ava's speech became hurried.

"In a way she is. The world is very different now than it was before we found her, did you know that?"

"The war?"

I sat silent for a moment, running through all of the facts in my mind. Our gods, Sera and Klaus had created the world and had kept Gaia, the spirit of the Earth, healthy as we went about our daily lives. Legends had said they lived among us long ago, but only until the Reckoning — the dark days when evil roamed our planet alongside man, after destroying that evil they disappeared completely to rest dormant in the Earth to recover, while keeping our world in order. Since then, they were said to have watched over us, protecting us, and guiding us in ways that we could never understand.

About thirty years ago the world had been in a state of relative peace. Mother Sera had been found and captured. She was too weak to resist, and instead sent out the Pulse, a shockwave that rippled through the world touching millions with her grace. This was her call for help.

The Pulse awoke something darker as well, and something a lot less open to the idea of being captured. Klaus, had begun to tear through the world, in a desperate search for his love. Cities had burned to the ground, families were destroyed, and nothing but despair was left in the wake of his volatile path of vengeance. The world had wept for him.

It was then that Commander Zanin took power, feeding off of the public's fear of those who had the Gift and their angry god. The Gift quickly became stigmatized and that's when the persecution began. It was then that Klaus turned his back on us as well, abandoning his children amidst a world of fear and destruction.

My eyes fell on Ava once more while hers begged for answers with an innocence that pained me, oblivious to the state of the world outside the walled garden that was Terra Sera.

"Ava," I started in a soft voice, "how much do you know about life outside of the city?"

There was a moment of silence as she rolled the question over in her mind, grasping for an answer. The moment her mouth opened to answer my attention was broken, a churning in the shadows of the room's corner stealing my gaze. A moment later Demi was leaning against the wall, and I wondered how long he'd been watching from the darkness.

Demi looked right through me to his sister, "We need you in the barracks, now. I'll meet you down there in a minute."

Ava jumped off of the bed, making sure to give Demi a sour look as she walked past, "Overdo it in training again?" she asked as if this was an everyday thing.

Demi kicked off the wall, taking a strong stance before us, relaxed, almost cocky as he stood with his hands resting lazily in his oversized pockets. "Something like that, you should get there soon," he said, nodding his head toward the door.

Ava listened, turning to say goodbye as the door closed behind her. Once the door closed I shot Demi an accusing look, "There wasn't really an emergency was there? How long were you watching? What gives you the right?" I asked almost rapid-fire.

"Of course not. Ava is a delicate girl and we don't need her to know everything that's going on in the outside world right now. She, at least, deserves to be happy now while she can, she's just a kid." Demi said, his voice never faltering from remaining calm while still offering a subtle forcefulness.

"What," I rejected, before he even had the time to finish, "she deserves to know! There are some things you can't hide once they exist, some things you can't forget."

"She doesn't have to carry that burden so soon, she doesn't have to forget because there's nothing to remember, not for her, not yet. I'm trying to give her a chance to live a life where the Stigma doesn't exist. At least she can be spared that fate."

"Well the Stigma does exist Demi and we can't hide from that fact, it would make us cowards. She has so many questions about life outside this city. Tell me you've at least told her what happened to Mother Sera?" In a way I shouldn't have been surprised Demi would try to protect her in that way, I knew his heart was in the right place, but I just couldn't fathom the idea of hiding the deeper truths of our existence. I knew her failure to know these truths would only hurt her in the end.

"What do you want me to tell her?" Demi began, his voice rising slightly, "That we are all hated, all hunted? Ava, at least, knows the world doesn't want us, and she knows that this Gift is what grants us our power. That's all she needs to know."

"And what of Mother Sera?"

"What of her? Ava will feel better not knowing that our Mother is stuck in some research lab or trapped in a cage because we failed to save her. If you haven't noticed, the world has gone to hell and all people like us can do in this age is survive. I'm just trying to give Ava a chance at having a normal life," he said, as he turned to look out beyond the balcony.

"What do you know of surviving? From what I can see you've done nothing but hide under the protection of the Council."

My face was hot with a newly boiling rage. I'd spent my entire life on the run, surviving on nothing but my own will and the land — I wouldn't let him believe that his life was so hard here in the city.

He shot me a piercing glance, "You know nothing about me. If I've spent my entire life cowering in the shadows of this city how was it that I was the one who found you on the brink of death on the outside? I could have left you there and we wouldn't even be having this conversation, I'm starting to think I should have."

"Is that why you walked away before when I tried to thank you? If you hate me so much then why did you bother saving me?"

He scoffed, amused by my question, and his response bit harder than I expected, "That's cute, you think I saved you? No, I was there to watch you die."

It took me a moment to recover from that fact, "Then who?"

"Don't play that card on me," he began, pacing back and forth on the balcony as he spoke, "you saved yourself. It was after I saw what you did to those Agents I decided to bring you here. You passed out after you finished toying with them. Really, I find it amazing to think a girl like you could control that power."

Was that weakness in his voice, or curiosity?

"I have no power," I protested.

Demi came back into the room to lean back onto the wall he'd originally spawned from. The shadows behind him began to churn once more, letting a thin black mist creep over and around his body. He smiled a sort of half smile and began to fall back into the void. As it began to consume him his last words were a mere whisper, "Who are you, really?"

"I don't know," I returned, solemn, and more so to myself.

In that moment, as the shadows faded, I found myself alone for the first time since waking up in Terra Sera.

# **Chapter 2:**

Aside from Ava's short, sporadic, visits I'd spent most of my first days alone Terra Sera. Whether Demi had kept her busy or she had better things to do escaped me, but I used my newfound free time to explore the every corner of the city.

Finally managing to pull myself away from the rare luxury of a real bed, I walked over to the balcony; where the rolling sweet scents of the gardens were washed over by the inciting smells of a fresh breakfast drifting over from the market district—as always, there to greet me. Looking down, I could see the same thing I'd seen each day before; the elders would wash their clothes in the spring, or twisting banks of the free flowing stream, as their grandchildren played in the fields behind them. Every now and then I'd see a quick flashes of power as the children tested their new abilities, still unable to control them.

Sometimes I'd watch Ava as she danced through the gardens, stopping occasionally to raise a flower to her nose so close I wondered if she was trying to dive into its core. I'd asked her once, if she loved the flowers so much why doesn't she pick them so that she may bring them home to admire. She gave me a very stern look then, and told me that if you love something beautiful you should leave it as it were; that at the very moment a flower was picked it would begin to wither and die, and there was no beauty in that. She told me that loving something, like a flower, was about appreciation and not ownership.

I'd left that conversation with the thought weighing heavy on my mind and wondering if it was because of her gift that such a young girl could be so kind. At first, I'd thought her ignorance of the outside world had been a plague to her mind, but more and more I found myself agreeing with Demi's decision to keep her shut off to those truths; allowing her an actual childhood and an unclouded mind. For Ava, ignorance was a special kind of bliss.

A new wave of delicious scents hit me, pulling me away from my thoughts and causing me to flirt with the idea of making the trip over to the market district. Moments later I found myself rushing down the stairs leading away from my single room and navigating the narrow streets and alleyways with a flow that had become second nature.

Running along the adobe walls on either side of me sat the open windows and doors that were the gateways into the homes of the other citizens; looking like a staggered line of building blocks, most two or three stories high. There were scattered balconies here too, connecting to another home across the way, likely a clever extension to growing families homes. Few shops passed me by, and were generally reserved to the street corners or were tucked into the shadows of dead end alleys; only offering the most basic necessities.

This was a quiet part of Terra Sera aside from the dull hum of conversation, and sometimes music, flooding out of the passing homes, finding freedom in the streets. Occasionally an echo of child's laughter would ricochet through the narrow streets, hitting me in waves; or excitement in the market district would cut its way through this hollow shell of a mountain from the far corner of Terra Sera.

There was incredible unspoken order here, something that had taken quite a few days to truly adjust to. Others in this area all dressed the same as I, with matching burnt orange pants and similar green sash. I'd even begun to feel a certain sense of comfort around those of my order that I couldn't explain, and another sense of ware around those who were not, despite neglecting to mingle with either as much as I might have been expected too.

It all felt so wrong; I'd never dealt with social classes while living with the Cekrit camps, mainly because few camps ever survived long enough for a solid structure to form. There, rank generally came from whoever had the most immediately useful skills, but with every new camp that was built there was always new faces and new needs. There were few people that could even be considered leaders in the movement, mostly stubborn Stigma holders who refused to die; fewer still had given themselves a sense of authority by that. Power there meant little, decisions were made by each and every member out there independently, but were all driven towards the same ultimate goal; unite the people, all people.

Here in Terra Sera the story was entirely different; the section I lived in all matched the same colors as I, being of the second order—just under the Council members and their families who wore the same colors as well, but inverse. All of it was very odd to me, and I felt uncomfortable speaking with those who were considered to be of a lower class, trying my best to treat everyone the same; sometimes, even, they were so reserved and broken into the system they had belittled themselves voluntarily. Even for me, it was an easy way to tell if someone you were speaking with outranked me or not, which certainly helped me to not cause any trouble for myself.

Walking through the streets of the residential district the towering apartments to my left only slightly leaned inward with the curve of the mountain wall, as if trying to catch me in its embrace. In the scattered windows on either side old woman would sit, watching the passing people below. Their eyes would fall on me with curious intent, but were never hostile though they would sometimes whisper too loudly, "Look, there she is, that's her!"

They weren't trying to be rude, and I knew that. Rumors were bound to spread like wildfire by woman with nothing better to do, especially while an outsider walked through their streets. It was only natural for them to talk; I was something new, something undiscovered, something that made their imaginations run with the mystery of who I may be. I looked up to them with a smile as warm as the spring-like air around us, before disappearing around the corner.

I'd only managed a few steps before I was forced to back into an open doorway as two children rushed past; a young girl only steps behind a slightly older boy, the look of desperation and sadness painted clearly on her face.

"Hey, no fair, give it back!" she shouted after the boy, and I caught a glimpse of a rag doll clutched firmly in his grasp.

"Only if you catch me," the boy called over his shoulder as he took a hard cut around the corner I'd just passed.

"Don't make me use it," she threatened, turning the corner after him and planting her feet with two solid steps that kicked up plumes of dust as they fell.

I snuck a glimpse towards what was about to unfold to see the boy look over his shoulder as a cocky smirk pressed his lips, "You wouldn't," he said, trying to mask the slightest hint of worry in his voice.

The girl's hair had begun to rise parallel with arms that were outstretched before her, "You made me," she warned, her fingers twitching in a swift, patterned, burst as if she was playing with a puppet on strings.

The boy's steps faltered then as he turned to face her in a brief fit of stupor as her palms rotated towards the ceiling as if cupping an invisible bowl. The boy's shirt began to ruffle as if kissed by a gentle breeze in a breezeless city; in an instant he was suspended several feet in the air.

"Give her to me," the girl ordered, her fingers still twitching, eyes locked on the boy with a deadly gaze; rendering him little more than puppet suspended in the air by invisible strings.

His head tilted curiously to the side as the ground began to tremble. Pebbles began to rattle like popped corn and a square outline shivered its way into existence below the girl's feet before launching skyward with such force that I was blasted with a gust of wind even from where I watched.

The girl lost focus as she rose, jumping off the block of displaced earth as the boy fell to the ground cushioned by a bed of sand that had formed below him. His arm extended towards one of the adobe walls, his fist clenched, and he swung his arm in her direction. Another block shot out from the wall beside her with incredible speed and I watched in amazement as she faced the coming chunk of earth mid-decent; seeming to pull herself up and over the block without ever touching it to do so in one fluid movement as if she were simply plucked out of the way.

"You don't quit do you?" the boy said, brushing the sand off as he stood.

The girl jumped off of the suspended block, which reverted to nothing more than sand as she did, landing lightly back on the ground.

"Hey," an old woman yelled from the perfectly square hole the young boy had made, "none of that here or you're going to hurt someone, and fix my damn wall!"

A new kind of fear struck the boy as he passed a worried glance to the woman above before looking back to the girl, who hadn't dared to break her deadly stare, and tossed the tattered old doll towards her. The doll drifted gently into the girl's arms, and she held it tightly for a moment before skipping back in the boy's direction with a beaming smile.

I left them then, amused, to say the least, and made my way back to the market district. Walking over one of the main bridges I was amazed by the swarm of people making their way to the colosseum which sat perched atop one of the central most spires. There was a steady line of soon-to-be spectators climbing the staircase carved into the spires rock face, and passing over each bridge that connected to that spires plateau.

Everyone had been flooding into the open, oval shaped, building that bore large stone pillars along each tier of its outer wall, peppered with people. The front entrance was a series of three archways that took up the entire height of the four story building and as I passed by I could see a short hallway that opened up into the arena. Beyond, I could see only the packed stands of the far side, and the occasional prismatic flare escape the field's high walls. Even from where I stood the crowd's deafening roar hit me like a crashing wave, and I could only imagine the excitement inside.

Despite the commotion in the colosseum the market was bustling nonetheless, a place where at all times a sea of people overflowed into the streets to visit the countless shops along every inch of the district. Over the booming sound of vendors pitching their goods and barter I found it hard to concentrate enough to tell exactly what was being sold, never mind for how much; it was only between small gaps between the vendors that I could find the doorway to an actual store where I might be able to gather my thoughts.

On each table I passed by were a laid out array of food, decorations, and weapons from all over the world. It seemed as if there was little that couldn't be found here.

The rich scent of exotic spiced tea peaked my interest, as always, as I passed by what had become my favorite restaurant. I took one of the only four barstool seats that hugged a counter wrapping around a street's corner.

"Look who decided to visit," the bald man behind the marble counter said with a slight nod of his head and a smile through a rough beard as he dried off a glass with a black sash.

He was a burly man, actually, one of the largest I'd seen here in Terra Sera, and packed with muscle.

He wore a sleeveless shirt, revealing a wave of tribal patterns tattooed over the caps of his shoulders. He was a brute, but one with the kindest heart.

By the time I found myself comfortable he'd already placed a tall stone cup before me, filled to the brim with a type of creamy spiced chai that had brought me back here time and time again. As always, his overused hands dwarfed the cup as he held it; small shards, almost like snowflakes, spreading over the stone and chilling the drink inside.

"The usual?" he asked, though he knew the answer, with a strong accent that immediately gave away the fact that he wasn't native to this area at all. I'd always wondered where he'd come from, but he would never tell.

"You know me so well Baron," I returned, sipping my tea, seeing he had already begun to prepare a bowl of white rice doused with the juices of a fruit he'd called a pineapple and peppered with foreign spices, all topped with a green leaf that already had my mouth watering in anticipation.

I liked watching him work; his black sash and white pants meant he was a man of third order, the merchant class, a class that would hardly get their hands dirty for their coin. Baron was the exception, only accepting the hand of one other man wearing the opposite arrangement of colors, meaning he was of the fourth order, the working class.

The whole class system here had confused me. As I looked around I noticed very few people in the crowd sharing my colors, which might have bothered me if I didn't feel so comfortable around those of the lower orders—feeling as if I belonged with them from the start. Here, the soot-ridden fourth order workers bringing their goods to the merchants who sold them, though still detached from my reality outside, felt more like home. Still, even in this little pocket of familiarity tucked in the corner of the city, I still felt uneasy knowing that the merchants, who hardly did anything other than talk, pocketed most of the profit from the goods the fourth order workers tirelessly produced for the city. Worse still, those of my assigned order could hardly be bothered to do much of anything, feeling some misplaced sense of entitlement that I would never understand, all while living, not surviving, with the once lost comforts of a civilized world.

In the Cekrit camps, only those of the fourth order would truly have the tools and skills needed to survive. Even the merchants, with their perfectly white pants and quick tongue wouldn't last long out there. Those with valuable skills would earn the respect and prestige of the others in their camps and would never be judged by what colors they wore.

That's why I liked Baron, he wasn't afraid to dive into his work, and treated his partner with the equal respect he deserved.

"Slow down," Baron began, "you eat as if you hadn't in days."

He was right, though that was more so out of habit than hunger. The bittersweet tinge of the pineapple bit my lips with every spoonful, and the rich spices, the identities of which Baron refused to share, left an aftertaste that had be diving back into the bowl for more.

"Another bowl?" Baron asked, seeming to sense when I swallowed the last bite, briefly breaking from his conversation.

"Oh no! That's plenty, thank you," I returned, fishing out two coins from a silk pouch Ava had continuously filled for me, placing them down on the counter.

Baron slid the coins off of the counter, placing one in a jar behind him and slipping the other into his pocket with a smile, "Anytime dear," he said, returning to his conversation.

I tilted the stone cup until every last drop of that tea fell onto my tongue and placed it back onto the counter before disappearing back into the commotion behind me, which was still a little overwhelming.

My hunger satisfied, I dipped into one of the dimly lit shops I was already familiar with, looking for a quiet place to ease my mind. The soft orange flicker of candlelight painting the countless books which lined every inch of every wall welcomed me in. Every shelf teemed with possibility and adventure, and those books begged to be read; I told myself I would, eventually. Placed on the scattered table, always beside a half burnt candle, were loose artifacts that I couldn't tell were true antiques, or just another one of the cheap knockoffs sold outside.

I gravitated towards the back corner of the room where a cluster of plush couches surrounding an antique wooden table called to me. At the center of the table sat a leather-bound tome with red foil pages, held closed by a thick leather strap. The front cover was built up in layers, a worn silver circle sitting atop the grey leather hide tucked into each corner, golden details flowing over the silver's edges in an ornate design of stacked metal that churned like a fractal wave tracing the borders. A distorted grid made up the space between, connecting the golden border to a golden crest, a vertical figure eight fixed in the center.

I turned the tome over to study its back, which was identical to the front save for the centermost crest. An elaborate golden print ran down its binding, it was beautiful looking language, but one that had been lost with the times. My fingers ran over the golden words, perhaps wishing that if I could feel them something deep within me might remember their meaning. No matter how many times I've felt myself be drawn to this book, no amount of contemplation or wishful thinking offered a meaning.

I opened the cover with care, beginning to shift through the thick pages, studying the diagrams and glyphs scattered throughout. On some, rough sketches of the human body had a certain intricacy in their detail, showing the way each muscle works in unison, or how energy flows throughout. Others were filled only with a rushed handwriting in the same unfamiliar language that I couldn't begin to understand. Still, I tried to make sense of what I saw, grasping for some clues of form or meaning until the text began to fade, leaving only a blank page before me. I flipped through the next pages with confusion, hoping to catch just one more glimpse, one more clue into the mystery trapped within, looking for an answer that would never come.

"Such a temperamental book that one is," a woman's voice said from behind.

I pulled myself from my empty gaze to see the shop owner; a middle aged woman of second order. Her voice always had a soothing effect for me, with her soft tone and perfectly articulate speech.

"Out of all the books here," she continued, her words floating like a feather through still air, "this one in particular gives me the most trouble. It hardly allows anyone to see past a few pages until the words just fade away. "

She reached over to take the book from my lap while pulling out a pair of glasses that accented the newly formed wrinkles below her eyes which were magnified by the lens. She wore the same warm expression as always, the same that had first welcomed me in.

"Hi Ms. Ingalls," I said.

"Hello Sage," she said, shaking her head with disappointment as she flipped through every blank page, "I'm surprised to see you here today, the whole city is up in a frenzy about the games you know."

"Are they? Actually, I came because of something in my dreams that's been bothering me," I said, pointing to the binding, "Those symbols, I've seen them before, they are written all over the walls in my dreams and I feel like I know them, or, should know them but I don't."

Ms. Ingalls smiled, closing the tome to run her fingers over the symbols pressed into the leather binding, "Of course you know them, these words are written in the language of the gods, they are part of our history—but it is not our place to know what they mean."

"What good is the language of the gods if we don't have any? Sera is being held captive, and she only knows where Klaus might be. Do you ever think if we learned how to read this book we might be able to find him? Or we might learn some secret that could save us?" I asked.

Her expression grew dim, troubled even, but I could see a glimpse of the same wonder and curiosity in her eye, "Of course I wonder Sage, but I fear that some things in this world are better left undiscovered."

"Than if it's not our place to know, what of Klaus? I feel like I know so little about him, other than the fact that he abandoned us. I want to know why. Do you have anything about him?"

"I'll look through what I have, if I dig anything up I'll let you know," she said, "now as for the games, Terra Sera needs a new Guardian and if you're to be a part of this city I'll have you off to see them, you simply must!" she said, passing me a look that said 'well-what-are-you-waiting-for,' before closing the book and placing it back onto the table.

I gathered myself, stood up from the couch, and headed to the door, but before I left I called over my shoulder to Ms. Ingalls, "Don't forget to look!" before stepping back out into the bustling market district.

It was almost as if every vendor could sense the presence of someone new. Each began to shout and rant about their goods, trying to out-yell the vendor beside them. I weaved my way through the countless people, misplaced tables, and children running about in between following the crowd and made my way to the arena I'd seen before.

Surrounding the arena's many entrances small groups of men huddled together, arguing over who would become the next Guardian. Behind them, scattered stands were surrounded by gambling spectators or those looking for a quick meal. The smell of spices lingered in the air, tempting me, and my stomach ached for food with flavor, but, I resisted—not wanting to get too used to the luxury of good food. Children fought playfully with their still undeveloped skills, trying their best to mimic what they'd seen earlier that day but with their own unique power.

I could see Demi in the distance, near a side gate with thick iron bars, looking almost ceremonial. He wore a long white jacket that narrowed down to a singular point in the back just around his knees with detailed black tribal patterns running the length of its flared arms. His hood hung just above his eyes, causing nearly half of his face to be engulfed in shadow. Long, metal tipped spike-like tassels hung from either side of the hood's drawstrings. His shirt hung half open, and I could see his chest bare beneath it. His matching pants flared towards the top and narrowed with his taped ankles, much like the pants I had seen him wearing while by the falls.

Demi was surrounded by girls, all lost in his charisma and hypnotizing smile. I pitied them for their weak hearts. He had both arms draped around the shoulders of the girls beside him as others circled around, all believing that the words he spoke were directed to her and not the girl beside them. It was obvious that he loved the attention and ill-deserved fame. His head poked up from the crowd around him, looking like he was scouting for more hearts to draw into his trap, as if the ones he'd already stolen weren't enough to quench his thirst. When his eyes fell on me his carefree smile instantly vanished, and he leaned to whisper into the girl's ears under his arms. They giggled amongst themselves, love-struck, as he walked away into the arena.

I tried to catch up to him though I didn't know why, perhaps wanting to ask him what his issue was or maybe just to annoy him, but he was lost in the crowd before I could even reach the gate. The crowd's excitement boomed through the arena, hitting me with tangible waves of paralyzing sound. I managed to weave through the undulating sea of people, struggling to find a place to watch with a decent view. Never having truly been around more than a dozen others, the magnitude of people surrounding me was overwhelming and I felt short spikes of nervous energy ripping at my insides, a feeling I hoped would fade away as I became lost in the infectious energy of the crowd.

The center of the arena was flooded with water only a few inches deep, but raged like the ocean amidst a storm, leaving only a few scattered islands of dry land. The waves would crash against the arena's walls, drenching the crowd in sheets of ocean-like spray.

On one island stood a lanky, light skinned boy in a grey sleeveless shirt holding a metal rod that jolted sparks of electricity out from its either end. His hair was bleach blonde and spiked to sharp points. He was watching the waters ebb and flow intently, shuffling in circles away from the tides that would inch closer, in an attempt to find some meaning to even the slightest shifts in the tide.

A swell broke behind him, shooting a slew of liquid darts toward him as it did, he quickly turned to deflect each with a show of a masterfully trained hand. Suddenly, more darts came from other directions and for a terrifying few moments the crowd stood on edge as he was engaged in a full flurry of defensive strikes, desperately fending off the bombardment. His body twisted and turned, danced even, through the storm as he wielded his staff with practiced skill to deflect every dart effortlessly. Bolts of electricity jumped from the rod, striking whatever he couldn't directly impact.

"Yeah! Get him! You have him on his toes now!" an older gentleman screamed through cupped hands beside me, his voice dominating over those around him, it was joyful and proud, yet in a way very forceful.

"What's going on?" I had to ask twice before he heard me.

"What? Oh," he said, looking at me for only a moment then back to the fight, pointing in the general direction of the boy center field, "The electrician, that's Kai — and the one in the water, why that's my only son, Aydin. I'm so proud of him, look at him, he shares my gift."

Below, Kai's eyes were fixed on the water surrounding his tiny island. I tried to follow his glance but could see nothing but crashing waves and shifting tides with no hint of another fighter. Kai stood center island, lunging at times toward the skittish shore only to drive his staff into the ground where the water retreated.

Slowly, the same liquid darts that had threatened him before began to raise from the surface once more. There was a certain calm now as the entire arena stood still, paralyzed with anticipation. Kai's attacks stopped for a moment as if he'd fallen into in a sudden state of shock, fearful of what was to come but staying calm despite being veiled by a dome of darts. The darts began to rotate and stretch, forming needle-like strands, all aiming toward him. After a painfully long moment they turned sheer white, beginning to solidify into ice.

I looked back to the man beside me for answers, trying to follow his gaze in an attempt to find his son. His eyes were focused, shifting from left to right in short jittery motions. His shouting had stopped, and his arm hung as if in a sling by his side. His fingers were curled in on themselves, weaving within each other as he whispered beneath his breath.

"Sage!" Ava's voice shot out as her arms wrapped around my neck from behind, catching me off balance and sending me into the man beside me.

"Sorry," I said, catching myself on his shoulder.

The crowd's cheers boomed as Ava pointed over my shoulder, "Look!"

The dozens of darts that had surrounded Kai had lost their form, all liquefying in unison before falling back into the now raging swells. To one end of the arena, not far from Kai's small island, two waves violently broke upon one another. As the spray cleared and the waves settled I saw Aydin for the first time, standing on the water's surface, half of his body still in liquid form.

Kai acted the moment Aydin's body reached the surface, rushing to the edge of his island and thrusting his staff into the shifting waves. An electric bolt cut through the swells and struck Aydin, pulsing through his liquid body. His bloodcurdling scream boomed over the crowd's cheers as he fell limp onto to the ground, the water beneath him slowly evaporated to nothing.

"I—he was going to win that," the man beside me said, looking at me with disgust before disappearing into the crowd, cursing beneath his breath.

"Demi's up next you know," Ava said with a smile, snapping me out of my trance, "he's going to win I just know it! He's fighting Han, who's tough, but I think Demi is tougher."

"What is all of this for anyway? These games," I asked while Ava climbed down from my back and took the place of the gentleman who had just scurried away in anger.

"To choose a new Guardian of Terra Sera, of course," she said, "every five years, or whenever the old one dies another Guardian is chosen. It's one of the highest honors we have here and I just know Demi can do it!" she paused, now speaking in a more somber tone, "Our father was a Guardian before he passed, I think that's what pushes Demi to try so hard."

Ava motioned to the arena floor, where no trace of flooding remained. Rather, from opposite gates I could see Demi and Han approaching the center. Demi was relaxed, perhaps too relaxed, his hands still resting in his pockets as he walked and a smug expression painted on his face.

Han wore a more serious expression, fist clenched and ready. His clothes were dirt stained and torn at the pant bottoms. He had predominantly Asian characteristics, his skin sooty and his uncombed jet black hair hanging loosely just above his shoulders. He was thin, and short, but his arms had built muscle from years of hard work. His long strides shortened to a shuffle before halting altogether.

"How do you win?" I asked.

"The games last many months, and are broken into different stages. This," she said nodding to the arena floor, "is stage one, winner moves on. With stage two the winners are given a mission. Those who return successful move to stage three, that is different every time. From there no one knows how a Guardian is chosen except the Council."

As I watched the two men below Ava continued, "Demi wants to win because of our father, to show pride or something manly like that." She looked down for a moment as if her words brought her a pain she couldn't yet understand. Her head jumped back up and with a smile as she exclaimed, "But that's okay because if Demi wins he'll pick me to watch over and train as his student, and I can finally see what it's like outside!"

"They would let you leave?" I asked

"Of course, well, once you're a Guardian. You live on the outside, watching over the city," Ava said, looking at me for a brief moment before fixing her eyes back on her brother.

Demi was standing just the same as before, his hands brushing through his hair, pulling off his hood as he did. He slowly draped his robe off one shoulder, then the other, tossing it to one side to a heap on the floor. The same markings that laid out the detail on his robe were painted in black on his skin. I could hear a crowd of girls near the front shout his name but his glare towards Han was never broken. Demi was carved of stone, every muscle was in proportion with the next, determined and cold. He stepped forward to ready himself and waited for the judge's mark.

Han knelt down, placing a single seed in the ground, patting it down before he rose. He looked up to the judge, high on a stand along the border of the field, and nodded. The judge looked for Demi's approving nod and gave the signal to begin.

As the match began Han immediately leapt backwards, diving both hands deep within his pockets before throwing hundreds of seeds across the arena floor. His arms rose from his sides, and with them the seeds began to take root, driving themselves deep within the arena floor with incredibly rampant growth.

A thick layer of vines weaved within each other as they spread across the floor between swiftly sprouting trees, the single seed Han had planted before the match began shook the arena's walls as a great oak erupted from the earth. Its roots burst in and out of the ground as they reached every corner of the field, crashing up against the high walls and nearly flooding over into the stands.

Ava nudged me, "Han's responsible for the gardens that grow around here, not that it takes much effort given his gift, but he's why it's all so beautiful here."

As the roots cut through the earth below, the topsoil would burst in a near explosion of soil. One root broke through, driving itself at Demi, who pivoted, letting it pass mere inches by his face.

By now the arena had been transformed into a forest designed to protect the great oak. Han moved swiftly between the trees as those around Demi began to send branches like whistling whips, and petals like razors, through the air towards him. Demi effortlessly danced between the swinging limbs while deep puddles of darkness pooled beneath his every step, hardly phased by the attack.

At first one, then maybe a half-dozen pitch black spheres began to raise from those pools. Dark matter dripped from their ever shifting shapes, taking the form of an insect-like face with a strong set of mandibles extending beyond their lower row of teeth, lined with a more all their own. Their eyes were large and oval, a bright yellow, blinking rapidly as they scanned the forest, catching their first sight.

The creatures had undersized arms that hung like tiny claws by their sides. Their legs were long, too long even, entirely too big for their bodies and moved with a long sweeping motion as they ran. Two jagged antenna rose from the tops of their heads, and fell over behind them, masked slightly by the churning black mist that drifted off of their undefined backs. They were no more than three feet tall and swayed from side to side while standing, dripping with a black sludge that burned the ground below them. Everything they touched as they ran through the underbrush soon withered and browned like leaves in mid fall.

One of them spotted Han, who had perched himself on a high branch of the great oak, and tilted its head curiously to eye him. Thick strands stretched between its lips like baleen as its head cocked to the other side to let out a rattling click that echoed through the stands, calling its brothers. The others, whose heads were to the ground, all perked up and made a chorus of the same sinister sound before making a mad dash for Han.

Their arms flailed helplessly by their side as their legs made long circular strides. Despite being a pack of ravenous darklings, I found their movement almost amusing as they ran, leaning forward with the weight of their oversized heads. I couldn't help but chuckle to myself.

"Don't laugh," Ava said without averting her eyes from the battlefield, "they are called Kurki, and don't underestimate them; they will tear you apart if you let your guard down for too long."

I looked on more intently as a few jumped from tree to tree, others remaining on the ground. Everything they touched became withered and, with each dying plant, Han struggled to raise another in his defense, seeming to lose track of what seeds were left to grow. A couple Kurki dove head first into the trees, disappearing into the trunks. A trail of withering plants began to circle around the oak where Han watched.

Demi was now sprinting through the undergrowth towards Han as four Kurki scrambled up the oak. Han seemed panicked, but climbed the tree with a nimble grace that suggested he had memorized every branch. Han kept his composure, making sure to keep sight of the advancing Kurki while trying to keep Demi at bay.

Suddenly, a root erupted from the soil, wrapping itself around Demi's leg and sending him tumbling to the ground. More rose with it as nearby vines began to creep closer. A half dozen roots loomed over Demi for a brief moment of terror before driving themselves down with piercing blows. Demi struggled in an attempt to break free from this prison, twisting and rolling to narrowly dodge the spikes as they drove deep into the ground beside him.

The same black mist that had drifted from the Kurki began to drift from Demi's right hand, the darkness seeping into his skin as the mist settled. At first, I thought the mist was forming a type of armor, but as his hand jerked open and he let out a terrifying scream I knew this was something else entirely, this wasn't armor, this was a transformation.

"No Demi, not now," Ava said, her eyes filled with worry.

"What? What's wrong?" I demanded to know.

"He's losing control," she said without breaking her stare, more so under her breath than to me directly.

Demi's hand had become pitch black, with large plated scales creeping just past his wrist. His clawed fingers ripped at the vines as they attacked him, causing them to wither within his grasp. He broke free, standing up slowly with his head down and fist clenched, facing Han—hatred consuming him.

The Kurki clumsily slumped over one another as they moved up the trunk of Han's massive oak with incredible speed, forcing Han to climb further up the tree to escape them. With a sudden display of balance and concentration Han jumped from one branch to another as they erupted from the trunk to catch him while others burst out to pierce the Kurki as they closed in.

The summons would dodge the sudden growths, but eventually all were hit and reduced to little more than small plumes of black mist drifting through the canopy. Han relaxed as the last one fell, but a moment too soon as the two that still lingered in the nearby trees emerged, attacking him in tandem.

One dove from a branch above Han, who caught the creature in its descent with another swift piercing growth from the tree. Han side stepped on his branch, dodging his own attack, struggling to keep his balance for the first time in the fight. The other Kurki reacted to this moment of weakness, clutching to Han's leg and scurrying around his body towards his neck.

Demi watched from the base of the great oak tree, arms fully extended to either side, palms flat against two withering trees.

"He's calling another spirit," Ava whispered.

I watched him intently; he was cold, closed off, completely lost in his own world of rage and more than anything else, confident. Demi watched Han continue to struggle against the last Kurki, and, content that his creature had bought him enough time, began to summon this new evil. Demi's hands drew away from the trees slowly, as if being forced back by an invisible wall closing in on him. In a moment, two heads began to lurch from where his hands had been placed on either side. He stepped back, letting his hands fall by his side, allowing his new summons to pull themselves from the void.

"What are those things?" I asked, looking to Ava for an answer.

"Something new," she whispered, in a state of disbelief, "he'd been talking about them for months now. I can't believe he's actually managed to bring them from the other side in their true form."

"But what are they?" I pushed for clarity.

"The Vemosa," Ava said, "it's over."

The white heads that emerged from the trunks were long and almost birdlike, with large circular eyes holding nothing more than a black abyss in their center. Their faces were covered entirely by a white mask, reminding me of those worn by old plague doctors, hiding their faces. They had a long protruding nose, like the beak of a vulture and as their bodies stretched out from the trees I could see their arms were almost skeletal and grey in color like the body of a decaying corpse, with long, curved scythes running along their forearms towards them. There was a tattered black cloak masking the rest of their bodies, if they had one, that was little more than an ominous mist.

Above, the last remaining Kurki snapped at any piece of open skin it could find as Han struggled to hold the creature at bay. Every touch that met his skin left a deep burn. The veins around the scattered burns turned black through his skin as they spread across his body. Han finally found the strength to grab the Kurki, his scream shaking the stands as his bare hands were scorched by the Kurki's toxic fumes. As he threw the Kurki off of the great oak he'd either lost his balance or began to collapse from the pain of darkness spreading through his veins.

Branches grew in an attempt to catch their master's fall but he could do little more than scratch at every passing one, his hand burned too badly to hold on as he desperately tried to keep from crashing down. Below him, vines began to intertwine into a bed, ready to catch his fall as a last ditch bid for survival.

The two Vemosa sank into the ground beside Demi, who had turned to walk away, unfazed by Han's perilous descent. The bed of vines withered and died before Han could reach them and in its place a churning void had formed. Just before Han reached it the second Vemosa burst from the oak's trunk, grasping him in his descent and plunging the two into the void that was the first Vemosa's embrace. The void closed behind them as they disappeared into the darkness.

With Han no longer in control, the forest had begun to die, leaving Demi to emerge through the tree line amongst falling branches, decaying overgrowth, and plumes of kicked up dust.

While the judge called the match Ava grabbed my hand, rushing down to Demi. The crowd was quiet, unmoving, the low buzz of their collective whispers filling the air. Something was terribly wrong. Ava didn't give Demi the chance to speak, pushing his hands aside as he passed her a sly smile and tried to take her into his arms.

"Did you really have to call them? The Vemosa? Where is he Demi? You lost control and you know it!" her voice was fierce as her temper flared, and in that moment I felt as though I might be more scared of Ava than I was of Demi, despite what he'd just done.

Ava grabbed his arm by the elbow looking at it intently as she passed her hand over the plated armor that had transformed her brother's hand like scorched earth. As her green healing light washed over it, the darkness began to fade and his hand slowly began to take its human form once more. I noticed his hair, the few speckled white strands had seemingly multiplied, and as the darkness on his hand faded away so did many of those strands, though many new ones did stay.

Demi didn't seem fazed by his sister's disapproval, relishing in his victory. He passed a look over his shoulder, where two black pools had formed side by side; from them, the two Vemosa rose from the arena floor, holding Han between them. The moment the crowd saw Han return safely the dreadful murmur of concern subsided to a complete roar of applause, chanting Demi's name.

"Well, I won didn't I? Oh, and don't worry about the hand," Demi said, pulling himself away from his sister's healing touch, "it'll work itself out, always does."

"Demi," Ava began.

"Ava," he returned, raising a clenched fist to his fans, "my people love me."

"Well then," she sighed, defeated, "congratulations."

I watched Demi curiously, who still winced at the pain of a hand still regaining its color and form. I felt like I had to say something, but all I could muster was a, "yeah, good job," which was ignored, naturally.

"Demi, my boy!" a man's voice rang out, dominating over the cheers of the crowd, "I knew you wouldn't let me down."

Demi's relaxed posture straightened up instantly as the older man approached. He wore a long formal black robe with red trim along the edges and the hood, which was worn down at the moment. I could tell he was of the first order, simply by his posture, despite his colors. A man perhaps in his mid-fifties, he was full with rich, youthful, energy and held the air of a well-respected leader.

"Good fight, no, great fight—" he began, "I haven't seen something so entertaining since your father's first round in the games. He'd be so proud!"

"Councilor Madsen," Demi said, offering his only healthy hand—but the Councilor ignored the gesture completely and draped his arm over Demi's shoulder, "thank you."

"I trust you and Ava are prepared to join us and the rest of the winners tonight for the feast then," Councilor Madsen began before eyeing me by Ava's side, "oh? I see you've made friends with—Sage, was it? Why she can come too!"

Demi avoided eye contact with me when I looked to him for answers, "we will be there."

Councilor Madsen looked back to me, "You've stirred up a lot of talk around the city with your arrival you know. I trust you'll have something to wear?"

Ava jumped in then, "I'll take care of that."

"I'm sure you will. We will see you tonight then?"

"I wouldn't miss it for the world," Ava exclaimed, before hastily leading me away.

"Oh and Ava," the Councilor called to us, "please leave the hat at home this time."

# Chapter 3:

"Who was that?" I asked, watching Ava sift through stacks of clothes tucked into drawers I didn't even know existed.

"Madsen?" she asked without looking up, "Ah! Found it."

"Yeah, I mean you didn't seem too happy to see him."

"Try this on," she said, catching me off guard as she tossed a silky heap of a dress into my face.

"Okay, okay!" I said shuffling into the bathroom, leaving her to dig through the drawers while I got ready.

"After our parents died," Ava said from the other room, "and after we found our way to Terra Sera—"

I inspected the orange silk dress she'd given me as I listened.

"He sort of adopted us."

The dress reminded me of ones I'd seen in abandoned shop windows, their studded rhinestones still shimmering in the sunlight. I always guessed no one had a need for them anymore, being one of the few things left behind.

"I guess I never really accepted him as my father," Ava continued.

"At least he's there for you," I called, turning the dress to see it would swoop down to the small of my back, light green emeralds lining edges that would be pulled tight by an amazing lace design in the void.

"He tries—" Ava said with a pause, "are you ready yet?"

"Hold on," I called, quickly stripping down to try it on.

I'd never worn anything like this; for as long as I could remember I had either made my own clothes or scavenged whatever I could. I never had time to be girly because I had always lived on the run, and without having a special gift, I had to be a bit of a tomboy to fend for myself as well as everyone else could. Whatever it took to stay alive. The dress was alien to me; altogether too restricting and flashy. I had no idea why anyone would actually want to own one of these.

"How does it fit?" Ava called from the other room.

"Perfect," I said, looking at my reflection in the bathroom's marble wall, a bit surprised, "how'd you know my size?"

"Like I said, you were out cold for a while and I kind of got bored sitting there watching you talk to yourself."

"Oh," I said, blushing, now slightly embarrassed as I looked back down at my dress.

By the time I walked back into the room Ava was already dressed in a full gown of her order, cut off at the shoulders with an ornate golden trim and accented by loose bell sleeves tied down just above her elbow, hiding her hands. It was more formal than mine, but it suited her perfectly. She'd look like a proper young woman if it weren't for the fur hat still on her head, then again, I wasn't much of an authority on what could look proper.

"I thought the Councilor told you to leave the hat at home?" I asked.

"Always does, never will- my mother made me this hat when I was a baby, before she died. I won't take it off, ever, I don't care what he says," Ava said, taking a deep breath and straightening up into an entirely different posture than I've ever seen her wear, "Now, you're still new here so you need to make a good first impression. All the Councilors and city elite will be there, as well as the contestants in this year's games. Stick with me and stay proper, and you'll be fine."

I gave her an approving nod, slightly impressed by her change in attitude. "Well then," she sighed, "we're off."

Walking back out into the cool air of the city, it amazed me how the drifting sprites had a light cycle all their own, just as the world outside. Terra Sera was dark as night, lit only by the sprites dim blue-green glow, and the soft orange flicker of candlelight that sat above nearly every door. Some low floating sprites would blink yellow, then fade away now and again as if to mimic wild fireflies. Even the ceiling mimicked the starry skies of a perfectly clear night.

Ava and I wove through the city largely unnoticed among the excitement of an ever shifting crowd pushing towards a large stone building perched atop the city's centermost spire where Council and, for tonight, the feast was being held. The building's ancient architecture boasted rows of long pillars along its every side, holding up a large dome which made up its roof. Dozens of steps stretched over the front face of the building, and I felt as if they were punishing me for wanting to enter the open doors waiting at the top.

Small clusters of would-be guest were bunched together here and there on the steps, but most had been steadily flowing inside. As we passed the scattered clusters I caught curious glances tossed in our direction, but no one had been troubled enough to leave their conversation for the pursuit of ours. I followed Ava sluggishly as she greeted one person, then another, with practiced gestures and phrases, each delivered with a renewed sense of false enthusiasm.

As we entered into the grand hall I saw, for the first time, where we would be spending our evening. Five tables stretched the full length of the room, all topped with tablecloths died a deep red and lined with an ornate golden trim that oddly complimented the mis-matched silverware already placed on top. Ava lead us to a pair of waiting seats close to the head of the centermost of the five tables, and, taking her seat, sighed, brushing her dress free of any crease that may have appeared.

"Very," I began with a pause, searching for the right word to describe her behavior, "politic. I mean for someone who is usually so lively."

"I guess it's something you get used to with things like this," she responded dryly, seeming lost within her thoughts as she stared blankly into the crowd. It seemed as if she had shut herself off completely, working on autopilot to remain poised and true to this practiced behavior.

The tables themselves took up the majority of the space in the grand hall and all were topped with artifacts from far off lands, candles, and bundles of exotic fruits. At the head of each stood large chairs that looked much more like a thrown than the typical, though mismatched as well, dining chairs in the rest of the hall. Each table sat members of a particular order, with the Council member who oversaw them taking their place at the head of each. The middle table, where we sat, was the shortest of them all and was meant for people of special honor.

My eyes glanced over the crowd, finding mostly strange faces and only a handful that I had vaguely recognized. I decided to walk around.

"Ava?" I asked

"Yes?" she answered blankly, looking off in the other direction.

"The bathroom, where is it?" I asked, needing an excuse to get up.

"Sure," Ava responded, not breaking her mindless gaze.

"Okay then, I'll be back," I said, standing up and taking off into the crowd without giving her a second look.

The main hallway, leading into grand hall, was a river of traffic flowing both in and out as the last guests began to arrive. Weaving my way through the crowd I made it to one of the outer walls and away from the other guests. The dining area was surrounded by large pillars supporting a balcony on the second floor that circled the entire room. It was between those pillars and the wall that I found slight refuge.

Squeezing through a group of older gentlemen dressed in clothes foreign to Terra Sera, I found myself in a side hallway with a series of archways leading to a spiral staircase that I assumed would bring me to the balcony above. Along the walls hung portraits of Stigma holders dressed in black robes with red details, much like the ones Councilor Madsen had worn earlier. I took a moment to look upon each as I walked up the steps, realizing that these were the portraits of the five members of the Council. Labeled under their names was the city, and order, they were responsible for governing.

I looked over each one more time, five Councilors meant that there were five cities ruled by the Council hidden somewhere throughout the world. Hiding, surviving, waiting, but for what? The Council hadn't shown itself on the battlefield, or anywhere for that matter, in close to two decades. I'd be lying if I said it didn't bother me that they have been living like this all along while everyone I knew on the outside struggled to survive. Then again, I can't say I wasn't bothered with myself for staying.

I made my way to the balcony, looking over its edge to watch the sea of people below. Scanning the room slowly, I spotted Han in one corner, the boy Demi had just fought earlier today. He was smiling as if everything was fine, and was dressed just as formal as everyone around him, but was obviously more comfortable in his normal, worn out clothes. I couldn't say I blamed him, these clothes were altogether to restricting and impractical.

Ava had finally left her seat and was now beside Demi mingling with the other members of the Council near the head of our table. Councilor Madsen was there as well, though his back was turned to the group as he spoke with Ms. Ingalls. She wore a serious expression, and spoke quickly in little more than a whisper, leaning in close to Councilor Madsen's ear at times. Councilor Madsen listened intently, nodding every now and then, seeming to approve of what she was saying.

Ms. Ingalls conversation broke off as she caught glimpse of me on the balcony, her expression suddenly became worrisome. Her gaze lingered on me for a long moment before she continued her conversation with the Councilor, who placed a hand on her shoulder and sent her off once she had seemed more relaxed.

I continued to watch the other guest, tracing the cold touch of the balcony's smooth marble finish with my fingers as I walked along its length. Toward the back wall the balcony formed into an overhanging semi-circle where five large chairs of red velvet and black wood were at rest by each other's side, overlooking the hall below. I continued tracing the cold marble with my fingertips, watching the crowd below as I wandered closer to the Councilor's miniature thrones.

As I drew closer there was a certain degree of tension building, as if all eyes had suddenly fallen on me. I snuck a slightly paranoid glance back down to the main hall where, thankfully, the other guest were too caught up in each other than to notice me in the shadows above. Demi, however, held a piercing gaze in my direction and excused himself from his conversation before I had time to fake a smile. For a moment, I felt equally repulsed as he, then oddly curious as I wondered why I caused him so much discomfort.

Suddenly, I felt an overwhelming presence beside me and I turned to see a young man leaning against the railing just inches from me. He was tall, and thin, with pale skin unlike anyone else I had seen in this city—almost as if he hadn't seen the light in ages. His blonde hair matched the light shade of his hazel eyes and was tied back into a neat tail. He wore a slight smirk on his face as he reached an arm out in front of me, blocking my path back the way I came, the other swiftly swept around my other side, forcing my back to the railing as he boxed me in. His eyes remained locked onto mine as his face hung just inches away. I braced myself against the railing, too terrified to run, his intent a force tangible in the air.

"Spying, are we? You know, there's been a lot of talk about you Sage, which makes me wonder what a girl like you would be doing here alone. My name is Lain, Councilor Madsen's— other son," he said with a pause, "I'm sure it's your pleasure to meet me."

I didn't dare move, only hopelessly scanned the room over my shoulder for Ava as I tried to think of something to say, "Well—"

"Ah," Lain interrupted, offering a hand to me, "before you ask, my answer is yes—I'll be your date for the night."

"Well, if you'd let me finish," I said, pushing his hand away, "I already have one."

"I don't mean to sound rude—"

"Oh, you don't?" I cut in.

Lain sighed, "If that's true, he obviously doesn't care enough to stay by your side, leaving you to wander at an event like this could be dangerous. It'd be a shame if anything were to—happen to you," he said, brushing my cheek.

"Perhaps, if you had any real power you might hold my interest," I teased, allowing him enjoy this for just a moment, "but for a Councilor's son to go unnoticed at an event like this I don't imagine you're needed, what a shame—" I said sharply, changing my tone as I pulled away from his touch,"—besides, I think my date is just fine thank you."

His eyes narrowed as his grip tightened around the balcony beside me and I pressed myself against the railing, trying to steal what little space I could, but found none. His aggression intensified and for the first time in our encounter, I truly felt threatened.

"Still," he said through a soft laugh with a voice suddenly sharp with daggers thrown from his lips, and a desperate look of disbelief in his eye, "who could be better than a Councilor's son?"

"Oh Sage, that's where you ran off to," Demi's voice came from the darkness before I saw him. A moment later I felt his arm drape around my shoulder as he placed himself between Lain and I. "Come on, dinner is about to start and we wouldn't want to be late now would we?" he said, beginning to lead me away. He looked over his shoulder to Lain as we walked, giving him a slight nod of the head, "Lain, I expect you'll be joining us?"

"You," Lain hissed through his teeth, "it had to be you, didn't it?" He stepped away, letting his right arm hang limp by his side as he clutched it with the other. There was a faint glimmer of light beginning to form beneath the palm of his open hand. His piercing eyes remained fixed on Demi, "You don't deserve to sit with those of our class. Why should my family suffer when yours lost their honor long ago. We should have killed you like the rest of the filthy half bloods." Particles of light began to be drawn in from all directions, floating off the surrounding candles to an orb forming in Lain's palm.

Beyond Lain, pairs of bright yellow eyes blinked into existence, curiously watching from the wall behind him and I knew that the Kurki were waiting for Demi's order to attack, if it were needed—I hoped it didn't.

Demi held me close, leading me away, his eyes fixed on Lain, "Not here, let it go."

"Like hell I will," Lain muttered and before my back was fully turned I could see Lain's light pulse as if it could hardly be contained.

The Kurki jolted into motion, and soon the light became dim as they struggled to consume it.

Lain groaned in pain as the Kurki's touch scorched his skin, "Don't you know you're not supposed to use in Council?" he said, trying to rip off the bubbling mass of Kurki one by one, only to have another replace it.

"You broke that rule first brother," Demi called back over his shoulder.

"See, there you go using that word again, like you're anything compared to me," Lain spoke through his teeth as he focused on channeling his energy, the intensity dissipating the Kurki as his orb formed into a spear. "This is my right!" he yelled as he launched the spear to our backs.

I tried to watch, but Demi forced me back just as a Vemosa rushed past me, catching the spear before vanishing into a plume of black mist. Demi and I had made it to the stairwell by the time

Lain could attack again, and I could see Ava rushing up to greet us. Demi's arm immediately dropped from my shoulder to his side as he led me to safety.

"Where did you two run off to?" Ava asked, placing both hands on her hips.

"I—" I began, unsure if Ava, or anyone, had seen what had happened.

"She got lost, I found her," Demi finished, his tone emotionless.

"I guess this place can be a little confusing at first," Ava said, taking a broad look around as if it were her first time here before coming back to attention, "dinner is about to start soon, come on!"

I passed Demi a look as Ava grasped my hand to lead me back to the table, but wasn't given as much as a glance in response. As we left him, my mind was flooded with uncertainty and I needed to know if he had seen Lain follow me to the balcony, if he'd been watching me since I got here, or if him saving me was just another matter of chance. I knew I'd never have an answer, still, the question burned deep within me—for now, I silently thanked him.

By the time we made it back to the table nearly everyone had taken their seat. Though a few stragglers wandered about, the room had been transformed from the chaos of conversation and excitement to complete order as the five Council members began to take their place at the end of each respective table.

Lain walked past slowly, sitting just beside Demi, opposite of Ava and I, and closest to Councilor Madsen. His demeanor had changed significantly, his eyes hung low, and he moved with a smooth and practiced grace.

He looked up to me after a moment, "I'd like to apologize for my actions earlier. I sometimes get ahead of myself, it is a fault I am learning to control," he said before averting his eyes, his tone sweet and sincere.

I found it hard to believe that this was the same person I had just dealt with on the balcony a moment before. I faked a smile and turned to Ava but the room fell silent as Councilor Madsen stood, beginning to speak with a demanding voice of power.

"Many of you here today do not remember a time before the Pulse, even for me those days are masked with a shadowy haze, leaving some of my earliest memories to be when the skies began to rain fire and all those who held our Gift suddenly became something less than human. For near a quarter century, the people of Terra Sera have found this place to be their sanctuary and lived here in peace, protected by our mountain and Mother Sera herself. Our children have been born here, and though they will never know the evil of the outside world they need not forget that their fathers, and their fathers before them have been exiled, hunted, and killed because of our gift.

"The stigma that's become of our lives has forced millions of our people to live in squalor, to hide, cowering, in the darkest depths of this world, and live in constant fear that Zanin and his Agents of Death may find them. Since the fall of the free world we have won and lost many wars, but our struggle to survive continues daily.

The Councilor paused, his eyes seeming to meet those of each individual in the room. Every person was silent, watching him. He looked down, he had no notes, nothing in front of him to aid him in his speech—speaking only from experience and heart.

He lifted his glass to drink, placing it down before he began to speak once more, "For many, Terra Sera is a place of hope for our people; an example of what life could be. Outside of these mountain walls is a world that many of us have never seen, and never will see. There are camps of our kind that are raided and killed by Zanin's Agents nightly. There are some of us out there that do not sleep for days trying to escape the relentless pursuit of the Agency," he continued, nodding to me, "In Terra Serra, this is not a reality that we have to face. Here, we have thrived, turning a mere camp, a dream, and some luck into one of the largest concentrations of those with our Gift in the world today. To the world outside, we hold the Stigma, but not here. Here, we have a gift of our mother, and here, we are free. The best we can do for our mother is to survive—survive until we are strong enough to take back this world and reshape it in her light.

"However, we can't forget about those who have protected our gates through it all, those who have held vigil through our darkest days, our protectors, the Guardians. Because of them we remain safe and no longer have to live in fear of what we are and can instead stand and be proud!"

The crowd roared with approval and the Councilor raised one hand and lowered it slowly, their voices followed his cue for silence and he continued, "A new Guardian will be chosen, and like those before they will ensure the survival of this city. Today, we saw many great young warriors do battle, and though not everyone tasted victory, everyone that fought has done us a great service. They should feel pride in this day. Now, dine— the next stage of their challenge will begin shortly. Thank you."

The room was silent until his last word, then erupted with conversation as the Councilor took his seat once more with a blatant expression of self-satisfaction painted on his face.

It wasn't long until the room was teeming with life once more, dozens of waiters began to fill the empty aisles carrying large silver platters, all dressed in matching formal uniforms.

Their clothes reminded me of something I had seen in a photo album I had found a few years ago in an abandoned third floor apartment. I remember looking through the pages and seeing pictures with isles of machines and people sitting at them, of people at tables playing cards, of people drinking and laughing. It seemed like all of the workers had the same vest on with a long white shirt beneath it with un-cuffed sleeves. I had never been to or seen a place like this but on the front page was written the word casino—it seemed like an amazing place. I'd always imagined they must have been everywhere before the Pulse, before the fall of the free world, and I wondered if they still existed in the Domes. The clothes the waiters were wearing must have been salvaged from an old casino for events like this. I've always thought there was no better way to discover who someone was than to study the things they left behind—and I savored the memories of those friends I'd never have the chance to meet.

After the Pulse, the rest of the human race, those without the gift, the Pure, fled their homes to escape the violence of the coming war for the safety of the domed cities—I don't think any of them would have dreamed that they would never see their homes again. I'd never seen one of the domes in this lifetime, but I'd heard stories of cities that stretched the horizon, of massive airships hidden within the clouds, some atop spires in the furthest lands, and others left to drift in the security of a vast ocean.

The cities protected by Zanin's empire protected the Pure, leaving all others remaining in the world outside to become targets meant to be killed and nothing more. Because of that, the domes were under near constant siege—but have proved to be no less than an impenetrable fortress often protected in some way by the landscape on which they were built.

The rich aroma of steamed meats and vegetables replacing the dry, earthy, smell of the stone room brought me back to my senses and I welcomed the warmth that had begun to fill the room. Platters of turkey, ham, and chicken overflowed on the plates before us—all decorated with an abundance of fresh greens and fruits. My mouth began to water as I gawked in amazement, never before having seen such a spread of foods I'd never tasted. I knew that the city had grown its own crops, but this feast must have been a different project entirely.

Ava's soft voice broke me from my trance, "Sage?"

As I looked up she gave a nod to the food before me.

"Sorry," I said, blushing, following her glance, "when did that get there?"

She passed me another questioning look, raising an eyebrow. "You really are an odd one aren't you?" she said, putting extra emphasis on the 'odd' part of the sentence.

I offered only a shrug, looking around to everyone else buried deep into their plates—I don't think anyone aside from Ava noticed my absent mindedness. I looked back down to my plate where I saw more food than I've ever eaten at once, sometimes in a week. I had only managed to survive off what little I could grow, or trap—then, I thought of the others, still out there, rationing what little they had from premature crops harvested before they were found. I could have never imagined that others with the stigma would be living like this all along.

The next thing I knew there was nothing left before me, and as I stared down at my empty plate I somehow I craved more. The flavors surprised me, and many of them were brand new. Slivers of turkey were topped with crushed cranberries and greens. There were potatoes, bread, and fruits of every color and kind. I looked to Ava, who was doing little more than picking at her plate by now, and stole a glance over to Councilor Madsen who, at the head of the table, scanned the room with the same calculated movements as I'd seen from his son earlier. He would pause from time to time, giving approving nods, which I noticed were directed to the few winners from this afternoon. After a few long moments he rose from his seat once more after the majority of his guest had nearly finished their plates.

"Could the winners of the first event please gather in my quarters to be briefed on the next round of the games," he said, turning to walk towards a pair of large wooden doors that stood on the wall behind his seat—the other members of Council following close behind.

As the days four other winners began to gather and dismiss themselves from their groups Demi rose without a word or moment of hesitation, disappearing before any other behind those doors.

"So what now?" I asked, looking to Ava.

"I don't know," she started, offering little more than a quick look and a shrug, "we wait, I guess," she finished, before bringing her attention back to the dessert before her.

I left her to eat in peace, though struggled to find mine amongst the escalating hum of gossip that erupted the moment the last winner left the room. I tried to tune into the flow of conversation, but failed, finding myself lost within a near constant stream of references to past Guardians and memories made within Terra Sera—all spoken in a language that, though familiar, had evolved into an entirely new tongue that I could not recognize through a chatter which became altogether overwhelming.

Thankfully, it wasn't too long before the contestants began to Madsen's chamber and blend back in with the rest of the guest one by one. Now, there was an entirely new atmosphere lingering, fueled by both secrecy and the curiosity of what the next stage will bring to the remaining contestants.

Ava and I waited patiently for Demi to return, though it seemed as though he was being held for last. I wondered if there would be any special treatment for Demi, considering he's under the care of the head Councilor himself. I liked to think that he wouldn't, that all things would be fair—but I knew all too well the edge an abuse of power and privilege might bring to a man in his position. I found myself secretly cheering for him, hoping that he wouldn't accept that privilege if it was offered.

Suddenly, the double doors to the Councilors chambers swung open, causing everyone to fall silent as an enraged Demi stormed through.

It was moments later before Councilor Madsen appeared lazily in the doorway, as if Demi's actions were little more than an inconvenience to his plan. He called to Demi calmly, who ignored his order altogether. The councilor sighed as he seemed to reach to Demi with an outstretched hand and, after a moment, his index finger twitched ever so slightly. Something seemed to catch Demi by the leg then, tripping him so that he began to fall forward to the ground.

Demi was quick to summon the Vemosa, which formed a black pool below him so that he may fall into the void. Another appeared before the Councilor as Demi fell out of the portal with the same force he has gone in. In an instant Councilor Madsen had forced Demi to kneel before him, the portal closing beneath.

"You look surprised," the Councilor began, "the power of a true god courses through your veins, granting you immense power for someone your age. It seemed, even, to be a mere formality for you to be required to compete in these games—much respect toward Han," he said, pausing to acknowledge Demi's opponent with nod, "for even being up to that challenge. These little monsters you control are not beyond my authority—and neither are you."

"She's too young to come with me, if I'm so powerful then why is it I can't take my trial alone? I want to be the Guardian, not her, she shouldn't be dragged into this. Instead of testing my own strength you ask me to bring my sister and a stranger to our people as if she has some allegiance to us— what if she betrays me?" Demi interrupted.

"Pride, son, you hold the same flaw as your 'father,' should I call him? Even as a Guardian he fell to that flaw and though he never would fall in battle — he fell to his own insecurities," the Councilor paused, looking reflectively to the ceiling as if searching for his words before continuing, "Ava and Sage will accompany you on your mission. You are being blessed with one of the best young healers I've seen in Terra Sera—you may be surprised what she is capable of. As for Sage, she is a girl who has clearly proven her survival skills and wisdom of the outside world and someone who may very well keep you alive one day. You are in command, so use these resources. If your own selfish pride keeps you from maintaining a clear mind when needed than there is no hope for you as a Guardian and you will not be trusted to protect our people. My decision is final, you may accept it, or you may forfeit your right to compete. Do you accept my terms?"

If one were dropped, a pin could be heard in the now silent room for what felt like a moment too long, then another passed before Demi finally struggled to speak through grit teeth, the pain causing a tremble in his voice, "I accept."

The force placed on Demi seemed to lift as his body finally relaxed. He stood, and walked silently down the aisle and out the main door. The eyes of nearly everyone followed him, but their looks were brought back to Councilor Madsen as he called for their attention, "The matter of briefing the contestants has been completed. I suggest giving any goodbyes or blessings to those leaving within the next few days for I highly anticipate all will be on their way shortly. Now, please, enjoy the rest of your evening, for it is almost at an end, thank you."

Worry plagued Ava's face and I could tell she was wondering the right way to go about talking to her brother.

"Should we go find him?" I asked.

"Probably, but I know how he can be—he won't like being followed. Let's get out of here, it might be best to wait until morning," she returned with a hint of indecision in her voice.

I rose to leave with her. We gave our goodbyes to the Council and were on our way. The whole walk back to Ava's room she remained silent in thought for the first time since I'd known her. She said her goodnight with a quick hug and left.

I still wasn't exactly sure what had happened behind those doors, or most of what was even said. The blood of a god? What was he exactly, and how did I end up being one of the ones chosen to join him on his mission? There was a lot I needed to figure out, a lot I needed to ask Demi, though I was sure Ava could get a lot more out of him than I. All I knew was no matter how much I pondered over them, there was a lot of answers I wouldn't find until morning.

# Chapter 4:

Morning never had the chance to come.

A banging at my door woke me, soon to be replaced by Ava's frantic voice calling my name from the other side.

I sprung from my bed, my instincts taking over, a trained reflex from years of being rushed out of bed with death lingering just moments away. The moment I opened the door she grabbed me by the arm, leading me with a hastily spoken, "Let's go, I found him."

Ava filled me in along the way, about how she was heading back to her room when she walked past the waterfall where Demi and I had first met. She'd noticed dark shadows in the pool and realized they were the same that constantly lingered in Demi's wake. She'd gone down, hoping he was there but found him nowhere in sight. Her words overflowed over one another, making it increasingly difficult to follow what she was saying as we sliced around every corner. Though I couldn't understand most of what she said, her worry pained me.

By the time we reached the pool nothing had changed; the shadows still lingered, dancing amongst each other just beneath the surface, and Demi hadn't left any clue to where he may have gone. Ava walked the water's edge, seeming to be lost in her gaze, as if waiting to see something more than her reflection looking back at her. I began to wander, exploring the pool and the walls around it for any sign of where he may have gone. I found myself beside where the waterfall crashed into the pool by my feet, trying to sneak a look behind it.

"What are you doing?" Ava asked curiously.

"I thought there might have been some kind of pathway, somewhere he may be hiding," I returned, disappointed when I found nothing but stone, again.

"Nothing back there but a wall," she added, only verifying my discovery, "and the pool is shallow, nowhere he could have swam to. I remember we used to play here when I was young— well, younger than I am now. But the shadows are here, and those are his, which means—"

I cut her off, "Which means he's close, right?"

Her eyes were taken off the water and met mine, full of worry. She nodded, "Right."

I'd seen her expression before—it was an emotion I didn't believe could be felt in this protected camp. Still, despite the love and attention of all those around here Demi was the only family she had left and she would follow him to the ends of the world if he'd ask her to. The thought of him being in danger caused her incredible pain.

I realized then, after a few moments that Demi had left a clue behind that we had been overlooking—the shadows. I thought back to his fight with Han, and how the Vemosa worked to catch his fall after the Councilor tripped him. I knew they worked as a type of portal, one leading to the other—which meant that the shadows may have stayed behind so he may escape from wherever it is they brought him.

Ignoring Ava's warnings to avoid them, I wade into the pool directly toward them. The shadows didn't engulf me as I'd thought they might, rather, they seemed to shy away for a moment before starting to circle around. I closed my eyes, trying to feel their movement in the water around me, releasing myself to their will, silently asking them to show me where Demi had gone.

"Sage," Ava began, "you might want to look."

I opened my eyes to see the shadows had formed a void before me holding nothing but darkness, still, I knew it had to lead somewhere and that wherever that may be, Demi wouldn't be far. I looked over to Ava, who shook her head to me, looking at me with fear in her eyes, "I don't want to go in there Sage."

"You don't have to. I'll be right back," I said with poorly bluffed confidence before stepping into the void before me.

All was black, and silent, there were no matter of experience or sensation other than sheer nothingness as I was swallowed by the void. I felt as though I was falling though there was nothing outside myself that hinted to the idea and the uncertainty of my decision began to swell within me. I felt helpless, fearful even, that this vast nothingness would become my existence, and that I would be forced to live an eternity trapped within my thoughts with eyes veiled by darkness against the world. The air around me gradually grew thicker, heavier, and I welcomed the sensation until the void turned liquid, and I plunged into the depths of another pool.

I chased the raising pockets of air racing towards the surface but stopped short, losing what little breath I had left when I noticed the Vemosa circling above. They slowed, staring down at me, before disappearing over the surface.

I swam for the promise of a new breath as quickly as I could, gasping as I breached.

Around me, the Vemosa couldn't be seen and as I relaxed, I realized that I was in a cave lit by the same sprites in Terra Sera, only, there weren't nearly as many here. Their soft glow reflected off the water's surface and painted the walls with a dancing light of cool purples and blues, accented by subtle golden wisps.

There was a small cabin just beside the pool, a fire burning low outside. The same two Vemosa stood guard on either side of the cabin's door, motionless and unresponsive as I began to swim to shore.

The moment I pulled myself onto dry land, one of the Vemosa turned to the other for a brief moment, then phased through the wall into the cabin. By the time I had the chance to get on my feet the cabin door swung open, unleashing Demi with the ferocity of an angry god.

"Oh, you're here. Ava was…looking…for…you—" I began, but was slowed to silence, threatened by the anger in his eye.

"What are you doing here? Or better yet, how did you find me? This is my place of solitude. You have no right being here," his questions shot out, venom in his voice.

"Ava panicked when she couldn't find you, I followed the shadows in the pool— they brought me here," I returned, trying not to challenge him. I didn't want things to turn into a fight I knew I'd lose.

He looked at me as if judging the truth to my story, then to the single Vemosa that had remained outside, who gave a slight nod, and back to me. "Leave," he said before turning to walk back to the cabin.

I followed, "Why run? I thought this is what you wanted— to be a Guardian I mean, like your father right? Why hide now when you've come so far?"

He turned to face me once more, "Don't talk like you know anything about me."

"Then tell me," I begged.

"If I tell you, will you leave?" Demi asked.

"Maybe, maybe not," I said, looking around a bit, "it's kind of nice here."

He shot me a piercing glance.

"Okay fine, get it alright, it's your happy place and I'll respect that and leave if you tell me what happened."

Demi sighed, not very pleased with my response but relaxed himself enough to swallow enough pride to indulge me, "My family lived outside the walls of this city with my father while he served his term as a Guardian. He was a good man, and his death is something I hold myself responsible for, it's something I will always have to live with. My path towards becoming a Guardian in his honor does not need to involve a little girl who can hardly fend for herself, and a stranger who plays the ignorance card. I didn't save you that night Sage, I saw what you can do and I don't understand it. You're keeping secrets, and that's not the type of person I need joining me on this mission. Which reminds me, my summons only obey me — so please, refresh my memory, how exactly did you find me here?"

"I told you all I know, your summons opened some sort of portal that lead me here," I said, not knowing know what else I could offer but the truth.

There was a pause before he spoke, "Who are you?"

I was taken back by the question being asked again, though I knew he wasn't expecting an answer. There was a painful silence then, and I decided to return with another question, "Your father, how did he die?"

Demi's voice remained cold, but reflective, offering slight hints of comfort despite drawing from a painful memory, "When I was nine I watched him kill my mother, and I was forced to run with Ava into the forest to find my way here. He was branded a coward here in Terra Sera for taking his life before our courts could try him, leaving me to fend for Ava on my own—she was hardly a year old at the time and I was just a boy. Somehow, I can't allow myself to blame him for what he did, or not being able to stop him, I know he loved us, why else would he let us escape?"

I was beside myself, but the question still begged, "Why did he do it?"

"I didn't know, no one told me until I was older that I wasn't really his son—even before then that didn't stop me from blaming myself. I was told he'd overlooked the truth since I was born, but that truth drove him to madness, and eventually killed my mother over it."

*The truth?* I wondered, remembering Councilor Madsen's words as I pieced his story together, "You have the blood of a god, then you're—"

"—The bastard son of that poor excuse of a man we call a god, Klaus. I guess the heartbreak of knowing my mother's betrayal finally ate away at him, I must have been a terrible burden to bare all those years. I seem to be the only one to remember the good in him—and I will return honor to his name. My parents death was a consequence of my birth, Klaus is to blame for tearing my family apart—not my father. For that, I will kill him, I swear it."

It took a moment for what he had said to sink in, did he really expect to be able to kill a god? Realizing I had just been standing there in thought, the only words I could muster were a meager, "I'm sorry, I didn't know."

"I wouldn't expect you to. Now if you're satisfied you can stop acting like you know a damned thing about me and what I've been through. I don't see a point in bringing Ava headstrong into the very danger I've spent my entire life protecting her from, especially for my own personal goal though that can't seem to be avoided now. If you don't mind, I'll ask you let me spend the rest of my time here in peace. Go, get some sleep and be ready by evening, we'll leave by nightfall," he finished, his voice much calmer now, as if a weight had been lifted.

I couldn't help but smile, silently thanking him for his honesty.

As he left me, the two Vemosa began to drift toward me, giving my cue. I waded back into the pool without another word, watching the Vemosa glide through the water beside me without as much as a ripple—as if they were incapable of interacting with this physical world. Again, a void formed before me, and this time, I entered without hesitation.

I found myself back with Ava, who was leaning over the waterline looking for any sign she could of, well, anything below the surface. Before I had the chance to gather myself back on dry land she had clung to me with an exaggerated, "By Sera you're okay! They didn't kill you? Where did you go, wait, did you find him? What happened, where is he?" each question flowed over onto the next— starting a new one before she finished the other.

I let her finish, and waited and extra moment, until she took step back and give me the sort of face that asked, *Well, are you going to answer me?*

"Don't worry," I started, "I found him and he's okay. We leave tonight."

"Okay, but where is he?" she asked once more.

"I'm not sure exactly, a cave. The Vemosa act as some sort of portal to this little secret hideaway he has." I really didn't know what else to tell her, the Vemosa seem to have some sort of power over the world— like they can create a rift in time, in space, in something, I didn't know. They can take someone from one place to another. I wondered where they had taken Han during their fight and if it had been the same they had taken me, or if Demi had entirely different places he could go.

Ava looked at me, then the water, the Vemosa were gone. I could only guess Demi didn't want any more surprise visits.

"That must be where he disappears to when I can't find him," she said curiously.

I put my arm around her and turned her away from the pool, "It'd probably be best if we get some sleep, looks like we have a big day tomorrow."

For most people, I imagine it would be hard to sleep, but not for me. I should have known that I wouldn't be able to settle into life here for long. I always have a way of moving, though in the past it was because I had to avoid being killed. Being in a city as safe as Terra Sera, it seemed almost insane to intentionally go back into the world outside. I wondered how many of those who lived here actually knew the reality we faced, and of even how many of those competing in the games would make it back alive.

# Chapter 5:

I slept well that night, and late into the day, knowing that I hadn't come to this city with much of anything and I wasn't planning on leaving with much either so there really wasn't anything to pack. I've learned that the people who try to bring everything with them often fall behind, and are lost to us. It is only the ones that travel light, and don't fear losing what they do have, that fair a better chance. Anything that a person may ever need, the world provides naturally.

Knowing it would be cold, at least at first, I started to rummage through my drawers, searching for something that might keep me from freezing until we escaped the ice and snow that seemed to surround this mountain and the nearby valleys. Impressions meant little to me so I grabbed the warmest coat I could find despite the sleeves being slightly too long, then threw on a pair of black jeans, a tattered camo jacket, and plain white t-shirt before I felt satisfied that I'd be kept warm through the next couple of nights.

I took a moment to become familiar with every hidden pocket—knowing that it was much easier to find something stashed away than to fish through a backpack on the fly, though I knew I should bring one anyway. I just had to make sure to leave any weapons I had within immediate reach. Despite Demi's power I couldn't trust that he could handle everything that may be thrown at our way, even if he believed he could protect us— I've seen greater men than him fall and knew that I would have to remain on near constant guard.

Everything was in order not long after I dragged myself from the bed. I guess I had grown used to being able to pack up quick and be on the move. Still, I've only been in this city a few days and it was already starting to feel more like home than I'd like to admit. It wasn't quite evening, and I had some time to do a little last minute exploring before we left so I started my way through the market district once more, not looking for anything in particular, just random little things that might be useful while we were out.

As I passed a stand selling a mix of exotic weapons I realized I hadn't seen my knife since the night Demi had found me. I guess I didn't notice because there was truly no need for one in Terra Sera other than for show. I was never one to fight, mostly because I never wanted to be a hero in this war. I was a survivor, and I learned early on that surviving meant knowing the right moment to run away. I'd decided long ago that living another day meant more to me than dying in a battle I could never win headstrong.

Maybe if I had some sort of power I would have been different, but living on the run from agents trained to fight super humans as a person with no special ability has a way of teaching you when to back away from a fight; which is most often always.

"A fan of small arms are you?" a familiar voice spoke from beside me as I looked over the merchant's selections. I looked to see Councilor Madsen beside me, casually picking up some of the pieces on the table with gingerly care.

"I was never one for them," he said, reaching into his pocket to pull out small blade folding blade, "always found them to be far too messy."

Its handle was a pearly white, with golden details that swirled throughout, and the blade had the curve of a talon. I'd seen blades like this before, though never so well made—it was designed to be held with the blade facing the elbow of the user to be used for swift slashes. He unfolded the knife in his hands, the design from the handle flowed over onto the blade itself, but the coloring had changed. The golden swirls changed to swirls of shining light that seemed painted onto the metal and as he ran a finger across the sharpened edge the light flared with intensity.

"Save what money you have, you'll need it on the outside, I've no further use for this blade—take it," he said, folding the knife into itself and offering it to me.

This was the first time the Councilor had ever addressed me directly, rather than through Demi or Ava, and I wasn't exactly sure how to compose myself around him just yet so I simply accepted his gift with a smile and thanked him.

Before I had a chance to respond he began to speak once more, "You might be wondering why I made the decision to send you along with Demi on his mission, since you had only just arrived here in our city. There is a lot we don't know about you, but from what I understand you haven't fully developed your gift. I'm hoping that this mission will force situations that will unlock that ability for you. Living with our gift is a struggle in and of itself, living with it and not having access to it is another story entirely. It is because of that situation you are probably the most capable person in this city to survive in the outside world. I am prepared to grant you full citizenship in Terra Sera— in return, I ask only that you care for Demi and Ava out in a world that you know best. I have advised them to listen to your wisdom, for neither of them truly knows what is waiting for them beyond these walls."

"I'll do my best sir. Aren't you a little worried about Ava though? She had told me you took them in after their parents passed, so I'm sure you know her abilities. Demi can fight, but Ava is still so young, and out there her powers won't save her."

"I'm sure you will help take care of them. They were both vulnerable when I had found them. I needed to take them under my wing, especially with Demi's history. I couldn't leave a child like that to grow up wild, he would end up being consumed by the same anger and hatred that fueled Klaus' rage. As for Ava, it's time she sees the world as it truly is, and you are the only squad with the ability to heal potential wounds without the use of traditional medicine. I understand you will be leaving tonight, tell no one of your plans for once you leave these walls you will have no ally," he returned.

"I'll keep that in mind," I said, placing the knife in my coat pocket.

He gave me a warm smile, and said his goodbyes, quickly disappearing back into the crowd.

I fingered the knife into the corner of my pocket, already getting used to how it felt there, but looked around the stand a bit more. Suddenly the pieces I had just found so pleasing had lost their allure, so I gave the now disgruntled shop owner a friendly nod and went on my way.

I'd hardly taken a few steps before I saw Ms. Ingalls talking to someone in the entrance of her shop. She glanced over in my direction, then back to the person she was speaking with. I don't think she had realized that she had seen me until a few moments later. Her head did a sort of double take and when she realized it was me, quickly ended her conversation to start my way with an over exuberant, "Sage! I got the news, you'll be joining Demi and Ava on their little top secret mission I hear, how exciting! How are you dear? Come here I've found something for you," she paused, placing a hand on my shoulder and beginning to lead me inside,

"You'd mentioned you wanted some more information about Klaus."

"Other than the fact that he's Demi's father?" I pushed, suddenly wanting to know more than my basic understanding of the god.

"Oh, so you know his little secret then? Not that it's much of a secret anymore really, we all knew he had to be something special for the Councilor to take such interest— but a prince of darkness wasn't what anyone expected," she said, walking behind her desk, " Well, anyway, turns out not much was written about Klaus— or rather not much had survived the wars. We have volumes on our mother Sera, but that's of no help to you. He's sort of the god everyone just wanted to forget."

"Remember that temperamental little book you took interest in? I did some extra research on where it had come from, there's always a surprise with this one—turns out it was a relic found alongside our mother. I have no idea how it ended up being little more than a paperweight, well, that's probably because no one was ever able to see much more than a book of blank pages. Of course my curiosity got the best of me and I tried to read the damned thing again, only to have the words disappear on me as always, but not before I caught mention of Klaus' name. I want you to take it with you, even if it's just a glimpse at a time, I think it might point you in the right direction," she said, sliding the relic over the counter towards me.

"Thank you," I said politely, "but are you sure?"

"Any librarian would kill to have this book in this collection— but it pains me to see something that might offer so many answers do little more than collect dust and frustrate my patrons. It's one of the last things we have that connects us with our mother, but it's also the one thing that may lead us to her. Now, I think it's time for you to be off, you've got quite the experience ahead of you! Be careful," she said with a smile, and I took that as my cue to leave.

As I said my goodbyes and left her shop I tucked the book deep within my backpack and molded back in with the crowd. It was getting late, I had spent more time talking than wandering than I'd wanted, but it felt good to have made a connection with some of the people here before I left —it would give me something to look forward to when we returned. I hurried back to my room to gather a few last minute things.

It wasn't long before I heard a knock on my door, and a second later Ava walked in. She had the pep back in her step, and twirled her way toward me without a hint of concern about the dangers we would be faced with over our first night. "Almost ready?" she asked, "Demi's already waiting by the front gates, no real rush, he's just talking. I'm so excited! Are you? You must be, I can't wait to see everything out there!"

I wanted to tell her that it was dangerous where we were going, full of people trying to hunt you down, or others of our kind looking for any edge they could muster. I questioned if she was really ready for this, but Councilor Madsen was right, she needed to be exposed to the real world, and she is much older now than I was when I was faced with this reality.

"I wish I could have spent more time here," I started, "but I'm ready, and excited. I'm a lot more used to being on the move anyway," I finished, truly wishing that I could stay within the safety of the mountain.

She smiled, and made an exaggerated point towards the door, "Off we go then."

Demi was waiting at the gates as she had said, surrounded by a small group saying their goodbyes. He wasn't joking, or being boastful as usual. His body language was serious and firm, "Good for you two to join me, I was starting to think you wouldn't show."

Ava crossed her arms, "I would never."

He gave off a nervous laugh that was really more like blowing air out of his nose than anything. I could sense his unease with the situation, though he tried hard to mask it.

I was curious, I knew that we were going on some sort of mission but I knew nothing of our objective, I figured now would be a good time to ask rather than going blindly into the night, "This mission," I said with a pause, "exactly what do we have to do?"

His gaze broke from me for a moment, and scanned the surrounding area before he spoke, "It's best that you trust me for the time being. Before I say anything about where we are going I want to be far enough away from the city that no one can drop in on the conversation. I'll make sure to fill you in on the way. The sun has already set outside, if we move now we have a better chance to stay unseen, and if we move quickly we might find a place to lay low for the night. I don't want to risk being out in the open for too long."

I could understand his concern, as worrisome as it was to leave without knowing what was in store, I knew I had to show faith in him as a leader if I wanted to gain any manner of trust, "Fair enough, I'm ready when you are."

He looked over to Ava, who gave him an approving nod and a cheerful, "Ready!"

"Well then," Demi said, pausing for a moment as if to take in all that was going on, and what it meant to him, "let's go."

# Chapter 6:

We were met by snowfall, which would have been inviting if it weren't for the harsh bite of winter air that welcomed us with a cold shoulder. The warmth of Terra Sera had been a luxury I'd grown accustomed to all too quickly but I couldn't let comfort erase a lifetime of knowing what it takes to survive out here. Far too often the lives of those who let their guard down for the sake of comfort are taken by surprise. I wondered if the people of Terra Sera knew how lucky they were to actually be able to live at peace, to actually feel human.

The entrance to the city was an extension from the mountains face made by a silent man with the ability to shift the stone. We stood on a ledge, too far from the ground to risk a jump into one of the accumulating piles of snow at the mountain's base. I could hear the stone moving, and to my left saw steps begin to form along the mountain's side, leading us down.

As we made our way down, Demi looked back at us, giving direction, "We can't be out in the open for long or this storm will kill us before anyone else has the chance, we need to find shelter."

When we touched ground we immediately started for the tree-line. As I stole one last look to the hidden city I was frozen in my step, seeing the Agents that had chased me down still in a heap on the frozen forest floor, half covered with freshly fallen snow— soon to be forgotten. Their metal armor was slashed clean through, and I could see the look of shock and terror still visible through their broken glass visors.

Demi came up behind me, "Look familiar?"

"I did this—" I said, in shock. The scene before me was gruesome, the entire squad's lifeless bodies had been strewn across the ground in a ruthless trail of destruction,"—There's no way."

"You're lucky you chose a spot to hide so close to the entrance or else I wouldn't have seen you on my way in. Against a squad that well equipped, I wasn't about to play hero and step in, I know you'd do the same for me—but, I'll admit you handled yourself well. Whoever you are, I need you to stay alive until the end—I want to fight once you learn to control this power, the challenge is something I'm looking forward to," Demi said, before pulling his attention away from the scene.

I didn't know what to feel, or if I should have been feeling anything at all, but there was this unfamiliar energy burning deep within my chest. I felt a certain sense of joy in seeing them dead, something I wasn't sure that I was ready to welcome. I looked to the Agents once more and couldn't help but feel a slight smile press my lips, *I did this*, I thought to myself, *good*.

I'd never felt this kind of pride for taking a life, even after the few times I'd actually managed to take an Agent down, at best, I felt a sense of relief. I'd mostly spent my life running, or setting small traps to slow the chase only to offer a second hope at escape but not to kill. If I had ever actually killed an Agent it was mostly by accident, I could never take one on up close. It was crazy for me to actually see that I had defended myself from so many, but still the question lingered as to how. Was my power finally starting to show? The thought of it excited me, but at the same time the sight of my unlocked potential filled me with the fear of who I might become.

Ava came to my side, sharing my gaze with curious eyes, "It's been a long time Demi, why hasn't anyone come to take them home?" Ava asked after a moment.

"The Pure are cruel people Ava. Those who die in battle hold no value to Zanin so he doesn't waste time bringing them home. Either you come home alive, and a hero, or not at all," Demi said putting his arm around his sister and leading her away.

The forest, if you could even call it that anymore, provided little cover. All that remained was a shell of what once was. The brush had almost been burnt away in its entirety, and the trees that still stood showed only bare branches, though that could be blamed on the winter. Now and then I could hear the crunch of footsteps in the snow, which startled me, though it was never more than a passing hare. Demi had scoffed at my worries, explaining he had the Kurki circling our perimeter as well, if anyone was seen they would report back to him immediately so I could stop being paranoid.

I wanted to hit him, but didn't, knowing it wouldn't change a thing. Knowing the Kurki were keeping guard did settle my nerves, and I silently thanked him for that—though I still kept alert regardless. I scanned the darkness more intently now, spotting a Kurki standing in a clear patch with its head to the sky, jolting around in short, frantic steps. I stifled my laughter as I watched it move, but as funny as they were I also feared the ravenous beast and their corruptive touch. The Kurki's antennae shot straight up and its head jerked to one direction as something caught its eye. A moment later it was gone, disappearing into the brush in pursuit.

"The other teams have left already," Demi began," I made sure we were the last ones out so hopefully we won't be followed—But that doesn't mean no one waited around for us either so be ready—

once we are out here the fact that we are from the same place means nothing to the other squads," he finished with the slightest hint of worry in his tone, his eyes scanning the high up branches as if he expected an ambush.

A new Kurki appeared beside Demi and made its way over to the same clearing, waiting idly for a few moments before starting back on patrol. I realized then that this was a constant security measure for him, if one was destroyed or left its post Demi could easily conjure a new one to fill its place without a second thought.

I remembered the landscape well enough from my travels before my short time in Terra Sera, "If we keep going we'll end up coming over a hill that leads down over a valley, it's open, I know, which can be dangerous but there's a set of caves that we can spend the night in on the other side. We'll be safe there until morning."

"Risky," Demi began, "but I guess I can send out a few Kurki to see if it's clear before we pass."

"Do you know the way?" I asked, sheepishly, not wanting to threaten his leadership so soon.

He stopped, thinking for a moment, and pointed in a general direction, "This way."

"Uhm, try a little more this way," I said grabbing onto his arm and steering it in the right direction.

He pulled his arm away, and silently started in the direction I'd pointed, mumbling beneath his breath. I looked at Ava and who had covered her mouth to keep herself from giggling, I smiled back at her—finding a little too much pleasure in frustrating her brother.

It wasn't long until we could see the crest of the hill before us. We slowed our pace and kept low as we came up, the tree line becoming even sparser, so we had to steal what little cover we could. Demi signaled us to stop and the three of us lay prone on the hilltop, the darkness behind us giving enough contrast to not be seen. I could see the hills on the other side, a little over a hundred yards out. I pointed, showing Demi where I had in mind, "The caves are in there, we'll be well hidden and warm for the night. If we do have any visitors it's easily defendable especially with your little pets."

"They aren't pets," Demi spat sharply, sending one of his Kurki to investigate, "and I hate to admit it, but I have to agree with you. There's little else around here to shelter us that well. Normally I have to—"

"—Guys," Ava said interrupting Demi, "looks like we aren't the only ones trying to get through either, look."

Not far, to the left of us, there was a group of four just now breaking the tree line. They seemed less cautious, more relaxed in their movements.

"Agents?" Demi asked.

"No," I said with a pause, eyeing them carefully," They are our own, you said another squad might have stood back right?"

"It's possible," Demi returned, "there are five groups in all, this could be one of them, or just a group of wanderers."

"If they are one of the other groups, they were probably trying to intercept us," I added.

"Likely," Demi said, keeping his voice low.

The lone Kurki at the center of the valley sank down into the ground, becoming little more than a misplaced shadow, concealed from the coming group. They stopped for a moment, scanning the valley, before continuing. I cursed their ignorance for not taking more time to investigate, their zealousness driving them forward, completely unaware of us watching in the shadows—they are lucky it is only us with our sights on them and no the Agents.

The squad was moving quickly through the valley when they stopped abruptly, as another group breached the tree-line to our right. There was a pause for both parties, as if assessing the situation. The squad from Terra Sera let out into a sprint, ready to take on the new group headstrong—fully assuming they were a part of the Games themselves.

The second group immediately took a defensive position as a single shot echoed through the valley, dropping one member of the squad's party.

"Shit," I muttered, "Agents."

Ava began to move as if she were about to run toward the fallen Stigma holder, but Demi's hand forced her to the ground with a wet crunch.

"We can't let them die!" she cried, keeping her voice low.

"If we attack then we risk getting killed ourselves," Demi answered sternly.

Ava looked to me for another answer, and I didn't know how to respond. This was something that I'd seen so many times before and Demi was right, it wouldn't help us trying to save them. If everyone ran into a fight so recklessly than the Pure would have won this war by now. I could see the sadness in her eyes, but I had to shake my head no before I looked back to the fight in the valley, hopeful at least some of them would live.

There were three members left on either side, for what should be a fair fight, but the Agents had the advantage of range. Who looked like the leader of the Stigma group pulled a collapsible rod from behind his back, sparks shooting from its ends as he drove it into the ground, the bolts were visible as they cut through the snow in one solid bolt before splintering towards each of the Agents. Another shot rang out just before the bolts hit and another one of our own went down. The electrical current traveled up the Agent's suits and discharged from their visors, breaking the glass, but all of the men were still standing.

"That didn't do much," Demi said to himself.

The Agents rose their weapons as if to fire, but stopped, looking at their guns, dumbfounded that they wouldn't work.

"It wasn't meant to, he shut off their electronics. One flaw about the Agents is they rely heavily on their technology—but don't underestimate their physical strength," I returned.

By the time the Agents had dropped their weapons the leader of the Stigma group had already closed much of the distance by foot. The last remaining member of his squad stood back, looking hesitant to join the fight.

Ava asked, "Wait, that's Kai right? Why doesn't he just send lightning down on all of them and end it quick?"

I thought for a second, having the gift didn't mean you could use it to its full power whenever you wanted to. Someone who controls water wouldn't fare very well in the desert and the conditions outside weren't exactly thunderstorm weather. "The cold," I answered, "he must not be able to generate enough electrical energy in the cold to do much damage that way, only enough to short out the Agents electronics."

Demi looked at me, "Makes sense, so he cut out their weapons since he can't use his own leaving it up to a good old fashioned brawl, interesting way to level the playing field."

Kai reached the first Agent, who sent an uppercut with one of his enormous fist, but Kai ducked under, ignoring him for now, and using his low stance and momentum to sweep his staff through the legs of the second Agent, lifting him into the air. In fluid motion with his swing Kai brought one hand to the other end of his staff and shot it straight back under his arm and through the visor of the third Agent behind him. Kai's fist clenched and sparks ran up the staff and directly into the Agent's face, finishing him.

With the second Agent still in the air, Kai's other squad member finally burst into action. In an instant he was gone, and the next was clinging to the suspended Agent. The two of them disappeared with a blink and it took a moment for me to find them, in the sky, maybe a hundred feet above the ground. The second Agent was dropped, his screams silenced as he crashed to the earth. The Stigma holder blinked once more, appearing behind the only Agent left alive, ready to ambush him just as Kai ripped the staff out from the visor which it was lodged and lunged it toward the Agent's chest. The Agent dodged, and the staff pierced Kai's teammate instead.

Everything up to that point had happened so quickly that Kai must have not known his teammate was there. He hesitated, shocked by what he had just done, a fatal error.

Kai was soon met by a fist of the only remaining Agent, who connected this time square on Kai's jaw. You could see him go limp as his body fell to the floor, neck broken.

"Shit," Demi said.

"What do we do?" I asked.

"Well we still need cover for the night, and I doubt there is another squad this close by. We need to get across."

"And the Agent?" I returned.

Demi looked back to the lone Agent in the valley, he had begun walking toward the pile of guns they had dropped before the fight, "I have an idea."

A small shadow began to move through the snow toward the pile of weapons.

"The Kurki, was that there the whole time?" I snapped.

"It never moved, but I couldn't tell it to do anything or they would have known we were here," he returned, confident with his decision.

"And now it's okay to show him?" I asked sharply.

"Oh he won't be seen by anyone. They are very good at that, clever things. Watch."

The Kurki's shadow disappeared into the gun just as the Agent reached for it. The Agent began toying with his weapon, trying to get it to work. He'd aim down the sights and pull the trigger, nothing. Reload, nothing. It was only when he looked down the barrel as if to see if the malfunction was there that I understood the Kurki's plan. One last shot rang out and the Agent dropped to the floor.

"See, no one saw a thing. Let's move, quickly," Demi said as he pushed himself up and started down the hill and into the valley.

I grabbed Ava's hand and pulled her hastily. She was drudging along, silent, for once, but I tried to keep us up with Demi's pace.

The snow was painted red around each body, and I tried not to look as we passed—the sight of death never getting any easier for me. I felt Ava pull towards them, and as I looked back I could see her arm outstretched toward the bodies of the Stigma holders, her palm glowing that faint green. My heart was sad for her, knowing this was the first time she'd seen the evil our kind has to face and this was only a small battle, one that happens every day all over the world. Still, it hit home, stealing the lives of four people she'd spent her whole life with in a matter of minutes.

I stopped with her, "Ava, they are too far gone to be helped, even by you. I know, it's hard, but we need to move on or we risk dying with them."

She was crying softly to herself, "We can't leave them here."

Ava was right, but carrying four bodies the rest of the way would leave us exposed for too long. I looked to Demi, who was much further ahead of us by now and yelled after him, "What about them?"

He stopped, calling over his shoulder, "Leave them, for now."

"For now? Leaving them here makes us no better than the Agents who abandon their dead," I argued, for Ava's sake.

He started back our way, "You're right, but they're dead and we are still alive and I'd very much like to stay that way. We need to get to shelter, I'll send the Vemosa out later to retrieve the bodies, they won't be left behind— now, let's go."

I nodded, and pulled a still reluctant Ava along with me.

The entrance to the cave system was mostly covered by snow that had built up with the winds and I had to do a little digging to find the right way in. I'd spent a few months here in the peace of the valley before Demi had brought me to Terra Sera. I was hunting when the Agents found me during a large sweep of the area. Having nowhere else to run, and being unable to make it back to the limited safety of the caves they chased me until the mountain left me no more room to run. At the time I had no idea I was so close to such a large concentration of others like me, I almost felt silly now seeing where I had been calling home before then.

I'd memorized the layout so, despite the darkness, I led us through the cave with ease. Demi and Ava followed close behind until we got to a larger room within the cave. I had dry wood stockpiled, and quickly put to work on a fire to offer some heat and light. It didn't take long for me to spark a flame and the darkness was soon replaced with the soft orange flicker of fire, shadows dancing on the walls around us.

"It's not much, but it'll do for the night," I said, throwing more wood into the fire.

"Looks like someone's living here, are you sure it's safe?" Demi asked after a good look around.

"Well, it was actually me that used to live here and from the looks of things nothing has been touched since I left," I returned.

Ava giggled, "Then why does it look like someone went through everything?"

I looked around a bit more and realized I left the place a mess, and I'll admit I was slightly embarrassed at the state of it. After all, I wasn't planning on leaving it like I had that day and I guess from living on my own I worried less about keeping things neat so long as I knew where they were.

Demi broke the silence, "The Vemosa are retrieving the bodies now. We still aren't far from the city so I'm having them brought there."

Ava sighed with relief and smiled, a small weight being lifted.

"Thank you," I responded, sitting down by the fire across from Demi and Ava, "but now that we are settled and safe what exactly is it we're doi—"

"—The mission, yes." Demi said cutting me off, "I guess I probably should fill you in. That book that Ms. Ingalls had given you, I assume you still have it?"

It took me a second to realize what he was talking about, I'd almost forgotten about it to be honest. "Oh, yeah, here," I said, slinging my bag from off my shoulder and fishing it out, "It's an odd book though. Ms. Ingalls was telling me that most people can't read it, and those who can only get little glimpses at a time. What does it mean for the mission?"

"That's the point, it's a mysterious book, a relic from the gods, it's something that could hold some powerful secrets. If we were able to read it we might be able to stop the war, so we'll start with that lead. Our mission is to discover the location of Sera and report back to Council."

"So what's the plan?" I returned, realizing he knew more than I had realized about the book. I began to flip my way through the pages hoping to spot something of significance.

"There's a monastery near the city of MarSeir, I've been told the monks there will be able to help us."

"The whole region has been at war since I was young, are you sure the monks are even still there?" I asked, trying to gauge how much he knew. I was familiar with the area, and hearing the name had brought back some painful memories from my youth. I wasn't entirely sure it was a place I wanted to return to, though I knew it may hold some answers.

"There's only one way to find out, the things we can learn from what's in this book could change the fate of our people."

I wondered for a moment, if he meant all people or just the ones he'd sworn to protect in the Council, but the thought was fleeting.

Ava finally looked up, she'd been sitting beside Demi the entire time but her attention seemed to be elsewhere, "What if the Agents are there? Are we going to have to fight them?"

I tried to reassure her, "Hopefully not."

"But," Demi continued, "if they cross us we might not have a choice. We need to be prepared for anything."

I looked at him with disapproving eyes.

"What?" he responded, "What we saw earlier is proof enough that they are out here and we might have to defend ourselves. I'm not going to downplay the fact that we might end up in a fight or two along the way. Being as I'm the only one here with any real attack power it's something we need to be ready for, you of all people should know that Sage."

Ava faked a smile and gave Demi an approving nod, "And if you get hurt, I'll be there to fix you up right?"

He smiled back, putting his arm around her, pulling her close, "Right."

I stood up, and began to gather some things to make a bed for the night. As much as I hated the idea of traveling back to MarSeir, if it could help us discover what may be inside this book and save our people, I would have to face the demons of my past.

My attention went back to the book. The symbols on the page looked familiar and I began to trace them with my fingers, as I did more would appear on the lines under my hand. I remembered, they were the symbols that I had seen on the walls of that labyrinth I had been lost in. Words written in some abstract language, familiar, yet unlike any I've ever seen.

Flipping through the pages I felt the same energy I had felt after stepping out of Terra Sera to see the Agents I had taken down. There was something deep inside of me that seemed to be calling. I understood nothing that was appearing in front of me but my finger just kept tracing the symbols and more would appear. Though I didn't understand directly, it felt as though part of me did— and begged for more to be revealed.

As I feverishly flipped from page to page the words began to dance amongst themselves. I rubbed my watering eyes, trying to stop the tricks they were playing on me, but nothing helped. There was an energy within me building in intensity as the words lifted from the page and began to swirl around me.

My surroundings became hazy, and the words themselves were shining bright and perfectly clear through that haze. They began to organize themselves in space, until they finally rested in line. The haziness of my surroundings began to subside and I realized I was no longer in the cave with Demi and Ava.

The same labyrinth I had seen before in my dreams had taken its place. The words now rested on the walls to either side of me in one long corridor similar to what I remember from the last time I had visited this place. But the question remained, where was I?

Was I dreaming?

Or is this somewhere hidden deep within my mind?

I began to wander, the walls were still damp, and my feet would splash in small puddles as I walked. It wasn't terribly bright here, but there was light, though I still didn't know where it came from. To my right, were rooms that held visions of nearly forgotten memories. As I passed some of them I'd pause to watch what was going on inside and with others I was quick to move on to the next.

There was one I had stopped to watch, it was of the first Cekrit camp I had spent time in. I was young, maybe four or five years old, when things were simple. The younger children would play child's games together while the older kids were off comparing powers and playing gifted versions of every game they had grown up with. I felt warm as I watched myself play with the others, before we grew older, before I was picked on and left out for not having any special talent. Before all of that I was happy, and felt loved.

At first it was weird watching myself like this, it was like I was another person in the crowd watching my former self, little more than a silent spectator of my own life. I looked around some more, and recognized the family that had taken care of me here, talking to the monks that made frequent visits to our camp. I was the lucky one, most orphans wouldn't make it past their first couple of years, and in a way I envied them for their early escape from this hell. Older orphans would be forced to fend for themselves until they finally found a group to call family, but were too often left behind in the chaos of a raid. I was lucky to be taken in at such a young age, even if I would be on my own soon after.

I didn't know much about my birth family. I was told that my mother had died giving birth to me, and nothing was ever said of my father. I guess that was normal, with camps of our people constantly meeting and moving on I had assumed I was the product of a passing fling. That's realistically what happened, though I like to think he might have died protecting others against the Agents. Every girl wants her daddy to be a hero, right? This here was one of the earliest memories I had, and this family would be the only one I'd ever known. After a squad of Agents came through a couple years later we were separated and I'd spent the rest of my time until my teens bouncing from camp to camp—most often taking shelter in the arms of a mother who had already lost a child to the war.

The memory in the room changed with my thoughts—and I was now watching a still younger self sitting in our dug out home deep within the chasm's that hid the camp of MarSeir. I could hear screams and gunfire outside as I hid under a table along the back wall, cloaked by a tapestry that hung over its side. I was such a frail little girl, my skin was dirty from days without a wash, my clothes torn, hair disheveled—but innocence in my eye. The woman who had taken care of me came in, frantically telling me to run, so I snuck out of a small opening in the wall hidden beyond an overhanging tapestry on the table behind me and into an alleyway.

A moment later I could hear the Agent's demanding voice from inside, "Where are they? Who were you talking to?"

"May Klaus burn your soul," the woman cursed through her tears.

"Silence, filth!" the Agent yelled, the woman's threat silenced as a single shot rang out.

My heart raced in tandem with my former self as I had burst from the room into an alleyway amidst the chaos, vaulting over the fallen bodies of Stigma and Agents alike. Explosions and gunfire muffled the screams of nearly anyone that had called out for help followed by the silence of the gunmen as they were taken down themselves. With each pass of the main chasm I had stolen glimpses of the carnage, forcing me to stick to the maze of alleys to find my escape into the lands beyond the chasms.

I took a step away from the room, it wasn't anything I wanted to relive again.

# Chapter 7:

I kept my eyes to the ground, trying to avoid getting lost in any more of the rooms I passed by. My mind lingered on the memories of everyone I've seen killed by the Agents, and how angry I was with myself that I was helpless to save them. The pain of losing so many friends burnt deep within me, and with that energy rose something else entirely—an anger that had slowly begun to consume me. I could feel it building; my cheeks burned as if they were being kissed by a bitter wind, and the air around me grew thick as a swarm of hatred and regret surrounded me.

The darkness was an easy thing to feed into.

Like wood to a fire, my memories fueled my rage, my sorrow. I knew I could easily lose myself to a path of vengeance if I weren't careful—I wished I could be stronger, so I could protect those around me. Still, despite the cool emptiness I felt, it warmed me in a way. That power beckoned, with an insatiable hunger for the memory of every sorrow my life has given me. I was empowered by it, compelled to strike back.

I had always just run, run because I was never good at anything. I couldn't protect any of the people who had tried so hard to protect and care for me. I was vulnerable, weak, and finally at the point where I was tired of letting everyone down. Running for survival couldn't be my only option, not anymore.

I'd lost so many friends over the years that I simply started avoiding people entirely, choosing to live on my own. In a way, I felt a sense of safety in my solitary existence; knowing that if I were to die than it would be my fault alone and I was okay with that truth. It seemed as though whenever I began to get settled with one group the Agents would come, and amidst the flames and gunfire I'd always find myself running in the opposite direction as the best of us ran towards.

For too many years I have kept mostly to myself, wandering into a camp only to trade for supplies and any information that might keep me alive. But even then I could see the effect this war had—I'd watch as groups would dwindle in numbers with each passing, couples would be separated, leaders killed. I never asked where the missing had gone, silently I knew they were lost to us, and I could see that truth in the eyes of those who remained.

I'd always thought my way was better, I could stay under the radar, fend for myself, and worry less about drawing the attention of Agents. But, of course, they weren't completely unavoidable.

"Stop!" a demanding voice echoed from down the corridor. "By the name of Commander Zanin! Stop!" it rang out again.

I was hesitant to follow the sound, and my first thought was to run but, in this place, I didn't know if that would lead me right into an Agent's path. They couldn't find me here, could they? Hell, I didn't even know where *here* was, but I couldn't assume it wasn't possible. Stranger things have happened.

I kept moving forward, cautiously, peeking into every room to make sure nothing was hiding in the shadows.

There was a panting, and the sound of boots on the ground that echoed through these halls, and I found myself running as well.

I had just passed the room when I realized what I was hearing, stopping abruptly, I took a few steps back to see myself weaving through the scattered trees outside Terra Sera. The Agents were hot on my trail, demanding me to stop. I was watching the night that I should have died, the night Demi had found me and taken me into his hidden city. The night that I had no excuse to escape with my life.

It was equally as terrifying now as I watched myself. I wanted to scream, to warn my past self, to jump into that memory, to do anything to try and help. But I knew from where I stood I was helpless, I couldn't change the past—and no matter what happened something good must have come of it or I wouldn't be here today.

I looked pathetic, quivering, backed up against the cold rock face waiting for death to greet me. The order was given— and an Agent took his place before me, raising his rifle.

I watched intently, frozen.

The moon hung high in the sky that night, and shadows were cast from all around. At first, they began to move ever so slightly, until at last I could see the darkness begin to consume me. My executioner hesitated as a black veil hung like smoke around me, covering my eyes. The dogs by his feet tucked their tails and began to take nervous steps back as I rose to my feet with an air of confidence, before racing off the way they came.

"What the…? Hey!" an Agent said, cocking his head in their direction to see where they went before putting his attention back on me.

I stood there, arms hanging limp beside me, rocking my head from side to side as we were locked in a standstill. A smile creased my lips with ill intent, and an aura that reeked of death lingered around my body like black steam. My entire demeanor had changed.

I could hear a faint whisper, *welcome.*

I noticed my hands turning black and looking as if my nails had grown, almost as if they were blades, claws even. The darkness crept over my skin, and as it settled a plated gauntlet formed with sharp points on each section—stopping just above my forearm.

*Now*, the voice spoke again, *play*.

My head stopped rocking then, and I watched as I began to lick my lips. My fist clenched, then opened revealing the long plated claws that now extended from each of my fingertips made from the same kind of plate as the gauntlets, breaking at each knuckle. I smiled, and let out a blood curtailing scream before launching myself at the Agents with incredible speed.

I could hardly follow my own movements, in an instant I was dancing between the Agents, slashing my way through their advanced armor in a flurry. Gunfire rang out in short sporadic bursts as they tried to fight back but each burst worked only to lead me to my next target. Seconds after it had all begun every Agent lay dead, scattered on the ground, snow painted red beneath them.

I saw myself amongst them all, a dusting of snow falling gracefully over us. The darkness began to leave me, and with it the armor that covered both my arms and hands. As the last of the mist drifted from my eyes my body collapsed from exhaustion.

It was only a moment later that I saw Demi for the first time, jumping down from a nearby tree to investigate the scene. He took his time, examining each Agent's wounds before moving to the next, before finally laying eyes on me. After a few long moments of hesitation, or contemplation, he picked me up and carried me into the city.

I took a step back from the room, in shock and wonder about what I had just witnessed, until I bumped into the wall behind me.

The sudden jolt must have shocked me out of my sleep. I woke up in a frantic state, sitting up, I began to gaze at my hands. Everything was back to normal, but I tried to figure out how I could bring back those claws, or the armor. I was equally terrified and amazed at what I had witnessed.

Was this my gift all along? I blessed Sera for not forgetting about me.

I looked around. Demi had held vigil by the fire—keeping it alive. He looked up at me with curious eyes for a moment, then focused back on the flames. He spoke softly, I assumed not to wake Ava who was sleeping against him, "I take it you're starting to figure things out?"

Had he been watching me that whole time? By the looks of it he had been trapped under Ava while she slept, so he probably had.

"What are you talking about?" I said, wanting to play the game of ignorance until I found the answer. He wanted nothing of it, laughing to himself and shaking his head in disappointment before focusing back on the fire.

"Fine then," I said, getting up and making my way toward the entrance, using my need for fresh air as an excuse to get away from him.

Making my way out, I saw no light creeping in. For a moment I thought it may still be night time, but even the moon's silver glow offered no hint of light, there was only darkness, and I was forced to trace the walls of the cave by hand to find my way out.

There was a black wall blocking where the entrance should have been, almost as if someone had moved a boulder in the way. Looking closer, it didn't look like a wall at all, just a churning void, emptiness. As I crept closer it began to open, splitting in half to either side, letting in the fresh morning light. The two Vemosa stood against either wall, letting me pass and as I did, thanked them for protecting the entrance all night.

They let me leave the cave, but didn't acknowledge me in any other sense, standing tall and proud as they kept constant watch. I imagined them as Demi's bodyguards, and they carried the same sense of pride that would come with the job.

At first I was blinded as I stepped into the light. The morning sun reflecting off untouched snow worked only to add an extra glow to everything it touched. There was a mist that lingered beautifully, dancing ever so slightly in the still air. I could hardly believe that the world could still hold such beauty despite the destruction we have all caused. Nature always has a way about these things—that no matter its scars, it would always prevail.

I found a rock to rest on and watch, to enjoy the simple pleasures that I still held onto. The bird's songs soothed me, and the rabbits playing fast paced games of tag reminded me of a time before my worries had begun to weigh me down. A time before I realized that what worries you, ultimately controls you; a time where I could simply be, knowing that's all that any of us, Gifted or Pure really wanted, wasn't it? To simply be?

There was a rustling in the bushes that I thought may have been another rabbit. I always hated the idea of killing anything, especially on such a beautiful morning, but as my stomach rumbled I knew food was a necessity. We had a long day ahead of us.

I reached into my pocket, fishing out the blade Councilor Madsen had given me. It looked almost too pretty to use, like being tainted with blood would cause it to lose its beauty, and it would—but I needed to eat so I unfolded the blade and began to creep toward the bushes.

A moment later a Kurki hopped out of the bush, startling and causing me to fall back into the snow. It tilted its head to the side with a curious look and cautiously inched towards me, seeming as much interested in me as I was of it.

I thought of the pain these creatures had caused Han just a few days earlier, but remembered that despite Ava's fears even the Vemosa hadn't harmed me—I wasn't scared, and reached my arm down towards the Kurki as I got close. I'd forgotten I had the blade in my hand, and the moment it caught the Kurki's eye it backed away. I smiled, putting the blade back into my pocket and offered my hand once more. It flinched at first, but came closer, unsure how to react to this kind of attention. Every time I'd seen one it had been hell bent on killing whatever Demi had called a target. It was hard to imagine that they could be docile little things at times.

It seemed as though these creatures had caused everyone else so much pain, but somehow I felt as though I understood them, and because of that I didn't fear them. I thought for a second, that maybe all they needed was for someone to understand them rather than fear them—that maybe then they wouldn't cause such pain.

I smiled, "We aren't so different are we?"

The Kurki perked up, nudging my hand, rubbing its head against it like a cat might do when begging for attention. Its touch didn't burn and I felt no pain, which was a relief. Rather, it was cool to the touch, and smooth. It had no fur, rather, my hand flowed as if through an extremely thick mist down from its head to its back.

My stomach grumbled again, causing me to stop petting the Kurki for a moment, distracted. I had forgotten that I'd been hoping that the rustling in the bush was a rabbit instead and I suddenly felt more starved than before, and I knew it was never a good idea to set out on an empty stomach.

The Kurki seemed to know what I was feeling and came alive with new energy. Its two bulbous antenna shot up, twitching around sporadically until coming to an abrupt stop. It looked in that direction, then to me, before sprinting away. I stifled another laugh, forever finding humor in its step. Its oversized feet made it look like a child running in their father's shoes. One leg would swing out to the side before making its step in an exaggerated movement before the other did the same, its whole body leaning forward over itself as if it were about to tumble at any moment. The Kurki disappeared into a bush.

There was a rustling, and a high pitched squeal, then silence. A moment later the Kurki reappeared, holding a rabbit in its mouth.

*That's interesting*, I thought to myself. It was one thing for the Kurki to interact with me, but to help me was another thing entirely. I was curious if this was how Demi's relationship with these summons started, a chance encounter, a gain of trust, and then control? Would that mean maybe, just maybe, I'd be able to use the Kurki in the same way Demi can with time? Maybe even the Vemosa would take a liking to me?

No.

This was Demi's power, his Gift, not mine. I must just have this curious little Kurki's attention, or maybe Demi is playing some game with me? It didn't matter.

The grumblings in my stomach broke my train of thought once more. It was time to go cook my breakfast, so I made my way back toward the cave, the Kurki not far behind, still carrying the rabbit in its mouth. It was nice having a little helper to come along, and to know these creatures weren't nearly as menacing as everyone thought they were—there was so much darkness in the world, it was nice to see that even the Kurki could show some light.

We approached the cave with what I had thought was good timing, spotting Demi and Ava as they came to meet the morning sun. Demi spotted me first and I thought I almost saw a smile crack on his face, until he eyed the Kurki beside me. His expression went blank, and the careless energy of the Kurki beside me immediately escaped it. The Kurki hung its head low and placed the rabbit onto the snowy ground by my feet, looked up at me, and disappeared into a plume of mist.

"Curious little things," I said loud enough for them to hear, trying to start conversation despite the distance. I picked up the rabbit by the ears and began walking toward them, "It found me when I was out and caught us some breakfast. Did you send it?" I asked, directing my question to Demi.

"No," He responded, "and I wouldn't bother eating its kill either, the toxins in their mist have tainted the meat by now. You'll die if you eat it."

I looked to the rabbit, which looked fine, but realized this was the least of my worries, so I didn't argue. I placed the rabbit down on the ground and began to rub snow over the hand that had pet the Kurki earlier, realizing I'd be covered in its toxin too.

"You pet it?" Demi asked a bit too calmly, perhaps finding silent humor in my ignorance.

"Yes, but I didn't know it was toxic!" I said, washing it off a little more nervously now.

"Of course you didn't," his response was snarky, "keep making mistakes like that and we'll have Ava tending to you the entire mission."

I scoffed at him, but I also knew that he would be the only one to know how to fix this. My arm didn't burn, or feel any different from before, but I also didn't know how this toxin behaved, and was more so reacting to my fear of not knowing what to do.

"Let's go, we have everything packed up and ready. We need to make it well clear of Terra Sera by nightfall," he said, picking up his things and beginning to walk the other way.

"Hey!" I shouted after him, "What do I do about my arm?"

He stopped, looked over his shoulder and let out a sigh of annoyance, "I don't know how you did it, but if the Kurki took liking to you then you are immune to its touch, it won't kill you, you're fine."

"Jerk," I muttered under my breath, wondering why he hadn't just told me this to begin with, my arm now red and cold from the snow. What did he get out of that? Was watching me panic punishment for playing with his pet? I forced myself to stay calm despite my anger.

Ava was silent the entire time, sleep still fresh in her eyes. She rushed past me to the rabbit still on the ground where I had stood and knelt over it. There was the familiar green glow over her hands as she moved them over the body of the dead animal. There, in the space between, I could see strings of soft purple energy twisting amongst each other with what looked like tiny white spores being pushed into the rabbit's body. The glow faded, but the spores still danced around the body and a moment later the rabbit jumped up from its position, looked at Ava as if to say thank you and ran off back into the brush. She took a deep breath and clutched her chest as if in pain, but her expression was joyful.

"Ava—" I began.

She looked up, smiling, though her eyes remained deeply troubled, "Funny isn't it?"

"I—" I paused, thinking about the correct answer, "what do you mean?"

"I'm young still, and I know everyone sees me as weak but my Gift has taught me so much more than they realize. I learn more every day, and get stronger with it. But—" her sentence trailed as she looked toward the bush the rabbit ran off into, "—some things hurt to know, like the weight of that rabbits soul. It took so much out of me to do what I just did, and I wonder if our souls are worth the same. I wonder what it would cost to bring one of us back."

She was somber, sullen, her eyes held an expression full of thoughtfulness, her eyes glossed over with potential tears.

"I hadn't even known that you could have helped the poor thing, I thought your gift only let you heal what was injured but still alive, be happy you could save it's life," I began, trying to shed light on the situation.

It seemed to work and Ava gave me an approving smile, "It's—" she began.

"Something new," Demi finished, placing a hand on his sister's shoulder, "as we use the gift more it develops and grows with us. Ava doesn't have the gift of healing, but the gift of life, in all its phases."

"So that means eventually—" I began.

"My gift can also bring death," Ava whispered just loud enough to be heard. She shook her head, sending tears flying off her rosy cheeks, "I won't kill, I can't."

Demi sighed, "Even if your enemy is intent on killing you? You'll have to fight."

"I can run!" She shot out, standing.

I grimaced at the thought. I'd spent my entire life running, too scared to stand my ground, too weak to fight. I understood her pain. Her energy was too pure to kill. Though, in the face of an enemy bent on bringing your destruction it can be surprising what demons could come out to play.

# Chapter 8:

Ava and I walked ahead for most of the day, Demi straggling behind. He'd been distant since we had left the makeshift camp in the cave, lost within his thoughts. He walked slowly with his hands stuffed in his pockets, occasionally letting plumes of cold air escape from his mouth with a deep sigh.

I hadn't known if he had allowed me to take lead due to some newfound trust in me, or if his leadership skills told him my knowledge of the land was more important than a pride that may get us lost, or killed. Of course, it could be neither. He could just be falling back, sulking over his Kurki taking a liking to me. Either way, this was a step for him and I secretly smiled at that.

Our walk so far had been pretty quiet, aside of course for Ava—who'd come and go from our conversation once something new and exciting caught her eye, which was nearly everything. She'd made a habit of breaking away mid-sentence to rush over to some rock, or tree, or to stalk some animal. I smiled as I watched her, the poor girl hadn't seen outside Terra Sera until we left on Demi's mission, so nearly everything was a new discovery. She'd forgotten about the rabbit earlier this morning—and I was glad her lighthearted nature wouldn't let her stay sad for long.

"Sa—," She started in an excited call for my attention. After a short pause she continued in close to a whisper, "Sage, look!" she held up a nearly clear stone with a purple tint, begging me to look. I smiled at her, taking it in my hand to examine as we walked. This wasn't the first rock she'd given me, in most she'd found a beauty in them that I couldn't see. Each was special in its own way and she'd tell me why, if I'd asked, and probably even if I didn't. This one, however, reminded me of the satchel of valuable stones I kept in my backpack, a replacement for the paper money used before the Pulse.

"It looks like an amethyst, someone probably dropped it out here," I started, handing the stone back to her, "keep it—you might be able to buy something nice once we get to MarSeir."

Ava's smile beamed, placing the stone in her pocket, growing even more animated in searching for others that may have been left behind. It'd taken quite a few outburst for it to finally set in that she couldn't yell out here, and eventually her excitement disappeared with each valueless stone she found—the ordinary stones having lost their allure after joy of finding one that was actually worth something.

Now and again I would pass a glance over to Demi, speaking just a little louder while talking to Ava in an attempt to draw him into the conversation. He'd ignore me, most often letting out a sigh and trying his hardest not to meet my eyes with his. I wondered what was going through his mind and thought that if only I could take a peek inside for a moment maybe I could figure him out. But of course I couldn't do that. A part of me wished that we could have gotten along as well as Ava and I had, and another part of me just wanted him gone. He was spoiled, arrogant, and completely into himself, but at the same time I felt something deeper, some mystery, something hidden and I wanted to dig for that truth. I knew my curiosity might hurt me but I didn't care.

I thought back to Terra Sera and seeing him surrounded by girls, effortlessly passing attention from one to the other with them not even knowing, or not caring, I couldn't tell. I didn't want to be like them— but I did want to be able to have some form of friendly communication with him if we were going to be traveling together, at least, that's what I told myself. I laughed silently to myself thinking of what I've gotten myself into.

We walked through a cleared trail around the valleys and frozen lakes that formed between the mountains around us. The mountain range created somewhat of a circle around Terra Sera, like a natural wall to protect the city. Looking at those that we passed by, I wondered if there were entire cities in those as well. I doubted that, if there was then I'm sure Demi would have made us stop for food by now.

Or maybe he just didn't want me to know.

I was still an outsider, and thought maybe his silence was due to mistrust. I could feel him watching me as we walked, and that made me nervous. It was like he was sitting back and trying to work the facts out in his mind, trying to figure me out. What did he know?

I was a stranger.

I was found alone.

I had lead a squad of Agents to Terra Sera's front gates, however unintentional.

I was found amongst the lifeless bodies of those Agents.

I have no knowledge of my own power, a power that saved me that night, a power that challenged even him.

And now here I am, selected by Councilor Madsen to join Demi on a mission that may bring back a sense of honor to his family. That alone put a lot of pressure on me, a pressure that just a few days ago I didn't have to carry.

I'd stumbled through this same path on my way in, before all of this—and felt that this was the opposite of where I wanted to be going, away from the great war, away from MarSeir, away from the death and despair that came with living with the Stigma. But then, did I really expect to spend the rest of my life huddled up in that cave?

I shook my head, as if the thought would somehow become dislodged from my brain and fly out to be buried in the snow and forgotten.

The truth is I didn't know what I wanted. I simply existed here, anyone with the Stigma simply existed. We didn't live, how could we? We spent every day existing, and not knowing if we would be alive to see tomorrow. I had no clear plans, no real wants other than to make it through the day and even with that hope I fully expected to be dead by tomorrow.

I tried to clear my mind, telling myself that there was hope, if we could just find Sera she would save us, but everywhere I looked all I could see was the destruction caused by this war coupled with the everlasting peace I saw in nature. I wondered why we couldn't live like the birds, or the flowers, or the trees and why everything we touch must die. I thought about finding Sera, and what I expected when we did, if we did.

I thought about how impossible this mission was, but I found relief in the fact that we were only here to find her, not to save her—not yet.

For that, we would need an army.

# Chapter 9:

I stopped Ava short, pulling her behind me as I caught movement in the distance. I put my finger to my lips, signaling her to stay quiet, and crouched low to the ground, trying to get a better look.

I signaled Demi to do the same and thankfully he listened.

There was a camp up ahead, but from what I could see it had been abandoned, or worse. I wouldn't have been completely surprised if we had just missed a raid, and if we did than the Agents who did this wouldn't be too far away— if they weren't still rummaging through their own destruction.

Still, I was relieved that it wasn't an Agent I saw moving through the camp. It was difficult to see in the distance, but there was something large roaming through. Its grayish skin worked as a natural camouflage with the thin layer of snow still left on the ground. I couldn't make out any details but the animal was larger than anything I'd ever seen out here, or anywhere for that matter. I thought maybe it could be a bear, despite its color, or maybe even an alpha wolf, though I'd never seen one so large, and this animal moved unlike anything I'd ever seen.

The animal stopped abruptly, seeming to catch onto the fact that it was being watched. A moment later it lumbered back through the tree line, disappearing into the wilderness.

A few minutes passed as I waited to see if it would return, or if Agents would come to investigate. I saw nothing, and signaled Demi and Ava to follow me through the brush towards the camp. The fact that the fallen tents weren't covered with snow told me that this attack was recent, after last night's flurry at least.

Scavenging through what was left behind in the wake of another's death used to bother me, Sera bless them, but experience had taught me that the things left behind would be better served to help those still living escape the same fate. Despite my worries I knew we had to get down there to find whatever might be useful before others stumbled on our potential treasure. Over time, the site would be stripped down until there wasn't a single trace of it, not even a memory.

I used to worry about being ambushed as I searched through the remains, or become filled with grief for the deaths of those I hadn't even known. A small fire still burned low in a dug out pit, telling me this all happened sooner than I had thought, which worried me even more. I wanted nothing more than to have arrived soon enough to save them, though I knew I couldn't. The knowledge that this could just have easily been me, us, in our camp would have troubled me years ago but years of living with this fear eventually makes even the most caring hearts grow just a little bit colder. Despite their deaths, we still survived.

I could only hope the scene might work as some shock therapy for Demi, so that these pointless deaths could have at least some purpose to serve. I knew he felt he could handle anything, but that's the kind of ignorance that might get us all killed one day. He needed to see firsthand the danger we all face, though I wish I could still have shielded Ava from it, not wanting to steal her innocence so soon.

We made it into the circular break in the trees that surrounded the camp. There were only a couple heaps of thick cloth collapsed into each other, telling me this was a traveling group—nothing permanent. They had snapped branches off surrounding trees to use as poles for support, planning leaving them when they eventually left. The cloth could be used to help carry what little they held onto through their travels, nearly anything useful had to be made or found on the way. It was easier this way.

There was an arm stretched out from under one of those piles, a bright red stream of blood still soaking into the ground below. Behind me, Demi had begun to wander and Ava remained reluctant to come out into the open, and I used that time to pull the cloth over the arm, hiding it.

There was another body face down near the other tent. I walked closer to take a look, finding a hole the size of my fist in the man's back between his shoulder blades. It looked like something had been shot clean through, but there was no blood to be found anywhere around him save for a few rogue drops. His body was pale and blue, he'd been dead a lot longer than the person in the other tent who still had her color.

Had she just stood in camp with a dead guy lying just feet from her tent? It wouldn't surprise me.

Demi walked over beside me, curious, then immediately looked to Ava, who was following a few feet behind, "Ava, go try and find something useful, don't come over here."

"Why, what is it? I wanna see," she retaliated but Demi ordered her away, she listened.

"What happened here?" Demi asked after a few seconds of silence.

"I don't know. There was definitely a struggle, but I've never seen a wound like that, it's like an animal just tore into the guy."

"So then, it wasn't the Agents who did this," Demi said.

"No."

"Then that animal we saw earlier?"

I sighed, looking out into the tree line, half hoping to see the large animal that had escaped earlier and half relieved when I didn't see a sign of it, "It doesn't make sense, if it was an animal then these two should have been able to handle it."

"Maybe their gift wasn't combative?" Demi suggested.

I shook my head, "If you travel in a group at least someone has to be around for protection. It wouldn't be wise not to."

Demi gave me a sly look, "I see you were following your own advice when I found you."

I rolled my eyes, "Well, I'm different."

Demi scoffed, "I've noticed."

I looked back to the body, "What bothers me most is the fact that there's no blood."

"So not seeing blood bothers you? Isn't it normally the other way around?"

"Shut up," I ordered, "I just don't get how he can have a hole in his back that large and he's not lying in a pool of his own blood."

"I guess you're right," Demi agreed, scratching the back of his head as he thought about it more.

There were footsteps behind us, a crunching in the snow, and we turned to see Ava making her way back with a smile. There was a glint of light that reflected a silver pendant on a leather cord dangling from her clenched fist.

"Look at what I found, isn't it amazing?" she said, presenting a necklace.

"What is it?" Demi asked, taking it from her hands.

I smiled at the sight of it, but gave a second look to the man by our feet, this time with more respect, "These people were a part of Cekrit."

"How do you know?" Demi asked as I took the necklace from his hand.

"This necklace, it's our symbol," I said with pride as I took the necklace from her hand, tracing my fingers along the markings as I thought.

There was a circle resting in the innermost arch of two crescent shaped marks, each with a stem that pulled down to sharp points, like overlapping question marks without the dot. The inner circle represents the self, while the smaller and larger overlapping arch represents our mother Sera and Klaus respectively. There was a small gap between the two marks, and the larger of the two pulled down slightly past the smaller. I flipped the necklace over, the initial "M" was carved into the back.

Ava perked up with attention and gave an exaggerated, "Cool," before taking the necklace from my hand to look at it again herself, this time with greater interest.

Demi squared up to me, "So you're with them? When were you going to tell us you were a rebel?"

I gave him a serious look, "So you're mad at me now?"

"Yeah, kind of!"

"Oh, okay," I started, "coming from the guy who's lived in a secret city run by a Council thought to be killed off over twenty years ago and protected by them while everyone out here was busy surviving and fighting the war for you, and you're the one that's mad at me?"

"But you're on the wrong side."

I laughed at that, "What side? We all just want to survive out here, if you didn't just hear me we all think the Council was killed off. Or do you want me to go spreading your little secret?"

Demi took a step closer to me and rose a finger, "Don't."

"So why do they hide anyway? Did they just give up on our kind or were they scared?" I asked.

"We're waiting," Demi said through his teeth.

"For what?" I asked, "Everyone out here to die? For the war to be over? Or are they just waiting and hoping those of us left out here do all of the work for them?"

"You have no idea what we stand for."

"And neither do you, so drop it," I ordered.

Demi went to speak but I crossed my arms and gave him a serious look, letting him know I wouldn't back down, and he listened, surprisingly.

I looked back to the body once more, and made my way to the heap of cloth that had stood as the man's tent before being torn down. I took the cloth and covered his body, it was the least anyone could do for him now.

I took a quick sweep around the camp, looking for food but came up empty. Either these two were living day to day off what they could hunt or something had already run off with it.

There was little left to salvage outside of the tents, and I didn't want to disturb the bodies by searching through the heaps of cloth that now covered them.

Demi had already taken Ava and lead her back into the direction we were going before. I caught back up to them and took lead once more, still trying to wrap my head around what had gone wrong here.

I could only hope that creature was far away by now.

# Chapter 10:

It was night, and we trudged along a path that lead out of the mountain system and into the greener and warmer plains beyond. Even the surrounding forest would grow thicker, and teaming with life beyond this point. The mountains behind us had created a void of warmth and I could only assume that the drastic change in weather had something to do with the surrounding mountains themselves. That, or someone had taken control, creating a hostile enough environment to drive intruders away. I guess either one was possible.

We'd been traveling all day through the cold on an empty stomach, and I knew that the warmer weather beyond the peaks would make the night that much more comfortable. I remembered there being an abandoned railroad station just a little further that I'd passed on my way in. I hoped that we could find a way inside to avoid having to camp out in the open, vulnerable to the elements and whatever might be watching in the dark.

As we rounded a corner, I froze. Off the path I could see the station in the distance, though the sky was painted a bright orange by the light of a fire that pouring from its windows. I reached for Ava, pulling her close to the face of the mountain while motioning for Demi to do the same. I peered around the corner, watching, and cringing when screams that were far from human pierced the midnight silence.

A girl with vibrant orange hair stood in the center of her smoldering camp, her back to a semi-circle of abandoned train cars that opened out towards the tree line before us. She was spinning a staff above her head, creating a churning vortex of fire around her that came crashing down onto the surrounding tree line, forming a blazing ring around the camp.

I could see a large shadow looming in the brush, and a screech as it dodged the coming infernal whirlwind. I followed the sound of breaking branches as it moved, but couldn't see anything in the darkness.

I looked back to Demi, only to see a Vemosa holding him in its bladed arms, sinking back into the ground. My eyes shot back to the battle where a darkened circle appeared beside the girl. She looked down, noticing the area of blackness and jumped back in surprise, landing a few feet away in a defensive pose, ready to attack.

Demi slowly rose from the void, arms crossed over his shoulders, his hood covering most of his face. Typical, even in battle he had a flare for the dramatic.

I feared our sudden isolation, and blindly reached for Ava for a sense of comfort but felt nothing. I immediately spun around only to see her frozen with fear, facing a giant creature clinging on the mountainside above us. Suddenly the fire's light grew brighter as the battle behind us raged on, in the dim orange light I caught my first glimpse of a monster that would soon haunt my nightmares.

We were faced with a creature with pale white skin that looked slick to the touch, as if it was covered in some type of oily membrane. Its body was long, and thin, with its ribs showing through a starved frame. It clung to the mountain wall, head to the ground, using its elongated arms to slowly reach for another rock to grab hold of as it inched closer. Its back legs rested on the rock above, completely disproportional to its body. There was a transparent tail, red with flowing blood that ran up its back, fused to its body and connected to a head that could only be described as death itself. The creature had no eyes, no nose, only a series of slits running from its stubby, boxed, snout to its forehead.

*Kill,* a voice in my head whispered and for a moment I felt strong enough to fight back, though I knew I couldn't, I shouldn't, but I had to, didn't I?

I hesitated.

As the creature moved closer the slits running up its face flared open, illuminated by a blood orange bioluminescent light, then closed as it honed in on us Its mouth opened to let out a screech, showing the full set of its long dagger-like teeth. Its tail rose, aimed at Ava, and a glint of light caught my eye. I gasped, a barb at the tip was ready to drive itself into her. I dove to get Ava out of the way just as the spike came hurdling down into the ground between my legs. Holding Ava in my arms I shuffled backwards as the creature pulled itself free and jumped off the rock wall and onto the path before us. The creature inched forward, its head swaying close to the ground, arms bent and its backside high with its large hind legs. Its every movement was unnatural.

I held my breath, and shielded Ava from the creature. The slits running up its face flared out once more, and I realized that was how it hunted. It locked onto us once more and lunged, arms outstretched and ready to grab hold of us and finish us off with its barbed tail.

Shielding Ava, I closed my eyes to the coming blow, but it never came. I only heard another screech and a thud as the creature's body hit the mountain wall then fell to the ground writhing in pain.

Daring to look, I saw a flaming arrow shot deep into the leg of the thrashing beast as it struggled to find balance.

There were heavy footsteps crashing through the brush, and I jerked around to see a man running toward us holding a flaming bow. He knelt by our side, putting a hand on my shoulder as I stared blankly at the felled beast, "We need to move, you hurt?" he asked, looking at me, then to Ava who was still curled up under me.

Releasing her, I shook my head no.

The man smiled briefly, "Good, then let's go we need to help the others," he said, his flame burning out so he could help us up.

Closer to the camp plumes of fire flared out into the brush, holding off the still lurking creatures in the darkness. Afraid to be cornered by one of those beast again, I pulled Ava along as this mystery man lead us back *into* the fight.

In the darkness I could see the blood orange flares that were the monsters sensors picking up our movement. We rushed past and in the corner of my eye I could see them change direction and burst into the closest thing to a sprint they could manage directly for us. I pulled Ava harder, and ran faster toward the flaming camp.

Ahead, Kurki disappearing into the darkness on the other side of the clearing beyond a line of abandoned train cars caused an enhanced spike of fear to run through me as I realized how many of these demons we must be faced with.

"We'll be surrounded!" I shouted, the thought escaping my lips.

The man who led us turned to me with a wicked smile as we broke the tree line into the camp, "I know."

"Marcus!" the girl yelled, causing a gust of wind to send a fireball flying towards us with a wide sweep of her staff, "behind you!"

I snuck a worried look behind us to see one of those monsters breech the tree line, its tail arched over its head, ready to attack.

"Move!" Marcus yelled, grabbing the ball of fire as it nearly whipped past his right shoulder. He planted a foot solid on the ground, turned and pulled one arm back as if he was drawing a bow all in one fluid motion. The blaze took shape and the flaming bow was in his hands once more. He narrowed his eyes as the arrow formed, releasing it just as the creature dove over Ava and I to attack him.

The bolt hit the creature in the center of its head mid-dive, immediately causing it to go limp and crash to the ground just inches from Marcus' feet.

I stood, staring at Marcus, in awe of the couples's synergy in battle. He gave me a quick smile, and turned to get back into the fight, focusing his bow into an orb of churning fire before throwing it into the abyss that was the forest around us. I watched as it streaked across the opening, and hit a just emerging creature on the other side. It fled back into the darkness.

My eyes searched for Demi, who was fighting in tandem with the girl in the middle of the opening, a single beast struggling to manage a blow between them, stabbing with its spiked tail. Demi spun, catching the tail barely an inch from the girl's chest. Demi's hand looked charred as the darkness began to overwhelm him— lost in the thrill of the fight. The monster writhed in pain as Demi's grip tightened and the red blood that flowed through its tail became black as night. The beast snapped and clawed at Demi, trying to spin its awkward body around the reach him but never able to catch him in its jaws. The darkness crept up the beast's transparent tail, until it reached where it began at the top of its head.

The monster's head jolted to the sky and it let out a terrific screech, before falling to the ground, dead.

Three of the creatures lay dead on the ground and in the darkness I could see the churning shadows of the others circling around, reluctant to attack.

"Dodge!" Marcus ordered from behind me, pulling me from my trance.

I turned to see a plume of fire carried on a rogue wind spiraling towards us.

*Do something*, the voice in my head demanded but was unable to do little more than push Ava to safety as I stood there, frozen in the face of the coming blaze, shielding myself with crossed arms and eyes closed.

In an instant, I was thrown hard to the ground and though I could feel its warmth flowing around me I wasn't scorched by the searing flame. I dared to open my eyes only to see Demi over me, his face just inches from mine, a black mass behind him shielding us from the fire. I laid there suspended in time as the battle raged around us, the near liquid shell that arched over dripping as the fire crashed to the ground on beside us.

I found a certain peace in this silence, a moment of clarity, and thanked him silently for saving me. A storm of emotion rushed through me in the moments our eyes remained locked, and for the first time I found myself believing that beneath his cold composure there was a warm heart no one cared to notice.

Another screech in the darkness of the surrounding forest stole our attention as the blast settled, and one of the creatures stumbled out into the opening covered with Kurki. It took staggered steps with no direction, throwing its body from left to right in a feeble attempt to free itself of the swarm. The nearly ten foot creature rose on its hind legs, towering over us as it threw its arms over its head, grasping at the Kurki as they bit down, creating growing black spots wherever they did. Its tail swung wildly before suddenly rising high over its head and driving its spike into its own skull in a desperate act to escape the pain of the Kurki's corrosive touch.

"Marcus!" the girl said pointing to the small black creatures with her staff as they jumped off the beast, one fighting to free itself from under it's dead body.

"Got it," he said, as he ran beside her with an open palm, gathering bits of fire before hurling it as the group of Kurki.

"What were those?" the girl asked, looking to Marcus for an answer as the Kurki burst into plumes of black mist.

Demi lingered over me in momentary silence, as if waiting for something to be said, but I could do little more than stare back at him.

"Kurki," Demi answered, scrambling to his feet to leave me on the cold ground.

Marcus seemed to have forgotten we were there, snapping out of his blank gaze to give Demi a questioning look, "You know what they are?"

Demi smirked as he took a step back, stretching his arms out by his side, palms to the ground—again with a flair for the dramatic. Slowly, a dozen antenna emerged from black pits that formed on the ground, like puddles of darkness slowly drying up as the Kurki rose from it with their awkward shape and their large yellow eyes. Moments later a small group of Kurki danced around Demi's feet, sniffing the ground and jolting to attention whenever their antenna picked up the slightest movement in the background. They'd stare out into the darkness past the tree line, watching something unseen by us. Demi watched the Kurki with a sly smile as they played, for the first time I've seen finding delight in allowing them to simply be and not kill.

The girl's eyes grew wide, and a smile broke on her face, "Well now that's just amazing! If it wasn't for you I'm not sure we could have handled all of those things."

Marcus' head snapped to the girl, "Piper!"

"What?"

"I was doing just fine, and if he can create those how do we know he didn't create those monsters out there too?" his voice rose as he threw his arm out to the side, pointing to the darkness beyond the surrounding flames.

Demi chuckled to himself.

"Something funny?" Marcus scowled.

"No, nothing. I just don't know what you think I'd gain from summoning those things just to kill them myself. A bit of a waste, don't you think?"

Piper nodded in agreement, "See Marcus? He's just trying to help."

Marcus sighed in frustration, looking up to the sky as he ran his fingers back through his shoulder length hair, "I guess you're right."

"So," Ava began, " what were those things?"

"Don't know," Marcus said, "they've been popping up out here lately, usually alone, but once a fight breaks out more always come."

"They can't be natural," I started, looking over to one lying dead just feet from us, "I've never seen a thing like it. Think it's some kind of mutation?"

Marcus walked over to the corpse, squatting down to take a closer look, "Not likely, that would have taken millions of years to evolve and these things aren't exactly the best at hiding, or small enough to overlook."

"So we might have another summoner on our hands?" Demi asked.

"Likely."

"So we find him and kill him," Demi added.

Marcus shot Demi a sour look, "Yeah, brilliant idea. Let's go hunt down the bastard who made all these damned things. Like something worse might not be there waiting for us. I'd think he doesn't want to be found if he sends these creatures to fight in his place."

Demi squared up to Marcus, making a show of his size though he was still the smaller man, "You'd rather wait until one of them actually kills you? You weren't exactly handling yourself before I showed up."

Marcus spat at the ground, "You trying to start something?"

"Easy now boys," Piper said, stepping between the two arguing men, placing her hands firmly on their chest. She paused, turning to face Demi, and looked him up and down for an extra moment.

Marcus perked up, "So, where you from anyway?" he asked, scanning the three of us.

"Terra Sera!" Ava exclaimed, happy to join the conversation.

Demi gave her a worried look but stood silent.

"Terra Sera?" Marcus questioned, "Never heard of it."

Demi chimed in, "I wouldn't think so, we've traveled a long way."

"But—" Ava began again in protest.

Demi cut her off, "But, I doubt it's gone this long without being raided. Damn village probably doesn't even exist anymore."

"Sounds like a beautiful place, just the name itself even," Piper said with a smile.

Marcus seemed to be watching Demi, trying to figure out if there was truth behind what he said. He seemed to know Demi was trying to cover something up, but let it pass and relaxed as Piper went on.

"...And this is Sage, and my sister Ava," Demi's voice brought me out of my thoughtful daze and back to attention.

"Nice to meet you," I said, smiling as I took my first good look at our new friends.

Truly, I was taken back by Piper's beauty. The surrounding fire's glow tinted her pale face with soft shades of red and yellow, light freckles scarcely scattered across her rosy cheeks and over her nose. Snowflakes clung to lustrous orange hair, looking so hot and vibrant I was surprised they didn't melt the moment they fell upon her. She wore a light hearted expression, smiling from the endless depths of her light blue eyes and thin coral lips. A pure white baja hoodie and a pair of ripped jeans spotted and wet from the snow were the only thing that shielded her petite frame from the bitter cold. Even so, I figured she had no need to bundle up— the couples flame offering ample warmth through the night. Her hands were by her side, holding a staff that she used like a seat as she lingered in the air, her legs dangling several inches above the ground with a carefree attitude.

Marcus looked more weathered than his partner, his kind eyes seeming to disguise a painful past—it was a look shared by too many in these times. His disheveled shoulder-length hair was held back by a frayed red sash and ran along either side of a face covered in the rough stubble of a once shaven beard recently left unkempt, perhaps trying to cover a scar that could now hardly be seen along his jawline. He wore hooded cowl bunched up around his neck with cloak that covered only his left side, leaving his right uncovered—presumably in case he needed to form his bow. Beneath, he wore a close fit shirt and a pair of cargo pants with a number of corked gourds and jars hanging from the loops around his waist. His hands were covered in ash and both index fingers and thumbs were accented with black flintlock rings for a quick spark.

Piper looked over her shoulder to the fires behind her, "I don't see any point in either of us setting off this late in the night."

"Especially with those creatures still lurking around," I added, giving a double take into the darkness beyond the tree line.

"Right. So, what do y'all think about camping with us tonight?"

Marcus crossed his arms in retaliation, like an upset child after his mother told him no, but he kept quiet. I smiled at that, he was so much like Demi it was no wonder why the two bashed heads. I knew the more people we took on the greater chance there was we would be discovered, then again, the fires and smoke trail alone would have already drawn the attention of any nearby Agents. The fact that they weren't here by now meant the creatures might be holding them off for now, so I saw no need to push forward.

I looked to Demi for an answer, he was silent for a moment before he spoke, "Only if Mr. Hero over here can deal with not starting any more trouble."

"Hey you—" Marcus began.

I cut him off, passing Demi a serious look, "That means you too Demi."

He smiled, then nodded to Marcus, "I'll do my best."

"Well then, it's settled. Marcus?" Piper said, turning to him, "Mind setting up?"

Marcus made his way to one of the low burning patches of fire with silent obedience. I hadn't noticed that as we talked many of the scattered blazes had begun to die out, but as Marcus walked around the clearing the fires grew with a reborn intensity. As he did the flames beneath his palm spread, rebuilding the flaming wall that would protect us through the night. The new light illuminated abandoned railroad cars as he set the wall behind them, and through the open doors I could see the run down train station in the distance. I questioned it for a moment why wouldn't we stay in the relative warmth of the station if we could. I decided to trust our new friend's judgement.

Marcus had returned to the group, and knelt down a few feet beside us, creating a fire in the middle of the ring, "The walls will burn till morning. We're lucky, the damned things don't seem to like fire, I think it screws with those sensors on their face. It pretty much makes them blind."

I sat down beside the fire, which burned with no wood. The ball of flame simply sat an inch off the ground, burning on its own. I didn't understand it, but I wasn't complaining, the warmth on my body was the only explanation I needed. I looked to Demi in a way that asked if he'd join me, but he pretended not to notice my gaze and started after Marcus instead. I thought, for a moment, to chase after him and tell him to stop harassing Marcus but I knew he wouldn't listen if I tried. He can be such a child, and I cursed him silently for his immaturity.

Instead, Ava sat beside me and nestled into my arms. Her cheeks and nose were a rosy red, and I could tell she was cold in the nighttime air. I knew the poor girl had grown used to the constant spring-like warmth inside Terra Sera. Before long, she had rested her head on my lap and fallen asleep as we sat for a while in the relative silence of night. Behind the fire, I was happy to see Demi and Marcus talking with some sense of restraint, maybe even getting along. They were laughing, and I smiled at that. I didn't need Demi getting hurt or picking too many fights along the way, we have enough enemies as it is just by being what we are and I was glad to see him playing nice for once.

"Sage?" Piper's voice came from behind, and I turned to see her making her way to me, "got a minute?"

"Shoot," I returned, meeting her eyes before going back to watching the fiery dance of the flames, or using that as an excuse to watch the boys behind them, I couldn't decide. The boys had stopped chatting and seemed to be running through the slow motion steps of some martial arts move I'd never understand. They'd push and shove each other and escape holds, always falling back with a smile. The fire's light cast shadows that played games of tag on Demi's orange tinted face. I felt silly watching him like I was, but when he smiled so did I, even if I thought he was a self absorbed jerk. I knew better than this, yet here I was breaking my golden rule. Don't get attached.

"So—what's the deal with you and Demi? I mean, are you guys a thing?" she asked, though I wasn't paying enough attention and she had to ask again.

I let a single laugh escape me, flustered, but that couldn't show, "I'd hardly call it a thing."

Piper sat silent for a moment as we both watched Demi through the flames.

"But you *do* like him, don't you?" she asked, finally.

"What?" I started, more ashamed than surprised of the feeling in my stomach when she asked, "He's such a jerk. And he's so full of himself, just look at him," I said as Demi dropped Marcus to the ground in a chokehold.

Piper sighed, "That's my point, just look at him," she said, resting her head in her hands.

I shrugged and looked away, "I guess, but I mean, his charm fades once you get to know him."

Piper laughed at that, "Hun, I don't plan on getting to know him. At least not like that."

I gave her a curious look, "What about Marcus?"

"What of him?"

"Aren't you guys a thing? It's not hard to see how he looks at you."

Piper smiled, "Gotta keep a man around for some things! Besides, this life's too short for monogamy."

"Seems like you're into it a bit more than he is."

"Oh he can have his fun too, it's not my fault he chooses not to," she pressed on.

"So, what do you want from me?" I asked after a short pause.

"It's not obvious? Your permission to steal that hunk away for a night. It's not every day you bump into something so—*fine*."

I was taken back by the bluntness of her question, and conflicted with my own heart, stuck between a deep need to not care and what I had begun to feel for him. I decided I'd leave it up to him, if he felt the same then he wouldn't spend the night with her.

I looked back to Piper, "Go for it," I said dryly, trying to mask my concern.

A huge smile broke on her face and she threw her arms around me for a hug. "Thank you!" she said, her voice muffled in the embrace. When she pulled away she nudged me with her elbow before getting up from the fire, "Oh, and feel free to keep Marcus busy if you'd like."

"Yeah," I said with a pause, "I'll keep that in mind."

With that Piper jogged over to the still fighting boys. They stopped to talk, and I could see both Demi and Marcus break eye contact with Piper to look at me with questioning eyes before focusing back on her, who gleefully jumped into Marcus' arms for a hug. She pulled away and grabbed Demi's hand, leading him away to one of the train cars. He paused, looking over his shoulder to me one last time as if asking if this was okay. I offered a half-smile and a wave before he looked away, following Piper.

My heart sank as they disappeared into the car and the doors slid closed. I was hot, but not from the fire. Something was wrong, and I felt emotions coursing through me that'd I had abandoned years ago— feelings I'd shut myself off from to avoid the pain they would inevitably bring. It was easier that way, but how stupid was I? I knew Demi was trouble from the moment I met him, I'd watched him with other girls, and he'd been nothing but cold towards me. But still, I felt something that warmed my heart when we locked eyes, but now that emotion was replaced with overwhelming regret as I realized my foolishness.

I should have known better.

Marcus came to the fire soon after, sitting beside me, "Hey," he said shyly.

"Don't even think about it."

"No worries, this whole thing is Piper's idea not mine," he said, shaking his head, staring at the ground.

"So why put up with it?"

"Because, I love her."

I sighed with misplaced disappointment, "That doesn't make sense. How could you love her if she has no problem running off with another guy?"

"If I didn't I'd find her dead in a few days. I've sworn to protect her life, no matter how she decides to live it. I'd rather have her like this than not at all."

*Idiot*, I thought, at first. But in the silence that followed I took my thought back, "How noble of you."

Marcus chuckled, "I guess, but it never really gets any easier to see—even if I know that after tomorrow I'll probably never see them again. Things just go back to normal and she'll pretend as if it all never happened, as always."

"Why's she like that?"

"She thinks we're all animals, and animals don't have these types of relationships so why should we? She thinks people with our talents lost the luxury of having a family, and need to be free. So she thinks that everyone belongs to each other, and it would be against nature to claim someone as yours and yours alone. It's a little odd I know, but it's her," he said, staring blankly toward the car. After a moment his gaze broke away, and he fixed his attention on the warmth of the fire, then to Ava and I, "I see the little one's already called it a night and I don't want you two to risk sleeping out here in case we have company. There's another car open, let's move you two there."

Marcus stood, offering a hand and a kind smile. I didn't understand how he could stay, even after watching Piper walk off with another man who knows how many times. But then I thought about Demi, and how I'd somehow been dragged along on this mission. I could have said no, I could have ditched them by now, but I didn't. I was here, watching over Ava as Demi ran off with some girl that he hardly knew. But then again, what did I expect? For him to stay? For the three of us to be some kind of family? I hardly even knew him myself, yet here I was, jealous, and disappointed.

I snapped out of my daze, realizing Marcus hadn't moved, his hand still outstretched.

"Sorry," I said, and went to take his hand before realizing Ava still held me down, "Maybe you could just help by carrying her. I think she's walked more than her legs could bare."

"Sure thing," Marcus said, walking around me and taking Ava in his arms before making way to another open train car. I rose slowly, and followed.

Fear surged through me as I caught sight of the still moving shadows beyond Marcus' flaming wall, telling me those creatures still lingered behind the veil, waiting for their chance to strike. I tried to look away, to find some semblance in safety. Though my instincts told me everything about staying here was a bad idea, I had to escape that the very demons who held us captive would act as our guardians for the night.

"You're not coming in?" I asked, surprised.

"Looking to get back at Demi?" he returned, stopping to face me with a cheeky smile.

I gave him a stern look.

He laughed to himself, shaking his head, "I know, I know. Wait here."

With that he turned back to the fire. I watched as he put his hands directly into the flame and pulled out a smaller orb. He returned, holding the flame in his hands, and climbed into the car.

"It's good to see others from Cekrit out here, I was starting to worry our numbers were getting smaller than they already are, "Marcus said, stepping up into the train car.

I eyed him for a moment, "How did you know?"

He pointed to Ava, "The little one's necklace," he said, pulling up his sleeve to show a tattoo with the same symbol taking up most of his left forearm before quoting the group's motto, which we both said in unison, with a beaming smile, "Keep it a Cekrit."

We laughed for a moment, and I relaxed as I felt the familiarity and positive energy that came with being with others that were fighting for the same cause. It'd become more and more difficult for me to find those moments, and this one was short lived as I looked back to Ava, remembering the camp from earlier, "To be honest, she found it on the ground earlier today and took a liking to it. We had the misfortune of having to pass through a destroyed camp. I couldn't understand what happened at first, but I think these creatures killed the people there."

Marcus walked over to Ava who stood beside me and examined the necklace, flipping it over to look on the back, "Ah, so that's where it went."

Ava shied away, protecting the necklace.

Marcus smiled, "No worries, you can have it. I lost it earlier today, but it's yours now."

"So you were there?" I asked.

"I was, and these creatures have been hunting us since."

"That explains a lot. But something bothered me, why wasn't there any blood?"

Marcus turned, looking back outside, "Damn things stab you with their tail and suck you dry, it's how they feed—it wasn't just that either, our friends eyes and mouths burst open with purple light as they were killed and I saw a thin mist escape them," Marcus spat at the ground outside the car, "it was almost as if their souls were drawn out of them."

Ava covered her mouth, "That's terrible."

Marcus simply offered a nod in agreement, before moving deeper into the car. The darkness soon faded away and was replaced by a flickering orange glow. My eyes shot to the far corner, and I pushed Ava along the back wall, jolting to attention as a jagged metal bar pushed up against my back. I spun to see a metal cage with torn out bars, broken and fractured out into the car. Marcus directed the light towards us and I relaxed as the cage came up empty. I turned, remembering the other on the opposite side of the car. Marcus moved between us, investigating, the fire in his hand growing brighter.

Inside of another cage lay the lifeless body of one of the creatures. Marcus moved to take a closer look, daring to nudge the beast with a broken off shard from the cage behind us.

"Damn thing starved in here," he said, after the beast remained motionless on the floor, "must have not been able to break the bars like the others."

I relaxed, "I guess that's assuring. Still, the thing creeps me out."

Marcus took a step back and ran his fingers through his hair, staring at the dead beast for a moment, "I guess they aren't the prettiest things are they?"

"Not at all!" Ava blurted out, taking a peek from behind me.

Marcus sighed, and turned towards us. He was watching the fire in his hand and looking around as if trying to find someplace to put it. There was a stack of metal containers to his right and he stretched to place his warm ball of light on top. He began moving around the car, looking for boxes or pieces of wood to stack up in front of the cage. Within minutes, any loose scrap that could be used had been, and he even found a nice sheet to drape out in front too add a little flavor.

Marcus stood back, looking at his makeshift blockade as he smacked his hands together, brushing off the dust. He smiled and took a look around, "Well, she's a bit of a fix-her-upper but she'll do for the night."

I shared his smile, taking another look around. I'd slept in worse places, though the vulnerability I felt here with the fires outside still haunted me, but I knew we had no other choice.

Ava yawned, and sat down by my feet, "I'm tired."

"I guess that's my cue, "Marcus said, making his way for the door, "I'll be outside if you need anything."

"Wait," I called after him, "sure you don't want to stay in here? It's warm."

Marcus shook his head no, "Someone has to keep watch right? Besides, Piper would be furious if she found out we shared a bed."

I narrowed my eyes at that, she had no right to get mad at someone so sweet. Marcus didn't deserve her, he deserved better. I started to protest, but Marcus cut me off before I had the chance to speak, saying goodnight, before pulling the rusty train car door closed for the night.

# Chapter 11:

Ava had fallen asleep on my shoulder as I sat up against the cold metal wall of the train car. I tried not to wake her as I rummaged through my backpack, trying to find the book Ms. Ingalls had given me, hoping that maybe it would give me a glimpse of what these creatures might be. I knew they couldn't be natural, and my first thought was that they might be some kind of summon gone wrong, or let loose, but the question was by who?

The same symbols I remember from the labyrinth walls were handwritten in columns along most of the pages as I flipped through with my free hand; I saw no pictures, and nothing to be read about the creatures but I was entranced nonetheless.

I flipped to a new page and paused. The symbols had begun to move, now forming words that I could easily understand on the page before me, as if the book was reacting to me.

*From trust, to betrayal.* The first line said, under it more words began to form and I waited patiently as they arranged themselves.

*Friends close, enemies closer*, the next line said.

I waited for more, but the symbols had stopped moving. I turned the page. There were no words here, only a rough sketch of two men looking at me, as if the drawing was from the eyes of someone laying down with the two men standing over them, watching. The sketch took on more detail, and I looked more intently.

I recognized one of the men, Dom Seir, an elder monk who lived in the monastery just outside MarSeir. I suddenly became overwhelmed with memories of my youth, the sight of him catching me by surprise. The man was the closest thing I ever had to a father and had taken care of me until I was old enough to be adopted by my first family in MarSeir. I was troubled by the worry written across his face, a look of uncertainty, of regret, and sorrow.

The other man was darker, and set with deeper shadows, as if he had been forgotten, left in a distant haze. I couldn't recognize him, and I had to assume that he was another monk in the monastery. The idea of someone from outside the monastery forcing Dom Seir's hand upset me to no end, so I forced myself to forget that possibility.

In the background I could see swirls of energy, churning on the paper behind them.

*From trust to betrayal*, the words echoed in my mind — but in a voice that wasn't my own. I ignored it, thinking my mind was playing tricks on me.

What happened between these two men?

I tried to wrap my head around the possibilities. I remembered the Dom as a kind man, loyal to his work, and caring for all those around him. I couldn't picture him in any form of trouble.

Who did they betray?

I turned the page once more, not wanting my mind to delve too deep into what the Dom may have been involved in.

*Friends close.* The words arranged themselves once more on the top of the page. Below, faded into focus a picture of Demi and Ava, walking through a torn city. Ava had clung to Demi's back and he bent over slightly to support her weight as they walked. They were both smiling, happy.

I thought for a moment, trying to figure out just what was going on. I'd thought this book had dated back to before they would have even been born, and thought that maybe someone had used their power on it, causing the book to take in things from its surroundings, only revealing itself to who it wanted. It might be a stretch, but that's the only way I could make sense of what was going on.

I turned the page once more to see the words, *enemies closer*, written on the top of the page.

Below, another sketch began to work itself out.

At first, I couldn't recognize who it was, but the more detail that was added the more I began to recall. I saw Lain standing on the edge of a ridge looking down on a world in flames.

Closing the book and tucking it back into my bag, I realized I'd seen enough, and the book was obviously playing tricks on me.

Lain was the son of a councilman who had made a point to keep him inside and out of danger. There was no way that Lain would have ever left Terra Sera, he was too important.

I tried to keep my mind off of the book, thinking it was playing games. I wasn't expecting to see anything that reflected what was going on here. I was looking for answers, not false prophecy.

I tucked my head close to Ava's and focused on falling asleep despite my hunger, tomorrow would be a long day and I needed all the rest I could get.

It wasn't long until I was dreaming, though, at the same time I wasn't. I was completely lucid and floating through the scattered trees. I tried to look down at my body, or to stretch my arms out, but found nothing. I had no body, I was just a little spec of floating perspective.

I came out through the tree line to see a camp ablaze. There were a few Stigma holders still alive, fighting desperately to fend off a larger group of Agents. It was early morning, and I assumed the attack had caught the entire camp off guard.

Stigmas struggled to fight back, only to be shot down by the Agents who had the advantage of distance. Then, in the middle of it all, I saw a familiar face and I realized I knew where this was.

Vatz, the leader of the camp, an old friend of mine, tore through it in a rampage. The Agents fired upon him, but each bullet was blocked as small chunks of earth ripped from the ground into the air, bursting into a hundred pieces as they took each bullet. A thousand razor sharp shards now surrounded Vatz, who spun to face the Agents for a step, sending the shards to slice through his attackers.

There was a small cluster of three Agents in the distance, making their way into battle. Vatz spun towards them with an outstretched hand and clenched his fist, a circular rift formed around the Agents and the ground collapsed in on itself, plunging them into the void below. Others continued to fire, but Vatz had risen a wall that created a dome of solid rock around him, trapping himself inside.

Slowly, the Agents surrounded the rock sphere, hesitant to waste their bullets in a failed attempt to destroy the shield. After a moment one of them ran up to the dome, and attached a small device to the outer wall. He turned to walk away but before he had the chance the wall opened, and spread—pulling the Agent and his device inside.

A moment later there was an explosion, the dome split up into hundreds of smaller rock shards that shot through the bodies of the surrounding Agents. Many of them fell immediately, clutching their wounds, writhing in pain.

Another hole appeared in the ground behind them and I could see Vatz enter the battlefield once more, a smug look on his face.

Nearly every Agent in the field had either been killed or left injured, crawling on the ground with no real direction.

There was movement on a high up cliff that caught Vatz's attention. I zipped up there, knowing by now that I couldn't be seen, that I was simply an observer.

There were more Agents lined up now, watching the carnage below. Among them I could see Lain, standing over the destroyed camp.

Could it be the book was true?

What was he doing with the Agents, why weren't they trying to kill him?

He looked to the Agent beside him, "Get down there and make sure the job is done. I don't want to have to do this myself."

"Sir, Vatz seems to be causing a lot of problems. Are you sure it's wise to get down there, we're losing men," the Agent returned.

Lain turned, placing one hand on the Agent's shoulder, and the other flat on his chest, "Well isn't that just sad?" Lain said, patting the soldier's breastplate.

Once.

Twice.

On the third, the Agent's head threw back, and his mouth and eyes shot wide open as light poured out and, as Lain pulled his hand away, the man went limp in his arms.

Lain took a step back, letting the Agent fall forward to tumble down the ridge.

He looked at the other men, "You are worried about losing men? Well, we are losing a war!" Lain began, furious, "I am your commander here, so does anyone else want to question me?"

There was a long pause, no one wanted to speak.

The light in Lain's hand dispersed and he faced the battlefield once more, "So," he began, shrugging his shoulders, "what are you waiting for?"

The other Agents shot to attention, and took position along the ridge.

They took aim at Vatz, who was now walking amongst the fallen bodies, searching for survivors. There were few, but some had managed to make it through the attack.

Back on the ridge Lain gave the order to fire, knowing Vatz had been left off guard. On his demand the line of Agents sent a rain of bullets down on Vatz's position.

I wanted to rush down there and warn him, but I could only watch in terror as a bullet clipped him in the shoulder. The force of it spun him around in time for a second to him in the other shoulder. A third landed in his leg and he fell to one knee before slowly collapsing onto the ground.

I felt helpless as I watched him fall. Around him, the surviving Stigma holders scrambled to their feet and fled, running for their lives as the Agents continued to fire from the ridge. A few of them managed to escape, but even more fell into a lifeless heap as they were struck.

I awoke suddenly, gasping for air, struggling to wrap my head around what I had just seen. There was no way, there was no way that could have happened. What was this?

*A dream*, I told myself, *just a bad dream.*

I struggled to keep my mind off of it as I found another comfortable position. I told myself that the book was just playing tricks on me, and my imagination was going wild.

I closed my eyes once more, and drifted back into sleep.

# Chapter 12:

I awoke to the screech of the rusty train car door opening and the bitter kiss of morning air. I opened my eyes to see Demi standing outside, looking in, and I rolled back over towards Ava for warmth, ignoring him. He climbed up into the car and started to gather up our things.

"What are you doing?" I asked, already annoyed.

He stopped, holding my bag in one hand, and his other on the strap around his shoulder, "It's nearly noon, we need to get moving."

"Where's Piper?" I asked, with a bit of venom in my voice.

"They left," he said.

"Oh, didn't take you long to drive that one away now did it?" I shot back, spiteful.

He shook his head, "They left in the early morning, a while ago. I don't think it's smart to stay here either. A lot when on last night and I don't want to be here when the Agents come to investigate."

He had a point, and I didn't much feel like having to hide out in a train car listening to Agents search for us outside, but, I didn't want to agree with him either.

"I'm sure a lot did," I said scornfully.

"Do you have something to say?"

"You already know."

"Whatever you say Sage," he said, turning to jump out of the car with our things.

I wanted to let him know I was angry with him, but doing so would mean admitting I actually felt something and he would get some sick pleasure out of that.

I got up slowly, sore from sleeping in the car. My body ached, but I had to ignore it, knowing I would feel better once I moved around a bit. Leaning up against the door, arms crossed, I watched Demi move about the camp, tucking whatever was left scattered around under the cars in hiding.

I guess he wanted to know where things were in case we ever had to come back here. He was picking up on things quick out here, I could give him that.

"So, where are they headed?" I asked after a few minutes of watching.

He looked up to me for a second, then went back to work, "Supposedly there's a decent sized camp not far from here. They said they were headed there to stock up on supplies before heading out again."

"Which way?"

Demi took a step back, trying to recall which way they left, and pointed.

I saw a flash from my dream, the village on fire, Lain's murderous intent. Vatz's camp was in the direction we were headed, and my only worry was if it would still be there once we arrived. I shook away the thought, the possibility of stopping in an actual camp sounded good to me. It had been a while since we had a legitimate meal and I'd be able to trade off these heavy clothes before heading out into the relative warmth of the plains beyond.

"At least it's in the right direction," I said after a while.

Demi nodded, "I'm thinking we should make a stop."

"Trying to score another night?" I teased.

Demi looked at me with surprise, "What's up with you?"

"Nothing," I said jumping down from the car to make my way towards him. I placed my hands on his shoulders, "I just thought with all this pressure on you that you could use another night with a girl like her."

He looked at me with disbelief, "If I didn't know any better I'd think you were jealous."

He wasn't going to tell me was he? I figured he was smart enough to know that I knew by now, or did he have some shred of respect somewhere in that shallow mind of his to not share who he's slept with?

I heard another crunch in the snow behind us and turned to see Ava climbing down from the car, rubbing her eyes.

"Looks like it's time to get going," I said, brushing past him into the direction of the camp.

It wasn't long before I heard their footsteps follow.

# Chapter 13:

Thankfully, we reached the camp before nightfall after a few hours of leading Demi and Ava in a painful silence and I was relieved to find it still standing when we finally arrived. The entire way I'd been mentally preparing myself to walk into the charred remains of a place I once called home. Instead, the camp was bigger than I remembered though the layout was the same, only—expanded. There were several rows of tents surrounding a large circular commons in the center.

I lead Demi and Ava through the camp with an air of comfort, feeling good about being back in an environment I was used to. I nodded to the vaguely familiar faces I passed by as if they had been old friends, gradually making my way to the center. A few people were circled around a campfire there, and I told Demi and Ava to wait by its warmth as I searched for someone I could talk to about a place to stay and some food for the night. I remembered where Vatz's tent was, close by, and made my way over to speak with him.

There was a light shining inside the tent that caused the shadows of those inside to be painted on the rawhide walls. The people inside spoke in hushed voices, a heightened sense of tension radiating through the walls. I knew my place and didn't want to interrupt their discussion, especially to ask Vatz for a favor after my disappearance, so I waited for them to finish before I entered.

Moments later I could hear the argument inside had simmered down, so I waited patiently outside for Vatz's guest to leave. When the flap finally opened my heart dropped and a sharp spike of panic shot through me as my eyes fell on the man who emerged.

He made his way over, "So look who we have here, hope the mission is going well," he said with a pause, taking an exaggerated look around me on both sides, "Looks like you already lost Demi and Ava. Did they die so soon? That's good."

"Lain," I said, trying to remain polite. He eyed me with the same look he had back on the balcony in the Grand Hall. He looked—hungry. I fumbled for words to say, trying to keep conversation. "What brings you away from your father's cradle."

I had thought the whole reason that Lain despised Demi was because he had been allowed to explore the outside world leaving Lain to his father's politics. Even so, there was no reason for him to be outside of Terra Serra. I thought of my dream, but tried to mask my own concern.

What was he doing here?

"So much hostility, and here I thought we were friends," he said with a sly smile and a wink, "I'm afraid I'm here on…business."

"Business?" I asked, wanting to know what business a councilman's son had in some random camp outside.

"It seems as though someone's released their pets earlier than expected. I've come to investigate."

"Pets? Those creatures? What do you know about them?" I asked.

"I'm afraid that's all I can say. Now, if you'll excuse me, I have some things I need to put in order," he said before making his way past me.

I stood there frozen, wondering if I should go tell Demi what I'd seen. I looked to the tent before me, knowing I first needed to ensure our safety here.

Vatz was sitting behind a long wooden table littered with open maps and hastily written plans, two other burly men standing by his side with unmoving expressions. Vatz had been the youthful leader who took charge during my time here, and in a way I was surprised to see him still alive. He'd always taken a liking to me, after he took control of the camp he'd even tried to make me his own shortly before I'd left. Not that I minded—I'd always had a soft spot for him, but perhaps the idea of being tied down is what compelled me to leave.

He was still handsome, though the past couple years must have been tough on his now battle worn face. He was a tall, though you couldn't tell with him sitting down, with long strawberry blonde dreadlocked hair that he wore tied back in staggering tails—which was a bit of a surprise given I'd once ran my fingers through his silky curls. He wore a large fur that looked like it was from a bear draped over his shoulders and tied in the front with leather straps. The fur cut off along his chest, leaving his arms free to move as he wore it like a poncho. I wouldn't have been surprised if he told me he'd hunted the bear himself, even without his gift, the man was a brute when needed, forever lost in the thrill he found alongside death's door. Through a low cut short sleeved shirt he wore beneath his fur I could see that his arms and chest had been covered in more tattoos than I remembered, becoming a collector of sorts.

He smiled when he saw me, and he waved me closer.

"So, you came back for me!" he exclaimed, motioning for his guards to leave the room.

"Seems so, I see you've been well," I said, offering a smile to the guards as they left to wait outside, noticing that one stood out more than the other— barring the empty eyes of a true veteran and a horizontal scar that cut clean across his face and over the bridge of his nose.

Vatz laughed at that, "You see I'm getting, these young bones don't feel so young anymore."

"Those bones seem to have protected this camp just fine."

He leaned back in his chair, tracing a crescent scar with his index finger that ran down from his temple to his cheek, curving around his eye, "So what brings you back?"

"I have business in MarSeir—figured it wouldn't be smart to pass up a safe place to stay for the night."

"Unlike you to actually choose to be around others, especially how many you'll find once you get there. I'd heard rumors you'd gone rogue out there on your own," Vatz said, "I won't believe that you are going back there for fun, what do you have to gain?"

"I did for a while, but I found a small group willing to travel with me to see the Dom—I have some questions I need answered."

"I've seen him myself recently, you'll be happy to know he's doing well—didn't he raise you?"

"For a time, but there is a lot he didn't tell me before he let me out into the world," I returned.

"Like what happened to your parents?" he asked.

Vatz seemed to notice my distress in the silence, and called for his guard's attention, "Fix this young lady up with a tent in an open lot, rawhide, not cloth. I want her and her friends to be warm for the night. Oh, and fix them up a meal if you will if there isn't any more in the commons."

His guards simply nodded and made their way back outside.

"I see you've done well for yourself," I added, as I watched the guards leave.

"My men respect me, rather than fear me. It's the only way to keep them truly loyal."

"You've come a long way here."

"Did you ever doubt me?" he asked, raising an eyebrow.

"Never," I returned, searching for an explanation, "it's just you know as well as I do that surviving for so long out here isn't the easiest thing to do."

"True, but I'm confident in our defenses. So, where are your friends?"

"By the fire, waiting," I said after a pause, forgetting I'd left them.

"Well then, don't let me keep you from them. I'm sure we'll have plenty of time to catch up while you're here. My men will let you know when everything is ready."

"Thank you Vatz, and I'm sure we will."

I made my way back outside but this time with a more watchful eye. I felt safe here, but at the same time I was uneasy with Lain wandering about. He was up to something, I just had to figure out what. At the same time I knew that prying into his business might be dangerous, the man was unpredictable when pushed back into a corner, that much I knew.

Vatz's guards had already started work on pitching up the tent by the side of his own, in the center of town where it would be most protected. He'd always taken care of me, and I smiled at the fact that even with my absence he would continue to if I returned. I thought, maybe, I could play it up a bit to try to draw a reaction from Demi, but at the same time I knew it would be wrong to lead Vatz on just to prove some selfish point.

Back at the fire I wasn't all too surprised when I saw Demi and Ava had molded in well with the others. I wasn't surprised even when I saw Marcus sitting beside them, laughing as they told each other exaggerated stories with only half the truth.

I searched for Piper, but she was nowhere to be found and i figured she'd probably ran off with another guy, leaving Marcus on his own again. I felt ashamed to immediately put the girl down like that but a bad first impression tends to go a long way. I figured, with her not around, I could deal with joining their conversation.

I sat beside Marcus, putting him between Demi and I, trying to play a game that I wasn't even sure I knew the rules of myself. Still, the tactic seemed to work, Demi broke off eye contact with Marcus as they spoke to pass me a curious look that asked why I'd switched sides.

I ignored him, and listened to the conversation in silence.

Ava was holding Cekrit's pendant in her hand once more, "So what do they stand for?" she asked after a while.

"Freedom," Marcus said, "for everybody."

"Can that actually happen Demi?" Ava asked, looking up to her brother who held her in his arms.

Demi looked away for a moment then back down to her, "I guess it's possible, but I doubt we could ever live as one. The best I can hope for is for this war to end. The Gifted can live on their own, as well as the Pure."

"Separate but equal?" Marcus asked.

"I guess so, I don't see us ever being able to live together."

"But we can," Marcus said, "we can work as one to build a better future. I've heard of lands untouched by our war, where the Stigma doesn't exist as we see it. The Pure and the Gifted live together in peace."

"Where?" Ava asked with wonder in her voice.

"Well, I haven't seen it firsthand but I've heard stories of the lands to the north holding their peace," Marcus said, staring into the fire.

"So they are just rumors," Demi said, trying to shoot the idea down.

"I guess, but they have to come from somewhere right?" Marcus added.

Demi laughed beneath his breath, "It's just stories to give you false hope."

"Hope is all we have," Marcus defended.

"No, what we have," Demi argued, "is power."

I had to cut in, "I've seen it, I mean, not an entire city but I've seen exiled Pure live amongst us without any trouble. It's on a smaller scale but still, that has to mean something right?"

Marcus nodded in agreement, "right."

Demi rolled his eyes, "Believe what you want, I don't think it's going to change anything."

Ava chimed in, "What about Sera, what if we find her?"

"Peace," Marcus said.

"You think the Pure are just going to let us walk in and take her back, acting like none of this ever happened?" Demi argued.

"I don't know what will happen," Marcus said, looking around the camp, "none of us do, but saving her is a good first step."

"They aren't going to make it easy," Demi said, shaking his head in disapproval.

"Nothing as a Stigma holder is easy, but it's better than sitting here waiting to die," Marcus said as he helped himself up, "It's getting late, I need to find Piper and call it a night. It's been a long day."

I wished him goodnight and watched as he disappeared into the camp.

I looked to Demi after a moment of silence, "Why do you always have to be such a jerk?"

"I'm a realist. If this war is going to end, then we need to be the ones to end it. We have powers they can't imagine, it's a wonder why we haven't won already."

"You don't get it Demi, it's not total victory we are fighting for."

Demi sighed, "Than what?"

"Peace, and not just for us, but for everyone. What's the point of winning the war if it means doing the same to them as they are doing to us?"

"The point?" Demi began, "The point is to not have to live in fear any longer. We can't do that if they are still around."

I wanted to shoot another comment at him but Vatz's guards had made their way over to us.

"Your tent is ready, and your food has already been prepared. Follow me," one of them said before turning back to lead us.

I got up and followed, though Demi and Ava were slower to rise.

Inside, there was a table along the far back wall with a large pot and bowls stacked up along its side, bundles of blankets and soft skins took up most of the floor space, making up an oversized bed covered in furs that we would all have to share.

I walked over to the table and started pouring the thick soup into the bowls, handing them over to Demi and Ava as they came closer. The soup was steaming hot, filled with vegetables and meats that melted in my mouth. The combined flavor was amazing, though earthy, I couldn't have been happier to have a true meal for the first time since we'd left Terra Sera. It wasn't long before we finished, most of the pot had been cleaned out, leaving only a thin film at the bottom.

I laid down on the bed, staring blankly to the ceiling. Ava joined me, laying by my side, but Demi stood by the table scraping every last bit he could out of that pot.

"Do you think we are going to find her?" Ava asked after a while.

"Sera?" I asked.

"Yes, I mean, we know that they have her. But what happens when we find her?"

"I don't know," I said, trying to be truthful, "They have to be limiting her power somehow, if we manage to save her maybe she'll regain her strength and try to create some kind of peace."

"Maybe she'll give everyone the gift!" Ava exclaimed, excited at the thought of it.

I laughed to myself, "That would be wonderful, wouldn't it?"

"Right, then everyone could just be happy," she said with a smile.

Demi scoffed from behind his bowl, "If only it was so easy."

I passed him a sour look, trying to tell him to shut up before he got started. It wouldn't be fair for him to put down Ava's dreams. It was so hard to find anything to hold onto these days—she, at least, could dream of peace.

I'd decided I didn't want to deal with him anymore tonight, I was frustrated to the point where I felt like getting up to punch him right in the face, but I knew that was a terrible idea. The last thing I needed was for Demi to fight back or have the Vemosa take me into the void. Instead, I pulled the blankets over Ava and I to sleep.

She cuddled up next to me, and though my eyes were closed I listened to Demi stirring in the background. Before long I felt him lay down beside me, pulling the blankets over him and coming in close. The added warmth felt great, but I couldn't believe he had the nerve to put his arm over me when he did.

"What do you think you're doing?" I asked, bitter, not bothering to look at him.

"It's still cold, body heat helps," he said, adjusting to a more comfortable position.

"Listen, I'm not some toy. If you want body heat why don't you go cuddle up with Piper again," I said, shrugging his arm off of me.

"What? That's not what—" he started, but I cut him off.

"I know what happened Demi, she told me," I said, standing. I didn't want to be around him if he was going to think I would be as easy to take advantage of as all of his other girls.

"Sage," he called after me as I left the tent. I ignored him.

I made my way to the warmth of the fire and sat down, pulling a blanket that I took from the tent over my shoulders as I sat. There were few people left walking around. Some would join me by the fire, sometimes trying to spark up new conversation, but I wasn't really in the mood and sent them away.

"Oh hey there," a familiar voice said from behind me.

I turned to see Piper coming over to sit beside me, a smile on her face. I pretended to be excited to see her, "Hey," I said, holding my tongue.

She must have picked up on my frustration, "What's wrong?" she said after sharing my gaze into the dancing flames for a long moment.

"Demi."

"Oh, why? He's such a great guy, you're lucky to have him," she said.

"We're not like you and Marcus, Piper. We don't do that whole free love thing, well we don't do any kind of thing. We aren't together, I don't know, I'm probably being silly. I guess I'm not usually one to actually care."

"I see," She said after a pause, kicking at the ground, "you aren't the only one."

"Yeah, I noticed."

Piper shook her head, "You said it was all right when I asked you."

I sighed, "I know, I guess I was just hoping he wouldn't go through with it."

"Wait, he hasn't told you?" she said, surprised.

"Told me what? It's pretty clear what happened," I asked, annoyed for even having to talk about this.

She laughed at that.

"You think it's funny?" I asked, defensive.

"You've got it all wrong! We didn't sleep together."

I didn't believe her at first, "Then what did you do?"

"Nothing. We got into the car, and yeah, I tried coming onto him, I mean how could I not, right? But he stopped me, said it didn't feel right. Then he started talking about you until we fell asleep. To be honest, I felt bad for the guy—he was totally out of his comfort zone."

I couldn't believe it, and had to ask again, like my ears had failed me. I was in shock, suddenly feeling silly for being so nasty to him all day, "He did what?"

"What did I just say?" Piper said, "He didn't go through with it."

# Chapter 14:

I returned to the tent feeling a lot of things, mostly guilty. My stomach was in knots and I felt terrible for how I had been treating Demi all day, knowing now that he didn't deserve it after all and suddenly I felt like the jerk in the situation. The tables had turned on me.

I wondered why he didn't tell me, why he had waited for me to find out on my own. Instead of telling me what had really happened he chose to let me dig myself into a deeper hole as he watched, amused. I could get mad at him for that, but I think I was just trying to find somewhere else to place my frustration.

He was still awake when I entered the tent, hands behind his head as he stared blankly to the ceiling. He didn't bother to look at me as I walked past, but I knew he'd noticed me.

The tension in the air was tangible, but it wasn't a negative energy, and the smirk on his face told me he knew why I'd come back. He had to know.

I sat down by the table, trying to keep busy while I waited for him to say something. I gathered all of the bowls and silverware, taking the time to clean and organize everything. He said nothing, only watched me as I worked.

I was frustrated with myself for not giving him a chance to be an honest man, so caught up in my own judgements of him that I'd just assumed he'd run off with her, and now expected me to be his next fling. I remember telling myself before we set out that I wouldn't be like those other girls, and I wasn't. I found reasons to push myself away from the idea of wanting him, but I guess none of them truly worked. The more I told myself to stay away the more I found myself wanting him closer.

I spun around to see him staring back at me, a stupid grin on his face, "Why didn't you tell me?" I asked, finally.

"You wouldn't have believed me if I did," he said, looking back to the ceiling.

"So you let me be mean to you all day? You knew what I thought you'd done," I'll admit I was annoyed with him for that, letting me suffer within my own ignorance, but he was right— I wouldn't have.

"Well, you figured it out now didn't you?"

"Yeah," I started, standing to make my way over to his side, "Piper told me what happened."

"Ah, Piper," he said with a sigh, as if reminiscing.

I rolled my eyes, "So why didn't *you* tell me?"

"I don't know, maybe I thought you were a little cute when you're angry. It can be a good look for you, you know. Maybe I thought you could use some time to think about it, you know— really let the thought of me with someone else marinate in your mind a bit. I see it worked," he shifted to his side to face me, his head resting in the palm of his hand.

I gave him a serious look of disappointment and crossed my arms, "Demi."

He smiled and pointed to me, "See there it is again."

I sighed, I just couldn't win with him, "So, do you have anything to say for yourself?"

"Okay," he began, I'm sorry for testing you."

"And?" I asked, prying for more. My face felt hot, and my stomach felt as though it were filled with angry butterflies fluttering about in an increasingly desperate attempt to escape. I was nervous, which was a new feeling for me, still, I wanted to hear him say it.

"And—" he carried on, "I turned Piper down because once I was alone with her I realized there was someone else in my life that meant more to me than a fun night with some random girl."

"Oh, and who might that be?" I teased.

He passed me the same serious look I'd given him, "Seriously?"

"Well," I said, laying down beside him, "a girl can be curious, can't she?"

"I guess a girl can," he agreed, rolling onto his back to stare silently at the ceiling.

I inched closer to his side, "So?" I asked again.

"So," he repeated, "I may have realized that you might be starting to mean more to me than I'd like to admit."

"Yet here you are, admitting it," I teased, again.

"Shut up Sage," he said with a slight chuckle.

I felt his hand searching for mine, and soon our fingers interlocked. I couldn't see, but I could feel that we were both smiling together as we laid there for what seemed like an eternity just staring up at the sheer nothingness above us. This feeling terrified me—but I found myself, for the first time, allowing myself to let another stand by my side, no matter how brief this may turn out to be.

I was never one to get close to anyone, not that too many people were ever interested in the gift-less Stigma holder but there were a few, like Vatz, that had taken interest. When I was sixteen he'd even proposed to me in this camp—but like any other who tried I'd turned him down, too afraid of growing attached, too afraid of having them taken away from me. I'd rather deal with the pain of not knowing what may have been than the pain of losing someone I'd grown to love.

I don't know what had happened with Demi though, for some reason he'd managed to break down my walls, or rather, worked around me in a way that I'd begun to build my walls around us, until it was just the two of us standing in our own personal fortress.

I found myself gripping his hand tighter as I laid by his side knowing that this, I would not let go.

# Chapter 15:

The next morning came sooner than I wanted it to. I woke up in Demi's arms and would have been fully content to stay there for the rest of the day, but I knew we had to keep moving.

I opened my eyes to see Ava sitting on the other side of the tent, eating a fresh bowl of soup, staring at us wide eyed. I passed her a smile, and she returned it, though I could see she was trying to piece the sight together. I wasn't sure if she was the biggest fan of what she'd woken up to, even I found it hard to believe that I'd actually let this happen.

I got up and made my way over to the table, where a fresh pot of soup, still hot, was waiting.

"When did they bring us breakfast?" I asked Ava, who sat on the floor beside me.

"They didn't, I went and got it myself," she returned proudly.

I was pleasantly surprised by that, though I knew her brother would have been pretty upset that she ran off without anyone to watch over her.

"Let's just keep that our little secret," I leaned in and said quietly, and she laughed.

I finished eating and began to pack up our things, thankful that between us we only had to carry three bags, any more would have slowed us down. The key to survival was to travel light and to not bring anything you'd regret losing. It was much smarter to hide away anything valuable and return to it later, only carrying the essential. Granted, even now I carried more than I really needed.

By the time Ava had finished her bowl I had all of our bags lined up in a row by the foot of the bed.

"Stay here with Demi, I'll be right back," I told her, and she nodded.

I left the tent and entered the surprisingly warm early morning air, forgetting that we weren't stuck in the mountains anymore. I decided to leave my overstuffed coat behind, only bringing my tattered camo jacket with me and a plain shirt underneath and a black pair of jeans to hide the inevitable filth.

The camp was alive with traffic, small groups going out to hunt, others preparing new leathers, and more still by the fire. In the center, near the fire—there was a large pot with people circling around, pushing and shoving to win a chance to fill their bowls. I shook my head at their impatience, it wasn't like there was a shortage of food.

I heard Vatz's voice from behind me and turned to see him leaving his tent, talking to a small group of other men. I didn't want to interrupt, but at the same time I knew I needed to talk to him before we left. He seemed to feel my presence behind him and passed a look over his shoulder. When he saw me coming he excused himself from the conversation.

"Good morning Sage! I hope all was to your liking," he said, arms out wide as he brought me into his embrace.

"Morning Vatz, and yes, thank you," I returned, wanting to say more but he spoke first.

As he pulled away he kept his hands on my shoulders and looked onto me with curious eyes, "Something bothering you?"

I thought of the right words to say, I wanted to tell him about the dream I had even if I risked sounding a little crazy. After a moment there was an even greater look of concern in his eye.

"I had this dream the other night— there were dozens of Agents attacking this camp. I saw you fighting, they shot you. Almost everyone died, even the Agents," I struggled to speak through held back tears, trying to erase the images from my mind.

I found it odd that he managed a smile as he pulled me in for another hug, "Even the Agents?" Vatz jest, "Seems like we did a good job then, it's probably just stress Sage, but thank you for the tip. Even a dream like that should be taken seriously, I'll have my best men on guard. Thank you."

I looked up to him as he pulled away once more, "Just be careful okay?"

"Always am," he returned, before perking up as something behind me caught his attention. His hands left my shoulders, "So you're leaving then?"

I turned to see Demi and Ava walking towards us, "Naturally, we've got a long road ahead of us," I said as they got closer.

Demi acknowledged us with a friendly nod as he passed my bag to me, freeing up his hand to shake Vatz's.

"Take care of this one," Vatz said.

Demi smiled, and passed me a look, "Will do, and thank you for your hospitality."

"Anytime," Vatz returned.

We said our goodbyes and made our way out of the camp, but as we left I couldn't help but think of my dream, and how happy I was that it was only just that. Still, I hoped that Vatz would stay on guard. The last thing Cekrit, or any of us needed was to lose a leader like him.

Ahead, I could barely make out the towering skyscraper rooftops of an abandoned city in the distance. In between stood grasslands that stretched out over the horizon, peppered with underdeveloped neighborhoods left halfway through their construction—proof that man had been the scourge of this land, and that even in their brightest day, forever destroyed its beauty. I knew we stood no chance out in the open like that, but it was the only way forward. We needed to make it to the city as fast as possible or risk being seen with few places to hide. If that happened we would be nothing more than targets in a field, easy prey.

I didn't bother to tell Demi and Ava of the danger. I'm sure Demi knew by now, and I didn't want to worry Ava. I was on edge, half expecting to run into the force of Agents I'd seen in my dream on our way out but as far as I could see there was no movement ahead of us.

Thankfully Sera had blessed us, and the openness of the grasslands worked for both sides.

I looked over my shoulder, towards the camp which was now dwarfed in the distance, sensing tragedy, and I was right. A moment later the deafening boom of an explosion ripped its way towards us, the screams were audible from here as gun shots echoed through the fields in short burst.

I spun around, ready to let out into a full sprint back to camp, "No!" I yelled, bitter tears streaming from down my face.

It was happening, my dream, it was real.

Demi caught me by the arm as I tried to push past, and though I fought him, couldn't break free.

"Don't," he said, holding me back.

"We need to help them!" I screamed.

"It's too late, we need to move," he said, in a too-calm voice.

It was over in an instant, the maelstrom of bullets had stopped save for a single shot that would silence the cries of any survivors.

I knew then that we would be next if we didn't move quickly, we were wide open in the grasslands and it wouldn't be hard for the Agents to spot us from where they were.

I calmed down, collapsing into Demi's arms, short of breath. "Lain," I said through my teeth.

"What?" Demi asked, surprised.

"He did this. I had a dream about this, he's working with the Agents," I sobbed, pulling away from Demi and storming off towards the city.

"Sage, no," Demi said, chasing after me, "he's still in Terra Sera, he's always in Terra Sera. Madsen won't let him leave."

I wiped away my tears, "You're wrong, he was in the camp last night. I saw him."

Demi stopped, shocked, "You—he—what? Why didn't you tell me?"

"I don't know! I was still upset with you, it slipped my mind. When we got to the camp and it was still standing I just thought I had a bad dream not some screwed up vision of the future!"

Demi tried to hold me, but I pulled away, "We need to keep moving," I said, searching for Ava to make sure she was keeping up.

I wanted to go back, I thought, maybe Ava could heal everyone, and that Demi could kill all of the Agents, that maybe we could have saved them after all. But I knew if we went back we would only die right beside them. There were too many, and Lain was too powerful for Demi to worry about us being in the crossfire.

We wouldn't stand a chance.

I felt helpless, knowing that if only I had warned them sooner that maybe then they would have still been alive, or at least stood a chance.

I kept my eyes to the horizon, trying to block the pain of having known—we had to push forward.

# Chapter 16:

Everything was in ruins as we entered the forgotten city. Even the welcome sign had fallen. *Dodge*, the moss covered sign read, now lying defeated on the ground.

The freeways and roads that were once the lifeline of this city were now little more than grassy fields sprouting from cracked concrete. Giant vines climbed the faces of mountainous buildings and even some trees had managed to take hold several floors above the ground, their roots flooding out of the vacant windows and down the outer walls. Their thick trunks would break through multiple floors as they grew, branches extending out to shade the streets below.

Before the war, cities like this were a cancer spreading over the world. It was only now that nature had come to reclaim its land and I knew it wouldn't be long until even these buildings fell, leaving only the slightest hints towards what once was—a species with a grim desire to separate themselves from their own humanity, a species driven by greed that mistook possessions for happiness. If my life had taught me anything, it's that happiness can only be found within—no matter the situation.

Abandoned cars peppered the streets, now little more than mossed over foothills in the way. Some of the windows remained open, or broken, and every time we passed I eyed the inside, an old habit.

On my first night here, when I was about fifteen, I was forced to hide in one of these cars as I listened to a large group of Agents sweep the streets. I could hear them occasionally bashing the butt end of their rifles against the cars as they passed, trying to get a reaction out of anything that might be hiding inside.

I'd tucked myself behind the driver's seat, buried beneath a heap of trash and debris. There was a thud on my car, and through a small hole in the debris I could see the shadow of an Agent leaning in through the open passenger side window. I'd been frozen with fear, remaining perfectly still until he moved on, and thankfully he did.

So now, I kept my eyes fixed to the shadows, knowing that every abandoned building, darkened alleyway, and busted out or dust covered window worked both for and against us. There were others hidden amongst the rubble, or were tucked away in one of the countless skyscrapers that towered over us—too fearful to show themselves, but too curious not to watch. Most of the windows had been blown out, leaving the shadows beyond to dance and play, taunting me with their mystery, and I knew all too well that it wasn't just the Stigma holders that took shelter here. Zanin's Agents would sometimes be on patrol for days and would risk bunkering down wherever they could.

Even with the comfort I felt being here, with the thousands of open doors, broken walls, and blind corners that may help escape an attack—I wasn't in any particular mood for an ambush. Maybe I was over-thinking, too vigilant and still shaken by the attack this morning. I thought, maybe they had seen us, that maybe they followed. In the furthest corners of my vision the shadows teased.

I had to stay sharp, had to stay on point and ready, knowing I'd rather be paranoid than dead. I found comfort in the idea that Demi would have sent the Kurki to patrol our perimeter, and took a deep breath, trying to calm my nerves.

I liked to believe that I knew almost every nook and cranny of this place, having spent the better part of four years hiding in its shadows. By the time I was fifteen I'd met with death many times, though it seemed fate had always spared me, offering escape in the midst of the chaos and panic of a raid. It seemed as though death followed me like a lost dog, never far behind but too scared to confront me itself—forever a whisper in my ear. Sometimes, I wished this old friend would make its move, and just get this game we're playing over with, to end my suffering. Today was just another reminder of how close death lingers. The fact that a camp we spent one night in was raided the very next morning was a painful reminder to the life I so desperately tried to escape.

But even here the pain still came. Watching from whatever rooftop, or alleyway, or vacant parking garage, or skyscraper window twenty-something floors up I was always helpless as Agents would ambush others like me in the very places I'd walked just days before.

There had been others here hiding in the shadows of the city, but most kept to themselves. I believe we all found some semblance of safety in our seclusion, and at the same time a sense of hope in seeing others survive, coping with our reality in the same way. We had all learned that large groups could attract Agents, and Agents attracted death— the best chance for survival came from being alone.

I was torn, my mind still with Vatz and his camp. It was no wonder why I'd decided to leave his camp so soon after I'd arrived, to come back here. Over time even this city had become too dangerous for me, so I left to live alone in a cave a few months ago now. Vatz was right, the rumors were true and what happened in his camp this morning was the exact reason I decided to live alone.

There was a false sense of safety in numbers, I knew that and I damned myself for that mistake.

The only way to survive out here was to stay alone. There was no one to watch after, no one to care for, no one to drag you down with them.

I looked over my shoulder to Demi and Ava, who were following without question, like I had some master plan.

What did they expect from me?

I don't know how Demi could look so calm, though he always did—walking through the world without a single care. I wondered if he was starting to get a sense of what life out here was like, or if he believed he did simply because he snuck out of Terra Sera every now and then. I hated the smug bastard for that, but I also knew he was calculated, and his calmness was probably a reflection of that. I could understand Ava's joyfulness due to her ignorance, but Demi should know better.

*Run,* A voice whispered in the back of my mind and the idea tempted me. I could run, no, I should run, I told myself. I knew this city better and could just slip away to live on my own again. But to leave them lost in an unknown city so that I might get the chance to live, probably only to watch while they were shot down, didn't feel right either.

I passed another glance over my shoulder, nervous, feeling as if I was about to make a decision that would change my life back to how it was before I met them. I damned myself for breaking my first rule of survival. Never travel in groups. Worse still I'd broken another. Never get attached. Yet, here I was walking through these city streets like the dozens I'd seen here before being taken down.

I'll admit I was disappointed in myself. What did I care about the Guardian Games, or Demi's pride, or finding Sera? We were all going to die anyway. I'd seen dozens of squads rush off to attack a Pure city, and it was rare that anyone had ever returned so what made us think we could just walk in and save her?

That's why I'd chosen to live alone, being with others had only brought pain and suffering. Our jobs as Stigma holders wasn't to save the world like the stories told, it was to survive. That was the point wasn't it? To survive?

But watching them I felt something different. Ava's smile warmed me as she rode on Demi's back, too tired to walk, and so did his. I found myself smiling too. Their world wasn't any different from mine, our situation was the same. But they had something I didn't, something that shed some light on their lives, something I was slowly finding through them.

Hope.

# Chapter 17:

I reacted almost before it happened, my eyes shot to a third floor apartment window above a rundown cinema in time to see a darkened figure duck out of sight.

"We need to move!" I ordered, taking a sharp right turn and hurdling over a waist high tree root and into the closest building. I hit the ground and pressed my back against the root near the trunk, ducking for cover. The tree had grown out of the entrance of the office building, leaning out into the street for sunlight. Its overgrown roots blocked most of the doorway and tore through the pavement in the street. Its trunk hugged the buildings street-side wall, as if growing with it, and its branches stretched over the street letting off a shade that only made the vacant windows darker.

Demi had snatched Ava up in his arms before busting into the building behind me. I pulled him down beside me as he landed just as an explosion in the street shook the surrounding walls—bits of dust and the crumbling particle board ceiling creating a shower of debris.

Searching for an escape, I eyed a half detached exit sign dangling above an open door at the end of the hall, but I couldn't trust that there wasn't an Agent waiting for us to pass by behind one of the dozens of open doors along the way. There was a sign to my left too, hanging two doors down that directed me to a stairwell, and I'd hoped we could get there before anyone followed us in.

Still, something didn't seem right. Whoever was in that window would have had us in their sights long before I noticed them, and if it was an Agent we should already be dead.

I didn't have time to figure out who that was, all that mattered was that someone was attacking us and we needed to get away. Nudging Demi, I signaled to the stairwell, not wanting to take the bait and run the gauntlet of open doors to the end of the hall. We would have to lose our attacker in the maze of floors above us.

I broke for the stairs, with Demi and Ava short in tow. Rounding each flight to the next floor I could see Ava just a few steps behind me, and Demi just a few steps more. Despite the chaos I knew that if anyone were to come after us they would have to go through him first, leaving me to find a safe path out for us. We'd made it to the fourth floor when I stopped to scan the room it lead to.

The large office was divided into tiny square sections with old, broken machines sitting on the dust covered countertops. Paper and trash littered the floor, and the bullet holes peppering blood stained walls didn't work well to sooth my nerves. It wasn't a good sign, but the way the blood had lost its vibrant color, turning a deep burgundy, flaking as it dried, told me this wasn't anything recent, however unnerving.

Outside, I could hear the sound of boots falling heavily on the torn up ground and knew that if it wasn't the Agents who set off that explosion it didn't matter, they were here now.

My head began to pound and a jolt of adrenaline shot through me, giving me the urge to rush out into battle and kill them all. But how could I? Still there was that voice in the back of my mind whispering, planting these thoughts.

*Kill....them. We can kill them,* my mind repeated over and over again, but I fought the urge.

I threw myself into an empty cubicle, ducking under the countertop to press my back against the flimsy separating wall. I motioned for Demi and Ava to come, but froze once I passed a look over my shoulder to see only Ava crawling towards me, unaware that Demi was no longer behind her. Worse still, I had to drag her across the floor and into my arms as I saw the front end of a rifle peeking through the door.

We sat there in moments of petrified silence—with Ava tucked between my legs, and my hand cupped over her mouth to keep her panicked breaths from being heard.

I damned that smug little arrogant bastard for leaving us like this. This wasn't some game, or training, or a meaningless fight at the arena back in Terra Sera where even if you lose you still get invited to a fancy dinner. It was one thing to run out into battle, but the least he could have done on his way out was take care of this one damn Agent.

"Shh—" I whispered to Ava as I moved my hand away from her mouth. She was shaking, but her breathing had grown calmer.

Papers crumbled beneath the steps of the Agent's combat boots, and my heart raced as the sound drew closer, and closer still, until he had stopped just in front of where we had been hiding, standing sideways facing the door, back towards us. He took a strong stance and bashed the butt end of his rifle through the already cracked window.

He was small for an Agent, only slightly taller than me and outfitted unlike the juggernauts I was used to going up against. He wore lighter gear, a vest, armored gauntlets and thin pants with plate inserts, all fitted to and moving with his body perfectly. I was surprised to see that he had no helmet either, only a small device attached to his ear which he would press with his pointer and middle finger as he spoke, "Let's hurry up and get this over with, we all have someone we want to get home to. I've got eyes up top." His voice was calm, smooth, yet there was a sense of discomfort in his tone, unease.

A woman's voice chimed in over the device, "Roger that, we'll make it quick. He must be around here somewhere, wouldn't be surprised if the freak just blew himself up," she said with a laugh.

A third voice came on, "Ha! If only they did our job for us more often! I'm starting to think these freaks are hardly worth the ammo."

*Kill him.*

It was that voice in my head again. My chest burned, and my head became hot with an anger that I wasn't sure I could control. I closed my eyes, trying to focus on staying calm. I knew I couldn't take on an Agent alone, even if he was small. Still, all I could think about was lunging out from under the cubicle to push him out of the window. I opened my eyes and peered back around the corner, shaking with pent up energy that was ready to be released, though I was still unsure if I had the strength to kill him. I would need the element of surprise.

The woman spoke up once more, "Anderson," she began, and the Agent before us stood slightly more to attention, "Watch our backs while we investigate, but don't forget your own. These buildings can be death traps."

"Roger that Val," Anderson returned.

The woman chimed in once more, "Cut the informal crap Anderson. It's Patel to you."

Anderson didn't respond, simply smiled and took a step back, scanning the room behind him. I ducked back under the counter, hoping he would overlook us.

He began to pace around the room, and stopped in front of the cubicle that we cowered under. I pushed Ava behind me, shielding her.

Anderson squatted, facing us. One hand lazily resting over his thigh and the other on his rifle, which dangled by his side. He was young, perhaps in his mid-twenties. His hair was cut short, but still just long enough to misbehave, his beard just scraggly enough to show it'd been a few days since his last shave. His eyes were a soft blue, and he let a slight smile escape his lips. It was such a sincere smile. Dangling from his neck were not only his dog tags, but a silver locket. He was a beautiful man, a kind looking man, despite the fact that he was dressed to kill.

I should have been petrified with fear, but somehow, I felt more amazed by this man than I was threatened by him.

"Anderson?" Agent Patel's voice had been repeating over and over in the background over his device. "Anderson damn you! Don't make me go up there. Anderson? Are you clear?"

He stood, watching over us, and pressed the button on his device, "Anderson here, sorry, got caught up in a daydream again. All clear up here," he said, never breaking eye contact with me.

"Damn you Anderson. Stay sharp and get down here we've got activity in the cinema," Agent Patel ordered.

"Roger that Val," Anderson said, knowing that he was pushing her buttons. He took a step back and offered a smile before leaving the room, Agent Patel still yelling in his ear.

Ava and I both let out a deep sigh of relief.

Agent Patel had said there was activity in the cinema and I wondered if it could have been Demi playing some sort of game with them. Then, I remembered the figure in the window before the explosion, and realized that whoever that was couldn't have been an Agent. I crept to the street side wall, peeking over the sill of the freshly broken out window, signaling for Ava to stay hidden as I stole a look of what was going on below.

The cinema across from us didn't match the design of the rest of the city. There was a large triangular sign that came out into the street, with black letters placed on either side, though some were missing. To me, the entire city was something of the past, something I'd never have the chance to experience, but it was easy to see that the cinema had history and was here well before the skyscrapers that surrounded it. There were several floors built on top, with darkened windows churning ominously with the void. The ground floor had two doors that had already been broken off, and now rested on the ground beside where they once stood. The doors sat on either side of a rounded desk protected by thick glass. I hadn't an idea of its purpose.

There were five Agents in the street, all in position and aiming into the cinema. I looked over to them, studying them more intently, Anderson must have still been on his way out.

A high pitched mechanical squeal that tore through the streets, making the Agents tense up. A moment later a voice spoke over the mechanical sound, replacing it, "Well, what-do-we-have-here?" the voice began, the man's voice fluctuated in tone and followed some unknown rhythm, putting extra emphasis on each word that he spoke.

Agent Patel stood from her crouched position, "Surrender and we may show some mercy you filth!"

"Is that how you ask me to be friends?" the man laughed, "Want to try that again?"

"Screw you," Agent Patel spat.

The voice being projected over the machine laughed, but the sound came from my building now, and too close to me for comfort. I looked down quickly in surprise and saw a speaker resting on the sill of the third floor window just below me. The Agents spun to face my building, and I ducked for cover before they could see me, crawling a few windows down in case that speaker went off again.

The projected voice continued, this time closer to the Agents. I found the courage to peek back over the window sill now that their attention was drawn away from my building. The voice had come from a speaker placed on top of a light post that sat in front of the cinema. "You? Show mercy, on me? Ha! Do you know how many of you I've killed? Maybe, hmm, maybe I'll show mercy on you. I am feeling a little tired today."

"Eleven, you've killed eleven of my comrades, now come out and face us you coward," Agent Patel demanded.

The projected man's voice made a buzzing sound, growing with intensity as he spoke, "Wrong! I've killed sixteen agents!"

Agent Patel checked a device on her wristband, scrolling through paragraphs of information, looking confused. Her attention was brought back to the cinema, "I'm afraid you're delusional, now show yourself."

The speaker went off again, "As you wish." A figure appeared in a second floor window. Immediately an Agent shot it down, and the figure collapsed to the ground.

Agent Patel motioned for her men to move in, but called off her signal as the speaker placed on the dashboard of the car she'd been using for cover went off, "Why don't you want to play with me?" the man cried out, like a child left out of a game.

She slammed her hand down on the hood of the car, "Damn it, I thought this was over!"

"We could always try again? We can make this work I swear!" the voice jest as another figure appeared in a window. Like the first, it was shot down, but a moment later another would appear only to be shot down as well. What I watched then was a flurry of bullets fill the air, striking down dummies that filled their windows as quickly as they fell.

"Hold fire!" Agent Patel ordered, "The bastard's just trying to waste our ammo!"

She looked down into the car, reached in and grabbed the speaker, yanking it out of place. She looked at it curiously for a moment, holding it in the palm of her hand.

Another speaker by the cinema clicked on, "Oh, are you mad? Because I am—goodbye!"

Agent Patel looked up toward the cinema. There was a pause of silence, then, an explosion in the palm of her hand big enough to send her entire squad falling to the ground in flames. All of the remaining speakers had turned on at once, the man behind them was laughing, a sinister echo pulsing through the street.

A figure appeared out of the darkness and smoke that enveloped the cinema's entrance. It was the man I had seen in the window before the explosion that attracted the Agents in the first place. He made his way to the sidewalk with short, staggered steps, holding his arm, blood soaking through an orange jumpsuit. I couldn't see his face, mainly because he wore a large spherical helmet that needed shoulder supports just to support its own weight. The sun glared off the hinged glass circle window on the front and a hose dangled off the back of the helmet, though it wasn't connected to anything. On his feet were a rough, miss-matched, pair of combat boots.

I followed his gaze to the entrance of the building. Looking down I could see Anderson just now stepping into the street, rifle raised, and movement in the tree's branches above him. Focusing, I could see Demi balancing on an outstretched branch, crouching, like a predator waiting for the perfect moment to ambush its unsuspecting prey.

"Let's go," I said to Ava before rushing down the stairs. I don't know why, but I felt an overwhelming sense of urgency to stop Demi from killing the only Agent that had ever showed me any compassion. I couldn't let him die, I just couldn't.

I nearly ran down the stairs, reaching the main entrance of the building and jumping over the overgrown tree's root by the door just in time for Demi to land behind Anderson unnoticed. Looking up I could see the Kurki falling over each other clumsily on the branches above, trying hard to hold back their attack.

Anderson was focused on the man in the cinema's entrance. As he slowly advanced, stepping over the charred and lifeless bodies of his squad, Demi crept behind, looking like he was going to take Anderson on without the help of the Kurki above. I guess I was a little naive to think the summons were his only advantage.

I rushed up behind Demi, putting myself between him and Anderson with outstretched arms.

"No!" I shouted and Demi's expression instantly grew angry.

Anderson spun around and took a step back in surprise, tripping over a body to fall hard on the ground and shuffling back once he did.

I looked over my shoulder towards him, noticing the man in the cinema entrance retreating back into the shadows.

"Oh come on Sage!" Demi scolded through his teeth.

"He's not an enemy!" I pled.

Demi's words were sharp, "Like hell he isn't! Let him go now and he'll only kill us later!"

"But he didn't" Ava said from beside Demi, whose expression grew confused, "He didn't kill us. He could have, but he didn't!"

Demi looked back to me as if for reassurance, "I'm sure if it was any other Agent we would be dead right now. While you ran off on your own playing hero, he found us," I told him.

"I didn't—" Demi started, but I cut him off.

"Think Demi, you didn't think. You never think. It's not always about you and your needs! What kind of leader leaves his squad unprotected?" The words came out harsher than I had planned and Demi bit his tongue as I continued, "And we're lucky it was him this time. So, we are letting him go, understand?" I found the last part silly, like I was scolding a child that wanted so badly to take a wild animal home with him, but forced him to leave it as it were.

"It's true. He's a good one, I know it," Ava said calmly as her brother passed her a questioning look.

He turned, head hanging with some semblance of shame I'd never seen him wear before. He made his way past me to Anderson, and offered a hand, which Anderson grasped, and helped him up.

Demi looked Anderson in the eye, still firmly gripping his hand, "I had you for a dead man, but they tell me you let them live," he said with a pause, looking to Ava and I then back to Anderson, "thank you."

Anderson gave an approving nod to Demi, and then to Ava and I. He took a step away, looking down at his fallen squad, crossing his arms, "What a mess."

Demi looked to the cinema entrance, the heat from the flames still burning in the street twisted the scene as it fumed. "Who was that?"

Anderson stood beside Demi, putting one hand on the back of his head, scratching it, "The man calls himself Tinker out here. Real name Tracey Edwards and he's a real lunatic if you ask me. He was exiled a few months ago after setting fire to the capitol building," he said, looking to an illuminated screen on a band that took up most of his forearm, like the one Agent Patel had been using.

I looked over his shoulder, oddly comfortable around someone who should be trying to kill me. There was a picture of a man, who I assumed was Tinker, and a long paragraph beside it, which Anderson scrolled through. He continued, "We tried putting him in a hospital, but the man has some serious issues. He ended up running a mutiny, as he called it, with the other patients. Took control of the entire hospital for a week. He's been more trouble out here then we could have imagined though. He's the whole reason my squad was out on this mission. To hunt him down."

Anderson chuckled, "Never thought he'd give us more trouble than some of you Stigmas!" he paused, "Sorry! I didn't mean it like that," he said taking a step away with raised hands. He looked back to his fallen squad, shaking his head, "Still a shame though, they are going to give me hell when I get back to Hope."

Ava looked at him curiously, "Hope?"

"Ah! I've already said too much!" Anderson said with a lighthearted chuckle, "I'm in enough trouble as it is, I can't add treason to that list for telling you about the dome I'm from." I gave him a questioning look and he caught his mistake, "I'm not very good at this am I?"

"Not at all," Ava added with a giggle.

"She's right, I think you're the worst Agent I've ever seen," I added.

Anderson gave me a playfully sour look, "Not nice!"

"So what," Demi started, "you're just going to leave this guy out here? Not finish your mission?"

Anderson was silent for a moment, thinking, "What choice do I have? You saw what that lunatic is capable of, he took out my entire squad. I need to get back to Hope and regroup."

Demi was frustrated, "Well you're still here aren't you, we could track him down."

"I'm sorry, it's one thing not to kill a stigma holder, but if my commanders caught wind of the fact that I not only lost my squad but worked with the enemy, even to complete an objective, I'd be killed!" Anderson exclaimed defensively.

"Still, the objective would be completed. You'll return a hero," Demi continued, trying to persuade Anderson.

"I've seen what this man can do. I value my life over a little bit of honor. Live to fight another day right?" Anderson shook his head, "Be my guest hunting him down but this is his city now. I don't trust it. I'm sorry, but I can't help."

Demi would have kept arguing, his own pride not allowing for another to lose theirs. Placing a hand on his arm to calm him, I spoke up as he began another round of failed persuasion, "We understand," I began, shooting Demi a look that said *and so do you*, then back to Anderson, "and again, thank you for your kindness."

Anderson's expression lightened once more, "And thank you as well. I suggest you three get out of this city as well, you can be sure that he will be watching if he isn't already. I'd say hope to see you again, but you know—just stay safe." He turned, standing for a moment, silent, looking over his fallen friends before beginning to collect their dog tags by carefully removing the chain from around their necks, and saying goodbye to each.

"So what now?" I asked Demi.

His gaze was fixed on the smoke screened entrance of the cinema, "He did try to kill us. I can't allow that to go unanswered." His eyes narrowed, "I'm going to find him, and I'm going to kill him."

With that he gave a farewell nod in the direction of Anderson, who was still saying his goodbyes, and made his way into the smoky gloom of the cinema.

There was no fighting him, and as much as I wanted to just get up and leave for MarSeir, I wasn't in the mood for another surprise attack on the way out.

I grabbed Ava's hand and followed, pausing at the door to steal one last glance at Anderson, who now stood, watching us. He lifted one hand and casually waved goodbye as the drifting smoke consumed us and he went out of sight.

# Chapter 18:

For a moment, I was blinded as my eyes adjusted to the darkness inside the cinema. Smoke and still settling dust churned in the few stray beams of light that managed to penetrate the long hallway leading into the front lobby, and even so, they hugged the side walls, the protruding triangular sign that hung over the sidewalk blocking the majority of the sunlight.

Inside, a soft red glow radiated from the exit signs and the flickering arcade games that lined the far wall to our right. In front of us was a long, glass, countertop lit by a flickering yellow bulb and half filled with stale popcorn that moved like an ocean's wave with the rats beneath its surface still feeding on the years-old remains. Opened boxes and spilt candy were strewn all over the countertop and the floor, making each step stick to the ground ever so slightly as it pulled away from the sugary glue.

I warned Ava to watch her step, to be careful not to step on one of the dozens of rats that scurried by our feet, unafraid. Behind the counter was a mirrored wall lined with dusted over soda machines and knocked over cups. Looking into the mirror, I could hardly make out our outline in the entrance, but something did catch my eye.

There was a large, square projection to my left that took up most of the wall. I traced the flickering white beam to a high up square cut out in the wall above the snack bar where a projector was perched, then back to the granulated and choppy video. I was amazed by the sight, but more curious how this machine was even running in a city with no power. I assumed it was a trick, or perhaps somehow there was still a working generator here—though I doubted that entirely.

There was a middle-aged man in a suit in the center of the screen, as he spoke graphic images faded in and out behind him, "Fellow citizens...fear...Stigmas." The image showed a group of Stigma holders standing over a heap of bloody bodies.

"They live...kill." Another image faded into place, the images weren't actual photographs, but realistic art.

"Barbarians," the voice continued before cutting back out, showing a camp of Stigma holders in minimal clothing and with over exaggerated features. They were all dirty and unkempt.

I found myself growing angry, this wasn't what we looked like, this wasn't how we lived, or how we wanted to live at the very least. It was because of them that we had to live as something less than human! Or, perhaps, we simply became human once more, and that's what scares them. Maybe they wished to bring us back down the pit humanity had already fallen into. How are *we* the bad guys? For a moment I wanted to see all of them dead, every last one of them, an entire dome burnt to the ground, but that would make us no better.

"If you...Kill on sight," the next image was of Pure civilians holding rifles and firing upon the stampeding herd of Stigmas.

"Keep...safe. There's Hope," the man said, showing a picture of a large white dome city slowly zooming in. The man faded away, leaving only the city in the frame. It was beautiful, a large white dome that sat on a plateau that no one would dare to climb, protected by its landscape. There were windmills that lined its edges, their blades spinning gracefully with the breeze. The dome itself had hexagonal sections of glass spread over the roof, from what I saw those were the only places that sunlight could shine into the closed dome.

The man faded back into place, "Fellow citizens…fear…Stigmas," he began again, and the video continued on its loop.

I pulled Ava away and headed toward the only hallway I could see along the left wall. We had to find Demi, and I damned him again for leaving us behind although I knew by now he felt we were safer this way. Still, I didn't exactly like that fact. We rounded the corner, and the man's voice behind us slowly began to fade as we walked. The lighting was better here, with small circular lights spaced out on the ceiling the whole way down, though a few had blown out.

I snuck glances into the open showroom doors as we crept by. In some, the giant white screen had been torn down and frayed, in others the screen had been used as a canvas for graffiti. Others played the same kinds of choppy video loops that ran in the lobby. But one caught my attention as we passed and I took a step back to peer through the closed over door.

A video of a now recognizable Hope was shown, the image was from a circling aerial view. A woman's voice spoke, though she couldn't be seen. She was calm, soothing, with a soft voice, "Hope provides your best chance for survival in today's world, and we welcome you to our open and loving community. Here you can enjoy all the great pleasures of life from inside the dome. Think smart, be pure, have Hope."

The video ran on a loop like the others.

I looked back to the hallway to see a shadow run out of a showroom toward the end of the hall and disappear around the corner to the right. Behind it, smaller shadows scrambled to keep up, and I knew that it was Demi who they followed.

"Come on," I said, waving my hand toward the end of the hallway, and breaking off into a sprint.

By the time we reached the end of the hallway Demi had nearly disappeared around the next corner. We followed, catching bits of sound from each showroom door that we rushed past. At the end of the hallway a staircase lead down into the basement. I could see drops of blood splattered on the ground and smeared along the wall and as I remembered Tinker clutching his blood soaked arm I realized I should have been looking for a blood trail all along.

We pushed forward through the narrow corridor that the stairs led to. Rusted pipes and valves ran along the walls above us and the air was thick with an earthy smell, each breath I took had become more and more strained.

A demented laugh echoed through the corridor, and cut out suddenly only to be replaced with a dry cough and a gasp for air.

"I've got you, you sick bastard," Demi's voice rang through next, hitting us in undulating waves.

The booming sound of something solid being thrown against metal tore through the corridor.

"I see—" Tinker's voice began, pausing to take a short, but strained breath before continuing in a sarcastic tone, "I see you have A-mazing observational skills, how's that working out for you?"

We rounded the next corner to see Demi holding Tinker up against a locker. Ava gasped and jumped back, "Demi!" she started, pointing at his arm with one hand and covered her mouth with the other.

Demi was gripping Tinker's blood stained jumpsuit by the collar, holding him up against the locker. Black patterns twisted like sinister roots, intertwined and churning as they moved up his arm.

Demi rolled his head toward us, his eyes were a glossed over black void, save for the vibrant green crescent that was our mark.

"Oh?" Tinker started, tilting his head to the side curiously, looking beyond Demi with crooked smile, "You've got a touch of darkness about you."

Demi pushed Tinker harder against the wall, "Took you that long to notice? I see your observational skills aren't much better than mine."

Tinker rolled his eyes and laughed, "Oh not you pretty boy, you're all for show," he said, pausing to lift a quivering finger in my direction, "her."

Demi threw Tinker a few inches up into the air, and caught him by the throat as he came down, slamming him against the locker once more, "You don't talk to her. Damn it, I should have killed you before they came. Just like you were going to kill us."

Tinker's lips were painted red with the blood that came up whenever his strained voice escaped "If you're going to thank me like this then next time I'll make sure to finish you off."

Demi's grip tightened, and Tinkers veins began to show black through his skin, "There won't be a next time."

"Oh? I don't think killing me is in your best interest."

"And why is that?"

Tinker reached for his chest, and with two jittery fingers started to undo the buttons of his jumpsuit. At first, it looked like there was an open wound in the middle of his chest, but as I moved to get a closer look I could see a large metal ring surrounding the hole in his chest, with bolts and clamps helping it fuse to his still healing skin.

What I saw next surprised me, it wasn't his insides that I saw, but working gears that surrounded a battery and a single red light in the middle of his chest that blinked with the rhythm of his heartbeat. I was shocked, amazed, and appalled all in the same moment at the thought of what he must have endured to fuse that machine to his body.

Tinker smiled, "If I die, this machine stops working, and when this machine stops working well, let's just say things go *boom*!"

"So, I leave you here to bleed out, we'll be gone before you blow up," Demi shot back, angry at the threat.

"You're such a simple boy. No — I don't go boom, every charge I have in the city goes boom. You'd be doomed!" His head rolled back as he laughed, singing, mostly to himself, in an almost childlike voice, "Boom-to-doom-doom-doom!"

He stopped his chant abruptly, "Oh," he said, raising a finger, suddenly serious, "so I suggest you stop doing what you're doing, I'm weak enough already," he continued, tapping Demi's black hand, but pulling his finger away as he was scorched by the darkness.

Demi eased his grip, but still made sure to have a hold on Tinker, "So why did you try to kill us?"

"I didn't."

"Liar," Demi spat through his teeth, pushing harder against Tinker again.

"Ah, Ah, Ah! What did I tell you with that choking thing? I'm just not into it, is this how you thank someone who saved you?" Tinker said in a playful voice.

"You tried to blow us up." Demi hissed.

"Yet here you are, safe and sound— well, I'm not, but...you know. Amazing how that works isn't it?"

"Wait," I cut in, "you weren't trying to kill us, you were distracting the Agents weren't you?"

A smile pressed on Tinkers lips, "Ah, see she gets it. Ten points! Now, can you let me go?"

Demi dropped Tinker, who fell to his knees, and took a step back. The darkness on Demi's hand began to recede, but the pain it caused was clearly painted in his expression.

Ava came closer, placing one hand on Demi's chest and another holding his arm. A soft green glow began to gather at her palm and slowly creep up Demi's arm. The darkness that spiraled seemed to fear the green healing glow, dodging the parts of Demi's skin that it touched.

"What did I tell you about losing control? You aren't ready, the darkness is too strong," Ava said in a soft, worried voice. She focused on herding the darkness towards Demi's fingertips where it would gather, and ultimately disappear.

Demi scoffed and looked away.

"Interesting—" Tinker said to himself, using the wall to steady himself as he stood, "follow me."

He moved, slumped against the wall, painting it red with blood as he walked. We followed as he led us to a large room littered with mechanical parts, half built machines and broken trinkets. I was careful not to kick anything aside, afraid that he may have left something explosive laying around haphazardly.

There was a torn mattress in the left corner of the room by a portable heater, its blankets left bunched up near the foot of the unmade bed. Along every inch of wall were poorly built metal shelves with dozens of gadgets and spare parts taking up every available inch. I stopped, eyeing one small metal cube covered with illuminated lime green dots at the center of each sectioned out piece. It reminded me of a puzzle I'd played with as a child, and I wondered what might happen if I'd finally managed to solve it though I didn't care touch the thing.

A small television sat on a side table, showing only the jittery black and white lines of static, still without a visible power source. The drawers of the table hung half open, with strips of film and hoses cascading out and onto the floor where larger reels of film sat collecting dust.

I took a double take as I stole a glance through an open doorway leading into a room to our right. In the middle of the room was a human body lying on a hospital stretcher that was acting as a makeshift surgery table. On small, portable tables lie medical instruments of all kinds, and overhead fixtures created a spotlight in the middle of the room. On the walls, nearly illegible drawings, equations, and charts could barely be seen written in chalk through the darkness beyond the light.

My mind raced with the possibilities, trying hard not to imagine myself being the next person on that stretcher. But, there was something strange as well. The blood that stained the sheets didn't look like blood at all as I looked closer, rather, they were black and smeared, like oil. I thought that maybe the blood had simply dried, but as a shimmer of light reflected off the figures overhanging arm I began to think that it may be something else entirely.

Could it be that —

My attention was broken as Tinker put himself between myself and the door, closing it, before falling into a large revolving chair in front of a workbench that took up the entirety of the wall facing the entrance.

I couldn't help but wonder what this man might be hiding behind those walls so I tried to distract myself from what it may or may not be, not wanting to pry into something I shouldn't.

My eyes were drawn to a hole in the wall above the bench where he sat, reminding me of the machine that was placed in Tinker's chest, with large gears moving seamlessly within each other. Besides that, open cabinets with wired doors hung open, broken cups and silverware thrown inside without order.

"I fear I've bled too much," Tinker started, kicking at the ground and spinning around in his chair, "My world's begun to spin around, and around, and I'm afraid that when it stops, well, you know," he looked at Ava with a raised brow, a little help?"

"Me?" Ava questioned, pointing to herself, then looked up to Demi for assurance.

Tinker laughed, "No need to be afraid, I don't bite."

Demi nodded to Ava, who then walked over to Tinker and placed a hand on his wound and began to work.

Tinker sighed, "Damn Agents shot me! Can you believe them? What nerve."

"What did you expect them to do? Just let you kill them?" Demi asked sarcastically.

"Well, it's only proper manners. I hate when people don't have the common courtesy to just die when they are supposed to. It's rude really."

"How did you even manage to get shot?" I asked, "Weren't you inside toying with them the entire time?"

Tinker looked to the ceiling, thoughtful, "Well, although every dummy that appeared in that window was, in fact, a dummy—one was not quite as dumb as the others, or maybe he was more so. I really can't decide."

"So you used yourself as bait," I began, "why risk getting killed if you could have used the fakes?"

"Life's no fun without a gamble or two along the way eh?" Tinker said, smiling a bloody smile.

"You're mad!" I exclaimed.

"Ten more points to you!" Tinker started before looking to Demi, "You, on the other hand, have some catching up to do. She's on a roll, and this little one over here," he paused again looking to Ava, then back to Demi, "well, I feel better already. I think that's worth, hmm — forty? No, fifty points to be sure!"

Demi muttered under his breath before he spoke up, "I'm not interested in your little point system."

"Oh, I am *so* offended," Tinker said, rolling his eyes.

"Done!" Ava said, taking a step away from Tinker and clasping her hands behind her back, patiently waiting for a response.

Tinker began rotating his arm, and bending it, working it out before relaxing in his swivel chair, throwing one leg up to lazily rest on the other's knee. He looked to Ava with a kind smile, "I'm forever surprised by these little powers of your kind. Me? I'm stuck to my gadgets but what you all can do is truly a gift."

Ava blushed and her smile was suddenly beaming with childlike joy, "We can do all sorts of things. I met this guy, Marcus, and he could control fire! Can you believe that? And I have a friend back home, Han, that can make the trees grow into a beautiful forest, though, I never knew what a tree was until recently, but now I know all about them and all about other cool things too because I asked Sage and she's really smart. And then my brother," she said, pausing to look at Demi, "well he can—."

"Ava, that's enough." Demi said, placing his hand on her shoulder.

"What, why? I'm just trying to tell him how amazing we are." Ava argued, but didn't say any more.

"Before," I started, hoping to avoid the awkward silence that was sure to come while trying to figure how exactly to frame my question, "earlier you told me that there is a touch of darkness about me. Why?"

"Can't you see it? This boy, here," Tinker began, motioning to Demi, "he has obvious power, and he reeks of it. As for her," he said motioning to Ava, "she has such light. Both, have a noticeable aura about them. But you, no you have nothing. You are plain, boring, unoriginal, and that is what bothers me, or does it excite me? I don't know. What are you hiding? Why is your light, or your darkness suppressed?"

That same question is one that has haunted me for my entire life. The only thing that I could offer was a simple, "I don't know."

"Your power, then," he said with a pause, "is much larger than you realize."

"I'm starting to doubt that I even have one," I said, more to myself than to anyone.

"You must, else you wouldn't have survived in a world built to kill you."

He was right, but what? "So survival is my gift? You've survived."

"No, the universe doesn't want you dead, not yet, so here you are. As for me, I'm mad. These straight cut Agents will have to think out of the box to kill me, which they won't—I'll always be one step to the left of them."

"So then what's my purpose?"

"The truth of your existence is for you alone to discover, and is uniquely different for all of us in its own way."

There was a rustling under the bed and a hint of movement behind the blankets that hung half on the floor. I looked to Tinker, who didn't seem to be surprised by the noises that came. Why would he? The man lived in an abandoned cinema infested with rats. This was probably normal for him and I found a sense of relief in the calmness of his crooked smile that nothing dangerous would come.

"Ahh, so you finally decide to show yourself," Tinker began in a playful tone, letting the slightest hint of a genuine smile crease his lips, "Come on, Farrow."

A tiny, almost human-like hand wrapped around the edge of the hanging blanket. A small monkey's head popped out from behind the blanket, and passed a quick look to each of us. Farrow looked to Tinker, who nodded, then ran from under the bed, jumped onto his leg, and climbed up on top of his slumped shoulders. The small monkey, dressed in a pair of worn out overalls, which were made perfectly to her size, sat there picking off small flecks of dried blood off Tinkers face, occasionally looking to us only to make a small noise as if asking if we did this.

"Allow me to introduce you. This is Farrow, my lone companion, at least until my wife Lucy is ready to join us. But Farrow's okay with that now isn't she? You want to see mommy soon don't you? I know, me too," Tinker said, scratching behind Farrow's ears and seeming to forget that we were even in the room for a moment, "say hi to our guests Farrow!"

With that Farrow sat up straighter and let out a monkey's hello as she waved.

I looked at Demi, trying to stifle a laugh, but he just rolled his eyes at me.

I wanted to keep on track, "So, why are you out here, really? Did you seriously try to set fire to the capital, and overthrow the hospital?"

Tinker laughed, but his tone was more serious and his speech collected, "Is that the story they are running? I'll admit I kind of like it, a rogue doctor who lost his way and recruited an army of patients to take down the system—what a twist. No, I was on a team of bioengineers whose goal was to help harness the gift our mother Sera bestowed upon you to develop superior weapons and a reliable power source. I tried to resign after human testing began, and tried to inform the public of what was going on but I was already in too deep and the information was kept in the shadows."

I rose a finger to speak, not wanting to cut him off, "Wait, what kind of testing?"

Tinker relaxed in his chair, folding his arms, "We'd already learned how to extract what we called 'essence,' which is what grants the gift within people of your kind. It was a process that left the subjects powerless, and near-death, not able to live without the power that had coursed through their veins their entire lives. The process ultimately provided us with that power, that essence, it's how my department eventually managed to create weaponry that was more effective against those like you than anything we already had in production. "

"That's terrible," Ava said quietly to herself.

"But wait, there's more!" Tinker said, then continued with a dark tone of forced enthusiasm, "Another department was tasked with trying to replicate that power to create more powerful Agents. It started simple enough, nothing out of the ordinary for science. They would splice the DNA of animals with that of captured Stigmas, or would try to inject the essence into them directly, noting any change for better or worse. The results were promising, at first, though the subjects remained unstable—always dying within a few hours."

"But you said they were doing human testing, and from your perspective at the time I can only assume that by human, what you really mean is Pure," Demi pressed on.

"That's true, the ultimate goal was to find a formula that would grant the user the same powers as Sera and Klaus, to create a new god—we'd even extracted some of her essence for the job."

"So what happened next?" Ava asked.

"I couldn't stand for it—despite my research. I'd seen countless bodies being taken out after each failed test. We had the essence, we'd been using it to build stronger weapons for years, and it'd become a major power source in the domes but for whatever reason a human body that didn't already have the gift couldn't cope with that kind of power and they would die soon after. Even so, I couldn't understand our purpose. I thought the whole reason we were fighting this war was through fear of what that kind of power could do, yet here we were trying to replicate it for ourselves."

"Cut to the point—I don't think they would be going through all of this trouble to find a doctor that simply disagreed with them. Why are they really hunting you?" Demi ordered.

"Farrow," Tinker said calmly.

"The monkey?" Ava asked.

"The experiments weren't as much of a failure as they believe. I had an epiphany one night and came up with a solution—testing it in secrecy. Farrow here was my last subject, and the only known subject to survive the test."

"So," I began, looking more intently at his pet, noticing her eyes shifting for a moment to a vibrant green and back, "she has the gift?"

"No" Tinker answered, "she holds much more than the gift. In many ways she's equally as powerful as our gods as she is now. Lucky for us she just an innocent little monkey that doesn't know any better, but if that formula ever got into the hands of Zanin I can guarantee he would make himself a god and rule over this world now that our true gods have been sealed away. I couldn't forfeit that power over to them so I escaped the city with Farrow being the only one who could crack the code."

"And what of the fire and the hospital?" I asked.

"They'll take any opportunity they can to be rid of undesirables and my betrayal was the perfect chance to launch a public campaign against me. They must have set that fire themselves, and probably killed the staff and patients in that hospital before framing me for it."

"But they would kill their own people?" Ava asked, shocked.

Tinker grew solemn, "The world's darker than you know. The Pure live in cities with limited space, if you are a criminal or ill then there are two options, exile or death. They needed someone to pin their murders in the hospital on and set it up so I would take the fall in the public eye."

"Why not just say that they killed you and be done with it?" I asked.

"Propaganda. It's the only real thing that has kept this war going on for so damned long. Every now and then there's some story about how contact with a Sigma holder made someone crazy, or that someone living in the city secretly was one before going on a rampage. Either way, both of those excuses would be impossible, the Stigma isn't contagious, you are born with it, and the dome's security is far too advanced for a Stigma holder to go unnoticed in its streets. However, that information is a luxury very few were allowed to know. If Zanin had me killed then the public wouldn't demand answers, they would simply go back to being content with their limited lives. But since I lived, it gave them more to talk about, something else to hate."

"Propaganda," I repeated.

"It's what's been keeping that fire under their asses lit for so long!" Tinker exclaimed.

"Like those videos in the lobby," Ava blurted out.

Tinker motioned to Ava, "she gets it."

"So what do we do to stop this?" Demi asked.

"We? I stay here and keep playing with these Agents. They'll never learn. You can go ahead and try to kill Zanin if you'd like but you have a whole population believing you're evil standing in your way!"

"Kill Zanin," I repeated with another pause.

"You're starting to sound like a parrot over there kid. You want to be my next pet?" Tinker said, beginning to pet Farrow, who was now sitting on his lap.

I cringed at the thought.

"So where is it?" Demi asked more calmly than seemed right for that question.

"Boy, you can't just walk into the Devil's den looking to kill him and walk out with your life. You'd have to be a god!"

Demi gave him a smirk.

"You're madder than me," Tinker exclaimed.

Demi pushed for an answer, "So?"

"Hope," Tinker began, "it's a large dome city outside the sacred plains, past MarSeir. But don't you think for a minute it'll be easy to get close to that city, never mind Zanin."

"We'll see," Demi stated in a very matter of fact sort of tone.

Tinker shied away from Demi, catching him in the corner of his eye, "Your confidence will betray you if you aren't too careful."

"My confidence," Demi began, gritting his teeth and placing a hand down hard on the table, "is none of your concern."

Tinker passed a questioning look to Demi's hand on the table near him, "Oh, but it should be yours."

Demi's open palm curled to a fist on the table, "Your point?"

"You can't hope to save the world if you can't even save yourself. You'll die," Tinker noted.

"I'll die a hero."

"I don't think so, you'll die another Stigma who tried to rise against Zanin and failed. How do you plan on saving the world if you are dead?" Tinker said, toying with Demi.

I could see on Demi's face he was growing frustrated with the argument. "You underestimate me."

"What's worse? That, or the fact that you overestimate yourself?" Tinker teased.

Demi furrowed his brow and grit his teeth, "How dare you question my power!"

"How dare you not?" Tinker said defiantly. Demi looked away as Tinker continued, "I'd rather be happily surprised by your success than disappointed by your failure. It leaves room for, say, a little bit of a surprise happy ending if you succeed."

"And I will succeed. Zanin's death will come by my own hand, and I'll return to my people a hero."

"A hero who only became a hero for the fame, not for the sake of good. Even a positive action done with ill intent becomes negative," Tinker said, eying Demi's clenched fist on the table beside him as if waiting to be struck.

"A hero nonetheless."

Tinker shook his head in disappointment, shot a glance over to me, and smiled, "So, we know what he's in it for. What about you?"

I took a moment to think, really, I just didn't know. I'd never dreamed of returning to MarSeir, or trying to hunt down Sera. I didn't even know what I would do if I found her. What would it change? How could a Stigma with no gift hope to succeed when thousands her have fallen before they even reached the battlefield.

"Just in it for the ride?" Tinker pressed on.

"Not exactly, uhm—" I began, stalling for time, hoping an answer would come, "I mean, I want to stop living like this. On the run, always hiding, you know?"

"And how are you going to change that?"

"By saving our mother Sera. When I was younger the stories the elders told said that once mother was safe and out of the hands of the Pure she would rise up and restore peace," I closed my eyes, working to remember being a young girl sitting by the campfire listening as the elders and monks told us stories of why we were here, and how this curse is truly a gift from our mother. I felt warm, and filled with love.

Now, my only goal was to survive and I'd grown cold long ago. I had no past, no future, only the moment, no matter how terrible that moment always seemed to be. But still, even on my darkest nights, I could feel Sera's love warm me, as if she knew my pain. I think it's that feeling that has kept most of us going through these years, and that feeling kept us fighting, it drove us to be so much more than content with our miserable lives.

"A fool's story," Tinker began with a pause, I felt my stomach sink as I thought about what he said. It may be a fool's story but it gave me more hope than anyone knew. He continued, "Don't you think if she had that power she would have escaped by now?"

"They suppress her," Demi chimed in.

"Then what of the other being? Is he powerless to save her?" Tinker asked next.

Ava perked up and turned from playing with all of the gadgets on the shelves behind us, excited to have the answer to a question, "Klaus?"

Demi let out a grunt, "I think that bastards done enough already. If he never intervened we might not even be in this mess."

Tinker brought his hands to his mouth, resting his thumbs on his bottom lip and his hands together as if he was praying, He began tapping his fingers together starting with his index, then middle, then ring, then pinky individually as he thought.

I watched him, wondering what was going on in that mind of his. There was a reflection in his eye, a spark, something that begged to be set free. He was hiding something, and at first that bothered me, sensing danger. But soon I realized that if he wanted us gone he would have done so by now, and if we were in danger he wouldn't just be sitting here talking.

He knew something.

I thought of his research, then, it dawned on me, "You know where she is."

Tinker's empty gaze didn't break, he didn't move, he just stared into nothing as he tapped his fingers against each other one by one.

Tap.

Tap.

Tap.

I waited, but begged the question once more, "You know, don't you?"

He sat up straight, dragging his palms over his thighs where they stopped to rest. He faked a yawn and stood, he was a terrible actor, and stretched his arms out to the side — being careful not to move the one that had been shot earlier the wrong way.

"Tinker," I pressed.

"It's getting late, as you know it's been a long day. I think it's time I get some sleep. We'll talk in the morning," he said as he moved past Ava to slowly sit, then lay, on his bed.

Demi took a threatening step towards him, but I put my hand on his chest to stop his stride and gave him a look that asked him to let it go. Tinker wouldn't give anything up if he didn't want to and I knew trying to force it out of him wouldn't work either.

I saw a smile break on Tinker's face as he watched me out of the corner of his now closing eyes. After a moment of silence the three of us began to gather our things to leave.

Demi and Ava made their way back out into the hallway, and I followed — but as I reached the door I could hear Tinker shift on his bed. I took a step back to steal one last look, he was staring right back at me.

"One more thing," he said after a moment, "I doubt Zanin would leave something as valuable as Sera unwatched. If you find him, I'm sure she won't be far." He rolled over to his back and his eyes closed once more, a crooked smile broke out on his face, "Oh, and I hope I don't blow you three up on your way out."

Farrow sat on his chest and tilted her head, waving goodbye.

"Thank you," I said, turning to leave once more.

I could hear Tinker speak as I left the room, "Good luck."

# Chapter 19:

I hadn't realized how long we had been inside. By the time we made it back out into the street it was lit only by the moon's glow, and the nighttime air said hello with a chill that was anything but welcoming. I knew we needed to find a safe place for the night, somewhere out of the way of regular traffic through the city, somewhere warm.

There was an old theater that I used to live in through most of my teenage years. It wasn't a movie theater like Tinker's, but one with a stage and rows upon rows of seats. I'd seen pictures hung up on the walls there of people dressed up in amazing costumes as they performed for the audience. Sometimes, I'd imagine myself as one of the actors, and twirl about on the stage rehearsing made up lines in costumes I'd found lying around, though I doubt my plays were as good as those I'd imagined the ghost of the past acting out before me.

The walls were lined with several floors of special closed off rooms with few seats in each. I guessed the most important people would sit there and watch what was going on below, but I found that was the safest place to sleep. If anyone had actually stumbled into my little theater I'd watch them from above, hiding in the shadows or behind one of the still hanging curtains as they explored.

Hardly anyone ever made it past the stage, or even upstairs, since getting caught on a high up floor could be dangerous without a real place to run, so most of us with experience knew to avoid that. I used that knowledge to my advantage and went up there anyway, knowing that as long as I kept a low profile and covered my tracks not even other Stigma holders would find me.

It's a sad thing to admit but we can be our own enemy, fighting for food and resources, or simply for a better hiding spot—not to mention the threat of coming across a roaming gang with no allegiance to anyone but themselves. There wasn't a true sense of law out here, but most still stood to their basic human morals to keep the peace, and of course there were those who didn't.

Still, few ever bothered to go into that theater, and only once had I seen an Agent investigate. He walked all the way down the middle aisle to the stage and took a broad look around, scanning for anything more unusual than an abandoned theater all set up with props that were left in place and forgotten. I remember watching him light up a cigarette and say something into his headset, though I couldn't hear from where I was. He took a long drag and let out a plume of smoke before he turned to leave.

I knew that this was probably the safest place to go, so again I lead Ava and Demi through the city, trying to stick to side streets and cutting through the occasional first floor of a building and back out into an alleyway through a fire exit. My instincts had taken over again, and it felt good to be back on my toes. I hated how relaxed I had gotten, knowing that it had almost cost us our lives a few times already. I wouldn't make that mistake again.

We were in an alleyway when I saw someone ahead, walking in the middle of the street as if they weren't worried about anything at all. I knew it wasn't an Agent, they wouldn't be alone unless they were being used as bait, which was unlikely. So this had to be one of us, but why so bold?

I pressed my back against the wall and lead us through an open fire exit door to take cover. The last thing we needed right now was to draw attention, even from one of our own kind and I knew that being followed back to the theater wasn't an option.

There was a reception desk in the middle of the first floor, I told Demi and Ava to stay low as we snuck over to hide behind it. After a moment my curiosity got the best of me and I peered over the countertop to see the figure standing still in the middle of the street, looking up to the sky.

I ducked back down.

"What are they doing?" Demi asked.

"I don't know, they're just standing there staring," I said, not sure what they were doing.

"What?" Demi asked, surprised by my answer.

"They're just standing there, looking up to the sky."

I snuck another peek, and in the moonlight I could make out the slightest details of a man's face.

I cursed as I heard a can rolling on the ground behind me, and turned to see Ava hunched over, "Sorry," she said.

The noise got the man's attention and when I peeked over the countertop once more his eyes were locked on the storefront. I wasn't sure if he saw me, so I stood perfectly still, trying not to draw any more attention.

Demi tugged at my shirt, "Sage, what's wrong."

I paused, focusing on the man's face. At first I couldn't believe my eyes, but as I realized who it was I wasn't entirely surprised. I gave Demi a worried look, "It's Lain."

Demi grit his teeth and immediately stood up from his hiding spot, "That bastard."

Before I could stop him he was storming towards Lain, fist clenched. Ava had begun to follow her brother but I pulled her closer to me, "He'll never learn, will he?" I asked, having much rather run than confront Lain.

I felt Ava let out a relaxed laugh, obviously not as bothered by Lain as we were, "Nope."

My worried eyes went back to an unmoving Lain, who stood with his hands resting in his pockets as he waited for Demi to come closer, "So, brother," he said opening his arms as if for a hug, "you look well."

Demi didn't bother to respond, immediately landing a punch to Lain's jaw that sent him skipping off the cracked pavement.

"Whose side are you on?" Demi shouted as Lain wiped the blood from his lip and began to stand.

Lain spat at the ground and walked back up to Demi, unnerved by the attack, "Oh, touchy now, are we? The same side as always Demetrius, or have you forgotten our purpose here? I was simply tying up some loose ends."

Demi threw another punch, but Lain sidestepped and Demi stumbled forward, trying to catch his balance.

"That temper is still there I see, but really, I don't understand why you are so upset, it is only a matter of politics. It is what we do after all," Lain taunted.

Demi spoke through his teeth, "An entire camp was murdered because of you, and Vatz was a guardian. Since when do we kill our own? Never mind the fact that we were almost caught in the crossfire, or was that your intention?"

"Don't flatter yourself, my business with Vatz was, well, business. He'd forgotten his place and you know how I just hate that. You being in that camp was, should I say, a happy coincidence? Then I got to thinking about how your death was a pretty little consolation prize that I didn't quite want to let slip away," Lain said, sighing, "I had said no survivors, but it seems as though if you want a job done right you can't send a bunch of monkeys to do the job for you. I guess I'll just have to do it myself," Lain's palm opened by his side, and the moonlight itself began to be drawn to his palm in thin slivers, along with particles of light that pulled from any surrounding source. Soon the entire street was lit by the blinding flare.

"So what's killing me going to get you? Madsen will know it was you," Demi pushed on.

"How will he? It's simple really, his favorite son never returned from a mission that put him through a perilous journey. It isn't a far stretch, after all, two of the other squads have already been dealt with, and you're welcome for that by the way I really would like to think of myself as a part of team Demi for that effort—not that it matters now. As for knowing it was me, well, you never paid attention n much did you? While you were out being a playboy, I was stuck in the Grand Hall for days on end studying our law, or did you forget the purpose of a councilman's son? It seems daddy has finally remembered me, with you gone and all he has a need for my help. So is this what you've been doing all these years? These little side missions can be such an adventure, I'm really quite thrilled! Thank you, thank you! You've set me free, truly I am in your debt. It's a real shame you have to die. I liked to think that we were—friends," Lain went on with a smile.

"So you'll have us all killed for jealousy?" Demi returned.

"You know, I never understood why my father chose you over me. Look at you, you've grown soft, it's pathetic. It's not like it's really been that long since you've left Terra Sera and already you've seemed to develop something new for yourself, feelings. You expect to become a great Guardian but really you'd just end up like your own dead daddy, wallowing in your own misery. I like to think killing you will be a show of mercy. I'm the best kind of person, really."

Demi dropped his jacket to a heap on the ground. Already the darkness had begun to consume him, black mist was drawn from the ether to settle as fractured plates on his skin that slowly crept up his arms and cascaded over his shoulders. Small pools, like tar pits, began to bubble up from the ground sporadically by his feet. From them, Kurki pulled themselves from the sludge into existence and immediately into a reckless sprint for Lain. Within moments dozens of Kurki were appearing from all directions, bursting out of darkened corners of every building and empty window to flood the street before us.

Lain bolstered his step as the Kurki drew closer, some lunged towards him as others bubbled up from the ground beneath his feet. The aura in his palm grew brighter and the Kurki evaporated in its immense light, drifting away as smoke in the wind. Still, more spawned in their place in an endless onslaught. Lain formed a staff from his gathered light, and danced between every attack, seeming to have memorized their movements as he slashed through each creature. Through the flurry Lain passed an unamused look over to Demi and drove his staff into the ground by his feet, allowing the light to encapsulate him entirely and dissolving the Kurki.

The dome around Lain fractured into lesser shards that lingered in the night air as he relaxed. Demi was in step with the break, taking advantage of the moment Lain had screened himself to drive a scaled fist into his chest. Lain was quick to react, offering only a sliver of contact as his body rolled off the punch as he placed his left hand on Demi's shoulder and guided him into his right hand's open palm. Demi took the blow, refusing to falter as a thin white beam pierced his shoulder and grabbed hold Lain's vulnerable arm, using the leverage to throw him to the ground and into a bubbling pool of Kurki about to spawn.

The ravenous pack hadn't even fully formed before they began reaching for the fallen Lain, their corrosive touch leaving scorch marks on his arms and tearing at his clothes. The shards above Lain became pointed and as each new Kurki would attack a shard would hone in to destroy it. Lain scrambled to his feet, and was immediately on the defensive as Demi pushed forth with a relentless attack. With each punch Demi's strength intensified, the tempest within him brewing; and with each attack Lain managed to avoid his movements became more fluent as if he knew what was coming before it was thrown.

Between each blow, a Kurki seemed to attack from Lain's blind spot. Many were struck down as his peddled shards tracked their every moment to defend him, but there were some that had managed to break through to tag his bare skin with their corrosive touch and gradually slow him. Lain reacted off of Demi's shift in momentum, using it to guide an overzealous punch away from him to offer some distance as Demi stumbled ahead.

Demi found himself a few feet from Lain, standing amidst the scattered shards that had been driven into the ground after piercing the Kurki. He stepped to Lain, who rose a finger to stop him— effectively pulling one shard from the ground and slicing through Demi's shoulder to collect at a point at the tip of Lain's outstretched index finger. Demi took another step, and was met with a cut from another shard, this time on his ribcage, and again the light collected at the tip of Lain's finger.

Demi paused, realizing that Lain's defense played on is aggression and lead him into a trap.

"If this is all you have to offer than why don't you just go get yourself killed—save me the trouble," Lain taunted as he rose his hand above his head, allowing the rest of the shards to release from the ground and slice through Demi's flesh to collect in an orb at his finger tip.

Demi wavered as he fell to one knee, "You mock me, the prince of darkness?" he said through grit teeth.

A smile pressed Lain's lips, "The prince of darkness, eh? Don't you think that's a little self-absorbed? You're a walking trope if I ever did see one," he began with a snicker, "You're the son of a whore and a coward, that's all you will ever be. My light will wash over the world and destroy all that oppose me and I will be king—you will rule nothing."

Demi eyed the growing orb above Lain and bolstered his step, "Everywhere the light touches darkness is already waiting."

Lain let out a deep sigh and shook his head before locking onto Demi's eyes with a piercing glare, "You bore me, I'm done with you," he said, releasing the colossal orb above him with a mere flick of his wrist.

Demi hardly had the time to react, in moment his feet had dug into the ground and the orb was being held back by little more than a thin veil of black mist that was steadily growing. Demi pressed against the veil, desperately trying to push back as the ground fractured beneath his feet. He fell to one knee, and the mist protecting him reacted instantly, pulsing once before spreading across enough of Lain's orb to shield Demi from the blinding light.

The mist began twist within itself, creeping over the orb before consuming it entirely. In a blink both were gone and a moment later the thunderous sound of an explosion ripped through the city followed by a storm of smoke and debris that erupted from the alleyways as the buildings beyond began to crumble.

The only thing I could see was a steady barrage of light beams being shot through the cloud which illuminated Demi for brief moments as he dodged each attack. The light pierced the cloud, but stopped shortly after to form once more into a steadily growing sphere that hung like a faux moon above the street. There was a tempest brewing above Demi, splintered bolts of violet lightning ripped through the space around him and into the ground. Kurki bubbled up through each scorched mark and sprinted headlong into the fray to sacrifice themselves in his defense.

As the smoke settled Demi struggled to stand. His clothes were torn and blood pooled to the ground below, but he refused to back down despite Lain's advantage with distance. Ava jumped at the sight of him, but I was forced to hold her down, knowing if Lain were to discover us than we would only put Demi in more danger. He had become engulfed in a storm cloud, a maelstrom of energy that's static electricity seemed to be drawn to his wounds, accelerating the malefic growth of armor. Undulating white streaks frosted the tips of his existing peppered strands of hair, looking like shimmering fields of reeds kissed by a gentle breeze, though he was dancing on the edge of a tempest.

Lain's eyes grew wide with excitement, but he gave no time for Demi to recover. The faux moon that lingered above the street splintered into dozens of spears that rained down on Demi's turned back. The storm around him intensified, and a Vemosa burst from the ground below, absorbing the flurry. Suddenly, the spears shot out from a street side wall behind Lain full tilt. At the very last moment Lain turned, sensing the danger, and they connected with so much force he was pinned to the wall on the opposite side of the street.

Demi took slow steps towards him, the Vemosa taking formation on either side of him as the remaining Kurki did little more than play games of tag in the street.

I took Ava's hand and lead her outside, knowing the battle was over.

"You don't have it in you to kill me," he said, pushing himself up to sit at the beams dissipated.

"I don't have to," Demi said, motioning to the two Vemosa behind him, "you know, not wanting blood on my hands and all."

"Funny," Lain said with a laugh as he struggled to his feet.

Ava and I took a step back, as did Demi, all waiting to see what Lain was about to do.

Once standing, the wounds didn't seem to limit him that much, other than the fact that his left arm hung limp by his side. He smirked, as another ball of light began to form in his palm, "Than I guess this isn't over."

"Drop it Lain, you lost. Go home before I have to put you down," Demi said, actually sounding like he was giving brotherly advice.

"You'd like that wouldn't you?"

"You're embarrassing yourself," Demi asked.

The light in Lain's palm grew brighter, and behind Demi the storm clouds took more life, becoming more violent as it reacted to the threat. Demi stepped back, putting room between the two men once more, not wanting to be taken off guard by another attack.

Lain noticed us then, and passed a quick look back to Demi, judging their distance.

A moment later Lain's energy was fixed on us. I immediately shielded Ava from the coming attack. Demi reacted just as fast, moving towards us the best he could, the darkness behind him now a raging tempest.

In those moments everything seemed to move in slow motion, and out of that storm the face of a black wolf with four violet eyes, the top set smaller than the bottom, emerged between the crackling bolts of electricity within the cloud. Through its flowing black mane there were two pair of horns rippling into shape from the ether, like pincers on either side, folding inward towards its face. The lower, and smaller of the horns traced the wolf's jaw line with little distance in between, while the larger of the pair bowed further outward aligning with the beast eyes.

The mammoth wolf had leapt out of the cloud above Demi, and as it moved through the air its front legs were shielded by an obsidian flame that spread from its wrist to its elbows. As it landed, the flames solidified in place, forming a porous and wave-like blade much like the Vemosa's but less defined.

It landed in full stride, easily catching up to Lain, who had only taken a couple of steps towards us, in just one step. As time returned to its normal pace the beast's enormous paw had wrapped around Lain's face and forced him to the ground with an audible thud and the crackle of broken bones.

The beast only seemed to grow more massive as Demi walked up beside it. On all fours it was as tall as Demi was standing, and as Lain cowered on the ground beneath it the beast rose up on its hind legs, towering over them. It leaned forward and let out a vicious snarl that echoed through the streets before slamming its paws back down on either side of Lain's head, sending shards of concrete flying upwards and trapping him between its horns just inches from the creature's maw.

Lain shot a truly worried look to Demi as the fiend loomed over him, "You—you aren't really going to kill me, are you?" he begged, terror in his voice.

Demi pet the side of his new summon, seeming to forget he was still in the midst of battle as he admired it. After a moment he looked back down to Lain, "I think I'll leave it up to this guy," he said, nodding to the beast.

With that Demi motioned for us to follow and we left Lain to the beast.

# Chapter 20:

We moved in silence, Ava following close behind, and Demi using me as support as we moved swiftly to the theater just a few blocks away. He was in agony, not even trying to mask his discomfort as his malefic armor formed like a scab over every cut. He refused Ava's help—saying he'd never learn to bare it if she always washed it away.

It seemed that the more he used his power the more he'd begun to lose control of himself. The darkness was gradually taking over each time he reached into its well of power, and I was afraid that one day he would delve too deep. I wondered what would happen once the darkness spread over his entire body; and if the Demi I knew would even return once it consumed him.

I lead us through the closed over fire exit door that lead onto the main stage of the theater. To our right there were the same familiar props and forgotten racks of costumes, all unmoved since I'd last been here. Ahead of us was mostly darkness, save for another fire exit on the opposite wall. To our left, on either corner of the stage sat a pair of staircases that curled towards the center, leading from the ground floor up to the stage. There were two hollow cylinders where the stairs met the stage, with an open door and a spiral staircase that lead up to the private booths above.

The front entrance was a wide open double door showing the remains of a gas station across the street beyond the grown over foothills of abandoned cars, a grim snapshot into the past. Beside those doors hung two long tapestries, torn and dirty—and, too dark to make out the detail now it was only through memory that I knew Cekrit's symbol was proudly painted in the center of each, a soothing reminder that we at least had some allies here.

I led the two of them up the staircase and into one of the private booths. Ava rushed ahead to find a booth that had been mostly cleared of debris. As I walked in she was dropping the last bits of wood off the side of the railing and down onto the seats below. I wanted to stop her, to avoid the noise, but I let her be, sure that my nagging was the last thing anyone needed right now.

I sat down beside Ava, who was still insisting that Demi let her take a look at him as she cleared the last of our floor space. He turned her offer down again, at first, but finally gave in as she persisted.

I watched the volcanic skin on his arm recede, his breathing regulate, and after a long silence I finally had to ask, "Did you really let that thing kill Lain?"

Demi shook his head slowly, silent, as he stared blankly at the ground beneath his feet. Ava looked at me with concern, as if telling me now wasn't the time. A sense of both grief and relief washed over me, this had to mean that he was gone. I couldn't imagine what Demi was feeling, having just killed his brother, but I still had so many questions.

As Ava's light washed over the darkness disappeared through Demi's fingertips. He lifted his arm and flexed it, wiggling his fingers before resting his hands back down on his lap and pushed his head up against the wall behind him, closing his eyes.

"No," he said finally, "I figured Uru scared him enough that he might actually learn his lesson. I'm not the mindless brute he thinks I am. I know killing him wouldn't be the smartest thing for me to do politically. I would lose my honor, forfeit my place in the

Guardian games, potentially be banished from my home, and fail my father all for one satisfying kill."

"Uru?" I asked, confused by the new name.

Demi smiled, eyes still closed, "It's the name I'm giving the new summon, though I don't know what kind of creature it is—I'd never bothered to name the Kurki or Vemosa."

"So what makes this one different?"

Demi laughed beneath his breath, "I might just allow you to call this one a pet."

The thought lingered for a while, and started to make some kind of sense. Before now, Demi had detached himself from his summons. They were nothing more than tools in battle, so they never had a need to be named. But this summon manifested from something else inside him. When we were being attacked he reacted, thinking of more than just himself, and that's when Uru came. I thought that maybe that's why he felt a sense of attachment to this summon.

I remembered my book, and quickly pulled it out to flip through the pages, hoping that it might shed some light on this new beast. It told me nothing, the symbols that faded onto the page didn't shift into a form that I could understand, they only sat there, mocking me.

Demi watched on as I struggled to find a page I could make sense of. I wondered if he was even seeing the same symbols, or something completely different.

"Here," he said after a while, reaching for the book, "let me take a look."

He rested the book in his lap and slowly turned the pages and it wasn't long until he found one that must have caught his eye. I watched on intently as the word *Kurki* formed across the top of the page.

Beneath there were rough sketches of several Kurki, only, the sketches were moving and playing with each other. They were like tiny children, wrestling and chasing each other across the page, their two bulbous antennae bouncing over their head. Their arms were too small to do much of anything, but their oversized legs and feet gave them long strides, powerful for jumping. They'd tackle each other only to roll off, unable to hold on.

Demi turned the next page, the word *Vemosa* was written across the top. Below there was a sketch of the two familiar cloaked guards hovering just a few feet above the ground. Here, they hid their bladed arms beneath dark and torn cloaks that barely rested above the surface. Their faces were covered by a pale white mask, with a long beak and large, perfectly round eyes that were nothing more than a black hole, with protruding white ridges.

Occasionally they would form their black portals and show some object passing through from one to the other. They'd appear all over the page, toying with their own perspective, but before long they returned to their guard duty.

Demi fingered the next page, reluctant to turn it, perhaps anticipating what would come. When he turned the page the word *Naukri* sat on the top of the page. The wolf's head came out from the side of the page in a full sprint to the other side, its misty fur trailing behind it, seeming to drift off the page.

Demi closed the book as we heard a rustling down in the theater. The three of us snuck a peek down to the first floor to see the beast walking in through the double door and making its way down the main aisle towards the stage.

"Naukri," Demi said softly, placing the book to the ground and gazing at his new creation, wonder in his eye like a child who caught glimpse of a new toy.

A moment later Demi was gone from my side. A black pool appeared in front of the beast and Demi rose from it.

Uru sat before him, towering over Demi as it did. The wolf was much taller than Demi, even sitting, but it lowered its head to him as he approached. Demi placed his hands on either side of Uru's face, and the two stood there for a moment as they rested their foreheads against one another.

Demi pulled away, taking a better look at his creation, which sat up proudly as it was inspected. Demi ran his hands over the rippled horns that came from the side of the Naukri's face, and ran his fingers through its thick black mane.

Demi looked to Uru's enormous paws, eyeing the solid flame-like bladed shields that had formed up its forearms. Demi touched them cautiously, and the blade returned to a dancing flame as he did. Demi pulled back, watching curiously. He'd made it all the way around the Naukri, smiling, clearly pleased, patting the beast on the head once more before the Vemosa formed under him once more, bringing him back to our booth.

"He's going to watch over us for the night," Demi said, grabbing a torn cushion from a broken chair and laying down, using it as a pillow.

Ava took a second look at the Naukri, and turned with a smile, "Can I ride it?"

Demi laughed once to himself, "I don't think now's the time Ava."

"Okay," she said, disappointed.

I laid down beside Demi, only to have Ava squeeze in between us, which I didn't mind. They both fell asleep soon later, but I laid there staring at the ceiling, thinking of what was to come. It seemed like I'd already found a tip towards finding Sera, and despite Tinker being on the verge of insanity, I believed him. I wanted to tell Demi, but couldn't. No matter how much I dreaded returning to MarSeir the answers to my questions waited for me there. Demi was already committed to going, so for now, I decided to keep him in the dark. I couldn't risk him making us turn back now, and getting a second opinion from the monks there would only confirm what I already knew.

Still, what would happen when we did return? Did Lain seriously expect for us to pretend that he hadn't tried to kill us twice now? Or that he'd ordered the deaths of two other groups?

We had a new enemy, that much we knew, but an enemy Demi couldn't be the one to kill and an enemy Ava and I wouldn't stand a chance against. I secretly hoped that Tinker might do us a great favor and take care of it for us, but somehow that didn't seem right either. Lain was too important, and his death would change everything back in Terra Sera.

I now knew that we had to be even more on our toes. It was only a matter of time before he planned another attack. There was no going back for him now.

# Chapter 21:

Ava woke me in the early morning, holding a broken sheet of glass with a bit of charred meat on it.

"Hungry?" she asked, offering me breakfast.

I rubbed the sleep from my eyes and sat up, sore from a night on the hard ground and taking the shard of glass from her to inspect her offering with uncertainty. As my eyes adjusted I realized that Demi was gone, and at first I was worried, but Ava's cheerfulness soothed my concern.

"What is this?" I asked, after taking a small bite—now knowing that whatever it was had the taste cooked right out of it.

Ava shrugged, "Something Demi caught, you should go watch him, it's really funny!" she said with a giggle.

We made our way down to the main floor to find him, immediately catching sight of him rushing past the fire exit door to our left. Curiosity drew me to him.

Peeking around the door and into the alleyway to my left I could see Uru standing at the end, mostly in the street since he was far too big to squeeze into the alley. Demi's back was towards me, and he kept a wide stance. Between them, a small rabbit jolted from side to side. It ran closer to Uru but stopped short, turning back towards Demi, who dove trying to catch the animal as it ran past. I laughed as he fell to the ground, missing it completely.

I let the rabbit run past me, it'd earned its life for the moment.

"This is a lot harder than it looks," he said with a deep sigh when he saw me, getting up and brushing off the dirt from his clothes.

"Guess so, and it looks like Uru's been a big help too," I said, motioning to the giant behind him.

"It'd be a lot easier if I could just get the Kurki to do it for me, but that wouldn't be too wise."

"Looks like being spoiled your whole life has paid off huh?" I teased.

Demi scratched his head, "Yeah, because having servants bring your food is almost as hard as catching it yourself."

I smiled and turned to go back into the theater.

"Hey, where are you going? I'm still hungry, hey!" he said, his calls fading as I disappeared back into the theater.

I didn't bother to answer, and instead cut loose some rope from an unused stage prop, sitting down as I tied a looped knot on one end that doubled over so I could pull it tighter. I came back to Demi and handed him the rope, then fished out a few fresh vegetables I'd taken from Vatz's camp and placed them on the ground.

"What's this?" He asked.

"I believe it's called a trap," I replied sarcastically, as I took the rope back from him and went into the theater to climb up to the second floor. I found an open window and threw the looped end down to him, and told him to put it around the bait. "Now watch out!" I called down to him, and he went to hide back in the theater.

It didn't take long before another rabbit came over, cautious, but too curious for its own good. I waited for the rabbit to start taking nibbles of the bait before I sprung the trap, pulling on the rope and closing the loop around its legs. A moment later the rabbit was hanging upside down just a few feet from the ground. I tied my end of the rope to a pole beside me and made my way back down.

I passed Demi and gave him a sly smirk, motioning for him to follow and we entered the alleyway once more. He looked at me, impressed, and I handed him the knife that was in my pocket, "I caught it, it's your job to cook it, I hate this kind of dirty work," I said, before walking back into the theater.

A few minutes later Demi returned, rabbit in hand.

"Where'd you get that?" he asked, handing back the knife.

"The knife?" I asked, as I folded it back up and put it in my pocket.

He nodded.

"Madsen gave it to me before I left, said it might come in handy," I returned.

Demi looked thoughtful, but didn't say anything, only started to work on turning the rabbit into a meal.

"Why?" I pushed for a response.

"I've seen it before, I just thought it was weird that you would have it," he said, focusing on his work.

"Well I didn't steal it," I defended.

"Oh no, that's not what I was saying," he returned, passing me a smile to show his sincerity, "It's an artifact that was on display in the Grand Hall, I'm surprised Madsen let something so valuable go. I wish I had known you had it, I'm curious what he thinks we might need it for—"

I fingered the knife in my pocket, reflecting on the conversation with Madsen before we left Terra Sera.

"Not that it matters," Demi said after a moment of silence, "I'm sure he knows what he's doing."

Demi placed the meat on top of some flat stones he'd found and put them into the fire to cook. At the same time Ava made it down from the booth upstairs, struggling to hold all of our things as she did. She eyed the remaining pile of unused rabbit beside the fire and looked away in disgust.

I went to help her with her things, taking both Demi's and my own bag off her hands. I watched her, already the light that she had back in Terra Sera had faded, though only slightly. She'd grown to keep quiet, and though nearly everything still peaked her curiosity she tended to keep it to herself more often.

"It seems better this way," she said to me as we sat down by the fire.

"What do you mean?" I asked in return.

She looked out past the double doors in the front of the theater and into the street, "She's happier now."

"Who is?"

"Mother, and so is the spirit of our world," she said, solemn.

"Gaia?" I asked, remembering the stories I was told as a child.

She nodded, staring blankly out into the street as she spoke, "the spirit is healthier now than it was, I can feel it. The plants are reclaiming what people took from them. The world was sad when this city was built, it was dying, but she's healing now, Gaia is."

"All we've ever done is destroy," I returned.

She shook her head in disappointment, "I guess that's what happens when we try to play God huh?"

"What do you mean?"

"Look at what we did," she started, tears swimming in her eyes, "we took something so perfect, so beautiful, and made it so ugly because we were never content, we always wanted more. It's no wonder why us humans are going through what we are right now, we deserve it."

I didn't know what to say, but it was true. Everything else in nature seemed to work so perfectly together, and yes, there was chaos— but there was also a simple order in that. Chaos was somehow more predictable than we were, more blissful than our too careful control, and far more justified in its actions. Ultimately it was that same chaos we found in nature that was best to govern this world, not man. What if, perhaps, our manmade order was actually true chaos, true madness? In nature, everything was just a piece of the puzzle, nothing ever asked why, and nothing ever faltered, and no one being could manipulate the world for its own private gain.

Out of all of that peace in chaos, mankind seemed to be the misplaced, a rogue piece that had found its way into the wrong box and upset the entire balance of things. It was a stubborn piece that constantly changed its shape, trying to be something different than it already was, and by doing so became the architects of its own demise. Our species built cities that spread like cancer over the world, tried to control the natural laws with science and technology, and with each so called advancement we grew even further from our own humanity and place.

"You can't say that we deserve it Ava, no one deserves this— there's a lot of good we can still do," I said, after a moment to think.

"Not all of us, just the ones that did this," she said, waving her arm towards the rest of the theater, and I'm assuming the rest of the world beyond those walls.

"Who?"

"The bad guys, the ones that did this to our planet. I don't know, the Cortecs."

"Cortecs?" I asked, never having heard that word before.

She shook her head, "It's what I call the people who did this, the people who kept pushing and destroying our world, the people driven by greed."

Demi came over then and handed me a plate with the freshly cooked rabbit, "Ever wonder why only some of us got the Gift? While others remain untouched?"

"I guess so," I started, taking a second to bite into the better cooked breakfast, "but why?"

"There are people that want to live at peace with the world, true Gaians, like us. I call them Earthies, people that are still human. Then, there are people who want to control the world, to mold it to their will. They are driven by technology and society, power. They lost their humanity a long time ago," Ava said, confident with her answer. She nodded, after another moment of contemplation, "It may be silly, I know, but I call them Cortecs."

"So that's pretty much a deeper reason for what made us Gifted and Pure in the first place?" I asked.

"Right," Demi confirmed, "but it's just a theory, of course nothing can be proven."

"Sera had to know we were better for this planet's health than they were. Sometimes I wish we could just get rid of them all and finally live happily with the world," Ava went on.

"Ava!" I exclaimed, a bit upset with the thought, "Sera gave us our gift so we could save her, if we killed all of the Pure we would be no better than they are now."

"You're right," she started, shying away, perhaps embarrassed that she had such a negative thought, "it just upsets me."

I put my hand on her shoulder, "I know, it's hard out here. I'm sorry you had to see this, but we are fighting a good war, one that will bring peace for all of us."

"How can war bring peace?" she asked.

"Well—" I began.

"—It can't," Demi intercepted, "violence only breeds more violence. This was won't end so long as one side is still alive, even if Zanin falls. The only way this suffering will end is if we extinguish their race, I'll be damned if I let them build a new world atop the graves of our fallen."

"You're wrong," I responded boldly, "the front line fights to protect those without the ability to do so themselves, for those who have lost their voice, for those who have learned to live happily despite being Gifted or Pure, for those who have thrown away the entire notion of the Stigma. We are not of different races, we are still human."

"And how's that approach working out for you? The war is well into its second decade, our conditions have only grown worse, and our enemy steadily grows better equipped to take our lives," he said in retort.

"Then we die protecting those dear to us, and die better people than they will ever be," I returned.

"But dead nonetheless, leaving the victor to freely pen history in their favor. Who would remember what we have done?"

He had a point, our deaths would mean nothing if we ultimately failed our purpose, but I couldn't let go of the hope that the masses could one day live as one.

# Chapter 22:

The rest of the morning had gone smoothly, and it felt amazing to be back out in the fresh morning air. The springtime sun was out in full force, and the light breeze on my skin was all too welcoming. I was glad to finally be away from the frigid weather near the mountains, and out here the days were much easier to bare.

The vegetation around us wore a vibrant green and the wildflowers showed off a plethora of colors. It felt good to be on the move again, it always did. I really didn't deal well with spending too much time in one place, a free spirit at heart— but it was more than just that. I wanted nothing more than to survive and I knew that comfort fostered weakness.

As we walked I took in my surroundings, finding lost in the minute details. I was happy, for the first time since I had begun to shut myself off from the world. I was okay here, and that closed door had finally begun to creak open.

It'd be another few hours until we'd make it to MarSeir, and I'd hoped to get there before the sun went down, not wanting to spend another night on the hard ground—already missing the comfort of a real bed, or at least a stack of thick blankets. Not that I liked to admit it, but I'd grown too quickly accustomed to the luxuries that Terra Sera had to offer. Part of me couldn't wait for this mission to be over so we could return, and another wished we never would. Life was so much easier there, but with comfort there many natural pleasures were lost. I could see how easily humans could detach themselves from the natural world, and despite Ava's theory of those with the gift retaining their humanity and natural habits—

even those remaining in Terra Sera were guilty of choosing to live a life of comfort and pleasure.

Everything was quiet as we left, peaceful. I mused to the soft morning symphony of the bird's song, and smiled when I saw a group of deer crossing a fractured overpass above us. Thankfully, I saw no sign of Lain, and prayed it would stay that way. I'd had enough of him for this trip, and hopefully his run in with Uru had managed to send him cowering back to Terra Sera.

Up ahead I saw movement by one of the moss covered cars. At first, I'd slowed us down until I saw Farrow climb out from an open window and onto the car's roof, pointing to us playfully. Tinker pushed himself out from underneath then, and stood, wiping off his hands on a rag as he made his way towards us.

"Tinker," Demi said, trying his hardest to remain polite.

Tinker gave him a crooked smile, but his eyes fell on me next, "Leaving so soon?"

"Afraid so, long road ahead of us," I returned.

"Ah," he said, shielding his eyes to the sun as he turned in the direction we were going, "MarSeir?"

"Ten points!" Ava blurted out, and Tinker smiled.

Demi shot her a look, perhaps telling her to hold her tongue.

"Ah, well, happy travels," Tinker began, "I've got work to do, bombs to build—you know," he finished, excusing himself, crawling back under the car. We left him in silence.

As we passed the border of the city I could see another small group making their way in off in the distance, a welcome sight. There were four of them that I could count, and I was thankful that they didn't seem to be heading in Tinker's direction, rather, they were trying to sneak straight into the maze of less traveled alleyways. I figured that they already were familiar with the city, possibly traveling from MarSeir.

The group stopped when they noticed us and raised a hand, offering a peace sign with their index and middle fingers that told me the coast ahead was clear, and wishing us well.

I passed a look over to where Tinker was, taking a moment to decide if he was safe enough to not blow them up, and decided he was—so I returned the gesture, watching as the group disappeared into the shadows.

I was relieved by their assurance, having been worried about running into another group of Agents on our way over, but then again the closer we came to MarSeir the less likely it would be to encounter a squad.

The mountains that formed around Terra Sera now lingered on the horizon, the entire system creating extreme changes in the climate. Just as the frigid air and snow within the ring swiftly changed to lush grasslands and dense forest, the land changed once more the further we got from this city. The land would become more hostile, with the vivid greens of the grasslands slowly being replaced with the diluted colors of a desert.

The damage wasn't so extreme on this side MarSeir, and had managed to hold onto most of its color and life. However, the landscape on the other side, closer to the dome, had been reduced to an arid wasteland, cracked and scorn, leading to an ocean of undulating dunes for miles on end—a land utterly destroyed by decades of war.

MarSeir acted as a station resting on the outskirts of one of the last major battlefields in the region, a place where war raged since the Pulse, and since the Pure fled to the safety of the domes. Despite the fact that most Stigma holders could use their gift to gain an advantage, being able to outmaneuver Zanin's army in the shifting sands, the army they faced was incredibly well trained and far better equipped to fight a war—often gunning an approaching wave down before a legitimate fight had the chance to break. Whenever our forces managed to push past the assault would continue to Hope, but was always quashed before they reached the gates.

"Demi," Ava said, breaking the silence.

"Yes?"

"My feet hurt, can you carry me?" she asked.

Demi shook his head no, "I'm tired too you know, do you want me to carry your bag?"

Ava copied her brother, crossing her arms and shaking her head while kicking at a rock in frustration before sitting down.

"Ava, come on," Demi pled, "it's not safe to just sit out here."

"We'll, I'm tired," she argued, looking away thoughtfully, "I guess, if you want to keep going, you can just leave me here to die," she continued with an overdramatic sigh, laying down to stare at the passing clouds.

"Ava," Demi pushed, "let's go."

"I told you, I'm tired," she pushed, "if you want me to keep going, than I guess you're just going to have to let me ride Uru the rest of the way."

Demi sighed, "You're still on about that?"

A smile broke out on Ava's face and she rocked herself back up to sit, legs crossed and grasping at her ankles, "So can I?"

Demi went to walk away in a bluff to leave her, knowing that she would inevitably follow, but I placed my hand on his shoulder to stop him, "What harm could it do? There shouldn't be many Agents, if any, on our way into MarSeir—and if we do see any then they will be far enough away for us to find cover. Besides, look at her, she could use the rest."

Demi sighed, looking to Ava, "Will it make you stop whining?"

"Maybe," She teased.

"Promise me," Demi asked.

"I promise, just let me ride him!"

A moment later Uru came into sight from behind us, like a phantom materializing out of thin air, and Ava jumped up to pet the giant wolf's mane, nearly consumed by it. He was such a gentle beast, kneeling as Demi lifted Ava up onto his back, dwarfing her in comparison.

As Demi turned I noticed something, and couldn't help but laugh, "So what's the deal with the white hair? You're starting to look like an old man."

"Yeah," Ava started, patting her brother's head, "an old man! You're starting to look like Madsen."

Demi narrowed his eyes but, to my surprise, laughed as well, "Oh anything but that."

"Is there a reason?" I asked.

"I'm not sure, but it seems to spread whenever a new summon comes out, or whenever I use my power for too long. It has to be connected but I haven't given it much thought."

"Maybe it has something to do with you being a half-god?" I asked.

"Maybe, that would make the most sense. Either way it's really starting to grow on me—"

"Literally," Ava cut him off, trying her best to stifle her laughter.

Demi sighed, "What am I going to do with you?"

"Well," Ava started, "I really do like it. I think it's beautiful, even if it does make you look like an old man."

Uru stood, as if silently commanded while Demi looked over the horizon, "We'd better get going."

As we walked in near silence, save for Ava's constant singing in the background, I fell back into my reflections of MarSeir and my youth, after the monks outside the city had left me under the care of the families there. I could hardly remember a thing from my time in the monastery, only faded memories of the monks kindness, and Dom Seir's guidance. I silently wished that they would have just kept me there, so that I could have become a monk like them and lived at least partially shielded from the war, but I guess those things weren't meant for me.

By the time I was five I was brought to the city, which was minuscule in comparison to now. It wasn't long before those willing to fight came in droves and the camp evolved, the dry land began to be carved as water cut deeper into the chasms. A maze had been created beneath the surface in an extremely short time, perhaps hastened by someone's gift, and the city was built within the growing chasm. The ground was little more than planks of wood, with water rushing underneath, constantly digging deeper. Rooms and houses would be cut into the face of the chasm wall as the camp grew, and bridges connected the gaps above. From a distance the area looked like nothing more than deserted land, but below the cracks thrived the hardiest of our kind, creating a war camp in disguise. The safety of the camp had always come from this advantage, but still, I was anxious to return.

As we got closer I watched as Demi and Ava struggled to find the hidden city on the landscape before us. I said nothing, only lead, knowing my way. They had cut wide tunnels into the rock that worked as entrances into the city. I'll admit, they weren't very well hidden, but they didn't need to be—the city below was the equivalent of a hornet's nest.

When we reached the tunnel I came to Uru's side to help Ava off, but the Naukri shied away, instead, taking the lead. I tried to imagine a beast that size trying to fit down a narrow tunnel built for humans, and couldn't help but imagine him stuck head first and needing our help to get out. I wondered if his perception of the world was different from our own, and how he saw what was ahead, perhaps forgetting there was a human on his back that wouldn't be able to phase through a wall like he might. But as he drew closer, something amazing happened. The once beast began to grow smaller, and smaller, until he was just tall enough to allow clearance for Ava's head as they passed.

"Well," Demi said with a smile, as surprised as I was, "will you look at that."

The tunnel was lit by a glowing green moss that lined walls painted with the names of the fallen, and once we reached the end we were flooded with the many sounds and vivacious energy of what MarSeir had become known for. At the bottom of the chasm there were hundreds of others moving about, carrying supplies, or just talking—probably spreading rumors and I tried to steal fragments of their conversations as we moved. Shop doors were open and busy with a steady flow of traffic and the sounds of conversation and music that remained trapped within the chasm walls was deafening at first. I felt like we were back in the marketplace of Terra Sera, but to me—this felt more like home.

By the time we arrived night had already welcomed us and I knew that we needed both food, and a place to stay. I remembered my coin pouch, which mostly consisted of precious stones rather than actual coins. I lead Demi and Ava blindly through the streets, the chasm having been cut down further into the earth than I had last remembered, and anywhere that I might have known was now lost in the intricate web of bridges above us. Of course, after all of these years my memory of the city was a little foggy, and much more had been built. My main focus was staying safe, and that meant staying in the center of town—even with everyone here, the end of the chasm's felt closer to danger.

I found an inn a few doors down, with a sign that said *vacancy*. We entered to see an older man behind a wooden desk, he looked up for a moment, acknowledging us, before returning to his book. I went up to the desk to ask for a room.

"All full," he said, not bothering to look up from his book.

I turned, passing a look to Demi and Ava, "But the sign says you have a vacancy," I pushed on.

"Well now, that depends," the man returned.

I knew where this was going, "On?" I asked anyway.

"On how pretty a penny you have to offer," the man said, pushing his book aside to clear off space on his table, and looking at me with a hint of greed in an eye that lacked the Stigma's mark.

I took out my pouch and poured it on the table, being careful not to let one roll away on me.

"Ah," he said as he took a magnifying glass and began to pick them up one at a time, examining them. "Axinite, rose quartz, purple agate, oh—opalite very nice, malachite, and this one, hmm, oh yes—ocean jasper. And ah, what's this?" he said as he picked up one of my darker stones. It'd been polished, and the glare from a candle behind him danced on its smooth surface—but beyond that you could see the shimmer of golds and blues underneath, with deep black lines carving through".

"Labradorite sir," I told him.

"And where did you find this? This isn't anything I see too commonly around here," he said, beginning to put the other stones back into my cloth pouch, leaving the labradorite on the table.

"I traded for it, with some travelers from up north. They had loads of it," I said, proud of my find.

"Ah, well then—this will afford you, say, one night here."

I was baffled, wanting to snatch the stone off the table and find another inn, "But I traded them a deer big enough to feed them for a week, it has to be worth more than that."

"A week's worth of food for a stone they had loads of? Can you not see the error in your trade? You present me with a common stone, as you said, and expect to carry your ignorance onto my business. I'll have you know I'm a better judge than that," he said, picking up the stone and rolling it over in his palm. "Shame, and it has such beauty," he said, placing it back into the pouch and handing it back to me.

"But just a night?" I pushed on.

"You're in MarSeir love, if you're here to fight I doubt you'll be alive come tomorrow. I can't have you keeping my rooms empty for the night now can I?" he said, victorious.

I stood there a moment, and looked to Demi to take charge but he offered only a shrug— I should have known he wouldn't be of much help.

I fished the stone back out of my pouch and put it back on the table, "Do you like it?"

"You know I do," he responded.

"Two nights, if we don't return by sundown tomorrow you can keep it and sell our room," I said, hoping to sway him.

The man looked at the stone once more, and took it in his hand. He sighed and leaned back in his chair, grabbing a key that hung on the wall before handing it to me, "Sundown. Tomorrow."

"Thank you," I said politely, hiding my delight of this minor victory.

As we headed for the door he called after us with a touch of annoyance in his voice, "Wouldn't you like to know where exactly your room is?"

"Sorry, yes," I returned.

He pointed to the left, "Out of door there's a side chasm to your left, third door down."

"Thank you," I said as we walked back out into the street.

We made it into the room, and immediately threw our things onto the floor, happy to be rid of the extra weight. Ava had already collapsed onto the unmade bed and I was surprised to see a mattress beneath them, which was always a rare delight.

The grumbling in my stomach broke my train of thought.

"I need food," I told Demi, who was changing into new clothes he'd taken out of a dresser beside the bed. I passed him a sour look, realizing that the man at the counter had just sold us someone else's room, someone who'd probably just made the same deal we did and hadn't returned. I wondered if he would come back, though I silently hoped he'd simply gotten too drunk at a local bar to find his way to the room.

Demi shrugged my look off, and got comfortable, going over to his bag to fish out some coins from Terra Sera.

"And where were those when we needed them?" I scorned.

"You seemed to be handling yourself just fine, I thought you were a strong, independent woman?" he defended, handing me the pouch, "I've got dinner, I'm going to stay here with Ava, you know I can't leave her alone. Just bring me something back."

"Anything in particular?" I asked, tucking the pouch away.

"Whatever you can find, you can only get so hungry before you stop caring what it is you eat right?" he said, laughing as he fell onto the bed beside Ava.

"Right. I'll be back," I returned, heading back into the alleyway.

# Chapter 23:

I moved my way through the streets alone, thankful that so far that no one recognized me—I preferred to keep it that way. I felt silly in my concern, how could they? The last anyone here would have seen me was when I was a child, and even so, most of the people I'd known would have been killed off or driven out by now. Still, I recognized a few battle worn faces as I passed by.

Every corner was shrouded in darkness, the streets lit only with the dim flicker of candlelight that painted orange the moss covered walls of the chasm. Most of the people out at this hour were drunk and more than just occasionally I would see someone stumble out of a door onto the street, and only sometimes gather their balance before mixing back in with the crowd. Though many of the faces have changed, at least their habits hadn't in all this time so I shouldn't have been too surprised when I noticed some men straggling behind me.

Two men about my age, perhaps a few years older had been following me since I'd left the inn, now just a few feet behind me. Every now and then one would stop and talk to a passerby, but at least one was always close behind. I guess being a new girl in town had a way of catching a man's attention. I thought, maybe, I could just walk back to where Demi and Ava were, but then again I would show these creeps exactly where I would be staying.

I decided to my best option would be to lose them on my own, knowing I couldn't rely on Demi to save me—he would enjoy that too much. Looking ahead, I spotted an alleyway to my right, hoping that if I could duck around the corner and sprint to the other side than perhaps I would be out of sight by the time they came around. It was that or keep wandering aimlessly hoping that they end their pursuit, something had to be done. I took the next opening that I could and made a dash for the other end, but I'd only made it a few steps before my sprint slowed to a staggered walk before halting altogether.

"Shit," I murmured to myself—being faced with a dead end. I'd been calm until now, but suddenly I felt something drop to the pit of my stomach, I felt sick and alone. My eyes darted frantically for something to climb, knowing that even to escape the chasms would be better than to fulfill their intentions. There was nothing, not a bin to climb on, not a ladder to reach a high up window, and nothing I could hide behind. I had to have picked the worst alley in the damned camp to be trapped in.

I saw the silhouette of the first man enter the alleyway, he turned, facing the direction he came and yelled, "Over here!" The sound echoed, and with each wave that hit me I felt an increased level of panic.

The men started towards me, but I kept my distance, back pedaling toward the dead end, trying to buy whatever time I could. I thought about yelling for help, but feared that I would only provoke them into attacking me sooner. The two walked side by side, creating a wall in front of me so that I couldn't rush by. I clutched my hand to my chest, my heartbeat racing.

I remembered the knife in my pocket, and shoved my hand deep to find it, damning myself for stocking my pockets full with useless junk. My hand wrapped around its smooth handle at last and I used a free finger to unfold the blade. The men had almost reached me when my back hit the wall, the unexpected jolt pushing my finger into the blade's sharp edge. I let out a startled gasp, feeling like a bolt of ice had splintered up my arm, radiating from the small cut.

Suddenly my world began to shake, but not shake—vibrate. The walls on either side of me began to show pure white streaks, jittering as they came into reality, starting at the top and spreading downward. With every vibration they would split—creating more streaks that would run further down the wall. My heart raced faster and the ground began to quake, small pebbles now jumping off the ground. The view outside the alleyway began to sway as if the entire scene had been set on a hinge, until it was replaced entirely with white space, leaving only a thin black outline of what had once existed there.

I noticed the men once more, they weren't far now, merely a few feet from grabbing hold of me. They jest over their plans, nudging with their elbows and nodding toward me with sinister smiles as if this was a game to them. As if the world wasn't in a bad enough place already. Still, they didn't seem to notice what was going on around them, or was this only happening to me?

A moment later a black pulse burst from my body, ripping through the white space like a stone cast into a calm lake. My heartbeat slowed to only a beat every two or three seconds, and rang loud in my ears when it did.

Thump.

I was frozen with fear.

Looking down, I seemed to levitate over nothing but further expanse of white space as if I were suspended in the air by some unseen force. Beneath me there were more shapes, cubes and spheres drifting slowly in the void. They'd take different forms, as if trying them out, but always returning back to their original shapelessness. I felt like I should be falling through this space, though here, I didn't know which way gravity might take me.

My eyes focused on a black sphere moving beneath me, it began to bulge from one side, as if something was trying to force its way out. A small orb fell from the sphere, and took a form that I recognized immediately. The creature's oversized head, with its large oval yellow eyes stared up at me. Its two antennae shot to attention and it used its rabbit-like legs to sprint back over to the still moving sphere, which was now drifting upwards, and dove back into it head first. It was a Kurki, but what was it doing here?

Thump.

On either side of me were gelatinous walls that would ripple and roll like oil on the water's surface, but roughly held their shape. A thin smoke fumed off them, and I noticed small bolts of electricity spurting out of the larger plumes like a miniature thunderstorm.

Thump.

I looked to the men, they were of the same material but had taken a more solid form shrouded by a thin black mist as I'd seen linger around Demi's summons. Their pace slowed, actually they were hardly moving at all. Joyfully sinister expressions were still painted on their faces, ill intent shown through their now yellow eyes, and I could see slight movement on their lips. Everything around me had seemed to be frozen in time. Even I moved slowly, though when I looked at myself I wasn't of the same matter that everything else seemed to be. I was solid, and white—every detail was outlined in black lines.

Thump.

I felt sick, trying to wrap my mind around what was going on but the sound of my slow heartbeat kept ringing out in my ear, making it hard to focus. There was something brewing inside of me and suddenly, I felt a as if that energy began to tug at my very soul.

Slowly, a dark figure began to stretch itself out of me, an oily goo dripping off as it did. Its head was free first, and rolled forward—a black sludge strung between us, like a web, connecting us. Its shoulders came next and its whole body lurched forward. Its arms reached out in front as if finding stability on an invisible surface to help drag the rest of its body out faster. It drew out slowly, at first, but once free burst into a sprint for the men before me. The figure quickly took a solid human form once free.

I was terrified of what I saw before me—a mirror image of myself, only, transformed into something that chilled me to the core.

I gasped, realizing I'd seen her in a dream — remembering the night we spent after leaving Terra Sera. I had a dream where I witnessed what happened when Demi saved me. Whatever had just come out of me was the same creature from that night and killed those Agents, and here it was again.

Thump.

I watched in shock as this creature, this darker self-dipped in between the two men slicing through one of them with serrated claws that formed over its gauntleted hands. The felled man seemed untouched at first, but moments later his torso began to drift away from his body, separated in solid pieces. The figure stood up behind them, and made its way back to me with a slow walk, staring me in my eye.

It stopped just a few inches from my face, "Embrace me," it whispered softly in my ear, before stepping back into my body.

Everything went back to normal, the white space subsided and time continued its normal pace. I was short of breath, looking around me in wonder when the wet sound of a man's body hitting the floor brought me back to reality.

The man that was left alive stumbled back up against the wall in terror, covered in his friend's blood, he was trembling at the sight, and angry—but too scared to try act on that emotion. He looked at me, pointing with a quivering finger, "What power," he started with a pause, "you're a demon!" he shouted before running back out into the street.

*Worse*, the crept into my mind as if a word whispered in the wind.

I was panicked, but needed to stay calm, knowing I needed to get out of here before someone else stumbled in on this mess, I was lucky no one had already. I stepped over the halved body of my victim and made my way for the street. It was still busy as ever and little time seemed to pass through that ordeal, many of the same people were still walking about the street so I escaped back into the crowd as if nothing had ever happened.

I'd barely made it a few feet away from the alleyway before I heard Demi's voice call after me. I turned, to see him frantically dodging everyone as he made his way through the crowd.

"Are you okay? Where did the other one go?" he shot out, fuming.

I pretended that I didn't know what he meant, "What are you talking about, and what other one—are you okay?"

He sighed and gave me a look that shot through my bluff, knowing I was lying, "I know what happened Sage. I've sent the Kurki to track that man down, they were—"

He started but I cut him off mid-sentence, "Were what? Watching me? Are you having your little pets follow me now?" I spat out sharply, though it was ill deserved.

He watched me for a moment, silent, "That's not what—" he began again.

I talked over him once more, "Not what? That's not what you meant to happen? For me to find out? If you had such a close eye on me then why did you let those men get so close, the Kurki could have done something!"

"No, that's not it, listen!" he plead, a hint of frustration in his voice.

"No, you listen," I said in a calmer voice, I was angry and knew I was taking my frustrations out on him, but I couldn't control my temper as it flared, "You have no right keeping tabs on me." I didn't give him the chance to respond before I walked away leaving him in the middle of the street, looking like a lost child.

I felt childish myself, walking through the streets alone with my head to the ground like I had just been yelled at by a parent. I'd been furious, and lost control, but to some degree I didn't want to control this feeling. For once I had felt a power inside me stronger than myself and I relished in that sense of empowerment. I knew the outburst wasn't well deserved, but I was angry— angry at the men who would have attacked me, angry at myself for killing one of them, angry at Demi for having the Kurki watch over me and still come late to my rescue. I cringed at the thought, I'd spent my whole life fending for myself, relying on Demi's watchfulness I'd grown to let my guard down and it had almost cost me my life.

I'd decided to wander some more, figuring that word of a dead man in the alley would have spread by now, which gave me at least some sense of immunity while everyone stood on edge. It'd been an hour or so before I found my way back to the room Demi, Ava and I would share for the night.

I tried the door and it wouldn't budge. I cursed silently and knocked instead. There was a window to the right of the door, and I saw Ava peek through the curtain. I took a step back and smiled at her. A moment later I heard the sound of furniture dragging across the floor, and a number of locks being clicked open.

A barricade? So where was Demi?

Ava opened the door and pulled me in, hugging me tightly, "You're safe!" her words were muffled in my chest.

"Of course I am, where's Demi?" I was upset with him still but in a city foreign my concern outweighed my anger.

"You mean he never found you?" she pulled away, looking at me with worrisome eyes.

I rolled my eyes, "How could he not? With the Kurki keeping an eye on me and all."

"Sage," she paused, her voice low, "the Kurki weren't following you, they sensed an incredibly strong spiritual force enter their world. They came to tell Demi what was going on. Didn't he tell you?"

My heart sank, and I found it difficult to speak. He had tried to tell me, but I was too angry to listen. He wasn't keeping tabs on me, he'd come running the moment he knew I may have been in danger. I felt terrible, and now he was out chasing down a criminal in an unfamiliar place.

My head pounded and I winced at the pain.

Ava gave me a concerned look, "Were you hurt?" Ava asked.

"No, I'm fine," I lied, "let's go, we need to find him."

I wasn't fine, my head was pounding to the core, my vision had blurred at the edges, and that energy— it began to surface once more until I felt the same as I had in the alleyway. Ava followed me closely, though I hadn't an idea where I was going to look first. I was disoriented and confused, my entire world seeming to spin around me as even the simplest things like walls, or the ground became unfamiliar.

There was a buzzing in my ear not so much like a passing fly, but a chatter, and it drove me. I followed the noise, moving through the crowd, often stopping to look around before changing direction. I felt out of place, detached from myself and all else around me. I could hardly make out the faces of the people who passed me by, though I had an overwhelming sensation that everyone's eyes were drawn to me.

Ava's hand rested on my shoulder, "Sage?"

The chatter inside my head's volume had gone down significantly as I came back to my senses, I looked to Ava and nodded, "Sorry," I said before looking out into the crowd with new intent.

I tried to narrow in on the sources, picking them apart. As I watched I could see that their lips didn't match the words that had started to form out of the chatter as I isolated a source. I looked to another, a man passing me by, he wasn't talking to anyone yet I could hear him clearly, though his words made no coherent sense. It was a stream of unfinished sentences, and references to what I could only assume to be his memories. Occasionally an idea would pop up and be replaced, sometimes entertaining one longer than others. The stream was scattered and unorganized.

I looked to another, and pushed myself to focus in on the chatter. It was a young man, about my age talking to others in a small group. His back was towards me, though I caught short glimpses of his face as he looked over his shoulder often. His

stream was more organized, focused, yet panicked to a degree—
not matching his calm demeanor.

I pushed deeper, focusing in on the stream of thoughts, trying
to place them in order. It was difficult, his mind kept jumping from
one thing to another.

*Distractions*, a voice told me, and I noticed a pattern. He'd
entertain one idea for a short time until it began to stray, then look
over his shoulder before hastily forcing himself to put his mind
onto something else. He was using too much energy to keep his
mind off of something, but what?

He checked over his shoulder once more, eyeing me for the
first time.

*Is that her?* The thought escaped him, and I had my answer.
This man had been so nervous because suddenly he didn't feel safe
on the streets anymore, fearful that I might hunt him down. He
excused himself from the others in his group and began to walk
through the crowd.

I looked to Ava, who'd been trying her best to seem occupied
behind me, looking at fruit on a farm stand a few feet away. I
cracked a slight smile when I saw her asking the merchant about
nearly everything he had in stock.

She looked back after a moment, "Oh!" she said, thanking the
merchant for a gifted apple before skipping over and jumping into
place before me with a thud.

"Let's go, I have a lead," I said, motioning in the direction we
needed to go.

She nodded, "And I have an apple!" she said, taking her first
bite into a fruit foreign to her, wincing at its bitterness.

I gave her a stern, almost motherly, look trying to mimic those
from one of the many woman that helped raise me and the smile

faded from her face. I seemed to be worrying about Demi more than she had been. We followed the man through the streets, being careful to stay far enough behind to not draw unneeded attention to ourselves. Before long he'd ducked into a side alleyway and passing by, I saw a glimpse of him entering and closing a doorway partway down. I paused, if the Kurki were any good at tracking they should have found this place by now, meaning Demi would be close as well. I led Ava down the alleyway to the door, a sign hung above it, "BarSeir," it read.

I opened the door, flooding the alleyway with not only the sound of conversation and laughter, but the foul smell of spilt beer and poorly washed men as I lead Ava to an empty side table.

Demi was sitting amongst a few other men at a table in a darkened corner of the room opposite to us. From the looks of things he hadn't noticed we were here, and more so, had won the trust of those around him. He bantered with and talked to the group with overly animated gestures, seeming to tell a story that had made all of the others at his table laugh.

I took short glances around the room. There was a couple of girls a few tables over with one man who had propped one leg up on a pulled out chair, leaning over it while talking to them. Near the bar was another small cluster of men, ordering drinks. They kept gesturing over our way, stealing glances and nudging one of the smaller men, laughing as they did. A few moments later he gave in to his friends, ordered an extra drink and made his way over to me.

I shot a quick glance to Demi's table, hoping he had caught onto what was happening. I felt silly for chasing him down and coming here, for risking Ava's safety without a plan and I thought of what his might be.

The humor had left Demi's group and he, along with a couple others, had leaned toward the middle of the table to talk in hushed voices. The man that was speaking had his eyes fixed in my direction as he spoke, pointing, and I could see Demi slyly peek over his shoulder.

My attention was broken as the approaching man reached my table, "New around here?" his voice was smoother than I'd expected, "Care for a drink?" he continued before I had the chance to answer, placing a glass on the table before me.

I smiled shyly, but avoided his eyes, catching a glimpse of Demi rising from his seat. I looked back to the man at my table, "Returning actually," I started, "and thank you but no, a girl in these parts got to be careful these days."

His expression became more serious but he faked a smile, "I suppose you're right," he said, watching me a little more intently. He looked over his shoulder to the group that had pushed him to talk to me, as if for some sort of guidance before he continued, "I'm sorry, but have we met before?"

When his eyes met mine I felt as if a sharp spike had pricked my heart. Fear overwhelmed me and my mind was flooded with mental chatter once more. As I focused his thoughts began to make sense to me. I felt the now familiar energy bubbling up inside me, like a kettle about to boil over.

There existed nothing but myself and that man—rather, I saw him in tunnel vision, all else around us unmoving and blurred. I felt a connection between us and a swift sense of being thrust down that tunnel and into him.

Suddenly I was back in the labyrinth that had been in my dreams, only, this one was different. The walls resembled that of the chasm itself, and opened up to the nighttime sky. Here, like in my own maze, there were rows of rooms consisting of played back memories. The symbols on the walls looked like they had been painted on, but soon began to glow a soft turquoise against the red-orange stone. I began to walk through the halls, quickly realizing that the rooms I passed by hadn't consisted of memories that belonged to me, no, they were his.

When I stumbled upon the scene from the alleyway my heart sank when I found the answer to his question.

The kettle had boiled over at that moment, and there was a pulse that rippled through this space.

The white space had returned, and as before I felt paralyzed with fear. Around me, everyone had become made of the same gaseous, oily black matter that I'd seen before. Everything had slowed down. I spotted Demi off to the side, his stride was not broken, he was the only one who seemed unaffected, "What have you done?" he scorned.

I felt sick as the energy poured out of me. The darkened image of myself had started to pull itself out of me, with more ease than it had before. It stopped just an inch from the man's face and whispered, "I'm sorry," it said, pausing before continuing in a voice that was not my own, a man's voice, "but I'm afraid we have."

The figure leaned forward as if to kiss the man, brushing his cheek as it smiled and took a long stride through him instead. The man's form burst into small orbs of shifting matter in space, like water thrown into the air. A gas cloud had formed around the gelatinous masses sending off small bolts of electricity that shot between them drawing them closer to each other, connecting and forming into larger objects.

The black image of myself had burst into a frenzy, and after only a few moments it had made its way across the room, slicing through each person with ease. Demi kept his distance, and focused on the black orbs of matter that the figure had sent spewed across the room with every kill. Demi would raise a hand, focusing on one and it would begin to emit a gas that attracted the other chunks to it, building mass. As they grew they began to take the shape of Kurki, that once finished were already running towards the enemy. The Kurki thrust themselves at the figure, but each one that attacked was swiftly destroyed.

All had fallen.

I shot Demi a worried glance, paralyzed with a mixture of fear and confusion, he stood with two Vemosa looming behind him, their long white masks and giant circular eyes coupled with their bladed arms beneath a tattered black robe was menacing, even if I knew they were on my side. Demi was hesitant to send them to attack.

My copy stopped, and took a stance facing Demi, hunched over and letting its arms hang by its side.

It was remarkable, looking exactly like me but radiated evil intent. Her clothes were tight, and leathery— churning and oily like the matter everything else here seemed to be made of, and formed atop her lavender skin. A pair of gauntlets had covered her hands and forearms, forming long staggered claws on each finger that broke at each knuckle into inward points like scales—meant to pierce her prey easily and cause the most damage when ripping her hand away. A blindfold of black mist covered her eyes as if to shield her from her own horrors.

Demi grit his teeth, "I'll kill you."

The figure cocked its head to the side, and began to walk toward me. Its voice was not my own, it was the same man's voice it had spoken in before, "You can't do that."

"And why not?"

"If you kill me," the figure began pausing in front of me, "than you kill her as well," it finished, before falling back into my body.

I was shocked back into reality, gasping for breath, and left barely conscious. Demi had rushed to help me up, throwing one of my arms over his shoulder. I leaned forward with dead weight. It was difficult to walk, so I just stumbled forward, relying on Demi to guide me. I felt as if all of my energy had been drained.

Ava pushed open the door to the alleyway. She was panicked, silent. I rolled my head sluggishly to look at the bar, only to see the blurred sight of the bodies I'd left on the floor. What a mess I've made.

We made it to the alleyway, but before we could make it a couple of steps further a large man in a robe took the corner from the street in a hurry. I was fading in and out of consciousness, each time I closed my eyes I'd see a shutter image of that dark figure moving through the bar, stepping over bodies on the floor, a sinister smile on its face as it made its way to the door— following me.

The robed man ran up to us, immediately helping Demi support my weight.

"And who are you?" Demi asked curiously, though he didn't seem to mind the help.

"A friend," the robed man finally spoke in a deep accent, "It's best if we get you out of MarSeir as soon as we can. You guys just made a lot of enemies in there, not that there is anyone left alive to point you out."

Demi shot the man a look, "All but you," he said half-heartedly.

"No need for threats, I mean you no harm. Now let's go," the man said hurrying us along.

# Chapter 24:

I awoke on a bed hard as stone in a dark room, lit only by the soft glow of candles that sat in a row on a wax covered shelf and a single ray of morning sunlight that had found its way in through a high up window, a spotlight to a thousand dust particles dancing to the rhythm of a faint breeze.

My body ached when I tried to sit, and my mind was in a painful fog. I could hardly remember anything that happened, or how I ended up here, but still, this place was vaguely familiar to me.

The entire room was made of stone, even the bed which was topped with soft, but worn, blankets in the center as the only semblance of furniture. Carved into the walls were depictions of Sera and Klaus and the story of how they had used so much of their power to create the spirit of the earth, Gaia, and life, that they were forced to lie dormant in the rocks, spending their lives keeping constant care of the fabric that holds this world together.

I stood and began to walk along the wall, tracing the carvings with my outstretched finger and studying the objects placed in several long, cut out, rectangular inlets in the wall that acted like shelves. There was a top beside some books that rested overlapping each other, a doll, and some blocks. I smiled as I picked up that top, brushing the dust off, realizing life was much like the top's movements—everything thing seemed so smooth and beautiful in my youth, but one wobble could unravel my entire life.

A couple feet from the ground were crude stick figure drawings in chalk. Kneeling down, I took a closer look, one was of a young girl that had a shadow with black wings lingering behind her— the only break in the darkness was to show a sinister smile.

In another, the same girl was standing beside a young woman, both smiling and holding hands. I wondered who they were, and what they meant to this world. I wondered where they may be now, knowing that these drawings had been done years ago, and silently wishing that I could only just speak with them, hoping to share in their delight.

Besides that, another showed the girl surrounded by monks, all smiling.

My eyes had begun to water as my memories began to find me. I reached out to the drawing as if touching it would make the thought more real in my own mind. I was overwhelmed with emotion as suddenly it settled in, this wasn't just anyone's room—it was mine.

"You're awake, good. So nice of you to pay us a visit after all these years. I see you've fared well," an older man's voice rang out from the doorway, startling me to attention.

I stood to face him, and my heart was filled with childish joy, "Dom Seir!" I nearly screamed with excitement, moving across the room and into his embrace, "It's good to see you, but, how did you find me?"

The ridges I remember on his face had gotten deeper in the years I've been away, some seemed as deep as the chasm's themselves. It was hard to believe anyone could smile as much as he could in these dark times.

"Child," his voice was calm, "do you forget my gift?"

"No, you're a far-seer, but your visions would only have shown you that I would return—not when."

"This is true," he began, "your power has grown beyond my own expectations, but to be fair, you gave us warning of your arrival."

"I don't feel very powerful, or even in control of my own gift," I said with a sigh, "It's as if there's another force inside of me that pushes me aside and takes over. I lose control. Still, how did you know where and when to find me? Exact time is beyond your predictions isn't it?"

He nodded, and smiled joyfully, "That wasn't anything I had planned," his words came out with a laugh, "which is why I was so surprised when your power surfaced so close to home."

"So, someone told you I was in the city? Those thugs?" I asked curiously.

"Oh! I'd almost forgotten to thank you for that, those boys were causing quite a bit of trouble around the camp," he said, a bit too happy about their demise.

"Whether they were causing trouble or not, killing them doesn't feel right," I started, memories of last night beginning to form.

"You did the right thing, and the camp a favor, if it wasn't you than they would have targeted another girl and I'm afraid she may not have been so lucky."

I was troubled by the thought, hardly being one to kill, and though death had made a habit of following me I seldom was the one with blood on my hands. I was conflicted, having taken lives but ridding the camp of criminals. Was that my fault? What if I hadn't put myself in that situation? I shook my head, if it wasn't me someone else would have been trapped like I was. Those men were still bad regardless of my actions so truly my actions were a justice to the others who might have been a target. Still, the feeling didn't sit well with me.

The Dom must have sensed I was delving deep into an unwanted thought and changed the subject hastily, "As for someone tipping me off? Impossible. Fourteen years have passed since you left the monastery, and only slightly less since you left MarSeir, you hardly resemble the young girl those of us who are still alive remember. You tipped us off to your own return!"

"How?"

"We weren't sure it was you at first when we felt the first energy spike, but with sheer intensity of the second spike we knew it had to be," he said with excitement.

"That's interesting, the Kurki had told Demi of some sort of energy spike after my first attack in the alleyway," I said more to myself than to Dom Seir.

"The Kurki?" he asked curiously.

"Oh, they are these creatures that live in the other realm, Demi can summon them here to help him fight."

Dom Seir stroked his beard, grasping its long white hairs and pulling them down to a point in his fist, "Do you know if he can travel there himself?"

I told him of how I remembered being back in the bar, Demi had been the only one other than myself not affected by whatever was going on, though he did seem confused by it.

"This boy—" he began with a pause as if contemplating what he was going to say next, "I'd heard only rumors, but with that power perhaps they are true, he must be—"

"The bastard son of Klaus," Demi's voice came before I could see him.

"Oh my Goddess, you do exist," Dom Seir said, holding a gaze at Demi in a fit of stupor, then to me as if for reassurance. He sighed, "It seems as though I can't see all things and fate has brought you two together, however it may complicate things."

"As if things weren't complicated enough already," Demi scoffed.

I ignored his comment, "How so?"

"I've waited years to have this conversation Sage," the Dom said, pausing to glance at Demi, then back to me before continuing, "I just wish it weren't under these circumstances, but it's time for you to know the truth. Follow me," and with that he turned to lead us through the monastery.

He had lead us into a hallway with similar carvings as my old room, though significantly more detailed and in greater length. As we walked he told us of what had happened, "After the Pulse, as I'm sure you know, a gift was granted to a significant amount of the world's population. This was our Goddess Sera's call to arms after her discovery and capture—truly it was meant as a last resort. This was before the fall that lead to Zanin's rise to power.

However, a much darker beast had been awakened by the Pulse, and filled with rage for his lost lover, reaped havoc on all who stood in his way, Pure and Gifted alike. The gift had become feared, a Stigma, and the purge began. That is when a young Madsen had come to me and my brothers with a proposal," he paused, nodding to Demi who looked wholly uninterested. Dom Seir continued, "Madsen was convinced that with Klaus subdued, proper relations could form between the Gifted and Pure, and with the war's projected end, Gaia could heal. The idea was to stop Klaus' rampage, at least until order was resolved."

It was then that the I remembered the second man the book had shown me many nights ago, now knowing it was the Councilor looking down before Dom Seir.

Demi laughed beneath his breath, "I see that plan worked well, nearly the whole world is a battlefield."

The Dom nodded to Demi, acknowledging the truth in that statement, "It could have been far worse. The night of Madsen's arrival I had a vision, Klaus had been running into battle against others of our kind. I feared that power, and knew we needed time to create peace, at least amongst ourselves. We couldn't hope to kill him even if he wasn't at his full strength, and I wasn't sure if that would the wisest choice if we managed to succeed. However, we could defeat him by other means."

We paused along the wall, the carvings depicted a pregnant woman being carried into the monastery by the monks. Madsen and Dom Seir were standing atop the highest steps watching. The next scene was of a room with strange symbols painted on the floor, and a table in the middle where the woman had been laid on.

"Having been a monk here prior to the Pulse, we had certain advantages. There had been a ritual meant to call the god's, if done correctly they would be compelled to appear before us," the Dom continued.

We'd reached the end of the hallway, in front of us there were two giant double doors. I'd grown nervous, realizing it had the same markings as the door in the labyrinth of my dreams. Though, the patterns and shapes stood still, unlike in my dreams where they would shift and weave amongst each other.

It'd become difficult to speak, but I begged the question, "So what does this have to do with me?"

Dom Seir looked at me with kind, compassionate eyes, smiling before opening the door to reveal the same ritual room that had been carved on the wall. Before us was a staircase that lead down into a circular dirt floor. Around the ritualistic center as an incline were rows of benches, many of which were filled with monks waiting for our arrival. There were circular patterns drawn on the ground, and around those lines marked the same symbols that I'd come to recognize from that labyrinth. He motioned for us to enter.

The doors closed behind us, and locked into place. Dom Seir led us down into the ring. He looked at me solemnly, "Madsen had brought the woman to me after she sustained wounds during a sweep of her town for anyone who had the gift." He sighed, placing his hand on the bed in the middle of the ring, "We conducted the ritual to lure Klaus into our chambers just after placing an enchantment on the room. Once here, the Gift became useless and we would have to rely on our existing rituals and strength to succeed. It was the only way we could hope to trap him."

The Dom paced the floor, reflective, thoughtful, "The ritual had worked as planned, a rift tore into the center of the room from the other realm and out of it came Klaus. He was arrogant, rude, and demanding the reason of his summoning. The entire ordeal had been practiced a hundred times before, and timing was key. Another ritual had been finished the moment of his arrival, trapping the God, and placing him within the woman's unborn child. She made a sacrifice to help save our people and died giving birth to a child who ultimately held the key to our survival. That child—"

*Is you.*

# Chapter 25:

I clutched my hand to my chest, my heart pounding as I began to imagine that creature, that monster, that demon, our lost God trapped inside me. This energy brewing within that would sometimes boil over when I was in danger, was the same energy that caused the entire world to fear our kind, the same energy that built this world to begin with. I thought of the visions, of what I thought were false memories—and I thought of that voice, that faint whisper in my ear urging me forward whenever I was in danger.

But why? Why save the person who is acting as your prison? If I died wouldn't he be set free? I cringed at the thought but found peace in the fact that despite all that has ever threatened me, he has not let me die. He needed me, but why?

He must have still been too weak to exist in this physical world, too weak to fight on his own. He needed a vessel to grow, he needed me and, in a way, I needed him. He was growing stronger every day, and I wondered what would happen when my usefulness ran out.

I shot a worried look to Demi, tears swelling in my eyes, and reached out to grasp his hand for comfort but found only emptiness in its place. The look of disgust, of confusion, of hate, and of love washed over his too perfect face in one mangled expression. His eyes had glossed over, but no tears fell. He'd pulled away from me, as if my touch would burn him. Staggering back, he shook his head, "How could you do this to me?"

I let out a sob, fighting through the tears, "I didn't know," I said, trembling. In a moment he was gone, nearly sprinting out of the room, fist clenched by his side.

I started toward him, but Dom Seir's hand rested on my shoulder, holding me back.

"Klaus' bastard son he said?" Dom Seir asked as if for reassurance.

I nodded, biting my lip as I held back my tears.

"He'll be back," the Dom said casually, turning to face the stone bed that rested in the middle of the room, his fingers tracing the symbols carved into the stone. He sighed, "Let's just hope it's for the right reasons."

I looked to Dom Seir with a worrisome look.

"He will be back," the Dom assured me, "until then we need to make sure you are ready for when he does. Right now he's deciding whether or not to stand by your side, or kill you. Torn between his love for you, and his hate for his father."

"So what do I do? Just sit here and hope he doesn't kill me?"

"No," he said, using one hand to motion the other monks to close the door, "it's time now for you to realize your power, to learn to control it so that when he does return you will be ready."

"I won't fight him."

"Only because right now you can't. The time has come Sage, you must fulfill your destiny."

"To kill Demi?" I questioned, hesitating at the thought.

Dom Seir sighed in frustration, "No child, Demi is but an inconvenience to our plan—with Klaus reborn, there may be some glimmer of hope for our kind."

"How? Hasn't he done enough? Isn't he the whole reason people began to fear us? And isn't that the reason why you trapped him in the first place?"

"Lay down," the Dom said, patting the stone table with an empty palm, "it will all become clear in a moment."

"But—" I began, he put a finger to his lips, silencing me. I followed his direction, pushing myself up to sit on the table. Around me the staggered piers circling the room were being filled by more and more monks making their way into the chamber. Candlelight flickered and danced with an invisible breeze, and though dozens burned I felt a chill to my very core.

Dom Seir placed a hand on my shoulder, easing me down to the cold stone, "It'll all become clear," he repeated, hovering a hand over my body, "Soon, you will realize your power."

My eyes rested closed, but I could feel the presence of his hands over my body, his energy passing through me like an invisible wave. "What are you doing?" I asked.

"Quiet. I must focus," the waves passing through me intensified, "I am going to help you awaken your chakras."

"My chakras?"

"It is the energy that flows within you, like seven dams holding back a once raging river. If blocked, the river grows stagnant and withheld. Your energy is trapped within, but once unleashed you will know power beyond your current dreams. Your chakras have been blocked since birth, to help hold Klaus behind those dams."

I smirked at that, "That would explain why my powers never came."

"Indeed it does, now, quiet."

I nodded my head, and adjusted my body to be more comfortable. I would have hoped for some soft blanket to fit between myself and the stone but I guess the monks here didn't believe in comfort. I relaxed, and began to focus on the energy moving through me. It was an odd feeling as Dom Seir hovered his hands over me, I couldn't see him, but I could feel his energy. Small spots ran up my body, feeling like a hot marble was rolling in place on my skin wherever the Dom's hands had stopped.

I focused on those spots, and the pressure would build as the energy crashed against those dams. I felt no pain but, as the tension built, the rolling energy became more and more intense until it began to overwhelm me.

I focused on the Dom's words instead, "You are traveling through a doorway in space, a portal to a new world. You are the sun, the moon, and the stars. You are the universe—and the universe is you."

As his words washed over me I found myself in space, walking on a thin film of water with grid lines just beneath the surface that gave off a soft white pulsing glow. The beauty of the universe above reflected off the water, looking like glass, but rippling as I walked past. The horizon was endless, in all directions, and above me I could see everything, all of the distant planets with their vibrant colors and gaseous clouds, all of the shooting stars, and all of the constellations. The entire sky danced around me, spinning slowly like it was trapped in some vast ocean's gyre as I continued to explore.

I wandered, lost, but feeling more found than I have ever been. I wasn't myself, but didn't need to be. I didn't need to be anything, I just needed to exist here. Everything was beautiful that way, everything was at peace—I had no needs, or fears, my only desire being to hold onto this feeling forever.

"Let's take this exercise further," Dom Seir's voice projected from nowhere, and everywhere all at once like some higher being watching over me.

I'd stopped walking. Instead, I drifted, dragging the tips of my toes through the water and watching the ripples as they distorted the perfect reflection of the sky above. I was truly at peace.

"First—breathe," his voice manifested once more.

I closed my eyes, only to imagine the same world I was drifting in. I smiled at the fact that even my dreams couldn't conjure an image so beautiful. Every ounce of stress seemed to melt away. Every bad thing in my life no longer mattered. I didn't have to think about the war, or Demi, or Klaus. I was fully content drifting for an eternity in an endless sea of bliss.

"You've found your peace," the voice rang out once more, "now, it is time to go beyond."

*Beyond?* I thought. I didn't want to, I wasn't ready. I wanted to drift along this plain forever, being carried by a cosmic current of warmth and content.

"On the count of three, you will be fully integrated with your body, filled with renewed energy. One, come back in peace with all life. Two, find a balance in your power. Three, open your eyes and feel *alive*."

I felt certain thrill then, and my eyes shot open. The water beneath me rushed past me and I was engulfed by it. My eyes opened just in time to see the passing walls of water above me fold inward, crashing down on me. As I plunged into the depths, disoriented, I struggled to hold what little breath I managed to steal before going under.

The darkness of the sky above made it difficult to tell which way was up, but I caught a glimpse of light and rushed for the surface, gasping for air once I did. The waves were rough now, and threw me back under a moment after. I came back up to fight the waves, searching for somewhere that might offer safety, spotting an island not far off. I let the waves carry me to its sandy shores, too tired to fight them any longer.

I staggered to my feet, coughing up swallowed water and looking out to the island before me.

Where was this before?

A mountain towered over me, painted with the lush greens of exotic plants and serenaded by the roar of cascading waterfalls, the starry sky a shifting backdrop. I walked along the shoreline, exploring. The waves that rolled in past my feet seemed to wash up the stars themselves as bio-luminescent specs drifted onto the beach, and back out to sea. I paused as I passed a clearing in the tree line, following a poorly beaten path towards the face of the mountain, having to step over the giant roots of ancient trees and duck under hanging vines.

A stone door was built into the face of the mountain with intricate designs carved into its frame. Three large stones created the side walls and overhead arch that stood just further out than the door itself. As I walked closer, I began to recognize the symbols carved in the stone.

After examining the door for a moment I tried to pry it open.

It wouldn't budge.

I threw my shoulder into the door, but it remained unmoved.

I took a step back, taking a closer look.

"You've come far," Dom Seir's voice rang, "But to go any further I fear you must travel alone. I can no longer help you. Fully unlock the seven chakras within, you are the only key."

I am the key? What did that mean?

I looked back to the door, only this time more intently. To my left there was a palm print indented into the stone. I looked at it curiously, for a moment, before placing my hand up against it. I felt my hand sink into the stone, as if I was pressing against soft sand. Suddenly, the symbols around me began to glow a soft green, lighting up the darkest corners of the shrine.

A moment later the stone door inched open. Beyond, I could see only darkness, until the soft glow of the symbols began to spread down the long hallway ahead, illuminating the labyrinth from my dreams.

I took a step back, staring into the looming darkness. It drew me in, but I resisted, hesitant of what lie beyond.

I took a deep breath, closed my eyes and entered as the stone door closed behind me.

# Chapter 26:

The hallway before me seemed to stretch into infinity, the soft green light of the glowing symbols carved into the wall only worked to illuminate so much before plunging into darkness. I realized that I had walked in through the front door of the labyrinth of my dreams and I was nervous to be back here, my stomach twisting into knots as the darkness before me called, teasing to be explored. There was a force here, drawing me in, as if a phantom hand had reached out and grabbed hold of me, pulling me deeper.

I hesitated, wondering if I should turn around before I got lost and escape the labyrinth to return to my endless ocean of bliss. Doubt consumed me.

I didn't want this.

I didn't choose this, and I didn't think it was fair. Why me?

Not only did I have the misfortune of being born with the Gift, I had to have Klaus trapped inside me as well? Now I was expected to awaken him? To save the world?

It was a lot to ask of a girl.

I just wanted to exist, to simply be.

There were whispers in the distance that broke my trance, calling me in, and though I was reluctant—I pushed forth.

The hallway stretched for an eternity. As I walked, the soft green glow of the symbols illuminated my path for only a few feet ahead, and dimmed as I moved past. Everything looked the same and I hardly knew if I was going anywhere at all, my only notion of progress being the fact that I wasn't standing still.

Finally, the hallway let up, opening into a vast cavern.

I stood on the edge of a steep cliff, overlooking a series of underground pools that cascaded into one another. The biggest of the pools was directly under where I stood and ran into the smaller ones, falling deeper into the mountain before me. Green flames rested on stone pedestals, reflecting off the water's surface— painting the ceiling with a shimmering ribbon of green and white light.

I strained to see a door by the lowest pool in the dim light, two stone pedestals with green flames resting by either side.

There were narrow paths carved into the stone, zig-zagging from one platform to the next all the way around the oval cave. To either side I could see paths along the rock walls, some hugging the stone and others leading straight down into the pools below.

There was a carving to my left on a stone rising a few feet above the ground. The symbols on it radiated the now familiar soft green glow and it seemed as though the longer I stared at the words the more they began to make sense— shifting into a form I could read.

*Root.*

The symbols finally arranged themselves, and in the space remaining under the symbols an outline of a palm began to etch itself into existence.

I lifted my hand, but hesitated, thinking of what might happen. The last time I touched anything I ended up stuck in here, so I knew I had to be careful. I took a deep breath, and let it out, pressing my hand against the cold stone—accepting that I had no other choice than to push forward.

Green lines began to run from each of my fingers down the base of the rock and into the ground, spreading out over the entire cave. They raced to unlit pedestals only to run up their base, igniting a new flame on each as they did.

A moment later, from the darkest corners of the cavern I caught a glimpse of movement. Slowly, a too-long, pale, and bony arm reached out into the light, a darkened shadow looming behind it. I watched as the creature revealed itself, seemingly unaware that it was being watched. Its head remained low, the bioluminescent slits running along its face emitting a vibrant blood orange glow as it searched for any other sign of life, and I was struck with a flash of terror as I remembered it was one of the same creatures that had attacked us at the train station.

The creature lurched through the cavern, keeping its head low as it moved one arm over the other, its oversized legs holding its backside high in the air, its long transparent tail waving over its entire body like a pendulum as it meticulously combed the ground for any hint of prey.

Another appeared by its side, and another crept down from the ceiling to my right, clinging to the vertical rock wall.

I was trembling, my hand still on the stone. I looked down at it, too afraid to move, fearful that if I did they might rush after me.

*Run,* the voice manifested from nothing.

I panicked, ripping my hand off the stone to spin around, hoping to escape through the everlasting hallway and back into my ocean of bliss. But when I turned I found no escape. The doorway I came through had been blocked.

When did that happen?

I spun back around to see the three creatures staring at me in the distance, unmoving. But that wasn't all I saw. There were Agents now, making their way through the narrowly carved paths of the cavern that lead up to me.

The creatures didn't attack them, clearly working *with* them.

I rushed back to the stone, pressing my palm against it once more, desperately trying to shut off whatever was going on, but nothing happened. The stone had grown dim, its light escaping it.

"Stop! By the name of Commander Zanin!" the order echoed through the cavern.

They were close.

My eyes darted around for an escape, but I found none. To my right one of the creatures clung to the rock wall above one of the many narrow paths. I couldn't go there, knowing it would tear me apart. To my left a squad of four Agents rushed towards me, and I knew they would fire before I even had the chance to attack.

I was running out of time.

Tick.

Tock.

My heart was beating out of my chest as I was forced to make the decision of how I'd like to die. A moment later I'd made up my mind. I wouldn't give the Agents the satisfaction of killing me, I would have to risk rushing past the beast.

I darted for the narrow path to my right, only wide enough for one foot to land perfectly before the other as I hugged the vertical wall. What was I doing? I had to have lost my mind, I was trapped in a cave with the two things in this world that wanted me dead—and plenty of them.

The Agents had reached the entrance where I had stood a moment before, shouting after me once more. Or it could have been another echo, they always sounded the same. On the face of that cliff I could see one of the creatures climbing toward the pedestal, and I damned myself for not noticing it earlier.

There was a screech ahead of me, my eyes shot back in front, only to see a creature jolting to cut me off. I wanted to close my eyes, for it to be over, but I refused to just sit down and let myself die. I pushed forward, on a collision course with death.

My only hope was that the beast would miss, so that I could squeeze past. It was only feet from me now, above me on the rock wall, its tail swaying from side to side, testing its aim on me as we moved.

*Jump*, the voice rang out again, and as the creature's spiked tail lunged forward, I listened.

Everything seemed to move in slow motion as I fell into the pool. I watched the beast rip its tail back out from the stone as it let out another thunderous screech. I heard the echoes of the Agents commands, "Open fire!"

I prepared myself once more for the worst as I plunged into the frigid water. Around me, misfired bullets ripped through the swells. I gathered my bearings beneath the surface and let the current guide me over the next shallow falls.

I breached at the lowest pool, gasping for air.

Behind me, the Agents had stopped firing, and started to make their way back down. I couldn't see any of the creatures, but I could hear their movements as they sent fragmented rocks tumbling down into the pools below. I swam frantically for land. Ahead, I could see the door, two pedestals holding a green flame by either side.

*I made it*, I thought to myself, and rushed to the stone pillar by its door to see the same *root* carving, and a place for my palm. I slapped my hand down on the stone.

"Come on, open," I begged, but nothing happened.

Instead, new symbols began to align themselves, *Let go of your fears and you will be free.*

I looked over my shoulder, death close. I was terrified, shaking, too scared to act.

*Be free*, that voice again echoed.

I turned back toward the cavern to see the four Agents lining the shoreline of the pool, rifles raised. On either side of them, one of those beast sat perched on the lip of the rock wall, watching me.

The third creature came from behind the Agents, and slowly made its way to the front of the pack. It moved patiently, knowing I was trapped, looming with murderous intent.

This was it, all or nothing, I needed to let go.

I took a deep breath, clenched my fist, and started toward the beast. If it was going to kill me, it would be by my own terms.

The creature stopped just inches from my face and I tried not to flinch as the slits on its nose flared out. Its tail swung above its head and it let out a blood curdling screech, its breath reeking of rotten flesh.

This was it.

Its spiked tail shot directly for my chest.

My eyes closed, and I relaxed.

I felt nothing, no pain, no stabbing.

Nothing.

I dared to open my eyes only to see the beast before me, the Agents, and the two beast by their side all transform into water and come crashing to the ground.

I heard the door behind me open, and a quick release of energy come to life at the base of my spine.

I turned and made my way to the door, turning to steal one last look at the chamber I'd be leaving behind before entering the next room.

# Chapter 27:

I was lead into an alleyway, lit only by the soft light of overhead moon and the orange glow of a lit torch by a door to my left which reflected off the pools of water that had gathered in the middle of the alley. Drops of rain, too small to see, would hit the water, causing tiny ripples to spread through the pool. I watched as the waves crashed into each other, creating a thin line that would spread outward infinitely if it were not contained.

A cold shiver ran down my spine as I wrapped my arms around myself for warmth, rushing to the only door I could see—but it wouldn't budge. There was a plaque on the door with words I struggled to read, but after a moment the symbols began to move into a form I could understand more clearly.

*Sacral,* the plaque read, and beneath it was another outline of my palm. I pressed my hand against it without question, hoping only to reach the promised warmth of being inside.

At first, I was overwhelmed by the noise, and lingered off to the side for a moment while I tried to gather myself and my surroundings. There was a terrible air about the room, a dark energy brooding, a vibe that separated me from everyone else here. No one turned to face me as I entered, not even out of curiosity—no one cared. Everyone simply stuck to their own group, their own conversations, completely incapable of distraction. Despite being in a crowded room I felt completely alone.

I looked around more intently, beginning to feel a sense of familiarity about this place, though I couldn't place the memory.

Another man came in through the alley's door, allowing a burst of cool nighttime air to enter by his side, chilling me to the bone.

The man looked over his shoulder, toward me—his face clouded by the shadows of cast by a pointed hood, the only hint of color being the vibrant green of his mark through the darkness. I noticed the detail of his clothes first, they were clean, and well made. Unlike the sooty browns and torn jean the rest of the men here wore, this man seemed—royal.

He stared blankly in my direction, as if not sure what exactly he was looking at, if anything, as if he had a feeling something was there, but saw nothing.

I felt utterly invisible.

The man looked back to the others in the bar and casually removed his hood. I clutched my chest in shock as I realized it was Demi who'd revealed himself here and suddenly the memories of this night surged to the forefront of my mind.

My eyes closed as I tried to calm myself, but I only saw flashback images of that night, the sign, the bar, and the bodies. So many bodies. I opened my eyes looking straight to a sign above the bartender, *BarSeir*.

My stomach churned as I anticipated what was about to happen, cursing beneath my breath.

Demi made his way to the back of the bar, to a table with a group of rough men. They immediately noted his presence and smacked the smallest on the shoulder, telling him to leave, and he did, leaving an empty chair for Demi. They must have expected him.

I watched as they began to talk in hushed voices, too far for me to hear over the roar of conversation and laughter. I would have dared creep closer, but I feared being discovered.

A moment later the door opened again, letting through another burst of chilled air, and letting out another batch of fresh stank.

I watched on as I saw myself walk in, Ava short in tow, and immediately make way for an empty table to the right of the door to sit down.

I watched on as the men in the bar eyed Ava and I.

How stupid was I? What was I expecting out of this?

It all seemed so silly now, watching it like this. At the time I thought I was being brave, but I was being foolish. What I saw wasn't anything but a girl who'd just been attacked on the streets finding another excuse to put herself in danger.

I wanted to tell her, I wanted to run up to this image of myself and tell her to leave.

But I couldn't.

No one would hear me.

So I watched as it all unraveled.

Demi had it covered, Demi always had it covered.

I needed to trust him.

Demi hadn't noticed me, either of me, either of my selves? Whatever.

It's hard to think of yourself in two places at once, but I managed.

There was a group of younger men by the bar, I remembered them, and watched helpless as they pressured the one who'd attacked me before to unknowingly make a second advance on the very girl who'd just killed his friend.

In a way, it amazed me how well he'd bounced back from that. He'd just witnessed a friend be murdered in a dark alleyway by some stranger with a demonic gift and here he was laughing with his mates like nothing had ever happened.

I guess losing a friend is something you might get used to in this city. No one is expected to make it to tomorrow. Maybe this was his therapy, so I watched as he made his way toward this mystery girl in the shadows of this run down bar.

I closed my eyes, trying to avoid watching the coming rampage, to save myself from viewing my own power. It didn't help. I could *feel* the energy within me, counting down the seconds to destruction.

Three.

Two.

One.

Pulse.

*Open your eyes*— there was that voice again.

My eyes were forced open, and Demi seemed to notice me then, the real me, "What have you done?"

I didn't know what to say, I wasn't prepared for this, everything was out of my control. "I'm sorry," I whispered before trying to escape the bar.

"I'm afraid we have," the words came from the lips of my dark other from inside the bar, but it was the sinister voice of a man that came out of her mouth rather than my own.

*Klaus?* I asked.

*Yes.*

A moment later little more than a black ribbon streaked through the room with incredible speed, slashing through each victim with ungodly efficiency. Demi's Kurki stumbled after that unstoppable force, desperately trying to end its rampage but were lead like lambs to the slaughter.

Helpless.

Everyone was helpless.

Demi stood amongst the bodies, staring at this other me.

She was reeked of evil and despair, bathing in the pain and despair of her victims. She stood, slightly hunched over, the oily blackness forming a skin tight armor that churned like the void. There was a veil over her eyes and her tongue hung out, licking the sprayed blood that painted her face.

I rushed away, cutting back into the street, brushing past the others who were still unaware of the horror that happened inside the bar.

I didn't feel invisible anymore.

No.

I felt something else.

I felt watched.

I felt guilty.

I wanted nothing more than to have stopped myself from killing so many but I couldn't change the past.

Everyone's eyes seemed to follow me as I made my way through the busy streets, or maybe I was just being paranoid.

I felt like I *should* be watched.

Out of an entire city of the finest gifted warriors somehow it was me that was the most deadly.

Somehow, I didn't find any sense of pride in that.

I needed to get out of the streets, I needed to be alone.

I remembered the room Demi and Ava and I had been staying, and figured that would be my best bet.

Walking up to the front door my mind was racing, weighed down by my own sorrow and self-pity. I wrapped my hand around the handle, and paused, taking a deep breath to clear my mind before I opened the door and entered.

I pushed the door open and stepped in, expecting to walk into a room of solitude where I could collect my thoughts. Instead, I had become fully immersed with the sounds and excitement of the bar once more. I stood there for a moment, scanning the room in confusion. Everyone was sitting, drinking, and laughing like nothing had ever happened. There were no bodies on the floor, no blood, and no sign of struggle.

Nothing.

I turned around to walk back out into the street but cut my stride short when I saw Demi step into the doorway. I backed out of his way, and into the bar, watching him as he played through the exact same motions as before.

What was this?

It wasn't long before I saw Ava and myself arrive once more, again, sitting in the far corner to the right, shrouded by darkness.

Again, the foolish young man made his approach, and again there was the pulse, then slaughter.

I backed away, terrified.

Demi stood in the middle of the room, "What have you done?"

Again, I didn't know. I wasn't in control, "I'm sorry," I repeated.

*It's not my fault,* I thought to myself, before stepping over the bodies to rush out of the bar once more.

I didn't run into the alleyway this time, or the busy street. I was on the sacred plains. The great battlefield where the best of us fought for freedom, fought against justice. I could see that we were losing.

I stood there, in the dunes, motionless, as my fellow Gifted fell all around me. Their screams rang in my ears. I watched, helpless, as bullets flew, tearing even the strongest of them down. No matter how many died the battle still raged, and raged, and raged.

I looked over my shoulder into the open door of the bar to see that dark image of myself leaning up against its frame, a cocky smile making it look as if she had just won some game.

The battlefield drew my attention once more. My people, we needed a hero—no, they needed a God, even if he was feared by darkness itself. We needed him, and all of this pain I've caused was because of my inability to control him, that was just Klaus trying to be set free.

I may have set him free to escape the pain, but he is a ruthless beast and we need him under control. I realized then that for his power to be used to help his children I would have to be his vessel—there was no other choice.

More of my people fell by my feet. I looked up to the red sky, like the blood that painted the ground beneath me, for answers but found none.

I faced the bar, hoping to confront myself but was stopped short. The battered door of BarSeir no longer stood, nor did the walls that surrounded it.

In its place was a large stone door, and a pedestal by its side. Above the door read *Sacral* in the same symbols as before, only now I could understand them without any help.

New symbols came into focus, emitting their soft green glow along the arch of the door. *Forgive yourself.* It read.

I sighed, closing my eyes, it was time for change.

I was forgiven.

The door opened, and I entered.

# Chapter 28:

The sunlight peeking in from a bedside window woke me atop of a bed freshly made in a room I'd never seen before. For a moment I was content simply lying there, but my curiosity drove me. I knew I'd never been here, I couldn't have been, this place was too—clean.

I stood, rubbing my eyes, before making my way to the window to close the blinds. My instincts told me that an open window was always an open invitation for trouble, if the blinds were closed then at least I could move about the room and not risk being seen.

What I saw outside shocked me. I was in a high rise, dozens of floors up. Beneath me, the layered walkways created an intricate web throughout the city. Everything was pristine and white, with burst of color strategically placed in scattered gardens and parkways. The streets below were teeming with life as hundreds of people walked freely. There were bridges, pathways, and a narrow stream running through the center.

Across from me, there was another tower, and looking down the entire street was lined with them. I could only assume each room was one much like the one I was standing in, basic living quarters.

Above, there was a honeycomb of hexagonal shapes that made a dome overhead. Some were solid and white, blocking the sun, while others were made of glass, allowing the sunlight to peek into the city.

I gasped, and ducked down, pulling the string to close the blinds all in one motion.

I was in a Pure city, I was sure of it. A dome city, behind enemy lines, and I needed to escape, but I tried to stay calm. I told myself that this was just a dream, a test, and maybe this chamber would be like the last. Maybe, they wouldn't be able to see me. Still, I had to play things safe.

Immediately I started going through the drawers by my bedside, searching for some clothes that might be able to hide the fact that I was a Stigma holder better than what I already had on.

I found only a sundress, actually, many, but all were far too impractical, and all of which fit me perfectly as if tailored to my exact size. I picked one out and moved to the bathroom to clean myself up.

There was a mirror above the sink, and as I cleaned my face with water from the tap I took a moment to look at myself, trying to figure out how I was going to pull this off.

It took a moment, but I noticed that something was different.

My eyes.

I didn't have the Stigma's mark.

At first I was relieved, but grew worried about what this might mean, naturally. I decided that for right now, not having the mark made me invisible in this city so long as I acted normal. I'd have to figure out what happened to my mark once I escaped.

I got dressed, and made my way for the door. There was another plaque to the left, the symbols on it had already begun to churn into place as I got closer.

*Solar Plexus*, it read, and like before, I placed my palm on the indent.

The door slid open with an electric swoosh.

I poked my head out of the room, looking both ways down the white walled hallway to check if the coast was clear before stepping out.

*Act natural*, I told myself, but it came to me that natural for me was far from natural for the Pure. I'd have to pick up on their behaviors as quickly as I could.

Rounding a corner, I saw another woman waiting, facing a metal section of the wall. There were numbers in a row lining the top of the door, with an up and down arrowed button by its side. I stood beside her, waiting.

I watched her out of the corner of my eye, she had her hands clasped behind her back, and stood perfectly still waiting for the door to open. Noticing that my hands were dangling loosely by my side, I straightened up immediately, trying to mimic her and caught a faint hint of a smile on her otherwise blank expression as I did. I realized I could be seen here. Still, I hadn't a clue what we were waiting for.

Finally, the door opened and two men filed out, another still inside. He smiled politely and took a step to the side, giving room for the woman beside me and myself.

The bell sounded, and she went first, I followed, the door closing behind us.

She turned around, facing the door once more. Her eyes scanned the selection of buttons to the right of the door and selected "G," which lit up with a white light.

After a moment, the man looked at me curiously, "Miss, are you going to pick your floor?"

I jumped to attention, startled, almost forgetting I could actually be seen here unlike the last chamber. "Oh, sorry. Three, please."

The woman looked to me, question in her eye, "Three? There's nothing down there but an office."

I scrambled for an excuse, "Uh, yeah, I work there, sorry."

The woman eyed me for a long moment, "funny," she said, "I've managed that floor for thirteen years and I don't ever recall seeing you there."

My stomach churned as I grasped blankly for another excuse, I could feel my head start to heat up as my body began to sweat. "I'm new," I managed to say, confidently enough.

"Hmm," she said, taking a moment to think, "you must have slipped past my interview. All well, these things happen. Welcome."

I smiled politely, but more because I was proud of getting myself out of that situation, "thank you, I'm sure it will be a pleasure."

The room we were in stopped, and the doors opened. Immediately I rushed out, only to hear the woman call after me as another man entered and the doors closed, "Excuse me, wrong floor!"

It was too late, the door had closed. Looking to a sign beside the door I could see that I was on the fifth floor. I shook my head at myself, I needed to keep my composure or risk being found out. There was a sign for stairs at the end of the hallway and was relieved to find something much more my style.

I made my way to the bottom floor, and into the lobby. I'd nearly made it to the door when there was a tap on my shoulder. It was the woman from that moving room.

"And where do you think you're going, skipping work on your first day?" She asked, crossing her arms.

"Oh, someone sent me on an errand." I returned.

"Hm, likely, I'm sure. And who was this?"

*Damn it,* "I'm sorry, but can't say I know his name. New girl and all, it'll take me a while to learn everyone's names."

The woman seemed to accept my answer, "Alright then, hurry up. And take the elevator when you get back, the stairs are so…primitive."

Elevator? I looked to the metal doors to the side of the main desk in the lobby. So that's what it's called.

"Will do," I returned, and rushed out into the street, making a good show of looking like I knew where I was actually going.

Everything was so structured here, orderly, pure, like the ideal image of what a society should be if everyone played by the rules.

Eying the people that passed me by, I saw hardly anyone dressed casual. Everyone seemed important and busy, rushing to and from nearly every open door. Nobody had any expression other than empty content.

There were large television screens lining the sidewalks every so often, and speakers tucked away and hidden in the scattered gardens, all broadcasting in unison to make a background narrative as you walked.

I thought of Tinker, and the projections in the cinema.

Propaganda, he called it. Supposedly it worked.

"The Stigma holders have forced us to live this life; hidden in giant domes, sheltered from our world, disconnected with our Earth. Soon, the war will be over. The world will be ours again, "a calm voice projected over the speakers and televisions as I passed by.

"Kill them, at all cost," the voice continued, "for the survival of our kind."

I thought of my youth, and everything up to this point. All I had ever known was war, death, and fear. I've known many of my kind that hated who they were, hated the mark that stigmatizes us all. At times, I found myself hating that too.

In our struggle for freedom and understanding we'd become something less than human, sometimes even wishing to be the enemy. Sometimes saying that we would give anything to be pure, to live a normal life.

That shame plagued us.

But what was normal?

I studied all that was before me, all of the high rise buildings, and too-well-kept gardens. I studied the people that passed me by, wearing formal clothes that, judging from my own, were near impossible to stay comfortable in. Everything here seemed too perfect, like a utopia, for sure, but more and more I realized that what I saw was a population that was mindless, a population who has forgotten the outside world, and caved into the political and social forces that governed them. There may have been the illusion of peace, and happiness, but I knew that this was no way to live.

What I saw was a way of life that didn't value what it meant to be human at all, or human happiness, it instead valued strict order and repetition without a single surprise or bend in the road. Anything that broke that order was cast away for fear of a reaction. The wheels of Zanin's machine needed to keep turning, and his citizens were the cogs, and their children but an echo of the same mindless life played on repeat. This was a life driven by consumption and gain, by working to achieve goals other than one's own, a life of blind content and ignorance wrought beneath the guise of security and freedom from the dangers of a foolish war.

No, this wasn't normal, and there was nothing natural about this life. This wasn't any way to live.

At times, I remember being filled with hate and fear. Ashamed of who I was, confused about who I might come to be. I absently listened to the broadcast as I wandered, and gradually my shame filled with hate for this system that holds us down.

My hate, turned to pride.

We weren't monsters, we were people. Misunderstood. Slowly, the rage within me simmered down, and as it did I found myself walking straighter, holding my head higher.

I'd rather live on the run, fighting every day of my life to be free and an individual than to become one of the standardized versions of a person everyone I passed by was. No matter what label the Pure could put on my life there was one true fact that separated me from them—I was still human.

I'd run out of room to walk. In my thoughts, I'd managed to climb a set of stairs leading up to a grand building that all of the pathways in this city ultimately lead to. A building that reminded me of the Council hall in Terra Sera.

Though, the door wasn't what I had expected. Instead, stood another stone door, and another stone tablet by its side.

I looked over my shoulder, seeing if anyone was watching what I had been up to. Then again, what did it matter? This was a dream. Wasn't it?

The stone tablet took a moment to arrange its words.

*Accept who you are, who you were meant to be,* It read.

*I am a stigma holder,* I told myself.

I have the gift, and I'm damn proud of it.

The door opened.

# Chapter 29:

I entered into a rawhide tent with dozens of tiny trinkets and tools scattered over the floor. There was a bed made, low to the ground and covered with thick furs. To my left was a wooden chest, closed, but with the long sleeve of a shirt hanging out as if it were reaching for the ground, or trying to make its escape. A feathered, white dreamcatcher hung in the middle of the room.

Outside, the sweet sounds of laughter, and happy conversation, filled the air though I couldn't make out any words. There was a fire that cast the shadows of dancers in its light. They'd lock arms and dance in circles before breaking off to find another. The shadows showed the heads of others as well, sitting by the fire. Sometimes the heads would roll back as they laughed, but not once did I manage to catch the joke.

The tent was larger than any I'd ever been in, the rawhide material was stretched from the center and out into the surrounding circle, wooden poles holding the structure up. The whole thing was very well made and I knew that this camp had been here for some time.

I was surprised, with all the noise I'd expect this to be an easy target for the Agents. I shook my head, finding my thoughts silly. Maybe the same rules didn't apply here in these chambers, maybe the Agents didn't exist in this one.

I was still wearing those stupid clothes I found in the dome, so I decided to find what clothes I could in the chest. I don't understand how a girl could dress like this and be okay with it. The too-loose skirt left me with no pockets, and would do nothing to protect me in a fight out here. I couldn't imagine the usefulness of such clothes.

I knelt down by the trunk and examined it. On the top the word *heart* was carved into the wood, and under the word rested another handprint.

I pressed my hand down, causing a green pulse make its way through the grain of the wood and into the ground. The chest unlocked and I opened the lid. The entire chest was a heap of clothes, poorly folded. It looked like someone had just thrown them in there haphazardly. Then, I was a little disappointed after I realized that in this chamber, this was probably a representation of what my tent would look like, meaning it was me that did this. I managed to laugh, and continued digging through the pile of clothes.

"Sage?" a familiar voice rang from outside, "can I come in?"

I scrambled to get out of my clothes, by now I'd figured out I had to be in a Stigma camp and didn't want to draw any extra attention by wearing the Pure's silly clothes, "Just a minute, I'm getting dressed," I returned.

There was a sigh, and the sound of hands fidgeting with the beaded lock on the rawhide flap that acted as a door.

"I said just a minute," I repeated, and grabbed the first thing I could see, a pair of hunter green harem pants and a loose fitting off-white tank.

I'd just managed to slide into my clothes when I turned to see Demi standing behind me, arms crossed, with a smile.

I gave him a stern look and sighed, "What did I tell you?"

He laughed, "You act like it's something I've never seen before. Come on, people are waiting for you."

"Demi," I said with a pause, "what are you talking about?"

He gave me a curious look and smiled, "You must have hit your head hun, come on."

I looked at him for a second, confused, but followed as I grabbed his outstretched hand. He led me out to the fire, surrounded by dozens of others. A ring of tents circled the blaze, and people came and went between them freely. The entire camp was enormous.

"What is this?" I asked.

"You must have hit your head harder than I thought! What were you doing in there? It's home," he returned with a chuckle.

"Home?" I repeated and took a better look at my surroundings.

There was a tall woman making her way to me, masked by the light behind her. As she got closer she spoke, "So the two lovebirds finally decide to leave their nest." She came up to us, stopping just inches away and leaned in to kiss both Demi and I on the cheek, "So good to see my baby find someone that makes her happy."

Demi nodded in agreement, "And she makes me very happy as well."

I wanted to take a step back and question what was going on, but knew this had to be another test. I couldn't go running off and losing control of my emotions. I might end up stuck here forever, not like that would be a bad thing given the way Demi was acting.

I looked up towards Demi with a smile, knowing I might as well enjoy this while I can, "You haven't a clue mother," I returned.

"Mother? Why so formal dear? Come join the others, we've been waiting so long now."

We followed her to the fire, towards an open spot already in waiting and took a seat. Ava was there, and before I even had the chance to find a comfortable position she'd thrown herself at me with a hug.

"So when's the wedding?" she asked, joyful.

"Wedding?" I asked, surprised by the question.

"Don't tell me you're getting cold feet!" my mother chimed in, putting an open palm to her chest as if she'd just lost her breath.

"No, not at all. I just didn't think everyone knew about that yet."

"Didn't know? It's the buzz of the whole camp dear!" she continued.

I faked a laugh, looking to the ground, "I guess I hit my head harder than I thought," I said, looking to Demi, who smiled and squeezed my hand just a little tighter.

Everyone laughed at that and the topic changed, thankfully. It felt weird being this close to Demi, but at the same time I wasn't complaining. I wasn't sure if I was ashamed of or surprised by my own feelings for him. I knew I shouldn't enjoy this too much, and that when I came back he would be gone, but I found this too hard to resist.

I began to scan the camp for other familiar faces and it wasn't long before I found things to be stranger than they already were. There were dozens of Stigma holders here, all going about their lives like there was no war going on, like none of them were being hunted. This was the most carefree camp I'd ever been in, which worried me. But there was something that worried me even more than this, I'd watched every single person here die aside from Demi and Ava.

Yet here they were, perfectly fine, smiling, living their lives as if nothing had ever happened. I felt ashamed to be here, unworthy to walk among them as one of the few left living. A hate boiled up inside me, a hate for myself. If only I had been stronger than maybe some of them might have still been alive today. I could have protected them, if only I'd discovered my power sooner.

With Klaus locked within me there was no excuse for so many of those who had been around me to die. I could have protected them, I should have, but I couldn't. All I had ever done was get in the way, and run, leaving them to die. I was weak, and I still mourned for them.

It felt so good to see them alive here, but the pain slowly set in. This was only a dream, only another test and these people may live here but they could never be alive back in the real world.

I watched them, at times our eyes would meet and we would share a smile, and share a memory.

The man across from me was much older than me. He'd been an elder who watched over a large area of land and the camps within them. He would travel to and from warning us of when a raid would come. He had great power, able to control the ground itself. I'd seen him bring up entire walls around a camp for protection, buying precious time for the others to escape. His name was Torro, and the last time I'd seen him was when I was younger, maybe ten or eleven years old.

He'd stayed back to hold back a squad of Agents as the rest of us fled into the surrounding forest. I remember a terrible sound, and a machine flying like a bird in the air. Torro had no trouble dealing with the Agents on the ground, but an opponent in the sky was an entire different story. It wasn't long until the rumbling of moving Earth stopped, and the roar of the flying machines followed us overhead.

There were others here who had died that day as well. As I remembered each of them, they would fade away, as if they never existed. I wanted to cry out, *not again*, I thought— but I knew it would do no good.

There was a woman, my first adoptive mother back in MarSeir, after the monks had dropped me off. Back then, MarSeir wasn't the city I returned to. It was still bigger than most camps but raids were still frequent. The last time I saw her there was a knock on the door. Outside, we could hear the screams and gunfire as the Agents made their way through the chasms.

She'd knelt by my side and told me, "Run child, you are the only thing here that matters. Run, so that I may die, and we may one day be set free."

It wasn't until now that I knew what she meant by that. I slipped through the escape hole and into the alleyway. Behind me I heard the front door open, a conflict, and gunshots as the Agents fired upon her.

The woman smiled at me from across the fire, nodding, and faded away like mist in a faint breeze.

I wanted to cry, the pain of losing so many burning deep within me. With each memory another would fade away, unnoticed. It wasn't long until few remained and ultimately I was left alone with Demi, Ava, and my mother, more beautiful than I'd ever imagined her to be.

I jumped to my feet and rushed to each tent, bursting into each with the hope that someone else still remained, thinking that they may have just returned to their homes. I'd searched each and eventually returned to the fire, defeated.

"Something wrong?" my mother asked.

"Yeah, everyone that has ever cared about me is gone and I can't do anything to save them," I said, trying to hold back my tears.

She got up and made her way toward me, placing her hands on my cheeks, holding my head up as she looked me in the eye, "Silly Sage, everyone who loves you is right here, and everyone who ever has will always be in your heart, no one is ever gone forever," she said and came in to kiss me on my forehead. I closed my eyes, and smiled as I felt my mother's kiss for the first time. She pulled away, and I opened my eyes. She was gone.

I thought about what she had said, and smiled. Everyone who had ever loved me was still right here, in my heart, and still, with all the pain I've endured there was a new love growing. I would make sure that this love would stay.

Demi and Ava had made their way toward me, "Looks like everyone else got tired," Demi said as if oblivious to the truth, "Time to call it a night?"

Ava let out a yawn and stretched her arms out to either side, "I'm exhausted!"

I looked at them and smiled, putting a hand on Ava's shoulder and the other around Demi as I brought them in for a hug.

"Yeah," I said with a smile, "let's call it a night."

I turned back towards our tent, and this time I wasn't surprised when a stone door stood in the place of the rawhide flap that was there earlier.

Above the door the words, *let your pain flow out and love, in,* were already illuminated on the arch above the door.

The door inched open and I entered.

# Chapter 30:

I was lead through a shallow hallway opening into a single square room with little more than a stone bed at its center and a wooden door at the opposite side of the room. At first, I dismissed the idea of this being the door I was looking for, seeing as it had no markings or unique characteristics. I decided to take a look round the rest of the room for some kind of clue. Tiny building blocks, dolls in tattered mismatched clothes, and chalk were scattered across the floor like dozens of playful land mines just waiting to be stepped on. As I drew closer a humming welcomed my ears with steadily increasing intensity, but as I entered I failed to find a source.

Chalk drawings covered the orange tinted clay wall. They were intricate and telling, but still, noticeably made by a child. I saw a drawing of a young girl with a darkened figure behind her baring enormous black wings and a sinister smile. Another still, showed a rough circle surrounded by many of the same odd symbols I'd grown to recognize and I wondered if this was some sort of ritualistic diagram.

The room was small, with blank walls on all sides that acted like a canvas and a few low hanging shelves. I noticed a girl, coloring a new picture in the corner. I couldn't see her face but I knew that she was a younger reflection of myself, maybe only three or four years old, and this was our room back at the monastery.

"Hey there," I said, with a kind voice, trying to draw her attention.

She said nothing, only continued coloring on the wall.

Maybe she hadn't heard me?

"Sage?" I asked, feeling a little silly addressing myself.

Again, she didn't respond.

I looked away, trying to find some clue as to what was going on in this chamber. I moved to the stone bed in the middle of the room and rested my hands on it. In the center read the word, *throat*, and beneath it the outline of another palm print. As before, I pressed my hand down to activate the chamber.

I sighed, watching the green light ripple down the bed and into the ground, glad that at least they kept things consistent.

A moment later my younger self perked up as if finally noticing me behind her, "I was wondering when I would finally show up," she said, not bothering to face me as she continued on her drawing.

"Uhm—you knew?" I asked, a bit surprised.

"Of course. It took us a bit longer than I expected though. After all, we were born for this."

I didn't know how I felt about being lectured by a toddler, but I let it pass.

"I guess, so what is it you have to show me?" I asked, passing a look to the closed door to my left, "I mean, that's the point isn't it? I'll learn something here and then the door opens right?"

She eyed me for a moment, and shook her head, "I can't believe how dumb I grow up to be," she said before returning to her drawing.

*Okay, so that didn't work,* I thought to myself, set back by how mature I had been at such a young age.

"Oh, and I know what you're thinking. After all, we are the same person," she added without bothering to pass me a look.

I sighed, "So what are you working on?"

"Don't you know?" she asked in a very matter of fact tone.

I came closer, looking over her shoulder to see a rough picture of the two of us holding hands and smiling.

"What the—" I began, remembering the very same drawing in the room when I woke up in the monastery earlier, "how did you know?" I asked, realizing she had already been working on it since before I walked in.

She let her chalk down and stared at the picture for a moment and smiled with content before looking up to me, "I've known my whole life we would come back, with questions—looking for answers that I haven't forgotten yet."

"So you already know?" the question sounded worse after I had asked.

Luckily she let this one slide, "It's our destiny."

"Our destiny?" I repeated.

"What are you a parrot?" she said with a childish giggle.

"Sorry," I said, bowing my head. I'd forgotten how ahead of my years I was, I could hardly keep up.

She got up and walked over to the other side of the room, looking at a picture of her and Klaus standing side by side, "It's not my fault that you decided to go and forget your own destiny."

"So what do I— I mean we, do?"

"Easy," She said, turning to face me, "accept it."

I pushed myself up on the stone bed, dangling my legs over the edge and my younger self joined me, only she leaned up against it with her arms crossed as we both stared at the pictures before us.

I thought about my youth, how I was raised in the care of the monks until I was five and finally let out into the world. I thought about how I was always protected by everyone around me. I'd seen dozens my age be left in the streets during a raid, or taken by

Agents as others fled, but never me. How had I thought that was normal?

"I think you are starting to understand," the younger me said, "You made the mistake of forgetting who we are."

"What a terrible mistake," I agreed.

The little girl kicked off the wall, and faced me, "It's a lot more common than you'd think. Well, if you've finally accepted who you are than I think it's time you meet the other Sage."

"Another Sage?"

"There you go again acting like a parrot. I'm sure once you're there you'll know where to find yourself," she said, nodding her head over to the wooden door on the other side of the room.

I hopped off the bed and took her in my arms, holding her for a moment before I pushed the wooden door open and walked into the next room, sneaking one last peek at my youthful self as I closed the door behind me.

I emerged from beneath an underpass in what I immediately recognized as Dodge, deserted as ever. I began to wander through the streets, as always keeping an eye on the shadows. However, the more I walked the more I began to let my guard down, realizing that the only other people here were reflections of myself.

I began to feel detached from my core self as I wandered, watching the scattered Sages, perhaps only fifteen at the time, act out my adventures in this city. I found one skipping across the rusted roofs of abandoned cars, arms spread wide as she felt the breeze, amidst a freeway frozen in time. Car doors were left open, windows broken, and scattered debris of what the citizens of this city thought important enough escape with littered all over the now grass covered road. Every now and then she would stop to gaze around or watch the clouds pass by, often pointing to one, or another, as if trying to draw someone's attention to it. I sighed, missing the sheer peacefulness I had found but knowing how lonely that reality was.

"Sage!" I called, but could not break her concentration.

I followed her gaze, catching sight of another self sitting on the edge of a skyscraper, legs dangling off the edge as if a fall wouldn't kill me in an instant. At first, from the distance it looked as if she had been waving, trying to draw my attention, but as I focused I could see she had been tossing things from the roof, finding delight in watching them crash down on the cars below.

I pushed forward, feeling as though these particular versions of myself would never offer a response. As I weaved my way through the busy city streets and along the cracked sidewalks I observed many more of my selves, all oblivious to myself and each other, all acting out on their own. Rounding a corner, I was confronted with yet another self, this time spray painting Cekrit's symbol to a white wall. Behind her, another laid lazily on her back, arms tucked under her head humming Sera's song.

None of these reflections would respond, which only added to my frustration with each failed attempt. All these images offered was a glimpse at the shenanigans I had gotten myself into. I wasn't sure exactly where I was walking, or if I'd just been chasing the image of each self hoping that that one would offer a response. Eventually, I found myself standing before the abandoned theater I had called home and realized that out of everywhere I had been, I was always most comfortable here.

One of those old style halls with rows and rows of seats leading up to the stage of my abandoned theater stood before me. On the high up walls to either side I could see sectioned off private booths, though the darkness had stolen them back. Many of the seats had been crushed by falling chunks of the ceiling or toppled over pillars, and even the main walkway in the middle looked more like an obstacle course in the rubble than an aisle.

I entered less cautious than ever, having been given no reason to be threatened in this chamber in particular.

I could hear footsteps coming from the stage as if someone had been dancing, pacing even, and my eyes followed to see myself dancing across the stage with a limp mannequin in my arms, rehearsing the lines to a play I'd never seen. I began to clap, applauding the image of myself on the stage, and, for the first time she noticed me. There was a long moment where she remained still before taking an exaggerated jump back into the shadows as if that would make me pretend I hadn't seen her.

"Wait!" I called after her.

She froze, pausing for a second to examine me with a confused expression before showing herself. She made her way towards me, cautiously, looking me up and down. I stood there as she circled me, taking in every detail.

"Is this some kind of joke? What power is this? Stop it," she ordered.

"Sage, no it's me. Well, you. I mean—from the future."

She stood up straighter then, at least somewhat content with my answer, "Prove it."

I sighed, was I really this difficult?

"Our favorite colors are lavender and emerald. Favorite animal is the fox. Our favorite food is eggs, if we can ever manage to get our hands on them. We were raised in a monastery before being given to be cared for by a family in MarSeir, and everyone around you dies," I returned, confident.

"Okay, I believe you. So what happened to our hair? You look like a pixie," she asked, seeming more than a bit bothered by the change.

I sighed, "I had to cut it off to get away from an Agent, long story."

"Lame," she started, but soon her eyes went wide with excitement, "wait, so my power. When it finally comes in I'm a time traveler? That's so cool."

I buried my head into my hands in disappointment. I guess I couldn't expect this one to be as well spoken as the four year old that just completely opened my eyes to my own negligence.

It took me a few tries to calm her down and try to explain, but I should have realized that by now I had already blocked out most memory of who we actually were and she probably wouldn't be as excited about the fact that Klaus was inside her as she was about being a time traveler.

"You're kidding me," she said after I had finally calmed her down enough to listen.

We laid on our backs, staring up to the age old paintings that were chipped away and faded with time on the ceilings of the theater, with our legs dangling over the edge. As I relaxed, my eyes closed.

Seeing myself as I was then put things in an entirely new light. I was naive, and hopeless as I was with no direction and no sense of who I was or who I could be. I saw a girl who lied to herself and everyone else around her about who she was to a point where she didn't even remember the difference between those lies and a truth she so desperately tried to keep hidden. I saw a girl lost in a world she couldn't understand, worse still, a girl who couldn't even understand herself. It didn't matter where she was, everyone in every camp had always given their lives to protect her even though she was completely useless as a fighter and she never questioned why.

Maybe the reason just didn't matter to her.

I thought back to that time, wondering if it did.

I knew her confusion. I'd wondered so many times why they hadn't just let me die, and why death had a habit of following me like a lost dog. I thought it was just a fact of life that the Agents would always be around.

Maybe they knew something I didn't, like I knew something she didn't. It felt worse now, knowing they may have known my secret even after I forced myself to forget. Maybe I told myself and everyone else around me that I was normal, just a regular Stigma holder—just a late bloomer. Maybe I lied, and believed my own lies in an attempt to save those around me.

Maybe I was wrong.

I opened my eyes and turned towards her to speak, hoping she had the same ability to know what I was thinking as the four year old before her.

I should have been surprised when I looked over and she wasn't there, instead, my more demonic self staring back at me with a crooked smile. I'd say I don't think I could ever get used to seeing myself like that, with skin tight leathery clothes made of gaseous black matter. My hair had a purple tint to it, and my lips, a burnt red.

And I was so pale.

"So," this version of myself began, "looks like you finally learned to accept me."

"Seems so," I returned dryly, still weary of this part of me, for good reason.

There was a shift, and suddenly we were standing in front of the stage in the main walkway. A shadow formed before us, and from it rose the next stone door.

The archway read, *what worries you, controls you. Only acceptance will light your path.*

I examined the door for a long moment, there was no place for my palm. I eyed the darker me curiously, asking for an explanation.

She only smiled and offered me her hand, "Accept your destiny, you can't run from it now."

I paused for a moment, but grabbed her hand in mine, shaking it.

The door opened.

# Chapter 31:

I followed a dirt road that lead into a village unlike any I'd ever seen before. It was easily the size of Terra Sera, but what had surprised me was that it was outside, and throughout the distant hills the homes and farmland stretched into the horizon.

To my right there was a large moss covered wooden sign with the words, *the greatest illusions* scribed across the top in an arch above the words *Third eye*. Below there was another arch that bowed downwards under the *Third eye* carving that read, *are those we create ourselves.*

To the side there was a place for my palm and when I pressed my hand against it the green pulse shot into the ground and rippled through the village ahead of me which then became alive with activity.

I entered cautiously, taking note of everything that was around me. All around people moved about the streets with carefree spirit. There was no sense of worry, no anxiety everyone simply went about their day like nothing at all was going on in the world. Even with a stranger walking their streets no one as much as gave me a second look.

There were men lying down low stone walls, separating their land from their neighbors. Others set the walls for new homes, while others prepared a wooden roof so it would be ready to be placed on top once the stone workers were finished. One of the houses was almost done as I walked past, the walls had been built and the roof ready in waiting.

A man walked up to the roof, which for the moment sat in the middle of the road, and examined it. He took a step back and slowly rose his hands. The roof lifted off the ground, kicking up swirls of dirt beneath it, as it was guided into place. The builders looked on with a slightly deluded sense of amazement, like they have seen this a hundred times before but were still taken back by it.

There was a blacksmith working in an open shop by the street, forging new blades and tools. He kept the fire burning strong as he controlled it with an outstretched palm. He'd take up balls of fire in his hand and work the metal in the blaze, often tossing the flame around like a toy as he worked.

There was a small river that ran along the village to the right, and cut in front of the road that I walked a little further ahead. They'd built a bridge over it to pass, and on that bridge there was a man patiently leaning over the railing as he fished. I wondered why the village hadn't sent someone who could better capture the food with their gift. Then again, I remembered running into some people who fished for fun even if their powers would land them a meal in just a few minutes.

I never understood those people, hunting was about survival, not fun.

There were monks here too, walking amongst the streets in small groups. They took the time to stop and talk to nearly everyone as they passed by, seeming very much welcomed here.

An older monk stopped before me and bowed, "Good day to you," he said kindly.

I smiled, and returned the gesture, but when he stood I noticed something in his eye. Or, rather, I didn't. There was no crescent shaped mark in the iris of the man's eye. He was Pure, but here in a Stigma's village.

It was rare, but not so rare that I hadn't seen it before. Nonetheless I was still surprised to see a Pure monk so old and out in a village like this.

I pressed on, watching the people of the village more intently as I passed.

Children chased each other through the streets, careless and happy as they tossed a ball between them in a fast paced game of keep-away.

"Hey, no fair!" a young girl yelled out as the ball hovered a few feet above her head. The others laughed as she jumped up trying to reach it, but every time the ball would hover up just a few more inches and out of her reach, teasing her.

I walked through the crowd of children and grabbed the ball from the air. She was right, it wasn't fair. She couldn't help it if her power didn't do her any good, the others shouldn't take advantage. I knew the feeling, when I was young they would do the same to me.

"Here," I said, handing the ball to her.

"Thank you," she said with a smile, but again, in her eyes I noticed something was missing—she was a Pure child.

The boy that had been teasing her ran up to me, "Hey you're no fun! It's just a game," he protested, a little extra bite to his words. I immediately looked to his eyes for answers—he had the gift.

In the background I could hear their mothers calling for them, "Come on, it's time to eat."

I didn't even bother to respond, using their parent's calls as an excuse to escape the boys judgement, I needed to figure out what exactly was going on in this village.

I'd run into rogue Pure before, like Tinker, but here they seemed to be living together with people who had the Gift in much larger numbers. There's no way that Zanin would allow proof that we all could live together in peace. If the word spread, then this entire war would be proven a waste and Zanin humiliated. The war would be over, there would actually be some hope for our race. This village here was proof that we could have peace.

I closed my eyes and took in the fresh valley air. Here, there were no worries. There was no war, no genocide, there was no fear. There was only freedom.

I imagined every village, every city, and every camp across the world being like this. Finally free of our own judgements. In time we could all learn to live together in peace, and not as two separate people—but as one. It didn't matter if someone had the gift or not, there was no need to separate each other with labels. One wasn't better than the other just because of a power or lack of. Everyone here was happy, they all had the same worries as each other and that wasn't about survival. At the end of the day we are all still human, and that's what mattered.

I smiled at this, and opened my eyes—but only to see that the skies had been painted red. All around me the stone houses had been broken down to their foundations, leaving only rubble. Fires raged in the streets, devouring everything in their path.

There were fallen bodies by my feet, and around me I could see the shadows of those who still walked. They didn't look scared. Why didn't they look scared?

Something was wrong. Those who remaining were transparent, like ghost walking through the village, completely unaware of the fires and destruction. They faded in and out, entering the doors of their once proud standing homes.

There was laughter, and out of the blaze before me I saw the children running my way playing the same game of keep-away as before, their laughter echoing through the streets. They had beautiful smiles—beautiful, carefree smiles, but those faded away as they ran past, leaving me as just another glimpse of the life that had existed here.

What is this? I asked myself, trying to find some hint of what was going on.

*Don't you see?* The voice in my head questioned, Klaus.

*See what?* I begged for an answer, *fire and destruction? The pain of watching a blissful village fade away amongst the flames?*

Beyond the bridge I could see large shapes making their way towards the village in the distance. I strained my eyes to make out the shape of several groups of Agents marching, with large vehicles by their sides. I'd thought at first that maybe the blacksmith had made a terrible mistake—but it was clear now. This was a raid.

I clenched my fist and without thinking started in their direction, ignoring the flames as I walked through them.

I was angry, and could feel Klaus' energy boiling up within me. I should kill them all—no, I would. I would make them suffer as they have made the people of this village suffer, as they have made the people of the entire world suffer.

My eyes swelled up with tears. It wasn't fair. We can't keep living as two nations fighting for their own survival. The war would never end, hate only breeds more hate.

I was stronger now, and I wasn't afraid, but I wondered if I would be able to kill in order to protect. Could killing others ultimately bring peace?

I understood now that we weren't two separate groups of people. The Gifted, and the Pure—no, we were one. Just like if this war was ever going to end I couldn't treat Klaus' like some parasite within me. Just like the people of this world had to be one, we had to be one as well.

I pushed past the bridge, focusing on the energy within me. I stopped pushing against the waves and let the energy flow, releasing myself to Klaus. His energy was mine, and mine his. I knew now that I couldn't fulfill my destiny if we remained separate.

*Now you're getting it, set me free*, Klaus' voice echoed in my mind.

I looked to my hands to see a darkness spreading up my arm. It reminded me of when Demi would lose his temper and release himself to the void. I couldn't let that happen here.

*I may be giving you your freedom for the moment, but I still control you*, I thought back to him.

The darkness had spread up my arm, my hands were covered by the same plated gauntlets I'd seen manifest themselves before, ready to rip into anything they swept past.

I paused over the bridge, waiting for the Agents to come closer but slowly they began to fade away until they were gone completely. The skies lightened back to a soft blue and the sound of crackling fire behind me stopped.

I looked over my shoulder to see no fires, no destruction, no death. Everything was back to normal, the builders continued building, the blacksmith sill forged, and the children still ran through the streets as if nothing had happened and I questioned if anything did at all?

"Don't look so confused," the fisherman beside me said, not bothering to look away from the water as he spoke. I jumped to attention and shied away, covering my arm as the darkness receded. I'd forgotten he was there.

"What do you mean?" I returned.

"Like the sun, the moon, and all the stars in the sky. Like the river, the fish, and the fisherman- everything is just one part of one whole," he said, looking over his shoulder with a sly smirk.

His eyes were beautiful, a vibrant green, and I stumbled over my words trying not to get lost in them, "I'm not sure what you mean?"

There was a tug on his line then, "Ah," he said, and brought his attention back to the river. A moment later he pulled out his catch, turned to me with a smile and said, "See, if I work against the fish, and the fish against the river, I'd never find my meal. All forces must be one."

With that he nodded his head, threw his catch into a bucket by his feet and started back for the village without another word.

I stood there for a second watching him as he left me, taking his words in.

I turned away from the village to see a door had appeared at the end of the bridge with the words, *all is one*, carved on the top arch.

I made my way to the door, placed my palm flat against it. The door opened and I made my way into the next room.

# Chapter 32:

I stepped back into the same expanse of space I'd been before. As far as I could see, in all directions, there was that same thin film of water atop a flat plane. White grid lines beneath the surface would pulse outward with extra flare with each step that I made. I watched as the ripples tore through the too-perfect reflection of the cosmos above. At first, it was hard to tell what was real and what was a reflection. All around me the stars glistened and planets slowly passed me by. Occasionally I'd catch a shooting star streaking across the sky until it disappeared over the horizon, seeming to collide with its mirrored image.

There was a tablet drifting in space near the door. I kicked off the ground, leaving tiny beads to float away as my foot left the water, and made my way to the drifting stone. I grasped it once I got close, and held it in my hands.

*Crown*, the tablet said. Below was the now familiar hand print, and beneath that the words, *accept the cosmic energy*, were carved into the stone.

I thought for a moment as I drifted in space, lingering just a few feet above the shallow water's surface, my back to the ground. I was staring at the stars above, watching as they slowly shifted in the sky. I clutched the tablet to my chest, not ready to activate this chamber just yet.

I really did love this place, and I wanted to enjoy it as long as I could, but I knew that it couldn't last forever, and after a few minutes of selfish enjoyment I took another look at the tablet and placed my palm onto the stone.

I almost expected another rush of water to overwhelm me as it had before. I'd even closed my eyes and prepared to take an exaggerated breath, not wanting to be surprised like before, but there was nothing.

I opened my eyes, looking for some level of change, but found none. I thought about pressing my palm to the stone once more, thinking maybe this one was broken, but the dissipating green pulse running through the water from me told me otherwise.

The light hit the horizon, but didn't stop there. Instead the pulse shot up into the sky creating a shimmering curtain of green and purple light that curled over me like a dome.

It was magnificent, and I watched as the ribbons of light danced across the sky.

I was at peace.

Before long the light took an entirely new life, beginning to create abstract shapes and forms. The light moved awkwardly at first, but soon everything it created had become clear.

The light took the shape of Ava, smiling as she pranced through the stars. I grew warm inside, and suddenly I couldn't wait to get out of here and tell her everything that had happened. I knew she'd love the stories.

Her laugh echoed and the shimmering picture of her seemed to notice me, she stopped and smiled.

"Sage!" But the voice didn't come from the picture in the sky. I turned, following the sound to see Ava with her arms spread out tiptoeing on the water's surface towards me. She collapsed into my arms and held me tight, "this place is amazing," she said, taking a step back to gaze upon the stars with wonder. She looked at me again, "When will you be back? I miss you."

I smiled at that, "Soon, I just need to figure this last room out."

She seemed content with that answer, nodding to me before getting lost staring at the sky above once more. She pointed to the ribbon of blue light still dancing in the sky, "Look, Demi."

I looked up to see a shimmering purple Demi pacing back and forth.

Ava looked to me with a smile, "He's worried about you."

"Is he now?"

"Mhm," Ava returned with a nod, "It's weird, and I think he might like you more than he admits."

"Oh really now?"

"Yup, why?"

I smiled to myself and wrapped my arm around Ava's shoulder, "No reason."

She just shook her head, "Adults are weird."

I couldn't help but let out a chuckle.

Before I met them, I never imagined myself even traveling with another person and now, after all this time, I'm not sure how I managed without them. Yeah, Demi drove me crazy, and Ava draws the attention of anyone within earshot but still, we were here together, and that made the struggle worth so much more.

I thought about what might happen if we found Sera, and what might happen if we actually managed to save her and bring some peace to the world. It was a crazy thought for me, even now. I'd never dreamed of seeing a day where the world may actually know peace. I know that's what Cekrit fights for, but still the reality that it may actually happen, that I may actually live long enough to see it still made me take a step back.

It wasn't even that I was just going to see it either. I'm drifting in some spiritual realm within myself trying to become better connected with one of our Gods. It was finally setting in that I wasn't just going to be watching, finally, I was going to be playing a part though I'd have to admit I'd always expected to die before that day came.

I'd never looked that far ahead. Even if Klaus hadn't been trapped within me, I'd never dreamed of living so long to see any of this happen. The life of a Stigma holder was short, painful, and I don't think many of us lived with a real plan for tomorrow.

We simply existed.

I didn't have a plan for after this.

When I first met Demi and Ava I'm not sure what my plan was exactly. In reality I fully expected us to die along the way. I'd given up on my own life before I'd even had the chance to live it. That, or I would have run off to live on my own once more by now, and if I did, well, I could be anywhere.

But something kept me here, and as Ava and I stared at the show of bright lights, showing the three of us together. That *something* started to become clear. The two of them weren't just people I was traveling with, I loved them. They were the closest thing to family I had.

It was true that Demi might be stubborn and hotheaded, that he might not tell me how he truly felt. Or that sometimes I had to swallow my own pride and take a step back to let him lead. And it was true that Ava broke nearly all of my rules for survival, and overall drove me mad— but I loved them both.

After all of this, I finally had a plan.

I would stay with them until the end.

"Sage, look" Ava said, pointing to two doors that were sitting on the water's surface just ahead of us.

Both were seemingly identical stone doors, the same that acted as a passage from one chamber to the next. The closer we got the more detail I was able to see. Both doors had a pedestal standing by its side, with another stone tablet resting on top.

The symbols on each door were different though. On the left the symbols arranged themselves into the word, *earth*, while the door to the right read, *cosmos*. I examined each before looking back to the sky, hoping to find answers in the ribbon of light dancing overhead.

*Let go,* Klaus' voice manifested in my mind. *Remove yourself from all earthly attachment.*

I closed my eyes, trying to focus on the words he was telling me, not believing that this was the key to opening one of these doors. I opened my eyes as I felt a void under my arm where Ava had been, she hadn't moved—only returned to a light energy that drifted back into the cosmic curtain above.

There, both Ava and Demi took shape and began drifting down to my plane before standing together by the side of the door that read *earth*.

"What is this?" I asked Klaus aloud, demanding an answer, "I thought the whole purpose of this chakra was to realize I loved them? To not think only of myself for once."

*And you are thinking of them, by letting them go,* he returned.

"What do you mean?"

*By removing yourself from attachment you are unblocking the path to the cosmic energy that beckons.*

"By letting them go? No, I can't, I won't," I retaliated, though I knew my complaints were in vain.

*What grounds you to this world, what you hold onto, are the only things blocking your path. Release them, and you will see your true, cosmic power,* Klaus explained.

I looked to the doors before me, Demi stood with his hand on Ava's shoulder, by the door to the left, and they waved as my eyes met theirs. To the right stood no one, the only thing I could see was a thin line of white light escaping through the bottom of the door.

"And what about them? When I wake up, will they be gone?" I asked.

*The fact that you release yourself from them does not take them out of your life, they will still be there. But understanding that they may one day be gone, regardless of your decision now, will open you to possibilities that may work to save them in the future.*

I had to think about that for a moment before it started to settle in. Letting them go didn't mean that they would be gone from my life. It just meant that with my attachment to them gone then I might be able to reach my full potential. A potential that once reached might actually help me keep them here with me, a potential that might actually save them.

I could decide to keep my path blocked, but that would mean holding myself back from my true power. Still, I didn't even know how Demi was going to react once I saw him. For all I knew he could be planning to kill me once I woke up, or he could already be gone.

My heart ached at the thought.

He could also be there waiting for me, holding back his own anger toward Klaus for me. Either way, if I kept my power blocked than both Demi and Ava could still be gone tomorrow.

I passed the shimmering projections of them another look, they began to drift away like sand in a windstorm, spiraling up into the curtain of light above us. I bit my lip as they left, holding myself back from trying to chase after them.

I stood there, fist clenched, for a moment as I felt my attachment for them escape me. It pained me to feel it go, but once gone I felt something more, freedom.

"I'm ready."

*Allow the cosmic energy to flow through you.*

The curtain of light in the sky stopped then and began to swirl, forming a cyclone of energy that crashed down into the crown of my head. I had little control after that, I could feel the energy rushing through me as all of my chakras came alive.

In a moment everything went still, the light fully absorbed into my body. There were twitches at first, but they faded as the energy settled within me. Suddenly I felt fully in tune with myself and everything around me. Every thought, every action, and everything beyond myself. I now became fully aware as the energy coursed through my veins.

The door opened on its own, flooding my world with an intense white light. I shaded my eyes, and blindly followed it in.

# Chapter 33:

I was back in the white space, an infinite expanse of nothingness in all directions. The only markers I had were the drifting shapes of dark matter that moved about on all planes. I had no real reference of which way was truly up, or down, only of where I was at this very point in this space, but nothing more.

The masses would take abstract shapes, some spheres, some cubes, other's seeming to imitate people, or other lifeforms, but only for a short time—always returning to a shifting shapeless form before it tried again. A mass drifted up towards me, from below. I reached my hand out, over it, stopping it. The mass compressed as it hit my palm, feeling like jelly, but moldable like clay.

I tried struggled to shape it in my hands, but my little creations only would hold their form for a moment before breaking down again.

*Well, that didn't work,* I thought to myself.

"That's because you are doing it wrong," Klaus's voice came out from behind me.

I spun around to see a black throne on a higher plane in the distance, seeming to levitate from where I was standing beneath it. Klaus stood and took a few steps in my direction, but suddenly, something shifted. With one step he had begun to walk straight down vertically, as if on some invisible wall that kept his feet grounded. He casually stepped back onto my plane and closed the distance.

I was in awe, he was a beautiful man, not at all what I might have imagined the famed god of death and destruction to look like.

He wore a pair of black harem pants with golden details running along the side and trim. Even his tasset had the look of polished obsidian ordained with an elaborate golden design. There was a gold sash, with black details, wrapped around his waist, with loose ends that flowed between and around his legs as he walked, seeming to dance around his bandage wrapped feet.

He wore a matching armored chest plate, though I was unsure as to why he may need it in a realm he controls. There was another sash, black, with golden designs matching his armor. It was draped over his shoulders, worn like a scarf and pinned into place with a broach on his shoulder, the loose ends flowing carelessly behind him. His arms donned the same black plated gauntlets I'd seen form on my own arms when he took over. There were four staggered plates, each coming to a sharp point that took up most of his forearm.

I was surprised by his size, expecting a giant, I saw only a man slightly taller than his son and even more surprising, sharing the same youthfulness. This was a man that had created life itself millions of years ago, yet he looked not a day over thirty despite his tied back white hair that fell just below his shoulders and a short, rough, white beard.

I saw so much of Demi in him, but his eyes were a vibrant emerald green. He'd even given me the same half-smirk his son does as he came closer.

The man was magnificent.

"You stare like I'm a stranger," he said, arms open to his side, now only a few feet away.

"I—" I started, trying to find the right words to say, if any, to a god.

"I'm not what you expected?" Klaus joked.

"Well, yeah, I guess," I returned, unsure of what I'd expected exactly.

"Lucky for you I'm not a ten foot demon with six arms and a mustache, though I could make a great impression if you want to see it?" He said, raising an eyebrow.

"I'll pass, thanks," I returned, shaking my head as he managed to draw a laugh from me—relaxing the situation.

Klaus folded his arms, "So, it took you long enough to finally get here. How rude of you to not return any of my calls."

He was sarcastic, I'd give him that.

"Well, I heard the whispers," I returned, then deciding to push right back, "but what kind of guy calls a girl and doesn't leave his name?"

His head fell back in a laugh, "Yet here you are, I guess you wanted me that badly."

"Well, I didn't exactly want you, but I figured if you were going to be freeloading off my body then I might as well get something from it. You're way past due on your rent, you know that right?" I said, mimicking him by crossing my arms and taking a strong stance.

"Ah, so the landlord's come to collect," he said, staring off into the distance before looking back to me, "And my power isn't enough? I've saved your life many times you know."

"But only to keep yourself alive as well," I said, testing my tone.

"True," he returned with a solemn shrug, "I never did figure out what would happen to me if you died."

"Besides, what good does your power do if I can't control it? I can't just sit and wait, hoping you'll come save the day."

"Ah, yes, well—I am a busy person you know. It takes a lot of energy to keep order here," he said.

I took a look around the void surrounding us, then shot Klaus another glance, "Yeah— I'm sure."

He bowed his head in defeat, but perked up again when he started to speak, "So, I've got a better idea. You've done a lot of work over the past nineteen years since I've been trapped here— you know, surviving and all of that. You've worked *hard*, so how about you let me take control for a bit, maybe—end this little war that's still raging outside, save my beloved—you know, end all of this foolishness. It seems as though Sera's little children have failed to save her as planned."

"What do you mean?"

"The doors are open, but you still hold the key. The world needs me, so hand over that key and bada-bing, bada-boom, I kill a few people, restore order to the world, and everybody wins right? Then we can all go on our merry little way," he said with a sly smile.

"And what do I get out of it?" I asked, trying to find some benefit to his proposal, but finding none.

"Peace, rest, I'm sure I'm not the only one who thinks you could use a little R&R, rest and reincarnation! You can stay here, safe, and keep order to this old place while I do all of the dirty work for you. Just give me the key."

"No," I returned, not trusting him.

Klaus brought his fist up to his chin and began tapping his outstretched index finger over his lips, deep in thought.

"Sage," he started, taking an exaggerated step closer, "listen to your elders. Give it to me."

"Rude."

Klaus sighed, as if I had offended him for being difficult, staring at me for a moment before lunging.

I stepped back, dodging his grasp, and as I did I could see a golden chain with a key drifting just above my chest and I wondered when that had gotten there. I didn't have time to think about those things, I needed to keep him away.

I ran, and as I looked over my shoulder I could see that Klaus was close behind. I couldn't run like this forever, I needed a plan. Then, I remembered what he had done as he approached—shifting his perspective as he walked, shifting planes.

Though there was nothing but white space before me, I imagined a wall a few feet ahead, perpendicular to my plane. As the wall drew closer I prepared myself for the shift, and stepped onto the vertical wall and instantly my entire perspective shifted over. The once vertical wall was now the horizontal plane beneath my feet, and once I dared a peek behind me I could see Klaus hadn't yet made that leap. He looked like he was running straight down a vertical wall.

I tried to understand the physics of it as I ran, but came up empty—deciding to simply trust it for now and understand it later. I needed to keep moving. I focused on imagining there was a slope further ahead. I pushed on, hoping to slide down to another plane and lose Klaus as I picked up speed. I hit the slope and slid down feet first, bracing for impact when I decided to stop on a new plane.

Dozens of shifting masses of black matter passed me as I fell, and as I did I watched them grow smaller behind me. I couldn't see Klaus in the distance, and I began to slow down— in full control of what was around me. I stepped off onto a new plane, checking my surroundings.

I felt ashamed for letting him get that close to winning, but proud that I had managed to get away. He'd actually seemed pleasant at first, but I guess his reputation was true.

There were other masses around me, drifting away in all directions as I passed by. I watched curiously as they took shape, and fell apart. Directly ahead of me there was one, staying perfectly still where it was. I decided I was going to give shaping it another try, maybe build something that could help me defend myself.

As I drew closer it began to take shape, which was normal— but as the matter took more and more detail I froze. Klaus formed from the dark matter and came into stride towards me, arms open as if to take me in his embrace. He wore a terrible smile.

"Do you forget, I created this place—you can't escape me here," he taunted.

I backpedaled, trying to keep the gap between us. I couldn't run, there'd be no point if he could just reappear at will. I needed a plan. I needed to contain him. I couldn't hope to fight him, could I?

My eyes searched for another mass, knowing it had to be useful. Still, I knew Klaus would react to it quicker than I could manage to create anything useful. I needed to trick him.

I passed a look over my shoulder, and saw one drifting up from a lower plane in the distance. I formed a plan, turned, and ran along my plane towards it— knowing it would be higher up once I got there.

Klaus followed, "Not this again!"

I pulled the same move I had earlier, only this time I waited for the mass to be above me before I shifted planes along the vertical intersection, now running towards it. I passed another look over my shoulder to see Klaus follow exactly as he did before. I tried not to think, I forced myself to keep my mind off of my next move, I knew he would be tipped off if I thought of my plan.

I waited until Klaus was a few steps away from the drifting matter, turned, and focused on making the matter form an orb around him— trapping him.

It seemed to work, but I could feel Klaus trying to push his way out, using his own control here to manipulate it. I focused, fighting back, holding him in. He may have spent years here, but this was my body, my mind, my realm, and ultimately I was in control here— not him, no matter his power.

He would have to learn that.

Eventually he stopped struggling, but I didn't let my guard down. As I approached he seemed more relaxed through the transparent grey film I'd formed around him.

"Seems as though I'm in a prison within a prison. Can't get much worse can it?" he joked.

I shook my head, trying not to let his charisma relax me, "Let's make something clear right here," I started, nervous to be putting my foot down. "You are inside *me*, which gives me control over what goes on. I understand that we need you, that's why I am here— but giving you power over me won't bring anything but more death to the world," I said, trying to hide the fear in my voice.

"Humans," Klaus scoffed, "always trying to control what they don't understand, rather than just accepting that it exist and moving on with their pitiful lives. As for this war, you've done this to yourselves you know."

"What do you mean?"

Klaus leaned back, eyes closed, resting his arms behind his head as he drifted in space, "The flaw with you humans is that what you don't understand—you fear, and inevitably destroy."

"Your point?" I pressed.

"Through its ignorance mankind has nearly destroyed themselves. I'm starting to think I might just let them."

"How could you say that?" I asked, frustrated with his abandonment.

"How could I not?" he defended.

"They are your people. You created them."

"Sera created them, and they betrayed her. Then, I was stuck with them and knew she would be so upset if I let them go. Even if we could just make a new batch."

"They didn't know what she was when they found her," I retaliated.

"And here they are, fearing me, destroying themselves. I wish that they had never found Sera and I."

"And why's that?"

"There are certain things people are not supposed to know, one of them being why they are here or who made them. You humans were never supposed to find us, you weren't supposed to care, you were just supposed to exist like every other species. But Sera and I watched as you spread cities like a cancer over our world and waged war over mere ideas of your own origin, many of them wrong, some hinting towards the truth—but until our discovery, all equally misguided. Some truths aren't meant to be known, which became quickly apparent. You were never supposed to find your gods, it wasn't your place."

"So we aren't supposed to question who brought us here?" I asked.

Klaus nodded, "What does it matter if you know or don't know? You don't see me asking questions about where I came from—yet here I am, existing, and I'm okay with that. It's simple, just enjoy the fact that you are here and suddenly the why doesn't matter."

I thought about that for a while, leaving Klaus suspended in his miniature prison. I'd found books that told of the time before Mother Sera had been discovered, the world was at peace—truly working together for the first time in history. There was a global democracy, a true democracy, all under one power. It seemed as though we had finally gotten it right. Before, there had been wars waged over false beliefs and ideas, prophecies and legends, but that had become something of the past.

It was only after we discovered Sera that the world was plunged into darkness once more. I guess you can never know how people might react when you finally find out that there is a god, or two. It should have been expected, and people had chosen sides even before there was time for the gift to become known. We'd become a target representing something others couldn't understand, so we must be destroyed.

There are some things in the universe we simply are not supposed to know, and we have to be okay with that.

"You're getting it," Klaus said, breaking the silence.

"What a mess we've made," I said, reflective.

Klaus nodded, silent.

I looked at him then, "I need to make it better, bring back the peace, but I am going to need your help."

Klaus finally reopened his eyes, "How noble of you, but can you kill to bring peace?"

He has a point, violence only breeds more violence— but it was obvious to all who could see that our enemy was not going to back down until we all were dead, this was not something that could be discussed to an end, we had to fight. There was no other option.

"Killing can bring peace, but only if the right people fall. I don't want to walk out of this stained with the blood of people who had no power over this reality," I said, finally.

"But don't they all? Any one of them could choose to fight against this system. Why don't they?" Klaus asked.

I pondered that for a moment, but it was already clear, "Fear."

Klaus looked thoughtful, "Fair enough, but what do I get out of this?"

I thought for a moment, searching for leverage until it came to me, "Sera."

"Oh?" He said, suddenly coming to attention.

"Yes," I said, trying to choose my words carefully, "but we need to kill Zanin first, once we do there may be some hope for the rest of us. I need full control of your power until he falls, and once we find Sera I'll set you free."

"You know where she is?" Klaus asked.

"Hope, one of the Pure cities, and I'm guessing Zanin won't be far," I returned.

"So, after Zanin falls you'll release me?"

"And after we locate Sera," I emphasized. "Once Zanin dies you will be able to take Sera to safety and let the rest of us clean up this mess."

Klaus put his hand against the transparent film acting as his prison, "Do you mind?"

"No more acting up, promise me," I ordered him.

"I'll behave," he said, like a child.

I stopped focusing on keeping the matter in its shape, and relaxed as the tension melted away.

Klaus offered me his hand, "For Sera."

I was reluctant, but took his hand, "Deal?"

"Deal," he returned.

# Chapter 34:

I was shocked awake, gasping for air as I sat up on the cold stone slab of a bed at the center of the monk's ritual chamber, feeling like there was an added weight pressing on my shoulders. I was sluggish here in this physical world, and everything around me lacked the mysticism that I saw in those chambers. Suddenly, normal life seemed—boring.

I clutched my chest. This feeling, this power, I felt as through a tempest raged inside of me— coursing through my veins, begging to be unleashed. But for the first time in my life I felt like I had control over my destiny.

It was an energy that had been brewing my entire life, a force that I had always fought against, rather than with. Just like the fearsome winds and torrential rains could destroy the landscape, those within me had begun to destroy me as well.

Not anymore.

The blur of the world slowly came into focus. Around me, the monks still sat among the piers, watching, waiting. In their expressions I could see that they were pleased, even relieved that I had finally come to. They relaxed, and a few rose from their seats to leave the room.

How long had it been?

I sat there in a daze, trying to catch up with my new sense of reality and responsibility to save our people, to bring peace to this world despite its many flaws. The thought of it was daunting, terrifying even, but only at first. I knew I was far from the late blooming ordinary, powerless, Stigma holder that I was at the start of this journey. I had the powers of a god at my fingertips, and had the power to change things.

I'd finally come into full bloom.

It was then that my world cleared up, and my thoughtful gaze became frantic as I remembered my impending conflict with Demi.

*What did he decide?* I wondered.

I spun around, looking for any sign of him, but there was none, only more monks. I saw Dom Seir standing by the head of my bed, hands clasped within each other, watching me with a too-kind smile.

"Welcome back," he said calmly, unmoving.

"I—" I began, but my thoughts were with Demi. I needed to know what he'd decided, "Where is he?"

The Dom smiled, and motioned to the door, "He's still here, don't you worry. Though, we chose to keep him away from you while we waited for you to come back to us. We couldn't risk any interference."

"How long has it been?"

"Three days. He's very stubborn you know, hasn't moved from outside that door since he stormed out."

"I need to see him," I said, moving to jump off of the stone bed.

Dom Seir put his hand on my shoulder to keep me down, "I'm not sure if that's wise. We still don't know if he is waiting to welcome, or kill you. He refuses to speak, presumably unless it's with you."

A sharp spike of energy shot up my spine as the Dom blocked my path. *I could kill you*, I thought, but instantly felt another spike of guilt as I did, "So what do we do?"

"Before I can have you risk confronting him we need to test your power. We need to make sure that all is working as it should, and in case he *does* attack—you can defend yourself properly."

The thought of fighting Demi pained me, but Dom Seir was right. I had no idea if he was planning to kill me, or take me in his arms. I hated having to not trust him, but I needed to make sure I kept myself safe as well.

Dom Seir was reading my expressions, and released his hand from my shoulder.

"Come," he said, as he motioned to a second door behind him.

I followed, reluctantly, passing a glance over to the large door at the top of the steps where I knew Demi was waiting. I wanted to let him know that I was all right, but at the same time I feared the conversation wouldn't even make it that far. I decided to follow Dom Seir into the next chamber. If Demi waited three days already, he could wait just a little while longer.

The Dom opened the door and led me down a set of stairs lined by lit torches. Slowly, I could make out a circular pit in stone floor, and the closer we came the deeper that pit came to be. When we got to the end of the staircase, I could see that there was a circular walkway surrounding the deep impression in the stone. There was a heavily reinforced metal grid that rested on top, making sure whatever was down there couldn't escape. At the base, there were caged doorways lining the vertical walls.

"What is this?" I asked, after walking around the cut stone to the other side. There was a section there on a hinge, working as a door into the caged in arena.

"Your proving ground," the Dom said, unlocking the gate and holding it open, "this is your final test, go on."

I looked into the pit, my stomach in knots, not exactly jumping at the idea of locking myself into a cage fight, but I followed his demands nonetheless. An instant feeling of fear and regret shot through me as the gate closed and locked me in as I descended.

*Klaus, I think I may need you,* I thought, as I began to see the darkness behind me cut out, barred, doors around me.

*Looks that way*, Klaus returned. *Relax, show them our power.*

"Are you ready?" The Dom called from below.

I nodded, and braced myself for the unknown.

The sounds of cranking gears filled the room as a handful of monks above pulled on chains that lifted the cage's bars. There was movement to my right, and before the bars were even fully lifted I saw my first foe. I felt a new kind of fear then, the fear of what it meant that I wasn't afraid of what was before me, and how my usual panic was replaced with a sense of power and confidence that truly frightened me.

The body of a starved beast ducked beneath the rising bars, the same ungodly things I'd faced in the root chamber. The slits running up its face flared as it honed in on me, and once locked, it snarled—showing a row of knife-like teeth.

I stepped back, falling into a stance that felt practiced, despite my lack of training. Passing another look to the dark cages around me there were three more opening, and in the darkness I could see the orange bioluminescent flares that were the creature's sensors just barely working to highlight their demonic faces.

There was a screech from behind me, and I didn't bother to look, instead focusing on the creature before me—I already knew, another one was coming.

I closed my eyes, focusing on the energy within me, for a moment not worrying about the harbingers of death lunging towards me. I inhaled, and behind my eyelids I had an understanding of everything around me. I felt no danger, only power.

*Open your eyes*, Klaus beckoned.

My eyes shot open, a black mist drifting from my open lips as I exhaled. As it did, all color escaped me—I was back in the white space realm.

Everything slowed down, but not too dramatically— there was just a sense of higher understanding as to what was going on. My body knew how to react. A black mist fumed off of me, lingering just above my skin, and as it settled formed the now familiar black gauntlets, though I wore the same armor Klaus had been wearing, with a ghostly black sash wrapped around my neck instead of golden like his. I smirked, embracing this power.

There was something behind me, I didn't see it—but I could feel it approaching. I tilted my head to the right, just as the dagger-like tail of the beast shot over my shoulder, dodging it. I grabbed the tail with my right hand and pulled it forward, my body unmoving.

The second beast before me lunged, and I took a step to the side, swinging the beast I had taken a hold of by its tail and sending it crashing into my second attacker. The two rolled together and crashed up against the far wall, lying there for a moment in a stupor.

I heard a screech, and passed a casual look to the left—another had escaped its prison and was barreling towards me. It had no color, and hardly any detail. It was black, oily, and a black mist drifted off of its rough frame. It reminded me of the drifting shapes of dark matter I'd seen before. No, it was that matter.

*Had I crossed over*—I wondered.

I decided to test it, and focused on what the creature was made of—rather than the creature itself. I lifted my arm parallel to the ground, palm facing the coming threat. I clenched my fist. The shape of the creature collapsed in upon itself, reverting to small drifting chunks of matter and black mist.

I smiled, pleased with myself, and after passing a look to the watching monks above it seemed as if they were as well.

By now, the two behind me had made it to their feet and sulked towards me, partially defeated, weary, but hungry enough to fight it seemed.

I knew they were coming, though I didn't bother to look. I *felt* their presence, but also knew they weren't a threat, not when I was like this. I brought my attention to the dozens of drifting bits of matter from the beast I'd just destroyed, and focused on them, forming each into thick needles. As I turned to face the two creatures behind me the needles shot over my head like a maelstrom of loosed arrows. Some drove into the ground by the creature's feet, but most made a direct hit, blanketing their bodies. Both fell, and I could only imagine that outside this realm there was no explanation, only death. I doubt the needles manifested themselves in the physical world, and for a moment I wondered what was seen when I reverted the other creature to mere mist.

There was a commotion up top, and I passed a look to see Demi weaving between the watching monks towards Dom Seir, demanding answers. He looked into the pit, and I could feel his terror as another gate opened, and another beast was let out to kill me. He hadn't a clue of what I'd come to be.

I ignored him, and circled the beast as it circled me, locked onto each other, so much deadly force held back like a spring ready to be let go. I wondered who would attack first, so I toyed with the creature, knowing I could handle whatever it had in store for me.

I no longer feared them, I owned them.

As I passed the heap of dead creatures I'd left covered in spikes I debated turning them into summons like Demi's. For a moment I tried to picture the Kurki, Vemosa, and even Demi's own Naukri, Uru. But I wasn't sure if that was wise. There was enough to talk to Demi about once I was through here—stealing his summons wouldn't make him any happier than he already was.

The last remaining creature closed the distance between us. I was growing bored of this game, knowing I'd realized my power— knowing it was time to end this.

There was a loud noise from above, and I shot a worried glance to the surrounding walkway—searching for the source. The gate had been opened and Demi scaled the full height to the bottom of the pit, landing in a crouch, and letting out into a sprint towards the beast, who took a surprised step back and lunged its tail for Demi's head.

In a moment I was between them—grabbing the beast's tail just below its sharp point and continued with its momentum towards Demi. From the corner of my eye I could see the shock in his expression as the death blow came closer.

"Move!" I ordered, and he did, stopping to stand back to back with me as I spun.

I carried the momentum of the creatures blow in a circular arch as its body had turned the other way, snapping at Demi to my left as I spun right—pitting Demi between us in a soon to be closed circle. I danced around Demi, trying not to strike him but trying to move fast enough that the creatures attack wouldn't land at the same time.

Demi was frozen, for the first time since I've known him.

I held momentum, and spun the creature's barb directly into its own face as I closed the circle. It fell immediately, leaving Demi and I both standing in the center of the fallen beast.

I breathed out, relaxing, as the monks above cheered, and a roar of gossip overwhelmed the room. All had returned to normal. I stepped away from the fallen beasts that circled us, taking a broad glance around the pit. The two in a heap to the side rested on top of one another, riddled with holes-- but there were no spikes that I could see.

Even more curious was the lack of the fourth body, the one that I'd reverted to matter and mist. It was simply gone, and I realized how amazing that must have looked from the monk's perspective.

I made my way for the ladder that would bring me back up to the monks, leaving Demi still standing surrounded by the last creature in a daze.

As I left he called behind me, "What was that?"

I stopped, looking over my shoulder, "What was what?"

"You could have killed me, you sent that dagger straight for my face!"

"I saved your life, I didn't tell you to jump in here—I was doing just fine on my own," I returned, and he knew it was true.

He set his jaw, "So it's true then? He's in you, you can control him?"

I didn't answer, only offered an open gesture towards the fallen creatures around us, letting them speak for themselves.

"I see," he said, looking to the ground with heavy eyes burdened by the truth.

"I don't know what you will do from here Demi, I can't tell you. You have your own paths in life, and I have mine. If killing your father is so important to you that you'll try to kill me then I'll have no choice but to fight back, and I have no intention of dying before I can save Sera."

I turned back to the ladder and gripped the first rung before looking over my shoulder once more, "You can try, but I *will* put you down."

# Chapter 35:

I'd left Demi in the pit, and brushed my way past the monks along with Dom Seir. As I did I took more than a few pats on the back and words of congratulations for what I had done, but few tried to stop me. There was a healthy respect in that, maybe even a fear, of being in the presence of a god.

Was I really a god? I wondered.

Or did I just control one?

The burden of being what I was that had weighed me down for so long had finally let off, just a bit—by my own strength. I relished in this new found power, but at the same time I feared that it may come to control me. I'm sure that's what Klaus wanted to happen, even with our agreement he would hope for me to let the darkness consume me, where he holds the most power. Living through me could almost be as good as actually living. It may have even been better, living with the benefit of not having to solve any of the problems he made himself.

On top of those concerns I was furious with Demi, though I wasn't sure why.

What did I expect?

He jumped into the pit to try to save me, I knew that, but I was upset with him for not trusting my power. Still, he hadn't known what I'd unlocked within myself and risked his life to save me, regardless of knowing Klaus is inside of me he still tried to protect me. He could have just let me die there, he could have let the creatures win and saved himself the trouble of killing me himself, but he hadn't and from his perspective I thanked him by sending a dagger swinging towards his face as if hoping to strike him down first, though that's what ultimately saved him.

Of course, he could have been trying to trap me in there with him so he could kill me. If so, why hadn't he tried?

The more I thought about it the guiltier I felt. The fact that he was still here spoke volumes, he could have left me. I'm sure by now he could have talked to the Dom, and found out that Sera was being held in Hope with Zanin. He could have finished his mission's objective on his own, found out where Sera was. He could have left me here and found me once he was strong enough to kill me. He could have fulfilled his dream of becoming a Guardian, of honoring his father's name—but he hadn't.

Why hadn't he? I thought, that maybe they hadn't told him, maybe he hadn't asked? But why?

I found myself angry with him for even staying, knowing that walking by my side now would only bring him pain as he held back his anger towards Klaus. Staying here with me was almost the same as accepting a man he's sworn to kill as an ally.

I wondered if he could ever truly love me because of that.

He was such a stupid, stubborn boy.

I passed monks as I moved through the monastery with no direction, fighting back my tears. Each would give me a smile, but that smile would fade when they felt my troubles. This whole time I'd been worried about whether or not Demi would still be here when I woke up, and at the time I wished that he would be, but here I was, wishing he hadn't.

I rounded a corner and froze. Demi was standing there, a few feet down, waiting for me to come. A sob broke out as I saw him, and I turned to go the other way, unable to face him.

"Sage!" he called, and I could hear footsteps coming up behind me.

I should have ran, I wasn't ready to face him, not yet— but I let him catch up, turning to him and punching him square in the chest with everything I could muster, "Why did you stay?" I ordered.

He looked surprised, hurt, but not physically, and took a step back, rubbing the spot where I'd hit him. He didn't look angry, only concerned.

"Why?" I begged for an answer, "You know it'll only hurt you in the end, why do this to yourself?"

He remained silent, calm. I would almost call it passionless, given his normal ways— but in his silence I could see more passion than he's ever shown me. It was painful to watch. I pounded my fist to his chest once more and he didn't flinch, or try to avoid it, only held me as I collapsed into his arms, holding me tight.

I sobbed, trying to hide my tears. He shouldn't be here, he should have left me behind. I couldn't understand.

"Why?" I asked once more, words muffled in his chest.

He said nothing, only held me tighter, and I finally welcomed his embrace.

"Why did you stay?" I needed an answer.

He pulled away, a smile on his face.

How could he smile? I was everything he wanted to destroy, I could see the pain in his eyes, the hate, and worse— the love.

He dipped a hand below my chin, and with gentle fingers tilted my head up, pressing his lips to mine.

Everything was calm then. In that moment the world around me seemed to melt away. The war, the loss of Sera, Klaus, Lain, the Agents, the camps outside— nothing else mattered—only us. I kissed him back, holding his frame just a little closer to mine, palms to his chest.

A surge of emotion coursed through my body and in those moments I knew now why he'd waited tirelessly for me to come out of that meditative state. I felt like a fool for ever doubting him, forever expecting him to attack me when I woke up. I was ashamed of how I'd treated him earlier. He had faith in me even when I didn't in him. I knew I didn't deserve him. I'd woken up expecting to have a new enemy but instead I found something that terrified me even more to welcome —someone who truly loved me.

I was forced to pull away as the sound of approaching footsteps grew louder in the corridor. I looked around Demi, to see Dom Seir, with Ava in tow, hastily making his way towards us, and as he saw that I was okay the blatant look of worry on his face melted away to be replaced with joy, as if he was expecting to walk into a war, but instead saw a field of roses.

I grasped for Demi's hand as the Dom approached with open arms, placing one hand on each of our shoulders, "I'm so happy to see you two aren't at each other's throats in the way I feared," he said, looking to the ceiling and walls around us, inspecting them. "Furthermore, I don't think this monastery would be able to contain your powers being unleashed on one another."

"Thankfully it didn't come to that," Demi said, letting out a light laugh as he squeezed my hand tighter and I looked up to him with admiration.

"Well," Dom Seir's voice broke my thought, "with this out of the way— we have some things to discuss. Come," he said, waving his hand and turning to walk down the hallway.

I looked to Demi one last time, and shared a smile. Then, I looked to Ava and called her over. She came, reluctantly, and I couldn't blame her. She was still a child, and Demi was the only family she'd ever known. She must have been terrified that I would take him from her or perhaps she feared what I may have become. Either way I took her in my arms and held her tight.

"I'm glad you're okay," she said, wrapping her arms around me.

"Me too, thank you for waiting," I returned.

She pulled away, "So what now?"

"Now," I said with a pause, "now we win this war."

# Chapter 36:

Dom Seir lead us into a circular room fit with floor to ceiling open windows that overlooked the chasms of MarSeir to the left with Dodge lingering on a lush horizon. To the right was an expanse of badlands, cracked, broken, and slowly being consumed by the dunes just below the horizon that ultimately separated MarSeir from Hope was thought to be.

The floor was soft as we walked here, and I could see that it had been padded and layered thick with the finest rugs. There were large pillows surrounding the walls, dozens of them, all overlapping into the next. Almost against the centermost window there was a low circular wooden table surrounded by a semi-circular section of the room that had been indented into the ground, then lined with more pillows.

The Dom stepped down into the indent, and sat— looking deeply out at the world beyond. We filled in next to him, sharing his gaze.

"It's been so long," Dom Seir said after a long moment of silence. "I've sat here and awaited your return. I would be close to saying I regret what we did—trapping Klaus. But we couldn't carry on as we were. I fear he would have killed us all. There were promises that were made in my agreement with the young Madsen. Some have been kept, while others still linger, yet to be fulfilled.

"This was all supposed to be over by the time you realized who you were. We weren't supposed to need you, else we wouldn't have kept that power suppressed for near twenty years. Every day I would sit here, watching as countless waves of our people, our best fighters, our bravest souls, would march out into battle never to return.

"I'd watch the horizon, waiting for the promised power of the Council to come marching over that horizon to save us. I kept my promise, I allowed them to live in hiding so that they may build an army strong enough to win back our freedom. Yet, enough time has passed that they have allowed for the very thing they needed to be kept restrained to manifest itself in you."

I stiffened at the thought, this had all been carefully planned, "So why did you help me release him?"

Dom Seir looked at me with tired eyes, "I couldn't let you suffer, let you wonder, but never know, never have control over your own life."

But he did let me suffer. I'd spent my entire life on the run, my entire life wondering why everyone else around me had died yet I was the only one to ever survive, no matter the odds. Some said I was blessed, but I had always thought myself cursed.

The Dom continued, "I have more loyalties than to Madsen, you are one of my own, like a child to me—I could not hold you back when you were ready to blossom. I may have done something terrible just now, but I feel that I have done worse suppressing it for so long. I'm not sure what the Council has planned, I've only heard faint whispers amongst the few who know of their secrecy, but if true are problems for another day, for now I know that it is time to try and end this war by our own means."

I looked out to the horizon, imagining having spent near twenty years waiting for a promise to be fulfilled—only to be forced to undo the very thing that brought those promises to be. Nineteen years had been wasted waiting for something that would never come. The thought of all of those lives wasted, of watching countless more leave the camp to fight, knowing they stood no chance, all while holding onto the hope for the promise of support to be close behind, yet knowing it would never come, weighed me down.

Nineteen years spent walking the streets of MarSeir, spreading words of hope to those who fought for our cause, answering prayers— always knowing they should have been answered by now, always hoping they would be soon. He'd sent countless men to oblivion with good will, hoping to buy more time for a promise to be fulfilled— all while knowing he suppressed the one thing that may actually have saved us this pain, even if his intent was just at the time. It was a terrible burden to bare, the end never came.

"So what do we do?" I asked.

"I'm unsure," the Dom said, never breaking his gaze to the horizon.

"I'll tell you what we do," Demi said, standing, breaking the silence that followed, "we fight."

Dom Seir waved the boy to sit back down, "We've tried that."

"But not like this," Ava said, "we have Klaus now right? And Demi."

"Two extra people on the battlefield won't change a thing," the Dom said, sounding defeated.

"Then I'll return to Terra Sera and bring back the entire force of the Council," Demi said, confident.

"More empty promises. They won't come, and likely won't allow you to leave," Dom Seir returned.

"Not after you tell us where Sera is, it's information that would change their mind. Look, we brought a book," Demi said, looking to me, and I began to fish it from my bag. He continued, "Maybe you could read it and it will tell us if there are any clues? This language, it's the same that's carved all over your walls, you must know how to read it."

"There is no need, boy, don't you understand? We already know where she is, we always have."

"Then why send us on this mission?" Demi said, lost in the possibilities.

Dom Seir sighed, "Sometimes the plots of old men aren't so transparent. Madsen built his wall of lies high, you won't see past them."

Demi grit his teeth, "I'm sure he has his reasons, even if they were just to make Sage and I stronger. He had to know Sage would realize what was going on? That she would learn to control Klaus, maybe he even knew that we would come to you for answers, and you would help her."

"Then it seems as though he has carefully planned it all from the start, but to what end?" the Dom pressed on.

"He now has two gods in his army." Demi said, proud.

Dom Seir shook his head, and waved an apology, "I'm sorry, I don't doubt your strength, but if we want to win this war then I'm afraid we need to try a different approach than Madsen has taken so far."

"Like?" Demi asked.

"I've thought of that for years, but the idea still escapes me. I haven't a better alternative, though I know our current method to be wrong," The Dom admitted.

"Why not hit them directly?" Ava asked.

"Right, but how would we get so close?" Dom Seir asked, and Ava shied away, having no answer.

"We would need to take the battle off of the battlefield," Demi said.

"Again, how?" Dom Seir returned.

"Leave it to me, I'll figure it out," I said, pondering the possibilities for a moment, finding few that might actually work.

I needed time to plan.

"So be it, we have time. But let me know what you decide," Dom Seir said, rising from his seat.

Behind him, the sun had just been rising, and for the first time I had a true sense of what time it really was. Everyone around me had looked drained, and I could only assume they all had spent the past few days watching over me. I still felt the slight surges of energy flowing through me from before and though the storm had calmed, the winds still churned.

"It's best if we get back to the city," I said, deciding that if there was a plan to be made- it would be found with the help of the others below. I couldn't see how this was something the three of us could do alone.

"Are you sure?" Dom Seir asked, surprised, "We have rooms."

I nodded, explaining my need for the creativity of others, if any of them would even agree to go along with me. I looked to Demi and Ava, asking them if that was alright with them. I didn't want to push them if they were too tired to follow.

"We're with you," Ava said with a tired smile.

I looked back to Dom Seir and smiled, "So that settles it. Thank you again Dom."

# Chapter 37:

As we walked I kept deep within my own thoughts, leading the way out of the monastery and back down into the chasm. There was this new energy within me, driving me, it was revitalizing yet relentless. I felt as though there had been a veil lifted from my eyes, and I saw the world in an entirely new light. I finally had a purpose to be here.

We made our way back into the early morning bustle of MarSeir. I knew we all needed rest and lead us back to the inn we had spent our first night in. Three days had passed, and I knew our room wouldn't be held but the sense of familiarity is what brought me back, despite the owners rudeness.

There was an odd energy in the air, and it made me anxious. As we passed others would stare, cupping their hand to one another's ear to talk in hushed voices. These weren't the curious looks given to newcomers, no, something else was going on here.

Gossip.

My stomach fell into knots as I realized that word must have spread about what happened that night at the bar. Now, with our return, the whole camp was alive with stifled excitement. My anxiety peaked, and I wanted nothing more than to be hidden away back behind the closed door of the inn. I worried, that perhaps they knew my secret—if it was even still a secret. I wondered if they might try to attack us, trying to avenge the fallen friends I slaughtered in the bar, or if it would be written off as just another day here.

I pushed forth with haste, avoiding their gazes, and not feeling like dealing with the owner, lead us to the same room we'd rented days before. Waiting for all watchful eyes to be gone, I closed my own, and focused on the energy within me, building it up, then releasing it out into the ground by my feet. There was a pulse, and I entered into the other realm. The door before me was black and shifting, I passed through it with ease, and looked around the room for signs of anyone still here.

I relaxed, letting out a deep breath, and everything returned to normal. I opened the door, and rushed the waiting Demi and Ava in, only slightly ashamed of having to steal the room.

Demi and Ava both collapsed onto the bed, exhausted, and for their sake I joined them, knowing that despite how I felt I needed the rest as well.

Demi held me in his arms as he slept, and Ava was curled up by me on the other side. I laid there, awake, for what felt like hours, stuck within my own thoughts, keeping a wary eye on the door in case anyone returned. I wasn't sure what I would do if they did, and I cringed at the thought of having to harm anyone— though I knew if I let them get away it wouldn't be long until the entire camp would be at our door with questions.

Luckily, I didn't have to face that, though there was a different kind of commotion outside, and it wasn't the angry mob I'd been expecting. A loud alarm shocked Demi and Ava awake after just a few hours.

"What's going on?" Demi asked, alert.

I had no idea, and reluctantly left the room to see everyone running about in a frenzy.

My first thought was of a raid, but here? Impossible, there were simply too many of us.

There was a boy, not much older than Ava running down the alleyway. I grabbed him by the arm as he passed and felt a tug as his body lost all momentum, "You, what's going on?"

He looked at me, confused, scared, "The Pure pushed past the frontline, our scouts say they just continued straight for us! We need everyone who can fight to ready up and go," the boy said, pulling away from me and disappearing into the chaos of the main chasm.

Demi came up behind me, resting an arm on the doorframe and yawning, "So what's going on?" he asked, oblivious.

I was frozen for a moment, trying to catch my bearings, wondering why I could never earn myself a single moment of peace. The entire city had burst into madness. I turned to him, but hesitated as I saw Ava come up behind him.

What do I do? Do I send us into battle or pretend we slept through the entire thing? Hiding away in the room and hoping the next person we saw wasn't a Pure soldier breaking through? A deep, dark, feeling fell into the pit of my stomach as I thought about that, there was no honor in hiding.

I cringed at the thought of watching that army overwhelm whatever forces we had left. The thought of having to hide in this single room as we watched them sweep the streets for survivors pulled at me the wrong way. I was finally strong enough to fight, finally able to do something with my power. I decided then, that I wasn't going to run—not anymore. I was going to stand and hold my ground, fight and take down as many of the enemy as I could. I wouldn't die, I couldn't—I'd lived my entire life surviving and knew their comfortable lives would breed weakness in their hearts.

MarSeir would not fall, not today.

If we could force the Pure back, we might be able to catch them underhanded. There was a glimmer of hope in my mind, knowing that if we could punch through then there might not be enough defense left back in Hope to stop me from rushing in and killing Zanin, from saving Sera. The thought of it all excited me.

"We have to fight," I said, defiantly, looking back out to the main chasm.

There were men sprinting towards the great plane, the expanse of dunes in the distance. They pulled on armor and tightened straps as they ran though many rushed into battle with nothing but the clothes on their back.

I could see Pure here too, not the enemy, but exiled Pure. They'd stashed the weapons of fallen Agents and strapped on their body armor. The armor was painted in tribal patterns, with bright colors that stood out from the original dullness of the armor's metal. On many of the plates Cekrit's symbol had been painted.

I made a mental note, not everyone dressed like an Agent is an Agent. I had to be careful.

I heard Demi behind me, "What?"

I'd made my decision, I had a god trapped inside me, I couldn't just sit back and watch as the people who needed me died, "I'm going with them."

"Sage, we can go warn the Council. The battle today may be lost, but we can come back with more force than this camp has ever seen."

"And with half the honor," I spat back at him.

"Sage," Demi began.

"Go back if you want, but I can't trust that the Council will come to help. If we return, then what? You'll get caught back up with the Guardian games and fall back into life there. You have your goals Demi, and I can't stop you, but I will not leave my people to die."

Demi set his jaw, and passed a worried look to his sister before he spoke, "I can't risk you getting hurt, stay here, keep the door locked, and hide if you need to. I'll be back for you, I promise."

I was already moving with the pace of the crowd by the time Demi caught up to me.

"You better know what you're doing," he said.

As we moved, the streets were chaos around us. Dozens rushed past as we made our way towards the dunes. Others ran the opposite way, fleeing MarSeir to escape with their lives.

*Cowards*, Klaus spat, *to think Sera chose you.*

He was right. There was no honor in their attempts for self-preservation, it was a Stigma's job to live and die in the pursuit of saving our mother, and if this battle meant the possibility of killing the ones standing between us and that goal it was an opportunity we couldn't let pass.

We'd made it out of the chasms and onto the vast desert plains that lead into the dunes beyond. I hesitated for a moment as the Pure's army peaked the closest dune a half mile in the distance. Already, there were heaps of bodies littering the ground where the dunes spilled over onto the cracked ground of the plains.

More rushed in, without order, every man for himself— but fighting towards the same goal.

Demi halted, letting others pass, watching the battlefield before us with empty eyes that had already become pits of darkness, "Are you ready?"

I clenched my fist, and let the pulse come more freely. The white realm didn't come this time, at least not entirely. I had a heightened sense of things, and as the pulse rippled through I watched others run headstrong into battle.

There was a storm brewing inside of me, a tempest coursing through, begging to be set free. It compelled me to move, urged me to fight, to be stopped by nothing that dare step in my path, to kill until there was nothing left.

"Let's go," I said, bursting out into a sprint as the black mist around me solidified into gauntlets and my armor, this time, mirrored what I had seen Klaus wear when we spoke. I wore a black chest piece, with golden detail, shaped perfectly to my frame, the same tasset, and the front of my legs were covered in a staggered armor that worked with my movements flawlessly. Even the golden sashes he had worn lingered over me, now little more than a black mist in their stead, but slowly coming to form. I felt as the wind itself— bursting into the heat of battle.

Demi struggled to keep up with this speed. A black mist had begun to form beside him as he ran and, in a moment, Uru burst into full stride. Demi immediately grasped at the beast's mane and pulled himself up onto its back without ever losing step. The Vemosa followed, as always— one to either side of Demi, drifting like reapers in the wind. Beneath, the Kurki breached in and out of oily pools as an angry school of fish might.

*No more distractions,* Klaus ordered.

I looked ahead and saw only chaos. Cekrit's force worked alone, individual fighters tried to rush the dune, but a long line of Pure soldiers fired down on them in formation, stopping them before they even had a chance to attack. It was a massacre.

I set my jaw and pushed forward, extending my arm to the side as a black mist lingered in my waiting palm. A moment later a long spear came to form, it's top quarter solidifying into the shape of the mist in which it was conjured—still weightless in my hands.

I focused my energy on the blade's tip, hoping that my idea would work as I'd imagined. I pressed on, passing a man who'd built a wall around himself as a shield, launching chunks of stone at the force atop the dune in a hailstorm. As I passed him I yelled, "Stop throwing rocks and make a damn landslide!"

I made sure he heard my order, watching as he shook the dumbfounded look off of his face.

A pulse shot out of my blade as I let out a broad swing before me, releasing my energy throughout. Only a few yards thick, the pulse rippled over the battlefield. As it passed through, all that were in its narrow field were slowed, ever so slightly, as I'd anticipated. The pulse pushed forth, moving past the Agents. Their bullets seized for a brief moment, giving our attacking force a narrow window to gain ground through the lag.

I spun around, yelling back to the man behind his wall, a bit frustrated that he hadn't done as I'd ordered. It would have been perfectly timed, "Now!"

The man jumped to action, swiping his hand to the side, his face contorted and strained having reached his limits, but it was enough.

Just as my pulse passed through the Agents fire began to rain once more, the ground from beneath them let out, sending them tumbling in an avalanche of sand towards us.

Demi burst past, barking out orders to those he ran by. I could hear him over the screams and cries of war.

"Form ranks!" he'd order, "You three, hold this ground."

He wasn't fighting directly, he'd sent the Kurki into battle. In the tumbling sand I could see bubbles of darkness form as the Kurki ambushed the falling Pure soldiers.

Beside Demi a single Vemosa now followed. I looked over my shoulder, back to MarSeir, and saw the second lingering in the distance, and was silently relieved that we had an escape plan.

The sound of gunshots brought my attention back to the battle to see the soldiers that hadn't been buried in sand managing to get up, desperately trying to fend off their attackers.

Above, I could see someone flying overhead, rifle in hand, firing upon any Pure soldier who reached the top of the now diminished dune. A moment later, they were shot out of the sky, and sent spiraling to the ground. I cringed at the crunch of their bones breaking and flesh smacking down onto the earth.

There was no helping him.

I pushed forth, but stopped short as the world around me slowed down. A stray bullet had made its way through the crowd and came straight for me. I focused on it—shifting the plane it traveled on, and all went back to normal. Just a few feet in front of me a small plume of dust rose as the bullet changed course and hit the ground.

*Pay better attention,* Klaus snapped.

The man who had caused the landslide ran past, the stone wall that had acted as his shield moving the earth before it as he ran.

At dune's crest there was a fresh line of Pure soldiers just now catching their first glimpse at the carnage below, some of them looked more heavily outfitted than others. I cursed, expecting Agents instead of regular soldiers, why had they come so late?

Why keep pushing?

The soldiers atop the dunes weren't Agents, instead, plumes of fire were let out of hoses that the larger soldiers held, not bothering to aim away from their allies on the ground. The inferno stopped short, as if blocked by an invisible wall, just as it hit the fighting Pure's line at the base of the dune, stopping the blaze from touching any of Cekrit's forces.

The flamethrowers cut out immediately, but the churning inferno stood in its place, contained. My eyes searched for the Stigma who controlled it, and I found him lying on his back at the front line, hand stretched outward as the blaze churned around him, narrowly escaping his death as the Pure's soldiers danced around him in flames, their cries a ghoulish chorus.

It was all over in a moment as he pushed the explosion back up the dune and into the forces above. The soldiers that held tanks of gas on their back tried desperately to remove them, but the fiery wave came too soon creating a chain of explosions down their line.

I could feel the heat from where I was, and when the smoke cleared there was little left of the dune. The explosions had left a crater, splitting the dune in two with the sand on the outer edges falling in.

Our army began to cheer, but through the smoke and heat distorted air I saw that we had nothing to be happy about. We had only just begun.

I found Demi, "What do we do?"

He paused, looking out to the approaching army, "They are relentless aren't they?"

"You have no idea," I returned, truly worried about what we were up against.

The soldiers around me looked weak, and tired, some must have retreated from the battle earlier— only to be pit up against the enemy once more here. We had to hold our ground, else we'd lose MarSeir.

"We need a plan," Demi said, mostly to himself, "these men know nothing of war. They fight for themselves, and not for those around them. There's so much potential if only they could work together, their gifts could complement one another."

"What do you expect?" I asked him, "It's an army of rebels and exiled. They have no order, no command. They don't train, they fight."

From behind us there was the joyful sound of laughter, and I turned sharply to see what had happened.

A man had begun to stand back up on his feet, beside him, Ava still knelt, the green glow of her healing power just now fading.

The sound of a single shot in the distance broke the silence, and not a moment later the same man she'd saved fell to his knees before collapsing to the ground, a fatal wound to the head.

Demi burst into action, leading Uru to Ava and snatching her up in his own arms as they passed. I followed, as we ran for cover by the sides of the dune that still remained.

Most of those who survived had done the same, ducking out of sight to either side of the dune.

Demi let his sister down, and jumped off of Uru.

"What were you thinking!" he yelled.

"I just wanted to help!" she yelled back, matching his intensity. I'd never seen her so worked up.

"That bullet," Demi started, calmer, "it could have been you it hit."

"And it wasn't me."

Demi gave her a stern look, "I told you to stay in MarSeir."

"No," she bit back, "I'm tired of always being left behind. I'm not weak. I can help."

Ava didn't give him a chance to respond, she'd turned and began to work on some of the injured that had been carried to cover. She worked quickly, and efficiently. Silent as she moved from one patient to the next, unnerved by their cries and blood.

Within minutes others were being brought over to her to be cared for.

"Demi," I said, trying to give him something productive to do, "get whoever is left into some kind of order. They don't have a leader, so become one for them or else we'll just keep fighting this losing battle." I passed another look to Ava as she took on another patient, this one looking as if he'd lost a lot of blood, or at the very least shed some.

"She'll be fine," I assured him.

Demi grimaced, but reluctantly did as I told. She was here now, sending her back over the planes would only put her in more danger.

More and more she took on the wounded, working tirelessly- and it wasn't long before I saw the standing force around us multiply as the injured became healthy again.

We had an army again but still, we needed a plan.

"Demi," I called, and waited for him to look over from giving commands to a small group beside me, "we need time. Send some Kurki over to keep them busy."

He nodded, and seconds later I began to hear gunfire on the other side of the dune as the Kurki tore into them. I wished, for a moment, that we could just sit here and let Demi continue to summon the Kurki until the Pure retreated, but I knew that wouldn't work for long. Eventually they would push onward.

As more shots rang out on the other side I could see the others around me grow tense, anxious, expecting the Pure force to storm through and take us down. None of them dared to steal a look to the other side.

I tried picturing the landscape from the Pure's perspective. The gaping hole in the dune offered only a glimpse of the vast expanse of cracked desert land ahead, littered with motionless bodies, and only a small handful of injured still stirring.

For all they knew there were no survivors and the only decision now was whether or not to roll the attack onto MarSeir. We could use this, the Pure force would walk past the dune expecting nothing but land between them and a raid of the Cekrit stronghold. We had the element of surprise, but that luxury could be easily lost. I knew no one here had the discipline to withhold an attack. Any of them could strike at the first sight of an enemy soldier, and the element of surprise would be gone entirely.

I looked around, and motioned the others to stay close to a dune that had the fingers and arms of those who were left trapped in the landslide, though I couldn't tell whose side they were on. Not that it mattered now that they were dead.

I looked away, searching for an answer, and it was only then that it hit me. My eyes went back to the buried, and I realized what could be done.

In a hushed voice I told everyone on my side of the dune to bury themselves in the sand, allowing only room to breathe. They were reluctant, at first, but as more and more disappeared into the sand others began to follow.

On the other side of the dune the others watched, and soon began to follow suit until every person was buried beneath the sand. I was the last to go, scanning the dune and contemplating the possibility this could actually work. If you knew what to look for it wasn't too difficult to see, but to an unsuspecting force, already expecting all others to be dead—it was perfect.

I buried myself in, and waited.

The minutes passed like hours. The gunshots had stopped as Demi called off the Kurki, leaving only silence. Soon, there was the sound of movement growing louder. I held my breath, sneaking a glance with my one unburied eye towards the opening.

The first line of soldiers broke into my field of view, and gradually there were several more marching behind them. My heart raced as the seemingly endless line of soldiers came through, but I found comfort in the fact that not a single one dared break their forward gaze. In this case, their training had worked against them.

It was a fine line to walk, the more soldiers I let through the dunes the more likely we were to be surrounded by those still coming. I couldn't let the front line get too far, but needed to maximize the damage done. I tested the cutoff point, letting them march as far away as I dared.

*One more*, I told myself and as it came, *one more still*.

I did that until my body reacted on its own, drawing away from the dune, spear in hand, and tore into their ranks. The others followed, and soon, all order had been lost for both sides. The battlefield had become a maelstrom of fire, bullets, and twisting sand. There was no order, only chaos, and in the middle of it all—I found peace.

A soldier turned, after shooting down one of my own, he was surprised, but raised a rifle as I lunged. A bullet ricocheted off my tasset, and another off my chest piece by my ribs. I slashed at him with my spear, cutting a deep canyon across his chest. Just as the blade began to tug it reverted to mist, allowing me to slice clean through and carry my momentum into the chest of another soldier just as the blade solidified once more.

*Feed me.* Klaus' voice rang in my ear as I slashed through another, and another, my bloodlust insatiable. With each strike my spear would pierce their armor before reverting to mist, always allowing me to slice clean from the void while never losing a step. I'd launch my spears into the chest of those who approached me only to have a new one seamlessly materialize in my grasp ready to meet my next target.

There was another soldier standing before me, hesitant, stumbling back and dropping his weapon in fear, "What are you?" He begged.

*I am your god, and I've come to bring the Reckoning,* Klaus said, though only I could hear him.

"Hungry," I returned instead, licking my lips.

I dropped my spear, which became a plume of mist as it hit the ground, and clutched the man's shirt with a clawed gauntlet and sent him hurdling into a triangular formation of his own soldiers. The men struggled to recover, and I turned to walk away as the ground beneath them began to collapse upon itself, sending the men into an abyss as they desperately clawed at the crumbling ground hoping for freedom.

I found delight in their peril.

What was I? I knew the answer, but the question came anyway.

Who was this?

I'd never enjoyed the thrill of battle so much. I was normally fearful, scared for my life, but as I walked amongst the chaos I found order, I found peace. I enjoyed this, and I was disgusted with myself for it— despite this overwhelming sense of joy.

As I walked I reached to the side, grabbing the only slightly too long hair of a Pure Soldier whose back was towards me. I pulled down, snapping his neck, and letting him fall limp on the floor. One of our troops ran to the fallen enemy, and stole his rifle, immediately letting out the entire clip into the still coming resistance. He was shot down moments later—I felt nothing for him.

"Fool," I murmured.

I approached Demi, who held a circle all his own. The ground beneath him had begun to pile with bodies of the fallen as more and more rushed him. Uru had been running through the crowd, tearing into anyone wearing the wrong colors. Bullets flew through the beast, never hitting him, he was like a ghost in the wind.

Around Demi, the Kurki took down anyone with a weapon, allowing only those without one to rush into Demi's circle of corpses. Demi fought only with his hands, and those who rushed him must have found a respect in that. On many, I could see daggers strapped to their belts, or leg, but none had turned to their weapon for help. I guess there was some honor among them.

Demi tore into them, sometimes facing two or three men at a time. He seemed to dance with them, weaving in and out of their blows, not once being touched as he snapped one's neck, disabled another, or chopped at one's throat—leaving them to fall to the ground coughing up blood. He was ruthless, efficient— nearly his entire body had been consumed by the darkness creating a thick black skin, cracked and plated, demonic even. He was such a beautiful monster.

A Pure soldier took aim at Demi from a distance, outside the range of the Kurki. I guess he didn't follow the same code as the others. I walked up behind him and placed a hand on his shoulder as he aimed and changed the inflection of my voice as I spoke, allowing Klaus' to come out, "Cease fire," we ordered.

The soldier lowered his weapon, "But sir," he began, and turned to look at the officer who issued the command.

When he saw me he jumped back, and rose his rifle once more, to me this time.

I reacted to what came next before he even had the chance to pull the trigger. I let out a pulse and time slowed only for the moment that he'd let his finger slip. I watched the bullet escape its barrel, and focused on it— changing its plane like I had before. I set it on a vertical plane first, then rotated it once more so that it was facing in the direction it came.

Time continued its course, and the soldier fell, killed by his own bullet. I stepped over him and made my way to Demi's circle, conjuring the spear in my hand once more.

Three more men attacked him, and as he took two of them down I cut down the third. We stood there for a moment, in silence, looking out over our gleaming sea of bliss.

There was so much death, so much destruction. Bodies from both sides littered the ground, but I was glad to see more of our own soldiers still standing than the enemy. The rest of their force seemed to be retreating, though whether they were abandoning or following their orders remained a mystery to me.

It wasn't time to rejoice, not yet. There was still more blood to spill.

Then, amidst the chaos I saw what was coming. The soldiers were not retreating, no, they were regrouping, ready to lead a new force into battle—though their numbers were clearly diminished.

I looked to the front lines, unsure of what was before me. Before us there was a line of a half dozen mechanical humanoid war machines, fully upright and standing with their own two robotic legs, their arms equipped with a plethora of weapons. Easily the machines would tower over any of us, standing around ten feet tall, large enough to hold a pilot in its center. The limited number of Pure soldiers followed behind these machines with what Agents had survived.

Instantly the machines let into those still standing to fight in a maelstrom of bullets. Demi and I acted swiftly, the Kurki already swarming one as the others fended off the last of our forces. I watched carefully, at first, realizing that raw firepower was not the only thing these machines had in their arsenal. The machines began to behave differently once approached, and some had seemed to possess the Gift themselves. I wondered what kind of technology the Pure had managed to create, wondered if perhaps they had learned to mimic the gift, to steal it—I wondered if this was all an illusion.

Either way, I didn't have time to wonder.

I sprinted for another, spear manifesting in my ready hand. Once solidified I hurled it at the machine, lodging it deep into one of its legs near the knee. In rhythm with my stride spear another formed, ready to be launched. I did this with nearly every step, sprinting toward this monstrosity now littered with my spears. The machine had fallen and as I approached the light in my world seemed to disappear. A dome of rock formed around me, leaving me alone with this machine inside once it closed over. I approached slowly, trying to study it as much as I could while I had the moment—feeling as if it were no longer a threat.

As I approached I noticed something, something that disturbed me, terrified me even. Fixed to the center mass of the machine there was no Pure pilot, rather, I saw a cold, near lifeless body hung at the center as if crucified. The closer I looked the deeper my heart sank as I realized what the Pure had done.

"Vatz," I cried, recognizing the man fused to this machine, "Vatz no!"

I looked deep into eyes that were glowing bright and fuming, as if ablaze by a ghostly green flair. Vatz's head rolled forward, revealing veins that looked as if they were trying to push out of his skin, throbbing, black, toxic veins. His gaze lingered on me for an eternal moment and I cupped his face in my hands, allowing his endless stream of tears to wash the blood from my hands.

"How could I let this happen to you," I sobbed, "I could have saved you!"

I looked back into his eyes, which offered little more than a window to his now vacuous existence, a look into a body whose soul had been broken.

I realized then, that this was the fate of those who were taken back to the domes. They were forced to kill those of their own kind, forced to witness the cruelty of this world with open eyes, forced to live out a fate worse than death.

I could hear but a whisper as Vatz's mouth opened, and I held him nearer, hoping to catch his words.

"Kill…me," the words struggled to manifest themselves on his lips.

"I— I can't" I started, but he only repeated himself.

I tried to think of a way I might be able to save him, but I only had so much control. I couldn't think, not clearly, his repeated words an echo in this shell he'd made. I knew even if I could get him out of here he would never recover, and I knew what I had to do.

Slowly, I rose his head up and kissed him on the forehead, bracing myself.

"I'm so sorry," I began, taking a step back.

The spears that had been wedged into the metal frame all turned to smoke once more, forming into a single spear in my hand. I rose the blade's tip to Vatz's head, holding the point steady with the center of his forehead. I lingered there for a moment before closing my eyes and lunging forward.

In that moment the dome around me began to fall as I stood there in petrified mourning. Falling stones crashed around me, but I remained protected by a deflective field I'd formed around myself, a personal bubble.

When my eyes opened I could see only red, feel only rage.

I saw a group of Agents still holding their own by the base of the dune. That was expected—they were more heavily armored than any of the regular soldiers, and far better trained. They'd created something much like what Demi had, a ring of bodies surrounding what little ground they held.

I rolled my head, cracking my neck, before I made a straight line towards the Agents, cutting down any soldier who stood in my way, enjoying the feel of my spear ripping through their flesh more than most should.

The Agents faced me, having killed all other challengers, and as they did I dropped my spear and interlocked my fingers in front of me, letting each pop as they extended.

The Agents dropped their rifles, and took a loose formation. I smiled, seeing they had a sense of honor after all.

As I entered their circle the closest stepped forth and sent a head sized fist soaring towards my face. I moved slightly to the right, letting him miss and extend his arm over my left shoulder. His body was close to mine, open. I took my left hand, formed a point with the claws of my gauntlet and drove it through the Agents thick armor and into his stomach.

"You forget your manners, you're never supposed to hit a girl," I said as I opened my hand inside of him, allowing the staggered sections to open, ripping chunks as I pulled my hand back out and letting him fall to the ground by my feet.

The two remaining Agents took a step back, but bolstered. This time they came at me together. The first Agent, to my right, sent a fist to my face as the second Agent swept low for my feet. They were trying to let me decide which way I wanted to fall. Dodge the fist and trip, or dodge the second and be punched. I decided I'd dodge both.

As his fist came I jumped into the air to the left, dodging it, as well as the second Agents swept leg. I grasped the thrown punch, wrapping my hand around his fist as my left hand found the Agent's shoulder. I pushed off of the second Agents face and my momentum carried me as I pushed down on the first Agent's shoulder while pulling up on his arm, popping his shoulder right out of its socket, for pleasure's sake. He screamed in agony as I released his fist and rose my hand to chop the back of his neck, crushing his brain stem. He fell instantly.

The last Agent scrambled to his feet, in a daze, immediately turning to make a feeble attempt at escape. I'd left his companions lifeless in a matter of seconds. They should have just shot me, though only I knew that wouldn't work either. They'd grown cocky— Zanin's best fighters, they'd grown cocky.

The fleeing Agent was no longer a threat, he didn't even bother to recover his rifle as he ran in fear. I sighed, remembering the good old days when an Agent would fight to kill until he was killed, and Agents were seldom killed.

That ticked me off.

I extended an open palm, placing my hand flat against an invisible wall. I focused my energy on that plane, and pushed, letting out a pulse that rippled through the landscape.

A darker laugh than I'd ever heard bellowed as I watched the Agent run, as if to escape the coming white pulse. Of course, it's not like he knew what was going on, he couldn't see it—this was purely for my own enjoyment.

I'd made a game of this shift, that white space that once would envelop my entire world was now focused in a pulse only a few feet thick, as before. The pulse rolled over the landscape, giving a short glimpse to the realm in which I had complete control. As the pulse passed over rocks, and fallen bodies, I saw them as the dark matter I'd learned to control.

The wave hit the Agent then, and like everything else he was seen in the same gaseous, oily, dark matter. I'd surprised myself with my own control this time, and I toyed with it. With the pulse just a few feet thick, I only had a moment to play my little game. I focused on the Agent as he became frozen in that sliver of space, his raw energy showing. I waved my hand, and the rough human shape of an Agent faded in the wind like the sand.

The pulse passed, and all that remained was a thin black mist, soon to be carried away with the breeze.

Around me, the fighting had ceased entirely.

We had won.

# Chapter 38:

I found myself back in MarSeir, sitting beside Demi and Ava in the same crowded bar that I'd massacred dozens in just days before. No one seemed to care, I'd left them as just a shadow in the night, an unexplainable disaster. I'd returned to them a hero.

The three of us sat along the bar's long counter, drained from the battle but the residual effects of adrenaline forbidding to grant us sleep. The storm inside me had calmed down, the crashing waves of energy had turned to a gentle roll that washed over my body. I'll admit it was soothing, it relaxed me as I emptied my drink, ordering another. Anything to keep my mind off of the things I'd just done.

There was a seemingly endless flow of now drunk Stigmas patting me on the shoulder, congratulating me for our victory. Somehow they seemed to credit me with that. I would smile at their gesture, telling them that we all played a crucial part today. Many couldn't accept the return compliment, and sent a volley back to me.

Eventually, I stopped pushing their compliments away, but tried my best not to relish in a sense of pride or honor for what had happened. I'd lost myself in the darkness, and I finally knew now why Demi struggled with it as well. Just like it consumes him in battle, it had consumed me. I'd killed dozens, perhaps hundreds, without a care, without a worry—I was callous.

Even Zanin's pride, three Agents in full armor, fell as if they were mere ants beneath my boot. I'd come a long way.

"You were amazing!" A man came up beside me, hand on my shoulder.

I nodded a thank you and lifted my glass, touching it to his, and he disappeared back into the crowd.

I eavesdropped on the conversations around me, though I tried not to be drawn into them.

"She was like a god," a woman said.

"I haven't heard of such power since the Reckoning," another joined in.

"Could it be? Has he come back?" A man asked this time. I could feel their eyes on me.

Demi sat beside me with arms lazily propped up on the counter behind him. He was surrounded by others, though they kept a healthy space from me. He relished in the attention, as always, accepting drinks as the cost for another drawn out story of valor. I let him have his fun, he'd lived with some level of what I just witnessed his entire life—he deserved it. He welcomed that darkness, and had obviously grown past the regret unleashing it would bring.

A man came up beside me, not bothering to sit, leaning over the counter as he ordered. "Rumors are spreading," he said, not bothering to look at me. He wore a large hat with a rim that extended outward, casting a shadow on his face.

There was an aura about him that drew me in and though I wasn't much in the mood for conversation he'd been the first not to congratulate me. The offer of something more than praise tempted me.

"Excuse me?" I returned, passing a quick glance toward him.

I saw a smile break on his face, "Sooner or later you're going to need to give them answers. You have no ordinary power, and if you let them talk who knows what they'll believe to be true."

I scoffed, swirling the rest of my drink in the bottom of my cup.

"Then let them talk," I said, before taking the last sip.

"Bold," he said, taking his drink and paying the bartender, "so what are you?"

I laughed under my breath, "Would you believe me if I told you I was a god?"

"I fear I've come to believe stranger things," he returned.

"Oh, have you now? Like?"

"That I would ever be driven from my homeland, forced to walk alone after losing everything I've held dear to me. That I would be here now, in a bar, surrounded by those I was once sworn to destroy," he said, looking down at his cup, thoughtful.

"So you're an exiled Pure. You're not the only one here," I returned, failing to see something hard to believe in what he'd told me.

"Ah, but there's more. I was once an Agent, but I'd lost my squad on what was supposed to be a simple mission—to kill one man. Instead, only one man returned home a failure."

I looked at the man beside me more intently then, "Anderson?"

He smiled, tilting his hat so that his face came into the light. He looked terrible, bruised, cut, and tired. His eyes wore deep bags beneath them, his once clean shaven face growing stubbly, "We meet again."

"I—what happened to you?" I asked.

The glimmer of light I had seen in his eye as he looked at me faded, growing cold once more, "I served Zanin my entire life, like all Agents, given that we are chosen at birth. In return, he murdered my fiancé in cold blood as punishment for my failure, banishing me from the domes to die out here."

"I'm sorry," I managed to say, placing a hand on his shoulder.

"But that's not what I've come to find hard to believe, and not why I've come here."

"Then what?"

"I want to kill Zanin," Anderson said, after taking a broad look around the room.

There was silence between us as the weight of the statement set in. I'm sure everyone in this room would be glad to kill that man by their own hands, but coming from an Agent the gravity of that could be felt.

"How?"

There was another pause before he spoke, he seemed to be choosing his words carefully before deciding what to say, "We sneak you in."

"Don't you think I've thought of that? The dome is a fortress, how am I supposed to walk in undetected, then expect to get close enough to Zanin to do anything?" I asked, shunning his plan.

"You won't need to go undetected. I have every intention of walking you right through the front gates. Well, more or less."

"I thought you were exiled?" I asked, looking for some clarity in his plan.

"I am, but I was also an Agent—that still gives me some leverage. If I return saying I have the second lost god as my prisoner, Zanin will be forced to let us enter. The possibility would be too tempting. He's already captured Sera, with Klaus captured as well the Stigma would have no hope of survival. Of course, you will only act as my prisoner until I can get you close enough to kill him."

*So she is there.* I thought to myself, happy for the extra validation. He had a point, but using myself as bait was dangerous-

and without Demi and Ava by my side I would have to rely on my own power to kill Zanin and then the force of an entire city that would come for me. I couldn't expect to walk into Hope, assassinate the most powerful man in the world and walk out without trouble, even with Klaus' power at my command.

The idea was daunting, but it was better than anything I could have dreamt of.

Zanin needed to fall.

"When?" I asked, finally.

"Tomorrow."

"Why so soon?"

"After what you, and these men, did to his army today?" He said, gesturing to the crowd behind us, "He must be low on troops, and I don't think you want to run against his army at full force, alone," Anderson said, eyeing me.

I sighed, "You have a point."

"Besides, he must be furious after this defeat— they'd been trying to take MarSeir. Well, until you showed up. I'm sure he wants you dead, or at least captured, and when I walk up to Hope presenting you as a prisoner of war there's no doubt in my mind that he'll see you as soon as he can. He'll want answers."

I passed a look to Demi and Ava, knowing that I would be leaving them behind. There was no other way, not without risking their lives and I couldn't stand to see either of them die. This was our war, but it had raged for too long. I debated slipping away as they slept, but the thought of our plan going terribly wrong didn't sit well with me. I couldn't leave them without saying what could be our last goodbye.

I looked back to Anderson, who waited patiently for my response. "Tomorrow, under the cover of darkness," I said.

He nodded, raising his glass, "It'll all be over soon."

I'd pulled Demi and Ava out of the commotion of the bar and lead them back out into the streets— towards the inn. I was drained, too drained, and the gravity of what I was about to do only added to the pressure I already felt. Again, I broke into the room and opened the door for them, not caring if anyone was already there or if they might return. I knew the second they saw me they would give up their place and leave, or if they didn't I wasn't afraid to force their hand.

Anderson was right, word had spread, and even people that bore no evidence of battle were talking about what had happened. The word of the lost god's potential return had spread like a wildfire.

I collapsed onto the bed, not bothering just yet to expose my plan. I didn't want to worry them, not tonight—they'd worked too hard for their sleep, they deserved this peace.

# Chapter 39:

I'd slept late into the afternoon. Opening my still tired eyes I could see Demi and Ava sitting by the foot of the bed, keeping themselves busy as I slept. On the nightstand sat a plate of cold food, I could only assume they'd gone out to get breakfast and brought some back for me. It would have been welcomed, if I hadn't slept past the offer.

I cursed myself for my laziness, and it seemed my stomach did too. Though, hunger wasn't my only problem—I'd woken up late, and troubled. Demi and Ava wore carefree expressions and I dreaded having to break the bad news. Then, I thought of my promise to Dom Seir, and how we would have to take the trip back up to the monastery to tell him of my plan.

I decided to let Demi and Ava enjoy the day for as long as they could. I would have to tell them of my plan later.

"Ah, there she is," Demi said, turning to me with a smile.

I couldn't help but return one, his smile was contagious—and, for a moment, I let myself be warmed by him. After all, I was walking straight into the belly of the beast and this may be the last time I enjoyed these simple pleasures.

I laid there silent for a long time, perhaps too long, running over the possibilities in my mind, preparing myself for anything that might come my way. I thought of turning back while I still could. We could return to Terra Sera and let the Council do their work, but the thought of ending the war now, by my own hands, was far too tempting. Then, I remembered the Dom's doubts about the Council and personally didn't feel we would be able to return and have the Council react in time to still hold an advantage. I wanted to avoid another massacre.

"We need to see Dom Seir," I said, breaking the silence.

"Already? We just left," Demi asked, and Ava laid back onto the bed in an over dramatic flair of disapproval of our coming trek back up to the monastery.

"I know," I started, but tried to find another excuse for the visit other than revealing my plan, "it's important he knows how well I fought yesterday. There's things that worry me about the darkness and I'm hoping he can help. "At least I wasn't lying, not completely.

"Why don't you just ask me?" Demi said, "I live in the darkness."

"It's different, something to do with Klaus—and I know you don't want to deal with him," I returned.

Demi looked away, hiding his expression, "Yeah, that."

"See? Dom Seir will be able to help, and maybe he's come up with some sort of plan to save Sera."

"And that too," Demi said dryly.

"What about it?"

"Don't you think it might be smarter to go back and let the Council take care of it? Once we get back we can mobilize an army, and not some poor excuse for one that we have here, an actual army, led by two gods. We could storm Hope and take her back," Demi argued.

"Still, that could take months and you heard the Dom, Madsen was supposed to be here years ago. He made it sound like they have known where Sera's been this whole time."

"Then why bother sending us to find something he's already found?"

"The Games, validation, or maybe they just needed you out of Terra Sera?"

Demi scoffed, "and why would they want that?"

"What about Lain and how he's acting? There's something we are missing."

"Like what?"

"I don't know Demi, but this isn't about the Games or becoming a guardian, and it's not about the Council, not anymore. It's about saving our people. Hope is right on the other side of those dunes and we have a real shot at saving Sera. We can't let that slip past and wait for the Council to act on it, if they even do."

Demi was silent in thought as I got up and gathered my things.

"If you want to back out, then now's the time," I said, as I finished packing anything I had laying around into my bag.

"It's not that. I just want to make sure we do this right."

He was over thinking, worrying himself over more than he should. He did have a point though, we needed to do this right—but we did have to do something, and soon. We'd come all this way to find her, and it was terrifying to think of the end, especially coming by our own hands, but sitting and waiting for a resolution that might never come didn't help either.

I wasn't sure what would come of it, or where we would go from here, no one did—no one could. Like Klaus had said, it's not our place to know, but it was my place to make a difference. Anything was better than how things were and I was willing to take it all as it came.

"So you're hoping he has more answers about Klaus?" Demi said as my hand reached for the door. I nodded, and he grew a little tenser, "I think it's best if I stay here then. I don't want to get in the way."

"Think about what you want while I'm gone Demi, if you want to go back to Terra Sera I won't stop you, and I won't be too far behind. But this is my war, our war, and it's time for a change in the tides. I will save Sera, and I'll find a way whether you are with me or not."

I left him there, sitting on the edge of the bed, deep in thought. I felt for him, this was his last chance to turn back, to advance in the games back home. But after all of this, those games seemed like a pointless memory, I knew—even then that they were, but for Demi that had been a goal he had wished to achieve his entire life. This was bigger than all of that, his sheltered and tiny world had suddenly grown vast and incredibly daunting since he left. Those games are meaningless when compared to what it will mean to save Sera at last, and I hoped by the time I returned he would see that too.

I walked in silence as I made my way back out of the chasm and to the monastery above, trying to suppress the storm that was already beginning to brew inside me.

*You should just go now. Leave. Save Sera,* Klaus told me.

*We both know we can't walk in there alone. We'll die,* I returned.

I heard a laugh, *you forget who I am. I'll kill them all.*

*And you forget who I am, you may not be able to die but I can.* I couldn't risk taking on the entire army myself, despite his powers. Anderson's idea would work, though it was risky it would at least get me further in than storming the gates alone.

*Then don't die,* Klaus said, as if it were that simple.

"Easy for you to say," I found myself saying aloud, and caught a few passing people stealing looks at me for it. Unless word about yesterday was still on everyone's lips.

*You trust him?* Klaus asked, referring to Anderson.

*I have to, he's our only chance,* I returned, sticking to my thoughts.

He sighed, *Very well, and what of my idiot son?*

*Demi?* I asked, surprised to hear Klaus talk about him.

*I don't have another do I?* He asked, sarcasm in his voice.

*How should I know if you do? And as for Demi, he'll do what he wants, there's no stopping that boy.* It was true, I couldn't keep Demi here waiting if he didn't want to, and part of me worried that when I returned from the monastery that he and Ava would be gone, leaving me to face this more alone than I already was.

It wasn't long until I found myself walking through the large open archways leading into the monastery that sat on the edge of a cliff overlooking the cracked plains and advancing dunes beyond.

There was an open courtyard in the center, and the surrounding walls held the quarters of each monk, but it was beneath the ground that the monks truly practiced their art. The ritual chamber where Dom Seir had sent me on my spiritual journey was built below, and judging by the second chamber with the pitted arena there was an entire system hidden here.

I'd spent the first five years of my life running through this place, and even then I hadn't a clue.

Dom Seir knew I was coming, he must have had a vision—and welcomed me in the courtyard as I entered. He looked troubled, and took me in his arms, holding me for just a second longer than usual.

"Come, child," he said, leading me to his quarters.

"I think I'm getting a little old for that don't you think Dom? I am a god after all," I bantered.

He let out a soft laugh, relaxing slightly, "You are not a god Sage, you simply harbor one inside of you."

"Then, I think I'm at least old enough to not be called a child," I pressed on.

"Ah," he said, sliding open the door to his quarter and letting me pass in, "this is true, but you forget you are a soul, not a human- and just like Klaus resides in you, you reside in that body of yours. You are not near your end, not yet, your soul is still young."

I didn't push it any further, knowing he would find some explanation carry this on. It wasn't worth the effort to fight him.

"Why do you seem so worried," I asked, "did you see something ahead?"

"As I saw your visit today, yes, though I'm unsure what to make of it," he said.

"What do you mean?"

"I see the world more torn than it has ever been. I see those with the gift using their power against themselves, though I am unsure why, "Dom Seir rested his arm against the glass of one of the tall windows that overlooked the battlefield. I could still see the tiny specs of color that were the unrecovered bodies of the Pure's forces.

"More war? But why?" I asked.

"Again, unsure, but there is a change in the winds, a terrible change. I fear that it will be storming for some time."

"Then enjoy the storm," I said.

"Perhaps I was wrong to call you a child," The Dom said, looking at me reflectively.

"Whatever it is, we can deal with it when it comes. After we kill Zanin I'm sure there will be unrest, people trying to move into power, but we can't let him live for fear of what might come next," I pressed.

"You're still on about that?" the Dom asked, a hint of surprise in his voice, as if I had discarded my idea.

"Yes, it will happen. Have you thought of a way?" I asked.

"I've tried, but I see no possible way to get to him without destroying the entire city. I thought, perhaps, we could send our entire force rushing his walls—distracting them while you sneak in to kill Zanin. Once he dies, may Sera save us all," Dom Seir said, still staring at the horizon.

Klaus seemed to like the idea, and I could feel him brooding inside of me, working the thought of being back in battle in his own mind. I tried to ignore the impulse to agree with the Dom's plan.

"No, that won't work. Too much bloodshed, and if we fail we'd have nothing," I said, not wanting to cause any more death than I needed to, trying to remember that the Pure citizens were human too. The world had been painted with enough blood already.

"Do you have a better plan?" The Dom asked, a bit defensive in his tone.

"Well—" I started, trying to frame my plan out in the right words before speaking. I'd already worked every possibility in my mind a thousand times, and Anderson had already seemed to have the entire plan worked out. I felt sorry for him, the pain of watching his fiancé die must have torn at him. I could only imagine he'd worked the idea to perfection as he made his way to MarSeir. He was missing a crucial piece once he arrived, but found that piece in me. Still, I was nervous finally sharing our plan with another.

"What?" Dom Seir asked, unable to believe my plan, "You want to walk right through the front gates and expect the Pure to bring you to Zanin? You'll be lucky if you even reach the gates before they have you shot down."

I tried not to let his disapproval get to me, "Even if they do attack me, I've proven I can change the course of their bullets. They can't touch me. I'll stay on my toes and at the first sign of danger, from that distance, I can escape. I think it's the only way. If your vision is true then we need as many soldiers healthy for after this war ends, so using them now isn't an option. Maybe this new approach might be what saves us."

"You hold a lot of faith in a *maybe*," the Dom said, shaking his head in disapproval.

"What else do we have?"

He lowered his eyes, "Nothing."

"I don't care what happens to me once I'm inside the city, I can release Klaus if they attack me. I'll kill anyone who dares come between me and Zanin. Even if I die, with Zanin dead—the entire war would change its course," I pressed, defending my plan.

"You're either incredibly foolish, or incredibly brave, I'm not sure which. Martyrdom isn't a dress that suits you well, Sage," he said in a solemn voice.

"To be honest I haven't found any dress that suits me well."

Dom Seir offered a sorrowful smile, worry in his eye, "So there's no stopping you?"

*There is no stopping me*, Klaus' voice echoed in my mind and I tried to silence him.

*Not now,* I returned, and thankfully he listened.

I looked out of the large windows that overlooked the dunes beyond. Somewhere over that horizon I knew Sera was waiting for me to save her, and I would. I don't even know what I expected after that, or how she would react to finally being free. I wondered if our betrayal would make her turn her back on us, letting us continue to squabble over our differences until we destroyed ourselves. I wondered if she'd rebuild.

Again, I couldn't know, but there was a driving force pushing me to save her— despite the outcome. I could not ignore it.

I looked back to Dom Seir, "It's time for a change Dom, I've waited my entire life to actually be able to have some effect on this war. I'm tired of running, tired of watching all of my friends die, I'm tired of the bloodshed and hatred. Suddenly, I have the power to make a change in the world and I have no intentions of sitting and waiting for a better option."

Dom Seir sighed, "So be it, you have my prayer. When do you leave?"

"Tonight."

He raised an eyebrow curiously, "Why so soon?"

"Why wait, when the opportune moment is now?"

He looked out over the horizon, "How kairotic."

The sun was setting over the horizon as we watched, it would be night soon, and Anderson would be waiting. I was exhausted and I knew that the trek ahead would only beat me down more. It might actually be a good thing if I arrived looking run down and worn, it might help explain how an unequipped Agent managed to capture someone who'd caused so much trouble.

It was a hole in his plan I hadn't thought of, but I was sure he knew what he was doing. At least, as much as anyone could when it came to assassinating the most powerful man alive. I tried to distract myself from picking out anymore holes.

This would work, it had to.

# Chapter 40:

I left Dom Seir just as the sun dipped below the horizon, though the sky was still painted a vibrant array of reds and yellows melting into the deep purples and blues that welcomed the coming nighttime sky. It was time, and I battled with more emotions in the time it took for me to walk back down into the chasms than I could cope with. I walked, silent, deep in my own thoughts, terrified of what was to come but knowing if there was going to be change then someone in this world had to be brave enough to take that leap.

I was unsure if he'd planned it or if this was just good timing, but Anderson met me on the surface, before I had the chance to go back into MarSeir.

"Glad you didn't bail on me," he joked, with a smile, and I wondered how he could as a time like this.

I bolstered myself, working up the nerve to speak, trying not to give my worries away, "And give up an opportunity like this?"

Anderson became more relaxed about this than he already was, how was he not worried? Still, his calmness was contagious, and it soothed me as well. As much as I wanted him to stay serious, I knew that his acting was what this entire plan relied on. I thought, maybe, this was just him getting into character.

He walked ahead, "So, you ready?"

"I—" I began, but paused, looking down into the tunnel that lead to MarSeir. I hadn't said goodbye to Demi and Ava, hell, I didn't even know if they were still there waiting for me—though I hoped. What would they think if I never returned? I shook my head, I couldn't think like that, I was going to return and I would see them again.

Still, the thought of saying goodbye to them now felt more permanent, like I was expected to die in my attempt to save us. I lowered my eyes, and turned to Anderson. I didn't need to say goodbye, not now, because this wasn't goodbye. I would return, I had to.

"Yes," I started again, "I am."

"Good," Anderson began with a nod, and started out over the broken plain, talking to me over his shoulder, "then let's go. We don't need to tie you up right now, but once we get past that first dune there might be scouts out there so we're going to need to look the part from there."

*I'm sorry,* I thought, taking one last look to MarSeir, before following Anderson. *I'll be back, I promise.*

We'd made it to the edge of the chasm, where the fissures in the stone closed back up and left only an expanse of wasteland beyond. We'd walked in silence, there wasn't much to talk about, we were simply tools working towards the same goal, not truly friend or foe.

"Hey, Sage!" I heard from behind me, and turned to see Demi rushing up, Ava not far behind. I froze as he got closer, "Where do you think you're going?"

"I—" I bowed my head, suddenly regretting my decision to leave without saying goodbye, "I'm sorry, I didn't want to worry you."

"So you just left? And to do what, take on everyone yourself?" Demi said, pain in his eyes. He looked around me, taking note of Anderson, "I guess I was smart to follow the Agent after all."

"It's not like that Demi, he's not an Agent anymore. He's— he's helping me get to Zanin."

"Then I'm coming too, Ava can wait at the monastery with Dom Seir," Demi said.

"No," Ava started but Demi cut her off, raising a hand to silence her.

"You. Will. Wait," Demi said, emphasizing each word before looking back to me, "I'm coming with you."

Anderson stepped up into the conversation, "This isn't a three man job, we can handle it just fine. You'll only get in the way."

I shot Anderson a glance, silently begging him not to cause trouble before trouble began. "Demi, I can't risk it, I'm sorry. He's going to turn me in as Klaus, I'll be close enough to kill Zanin once I'm inside. If you come with then we'll only draw more attention."

Demi was troubled by that, "And if they overpower you? If you die?"

"Then I die closer to victory than anyone before me," I returned. He looked away and I pulled his face back to look at me, "Demi, believe in me, I can do this."

"Fine," he said, looking to Anderson, "How long will it take for you to get there?"

Anderson turned to the horizon, judging the distance as if he could see Hope from here, "If we stop stalling now, we could be there by morning, but I'm sure we'll be picked up before then. I assume there will be a celebration, and a reveal—Zanin will see her by the afternoon at the latest, possibly immediately."

Demi worked through that plan in his mind for a moment, "All right, if you aren't back by tomorrow at midnight I am storming that damned city myself, with all of the help I can muster here."

I wanted to protest, but I knew if all went wrong I would need support despite my effort to keep others out of this. "Fair enough," I said.

Ava came up to me and gave me a hug, silent, clearly troubled by the fact that I might not return. She began to unfasten the necklace with the symbol for Cekrit that she still wore, and offered it to me.

Demi took it from her hands before I had the chance to, and for a moment I thought he was going to hurl it back down into the chasm behind us, but he didn't. Instead, he lifted the pendant, clutched within his fist, up to his lips and kissed it, then took the necklace by either end and fastened it around my neck. As he did, his hands brushed along my cheeks and he held my head in the palms of his hands, kissing me gently.

"I love you," he said as our lips parted.

"I love you too," I found myself saying, "I'll see you on the other side."

Demi and Ava stood there as I looked back to Anderson and nodded, "I'm ready," I told him, and we set off into the night.

# Chapter 41:

We moved in silence through what had become a graveyard not yet taken by the sands. Any of the Gifted who had fallen the day before were already brought back to MarSeir to be given a proper burial, and as we passed, I could see that the Pure had returned as well. Though the bodies of their fallen still remained, they had been stripped of all their armor and weaponry, unless that was of our doing as well, either was possible.

I was silently relieved that the two parties hadn't arrived at the same time.

Even though they'd been bent on killing us, I wished these men peace in death. It seemed as though I was the only one who cared to notice them, cared to remember them. The Pure certainly hadn't.

Anderson didn't seem phased by the fallen soldiers that were once his own either. He'd told me that was the way they lived, you fought to kill, knowing your enemy was fighting to do the same. He said that the soldiers were chosen since birth, or at least the Agents were—and trained to believe that death was glory on the battlefield. It would be a disrespect to move them from the very place they gave their lives to thrive on.

I didn't believe it, and in a way I felt his training veiled him from the truth. The Pure didn't care about their fallen, they were tools, and those who died were no longer useful. I almost felt sorry for them.

We reached the other side of the first dune, the hole that was once blown through it had become smooth— now resembling two smaller dunes resting side by side, dipping in towards each other.

Anderson turned to me, and began fishing something out of his bag. I expected rope, but he came up with a metallic cylindrical cuff, with a vial vibrant green liquid encased in the center. The light reminded me of the light that shone from the puzzle box in Tinker's lair.

"What's this?" I asked, taking a closer look.

"Stigma restraints, powered by extracted essence of what you guys call the Gift. It's the stuff the Agents use to make their weapons more effective against your kind. Lifted it off a fallen Agent on my way in, crazy what you can find if you look in the right places," he said, inspecting it, prideful.

"What makes it so special?"

"Easy, it puts out an opposing frequency to your own essence, jamming it. Once locked in it renders your gift useless," he said, opening the cuff and gesturing for my hand, "We're getting close, I'm afraid scouts might catch sight of us soon. Do you mind?"

*Still trust him?* Klaus asked as I stared at the restraint.

*Shut up.* I returned, though still questioning my comfort with this plan.

*No,* I thought, *I need to trust him.*

I offered Anderson my hands and he put the cuff around them, letting my arms rest as if my hands were clasped before me. I tried to adjust to find a more comfortable way to rest my arms, but found none.

I tried to humor myself, realizing that I'd just put myself in the very situation I'd been running from my entire life. No Stigma ever wanted to be caught like this, it was a death sentence.

*Does this affect you?* I asked Klaus.

*Oh, starting to get worried now?* He taunted

*Answer the damned question.*

*Hm, let's see.* He said, and I felt a sensation run down my legs and out through my feet to the ground. A small pulse rippled through the sands.

"Whoa, what was that?" Anderson asked as he slipped in the sand, his leg diving deeper down as if the ground there had let go.

I cursed Klaus, before addressing Anderson, "Probably just a shift in the sand."

"Probably," Anderson returned, "glad I'm going first, just watch your step."

*So?* I asked Klaus after long silence.

*Hm?* He returned, clearly acting oblivious.

*Damn you, you know what I'm talking about.*

*Everything's fine, doesn't seem to bother me,* he said, to my relief.

*Good, at least we have a backup plan.*

I let Anderson lead me as far as I dared, in case I accidentally spoke aloud to Klaus at least I could hope he wouldn't hear me. He didn't seem to mind, actually, he hardly looked back at all. I could only imagine the pain he felt returning to Hope, and the anger that had drove him there.

We'd passed over several dunes, and though the moon now hung high above there was a bright light that broke on the horizon. It was still too early for the sunrise, and this light was different. The stars above all seemed to vanish as we approached. I realized then that we were close.

Anderson paused, shielding his eyes to light, looking out over the dunes beyond, waiting for me to come beside him, "Hope."

"I'm ready, are you?" I asked, as we stared towards the city.

I took a step to push forward but Anderson's hand stopped me, "What's wrong?" I asked.

"No need to tire ourselves, they'll come once they see us," he said, sitting down atop the dune while throwing his bag between his legs to fish out a flare.

"Well aren't you resourceful," I said, sitting beside him.

"Like I said, you'd be surprised what you can find if you know where to look," he said, igniting the flare, standing, and hurling it upwards. I watched it as it streaked across the nighttime sky. It was beautiful, but solidified for me what was to come. There was no turning back now.

I told myself to stay calm as I saw darkened shapes moving quickly over the dunes in the distance. They were the Pure, that I knew, but I had to force myself to stay as my instincts told me to run. The lights in front were blinding, and soon I could hardly make out the shape of the vehicle that they belonged to. There were three of them, staggered as they moved with great speed over the dune.

They stopped by the foot of our own dune, and I could see the large shapes of Agents as they passed over the headlights, forming a line. Anderson stood, and placed a hand on my shoulder before he started towards the Agents.

"Don't move!" A demanding voice called from below and Anderson obeyed, lifting his hands to shade his eyes from the glare.

"State your business," another voice bellowed.

"I've brought a gift for Commander Zanin," Anderson said, proud.

"Oh shit, is that Anderson?" Another voice said, with a slight laugh of disbelief.

"Stay sharp, he was exiled remember? We don't want to end up like his last squad now do we?" The demanding voice spoke again. I could assume he was in charge.

"No sir."

Anderson waved his hands casually, "Now come on boys you know that wasn't my fault. Look, I thought I might be able to win my way back in after bringing the Commander this little treat," he said, stepping aside to bring me into the light.

"Wait, is that—" I heard an Agent say from below, a new voice, but was cut off. How many were there?

I recognized the next one, though I didn't know who it belonged to, "You're right, that's the girl."

The Agent in charge spoke next, "Well I'll be damned, how'd you pull that off Anderson?"

Anderson shrugged, letting his hands fall by his side, relaxing as they praised him, "She must have been exhausted from the fight, I caught wind of where she'd been staying done and found her asleep. Girl didn't realize what was going on until I had the cuffs on, I guess controlling a god takes a lot more energy than we thought. Tell that to the boys in the lab with Sera eh? Having a living host to work with could offer quite the reward."

Anderson relaxed some more, perhaps too relaxed, but he played the part well.

"A god?" another Agent asked.

"Word in MarSeir is our second lost god Klaus has been hiding in this one for years, and was just now awakened. I figured it wouldn't do any harm to capture her and bring her here, if I'm wrong we end up with another dead Stigma, but if I'm right. Well, if I'm right we might finally be able to win this damned war."

"Well damn, looks like you've got some balls after all Anderson," the leading Agent said as he started walking up the dune. He brushed past Anderson, despite his praise and stopped just inches from my face. The man took his helmet off. Even in the darkness, the light from the headlights cast deep ridges and scars covering this man's battle worn face, "You killed a lot of my men girl, a lot of good men, do you know that? I'd be in my right mind to kill you now, and I would if you weren't so valuable."

*I could kill you too,* I thought, narrowing my eyes.

He turned and walked back toward his waiting vehicle, "Tie em up, let's go."

Anderson backed away as the Agents approached him, "Wait, why me?"

"Sorry man," one of the Agents said, "but you're still in exile, you'll have to take your plea for freedom up with Zanin."

"Guys, come on. I brought you a god!" Anderson pled.

The leading Agent stopped by the driver's side of his vehicle, standing inside and looking over the door, "Anderson, you know the rules as well as any of us. Keep quiet and keep it moving."

Four Agents came for me, two picked me up off the ground by the arms and the other two walked in front and behind me. I didn't resist.

They threw Anderson and I in separate wagons, and as they closed the door on him he passed a glance of genuine worry.

*Stay calm.* I reminded myself, as they threw me into the empty wagon and the hum of the vehicle started up. I felt a slight shift in gravity as it hovered over the ground and sped back over the dunes to Hope.

I watched as we passed over the dunes, trying to take note of which way we came so that I could escape later. There was a luminous dome on the horizon ahead of us, painting the sky white, hiding the stars. As we moved, the soft tans of the desert sand slowly shifted to grey, and the ground become increasingly littered with debris until it had piled up into scattered mounds.

There were people here, even at this time, watching us with empty eyes as they huddled by small fires. Their homes were built entirely from the scrap, small shacks only big enough for one or two people. I saw no children and could only assume, or hope, that they had been sleeping. Everyone I saw wore rags, or mis-matched clothing, torn and dirty. I'm sure it was all they could manage, living off the trash of the city.

The Agent's paid them no mind, and the people here watched on with a certain kind of acceptance. I thought, maybe, that was why the Agents weren't shooting them down as we drove past— that perhaps there was a mutual respect. I doubted that, so many Stigma holders would never be allowed to live so close to Hope. So, that meant that these people must have been exiled Pure, still living off the scraps of a city that had forgotten them. To the Agents, they weren't even worth the cost of the bullet it would take to kill them.

I was saddened by that in a way, knowing that there was something worth even less than a Stigma holder in the eyes the Pure, though part of me was happy that they could share our pain—even if that was wrong.

Hope sat atop a large plateau overlooking the junkyard accumulating at its base. The main Dome took up the majority of the space, leaving little room around its edges. On the plateau's rock walls rested enormous tubes, spilling waterfalls of liquid waste and scrap out onto the already mountainous heaps of debris that surrounded the city.

The sound of the hovercraft's engine intensified and I felt a shift as we gradually began rising higher off the ground, aimed at one of the empty concrete tubes that I hoped wasn't about to send a river of trash crashing into us as we entered. We disappeared into the darkness of the tube and I braced myself for an impact that never came. I could hear nothing but the subtle ring of silence, and was blind, the already dim lighting in the wagon having gone out completely once we entered the tube that I could only assume now was a docking station.

The doors of the wagon opened after what seemed like an eternity later and two Agents called me out. Thankfully they didn't force me as before, seeming to relax a bit now that they were on their own turf. I thanked them silently for that.

My eyes searched for Anderson, without trying to blow our own cover. The Agents lead me through the bowels of the city, a long underground concrete hallway. There were dozens of multi-colored pipes overhead, some letting out steam that the Agents tried to avoid, but none seemed to care if I passed through it though I avoided it the best I could.

The hallway let up to a more spacious room, which was relaxing until I realized that the walls were lined with detainment cells. There weren't many, maybe a total of six all together and the reality of what Tinker had told me further set in. The Pure don't keep their criminals, they exile them.

The Agents lead me into a cell and the floor to ceiling glass door slid automatically into place. The cells were beautiful, well, as beautiful as a prison cell could be. The concrete was smooth as a polished stone, every bed was made perfectly, and the lighting was more than generous. The entire room looked like it had barely been used, ever.

I wasn't sure if I was comforted or frightened by that observation.

I was exhausted, and though I still felt Klaus' energy within me, ready to be released, for those moments the stone slab of a bed on the back wall of the cell was the most comfortable thing I'd ever felt.

I closed my eyes, trying to find some semblance of peace while I could but I was soon brought to attention by the sound of more footsteps entering the room.

I was relieved, when I saw two more Agents leading Anderson into his cell.

He gave me a sly smile as he sat, nodding his head slightly to signal that he was okay.

*Good*, I thought, *I'm not alone.*

# Chapter 42:

Despite my exhaustion I couldn't sleep, I simply laid on the stone bed and waited. There were no windows in my cell, or for what I could tell in the entire room. I had no semblance of time, though every second pained me as passed. Anderson seemed to feel the same, sitting back on his concrete slab and staring at the ground, occasionally passing a refreshing look my way.

Eventually, Agents came and released us from our cells, though we were both still restrained. We were lead back through the narrow concrete hallway in which we entered, into a large elevator, surrounded by Agents the entire time.

The elevator door opened and I could see the entirety of Hope before me. I shouldn't have been surprised when I recognized the city. It was exactly like the one I'd walked through in my dream, when I'd unlocked my chakra. Still, I was shocked at how accurate my vision was. On either side of me, hugging the walls of the dome were strips of houses and businesses, leaving way in the center for an overlapping series of lush green gardens overflowing over scattered land bridges and pearl white walkways. There were pools, and fountains, and trees that towered up almost to the top of the domes themselves.

Sunlight peeked through hexagonal glass sections of the dome that seemed placed in relation to the sun's path in the sky, sometimes letting it shine through, while blocking it during others.

This was paradise, a terrible, but beautiful, paradise.

The Agents lead us out into the streets beyond, and again we'd become surrounded as they made a tight square formation with Anderson and I in the center. Hundreds, maybe thousands, of people lined the streets and hung off balconies as they watched the Agents parade us through the Dome.

*This is a show for them,* Klaus hissed, and I agreed, *I'm a sideshow for these fools. I should kill them all.*

*Save it for Zanin Klaus, we need to be smart and save our energy, that last fight took more out of me than you realize,* I urged him as we were pushed through the city.

The Agents didn't bother to take the direct route either, it seemed as though we walked along paths that we'd already been over, as if the Agents themselves were somehow lost in their own city. But of course they weren't. We were a spectacle.

People cheered beside us, eyes wide with both horror and wonder. I smiled to myself for what was to come.

*Just you wait,* I told myself, and Klaus finished my sentence.

*Today, you celebrate for the wrong reasons. Tonight, we celebrate your defeat.*

The Agents lead us up the staircase leading to the grand building that acted as Zanin's hall. I passed a look to Anderson, but it was ignored. I didn't blame him. We couldn't break character, not now. I steeled myself as the Agents opened the double doors and lead us in.

Their formation broke, allowing Anderson and I to lead and falling behind us as we walked into the black and red marbled room, the doors closing behind us. Everything resembled the night, the floors and walls were all the same marble, accented with blood red trim, even along the pillars. There was something of a stage further ahead, with a shallow set of stairs leading from its lip to the floor below, fanning out into the room.

There was a man that stood at its center, hands clasped behind his back, in a red robe bearing black details. There was a tangible

sense of power about him. He was an older man, with short, but
wavy black hair that had greyed along the sides. He didn't move,
didn't speak as we approached, only watched as we did so. The
wrinkles on his face had me conflicted. I knew that I was looking
at Commander Zanin himself, and the reality of his ways did not
mirror the kind looking old man I saw before me.

I was troubled by that thought. A man who'd spent a life of
tyranny stood before me, looking almost blissful as he was. There
was no shame, no regret, and I realized despite the terror he'd
rained down on this earth the man was completely at peace with
himself for it. This wasn't a genocide he as committing, to him— it
was a cause.

I felt Klaus' energy stir up inside me, and I tried my best to
calm him.

*Not yet,* I pled.

Zanin raised an open palm, ordering us to stop where we were.
He eyed me for a long while, then passed a look over to Anderson
as he began to slowly descend the steps.

There was a voice from behind him, coming out from beyond
the stage but growing louder as it came, "You can feel him can't
you?"

Zanin said nothing, but lifted his hand for whoever had spoken
to be silenced. On the stage, making his way to stand beside the
one man who sought to destroy our kind, was Lain.

"You bastard!" I shouted to him, but silenced as Zanin shot me
a look of disgust.

Zanin looked to Anderson, "You've done well, you may stand."

Anderson obeyed, "I've brought you what you asked for
Commander, now, as promised—may you release my fiancé?"

My eyes shot to Anderson, the fire within me raged with the heat of his betrayal, becoming a tempest that I was just about ready to unleash, but no—not yet, not now.

Zanin's eyes were on me, "I'm afraid I can't do that any longer."

"But Sir," Anderson started, taking a step towards Zanin. An Agent held him back, placing a hand on his shoulder, "Sir, I did what you asked. Please, I just want to see her. "

Zanin sighed, and broke eye contact with me to Anderson, "She's been dead since you left boy. I never thought an Agent as pitiful as you would actually do something right for a change. Letting you believe she was still alive gave me leverage, and you the strength to actually do something. Call it—a tactical decision."

Anderson tried to lunge at Zanin but the Agent held him back. Tears flowed as he resisted, he looked to me, pure sorrow in his eye, "I'm sorry, I didn't know, I was just trying to save her. I was just trying to—"

"Shut him up!" Zanin yelled over him and an Agent punched Anderson in the gut, letting him collapse to the floor, writhing in pain.

"Now, what to do with you?" Zanin said, reverting his attention back to me.

I spat at him, but he was unfazed as he approached.

He eyed my necklace, "Ah, a member of Cekrit is it? What a troublesome bunch, don't you think?"

"Almost as troublesome as that Council," Lain said, appearing behind Zanin.

Zanin smiled, and tugged at the pendant, snapping it from my neck and hurling it at Lain, "You speak when spoken to. I see defending these Stigmas wasn't my brother's only failure."

Lain straightened up, but didn't speak. His face was bandaged, and his arm hung in a sling. Still, he held a certain aura of arrogance in the room, pretending that he was in control.

Brothers? Zanin and Madsen—one pure and one gifted. Perhaps that was a fuel that drove Zanin. Just as Lain's jealousy of Demi drove him, Zanin's brought him to destroy what he couldn't have. Though, that was only a possibility.

Zanin turned his attention back to me, but my eyes watched Lain behind him, hoping he would act up again so I could make my move. I noticed something though, by Lain's feet. The silver pendent slowly disappeared into the black marble. I blinked, my eyes must have been playing tricks on me, I was overworked, overtired.

Still, I watched that spot. The marble beneath Lain's feet began to churn, and a black puddle pooled beneath his feet. I held my breath, preparing myself for what would come next—I knew what this meant, and thought of how.

Then it came to me.

Demi had taken the necklace from Ava, kissing it in his clasped hand. Had he snuck a Vemosa into it without me noticing?

*My boy's clever,* Klaus boasted, a sinister delight in his tone.

My answer came when Uru caught Lain in its horns as the beast burst from the void, ramming him into the marble with a thunderous crash. Behind Uru dozens of Kurki flooded out of the Vemosa's portal, more than I'd ever seen summoned at once, and rushed for the Agents behind us in a mad dash.

*Now,* I ordered, standing, prepared to fly into the frenzy of battle. Something was wrong, nothing happened. *Damn it Klaus, help me.*

*I'm trying,* he said, *the frequency changed, I'm jammed.*

I watched, helpless as Zanin's supreme order spiraled into chaos within seconds. He'd spun around in surprise just in time to see a crazed Demi leap from the stage front and drive a clawed arm into the commander's chest.

Zanin hunched over Demi's shoulder, there was a sinister smile on Demi's face, "I told them," he said more to himself than anyone else, "you would die by my own hand."

Before I had any time to react the room was thrust into a frenzy. The spattered burst of gunfire rang out behind me as the remaining Agents struggled to fend off the ever coming wave of ravenous Kurki.

Demi left a Zanin to fall onto the stairway, clutching his wound, breathing deeply. It wouldn't be long until he bled out.

I felt powerless amongst the chaos, standing amidst a battle that had begun and ceased in a mere instant. I felt weak, as I once had, and though Zanin lay dying before me I felt defeat.

I took a sweeping gaze around the room as the gunfire subsided, Zanin had fallen with Demi before him, Lain sat up against the wall, in a daze, though he looked to be just now gathering his wits despite being contained by Uru, and nearly every guard lay either lifeless or wounded on the floor.

Ava had rushed to my side.

*Good,* I thought, *Demi let her come.*

But judging by his expression I couldn't tell if he was shocked at seeing me standing powerless, or her presence.

A soft clapping echoed through the room, breaking the silence that had taken over.

"Oh how the mighty have fallen," a familiar voice boomed.

Our attention was drawn to the shadows of a far corner, spoken by a silent specter of this slaughter.

"You, what did you do?" Demi asked, confusion in his voice.

"I've won the game son, don't you see? All of the pieces fell in perfectly."

My eyes struggled to focus, and I looked on in near disbelief as the man that stepped into the light was Madsen.

"You used us," Demi bellowed.

"Well now, *used* is such a harsh word. I'd prefer to call it—a tactical decision. Any great player needs to know how to use his pawns."

I heard another man cough.

Lain.

"It's useless to try and fight Demi, we've won," Lain said, I could see him beginning to stand out of the corner of my eye.

I struggled to breathe as I tried to remain calm, becoming filled with uncontrollable fury. I could feel my power surging from my body, feeling like an invisible flame had begun to engulf me. My restraints severely limited my ability to control my power from within, my only hope was to try to control this energy from outside of my body. I couldn't die here, no matter the means I knew I needed to save Sera, whether the Council would try to stop me or not I could stop at nothing.

Madsen spoke again, calm. I could see him pacing around the room, examining the bodies, "Don't act so surprised my boy, this is what we wanted. We can use power like yours you know— for more than just this here. Help us reshape the world. There's a saying you know, I believe it goes ' do unto others as you wish to have done to yourself.' Well, I believe it's time to do to the Pure what they have done to us. We're powerful Demi, we are the chosen race. I've waited too long for this and it's time we realize our destiny: to create a new world for ourselves. A better world."

"How did you know I would come?" Demi ordered.

"You're more predictable than you might imagine boy, I knew what she was," Madsen nodded to me, "and that she would be compelled to come here regardless of what you did. I also knew that you would follow, it's in your nature."

Demi spat at the ground, "you had no right to use me like this."

"My right," Madsen started, "is whatever I please. You need to learn your place."

By now, Lain had taken his place by his father's side.

"Come now," Madsen began, offering an open palm, "together we will reshape this world—starting with this girl. Kill her first, then with Klaus and Sera's powers we can cleanse the world of those who weren't chosen."

"And if I refuse?" Demi countered.

"Enough!" I screamed, allowing all of the energy I had left to swirl around me, the pressure nearly cementing me to the ground.

*What's this now?* Klaus asked.

The pain was overwhelming, but in order to save Sera I knew my body would be the sacrifice. The ground beneath my feet began to fracture as the energy around me manifested in reality and I was forced downward. My entire life had been a storm, a raging whirlwind of negative emotions, of doubt and regret, of self-pity. Now, those winds raged from within me, they fueled my every step, my every action. That tempest of energy swirled around me—freeing me entirely.

Like the ground beneath me, eventually the restraints began to fail, fracturing as well until falling to the floor altogether.

Somehow, I could feel Klaus smile as he spoke, *most impressive, it's a shame we'll have to part soon.*

"Shut up," I said to both Klaus and Madsen, "I will not die here."

"Oh but I think you shall," Madsen continued, "Demi, that was an order. Don't forget your place with the Council. Don't be as much of a disappointment as your father."

Demi's expression twitched with pain as he turned to me with sorrow in his eye, mouthing the word, "Run," before starting towards me, black pools forming by his side.

For a moment, in this state, I knew I could kill any of them in a head to head fight, but like this, the odds were against me. I was up against three of the most skilled Stigma holders I've met, and thankfully I wasn't blinded by my rage. I was compelled to listen, and ran, knowing that if I could free Sera that this nightmare would have been worth the pain.

I sprinted headlong down the nearest corridor, following nothing but my instinct. Before long, my world grew dim, the walls around me beginning to churn and bubble like tar pits, reverting to the black matter I'd grown all too familiar with. Kurki burst from the walls, from all directions, with open arms ready to grab hold. I dodged them the best I could, and dispelled those I couldn't. Their movements were unlike any I'd seen from them before. Now, they attacked with perfect synergy, the clumsy creatures I once knew were now perfectly controlled and lethal. As one burst from the ceiling, I dodged, allowing it to fall into the liquid floor like a breached whale might fall back to the ocean. Countless Kurki attacked this way, hurtling from the walls, or the ceiling, reaching from the floor. Somehow, I managed to keep just one step away from them.

I wondered if Demi had held them back just enough to not catch me, if he was putting on a show for Madsen. That's what I wanted to believe, but I knew that what we felt for each other couldn't erase a lifetime of loyalty to Madsen, couldn't erase his need to restore honor to his family, and certainly wouldn't allow him to put Ava in danger. Still, even if Demi did defy Madsen, the Councilor would merely use Demi's body as a puppet and force him to kill me out of spite—I knew well enough my fate here, and I wept for Demi as I ran, knowing he was powerless to save me.

I passed a look behind me to see Demi still sprinting toward me, a Vemosa by his side. As my attention was brought before me I took a sharp turn I nearly froze, realizing I was simply a rat in a maze, having been lead to the second Vemosa who awaited merely ten feet before me.

"Shit," I spat.

*Sage*, Klaus interrupted.

*Not now Klaus*, I shot back.

*Now indeed, remember our little chase?*

It hit me then, I could alter the plane which I walked. I focused on the ground before me and tore a hole into it, hoping to shift my perspective and run on the vertical plane down to a lower floor. As the hole opened and I approached I stepped into it, but instead crashed to the floor below.

When I came to my senses I was thankful that the Kurki had failed to follow, for now, and began to gather a sense of my surroundings. I found myself in a room that looked like something Tinker may have worked in. The walls were lined with machines, medical instruments, and shelves behind glass doors. The entire room was dark, but tinted with a soft blue-green light and all was quiet save for the occasional bubbling of water.

I turned, trying to follow the light and froze in place—suddenly filled with a mixture of both wonder and terror, hope and fear, relief and sadness, as I saw the motionless body of our Mother suspended in the green tinted water of a stasis chamber. She drifted there in silence, curled into the fetal position. Her snow white hair drifting all around her, only partially covering her naked body.

"Sera," I said aloud, in awe, immediately searching for a way to release her.

I found myself at a loss amongst the dozens of dials and buttons before me and found myself unable to muster the courage to try any of them, fearing I could harm her. I couldn't make any sense of the displays either, which were mostly flooded with charts and diagrams that I had no idea how to read.

The air in the room seemed to grow thicker the longer I lingered, knowing it would be any moment that Demi would burst in to take my life and the fact that being so close to Sera, Klaus' own energy begin to boil within me, begging to be released.

I felt magnetized to Sera, and left the displays to walk over to her prison. I was beside myself by her beauty, here, an ancient god, looking no older than myself, forever at the peak of her beauty. Her pale white skin was tinted by the green lights surrounding her tank, which lit the room as well.

"Sage," Demi's voice spoke behind me.

"So, you found me," I began, ignoring the threat of him being here, "isn't she beautiful."

I placed my palm to the glass, hoping to console her, so happy to have found her.

*Sera, I've come at last,* Klaus' voice rang in my mind.

As he spoke I felt a sharp pain shoot through my chest. As I fell to my knees I wondered if this was Klaus escaping, our deal having been fulfilled, or if Demi had struck me down. As I looked down I saw only a thin beam of white light had been driven through my chest, looking over my shoulder I could see Lain looking down from the floor above through the hole that still lingered.

"Madsen knew you were soft," Lain spat at Demi, who ignored him and had come to my side.

I tried to focus on Demi, happy that it wasn't him that would kill me, somehow at peace with that end—but my attention was brought elsewhere. Demi wasn't the only one looking back at me. Before me, Sera's eyes had shot open to stare straight at me, letting out a terrific water diluted cry. In a moment, splinters began to form and the glass shattered as the water pressure became too much to hold back, flooding the room.

I couldn't react, not like this, and it was then that I felt a deep tug on my soul. I felt spiritually weaker, drained, as if my energy had been sapped out of me. Slowly, like I'd watched in the alleyway the first real time I could remember Klaus taking over, his body began to push out of my vessel as if I was an old skin.

Before the goddess fell, Klaus caught her in step, caressing a fragile body that was hardly able to lift her arm to brush the hair from his cheek.

Everything in my world began to slow as the chilling water that had flooded the room seeped into my clothes, the only warmth I'd found being that of my own blood and Demi's embrace. Oddly, I didn't mind this feeling, it was as if my body was ready to sleep, finally able to rest.

The darkened shadows in the corner of my vision crept closer to the center until all I could see was Demi staring back at me as if frozen in time, and Klaus, holding Sera, watching us intently. In a moment, I found Klaus beside me and Demi's body against mine struggle to restrain his urge to lash out at the god.

Neither said a word, the only sound was my short gasps for breath and Demi's sob as he held me. Klaus looked to his son for a moment, before reaching over to take me from his grasp. Demi was reluctant, but didn't fight his father as he took me over his shoulder with care. In a moment, Demi seemed so far away as Klaus carried Sera and I into the void, leaving all else behind.

Then, just as it all had begun—my world faded to darkness.

Made in the USA
Middletown, DE
17 May 2018